NOVA ACADEMY

HEROES & VILLAINS

(A NOVA ACADEMY NOVEL)

SCOTT OLEN REID

Copyright ©2017 Scott Olen Reid
All Rights Reserved.

No part of this work may be reproduced or used in any form, or by any means, without the express written consent of the author.

THREE HELMETS BOOKS

Publisher: Three Helmets Books, Laguna Hills, California.
ISBN (Amazon Print): 9781521101278
ASIN (Kindle eBook): B071YJZ8M4

Original Version Cover Art: Samantha DeBie
Current Cover Art: Covermint Design
Three Helmets Books Logo: Samantha DeBie

First printing in any format: 2017
Printed in USA

This is a work of fiction. Names, characters, places, and events contained within this work are the product of the author's imagination and/or are used fictitiously. Any resemblance to actual, or legal, persons, living or deceased, is coincidental.

Neither the author, nor publisher, has control of or assumes responsibility for third party representations related to themselves or this work.

Dedication:

This book is dedicated to every person who has ever dreamed of writing their own book. Believe in yourself and never give up the dream.

Special Thanks to my Editor and Beta Readers:

A very special thank you to Sheri Clifton for the work she put into editing the book.

Thank you also goes to my family for their incredible support and encouragement to push through to the end and who gave me the confidence to go to print.

Lastly, a special thank you to my niece, Samantha DeBie, for working too many hours creating awesome print and ebook covers. And, to Chris Beccacio for his last-minute tweaks of the cover's size so the print version could be published on-time.

I could not have done it without them.

OTHER BOOKS BY SCOTT OLEN REID

Earth Interstellar

Nova Academy: Bases and Lairs

For more information go to:

Three Helmets Books

www.ThreeHelmets.com

Chapter 1

I hear the first-bell as I pull into the school parking lot. Most of the kids are ignoring the bell, which is what you would expect on the last day of the school year when no one has any fear of being tardy and getting another detention. For me, it is going to be great not only because it is the last day of school; it is going to be great because it is also my last year of high school. Today, I graduate from being a kid and start taking on the world. I have a plan. And, the first part of my plan is to have a great summer before I start college in the fall.

Lucky for me, my plan is wasting no time in getting started as up ahead is a key player in Phase One, Tess Evans. She's getting out of her mom's car. "Hey, Tess," I call over to her as I get out of my car.

"Hey, T. You going to walk me to class?" She asks as I jog up to her. Tess is stepping out of the car wearing black uni-body "super" tights with white stripes down the sides that highlight her long, athletic legs, among other assets. She has Ninjette's super suit look down effortlessly; it is hard to not trip over myself from the distraction.

"Uhh, Hey Tess," I say again, making a bad attempt at taking back control of my hormones. I can't allow myself to be distracted, because no matter how great she looks, walking her to class is not part of Phase One. She'll hang on me like we are going steady, which we are not, and I can't let that happen. Not today, anyway. I cannot afford it getting around today that we are an item. "I can't. Rain check?" is the best I can come up with in my current mental state.

"It's the last day of school, silly. Are you planning on coming back next year?" She asks, teasing, as she latches onto my arm. Tess is a senior, same as me, and neither one of us is planning on being back next year, "Are you going to walk me to class then?" she asks, not letting up.

I start walking with her while I work out how to pull myself out of this. I'm a mad scientist, not a mad Casanova, so it's going to take me a minute.

"Okay," she says, perking up as she thinks I've changed my mind. She runs her hand around my waist, getting snuggly as we walk across the parking lot in what I now recognize as her trying to close any outs I can use to get out of walking her to class. This would allow her to lay claim to me for all to see. She's playing a game as she has to know how uncomfortable I'm feeling right now. She's toying with me.

She knows because she's a strong telepath with emotional sensitivity. She can hear the surface thoughts and emotions of people she's near. That's not to say she can read my thoughts, because no one can. My brain has natural protections from telepaths. But, Tess and I have known each other so long that she's become attuned to me enough she can sense my emotions.

Tess is a bit controlling, and judgmental, and likes to play games, which is unusual for telepaths. They tend to be really laid back, live-and-let-live types. But, I am usually fine with how she is as she mostly focuses on others (and not me) when they violate her high standards. I think that not being able to read my mind makes it harder for her to catch onto all of my more personal thoughts, which allows her to give me the benefit of the doubt that she can't give others.

Tess has had a really strange social life as long as I've known her because she can't seem to keep a boyfriend. As beautiful as she is, and as good a person as she is, it is incredible that it is a problem for her. It seems every time she has to dump boyfriends because they want to cheat on her or are thinking some other stupid thing that gets them in trouble. She demands loyalty and respect, as any person should in a relationship. Because she's a telepath, she also demands her boyfriend not even think about cheating, or lying, or deception. Thinking it for her is the same as if you say it.

She knows what she brings to the table and fairly thinks whoever is with her should be happy and not want to think about other girls. She expects them to be happy with being with her, and she expects them to be a genuinely good person. Finding someone like that is hard, if not impossible, though, and I'm not sure she knows it.

I like that Tess has a strong set of standards, which she lives by, and which she enforces mercilessly. It may sound like she's a nightmare girlfriend to some people, but to me, she's like the ultimate superhero tough, with her *"Don't even think about it,"* ultimatum.

"Can I walk you to church on Sunday?" I finally throw out as an alternative to walking her to class.

"Sure." I'm pretty sure she knows my bow-out was coming, and she is nice enough to let me off the hook.

"Cool, I'll pick you up!" I yell as I run for Homeroom. I'm not worried about being on time on the last day of school, that's not why I'm running. The reason I'm running is I don't want to miss the surprise my best friend, Ernie Beck, has in store for our homeroom teacher, the old bat, Mrs. Frazier.

When I walk into class, Mrs. Frazier is already giving me her best Jack Elam, cockeyed, suspicious, I'm up to something, look. It's not that I'm late, or up to anything, she's got the wrong guy. Ernie's the one she should be watching. Because today the scales of justice will come back into balance after a year of misery from Mrs. Frazier.

Ernie gives me a smile and chin nod when he sees me, and I go sit in the back next to him.

"You doing it?" I lean over and ask him in a whisper as soon as I sit down.

He just smiles and says, "Just watch," as he turns to look at Peg Miller and gives her a thumbs-up.

Peg is a telekinetic who can move things with her mind. Right now, she starts using her power to plug in, and then turn on, a portable bubble machine Mrs. Frazier keeps in the corner that she uses in her drama classes. The machine immediately starts whirring; shooting bubbles out. Only the bubbles are coming out far faster and larger than anything that bubble machine is actually capable of creating. The extra bubbles are coming from Ernie. That's his power, making bubbles, and he's making a lot of them.

Mrs. Frazier doesn't notice the bubbles as they start drifting over to her desk. She also doesn't notice the whirring sound because she's half deaf. When she finally does notice, she runs over to the device to turn it off. When she gets there, she is completely engulfed in the bubbles that are also quickly filling the entire front half of the classroom. Kids in the front are scrambling out of the way while the kids in the back are falling out of their chairs laughing. Unplugging the machine does not slow the creation of bubbles and, realizing it is not the machine, Mrs. Frazier starts screaming for someone to go get help. She keeps screaming right up until she figures out the real reason for what is happening. Her wide open eyes and look of panic on her face transforms into a sneer of hatred and looming violence as she turns to look at the back of the class. She bellows out Ernie's name, threatening him with murder and mayhem. Thankfully, moments later the bubbles become too thick, and we can no longer see our homeroom teacher, the harbinger of death.

Hearing Mrs. Frazier yelling Ernie's name puts a temporary damper on how hilarious the whole thing is to me because I didn't know if she knew Ernie could make bubbles. Now I'm wondering if Ernie knows that she knew when he set this up. Then again, I wonder if he cared even if he did know. Ernie's a good guy, but all bets are off when it comes to Mrs. Frazier. Whatever. This is too funny to worry about consequences right now.

After a couple minutes of bubbles going everywhere, the five-minute bell rings starting Homeroom. Before it stops, Ernie pops the thousands and thousands of giant bubbles all at once. Bubble goop flies in all directions and Mrs. Frazier and a few of the slower kids from the front of the class are coated head to toe in the slimy stuff.

Everyone not covered in goop is laughing hysterically, with half of them now on the floor. Ernie is sitting upright in his seat; his hands folded in front of him and calmly looking to the front of the class as if he is the model student waiting for class to start. I can see his jaw clenched as he fights to not burst out laughing. What a great start to the summer.

Chapter 2

Lunchtime is tricky. I can't let Tess see me. And I especially can't let her trap me like almost happened this morning. But I can't look like I'm avoiding her. And while I'm avoiding Tess, I need to find Maria to ask her out. I am beginning to question my sanity in trying to date them both at the same time, but it's necessary. Hold on, I'll explain.

Luckily, I am saved by circumstance. Tess and Maria run in different circles, and they have different hangouts during school. So far as I can tell, they also don't have any crossover of friends. I just need to find Maria.

Now I know it sounds bad that I am trying to go out with both of Tess and Maria at the same time, but I need to do this. It has nothing to do with trying to be a two-timing dog, even if it looks like I'm trying to be a two-timing dog. The truth is they are representations of two alternative choices I have in becoming a super. They are polar opposites and represent the choice I have been struggling with for four years. The choice I need to make of who I want to be in my coming career as a super. My plans over the next four years will not be focused if I have not decided which direction I am going. I have this summer to figure it out so I can start school in the fall with a clear path to where I want to go. And, those two are going to help me decide. They just don't know it.

Tess and Maria are facsimiles of my path choices: hero? Or, villain? One of them has a strong code of right and wrong which reminds me of heroes. It's a standard you live by, and expect everyone around you to live by. It forms a foundation for your life and for everything you do that leads to stability, security, and hopefully, happiness. While the other is all chaos that reminds me of what it is to be free to do whatever I want. To get what I want from life without compromise. To do what I want to get the things I need, and to be what I want to be. This, in the world of supers, is a well-documented and classic villain's way of thinking. Tess and Maria are prime examples of these two ways of thinking, and I am using them to work out which appeals to me most, and which path I like most. They are my life path experiments. The best part is – they come with perks.

Okay, back to figuring today out. If I hang out with either of the girls at lunch, it will end with me not going out with either of them. Tess, since we are not official yet, will be all over me to make it clear I'm hers. She'll announce it over the school's P.A. system. Maria, on the other hand, will be cool about it. She's unpredictable though, and dangerous. I've watched her set a guy on fire because he pissed her off for a lot less than being two-timed.

Maria is a fire elemental, and on top of that, she's stronger than me. If she wants, she can burn the school down before the five-minute bell rings a second time. And I can tell you, that kind of ability can bring out the dominant personality in a girl. They came out big time in Maria. She's dangerous. A fierce woman, who takes what she wants, and destroys anything that gets in her way. It's awesome to see her dominate everything around her. And, yes, I'm more than a little attracted to that.

It goes without saying; this plan of mine is not without risks. If they find out, there will be consequences. Tess could decide we are already officially dating (aka committed) and never talk to me again for betraying her. (Note: We're not official, and I've made her no promises, real or implied. But I'd still feel like crap for hurting her feelings.) Maria? I'm not sure what Maria would do. She would either make us all die in a blazing inferno or make us all die very slowly in a blazing inferno. You never can tell with her. Whether we are already dating is absolutely irrelevant to her. She likes me. And until she decides she no longer likes me, she has a claim. I know that's how she thinks.

Rather than going to where Maria hangs out at lunch with her friends in the back of the parking lot, I drive over there and roll down the window of my car as I roll by her lunchtime hangout. When I see her, I get her attention, point to her, and shout, "You! Me! Tonight!" We've known each other a long time, so I know asking her out this way is actually a safer bet than how I would have to ask Tess out. Maria likes bold, she likes brash, and she even likes crude. And, she would torch me if I came up to her like some Rico Suave punk, being all proper, and tried to ask her out. The great thing is no one can see me with Maria if I'm not ever actually with Maria when I ask her out. Her friends don't count as none of them would ever be friends with Tess anyway.

Everything works out as Maria flips me off and shouts back, "Five o'clock! We're going to the river!" and then turns back to her friends. Phase One is complete.

The last class of the day is almost over, and I have to get away from school without running into either of the girls and screwing this whole thing up, so I ditch the rest of school rather than go back after lunch. Maria is on for tonight. I'm guessing she meant we're going out to the river to hang out with her all-girl crew at the lake. They're a pretty tough crowd, and more fun than any group I've ever run with, so it should be good.

Maria's dad lets her and her friends take their camper out and stay the weekend at the lake's campgrounds, which they do nearly every weekend. What he does not know is Maria and her crew goes out and does the occasional bit of super-villainy. The biggest job I know of they have done is an armored car heist over in Emeryville last year. And, the reason I know about that job is I was in on it with them. Hey, I only went because I was short of funds and needed the money for a project I was working on. Doing the job was an easy solution. Besides, I wanted to know what it was like to do a robbery.

That's right; I've been a supervillain. For a day. It's an option for me because I like it. Isn't that what I've been saying? That's right, so don't get all surprised with the revelation. I also volunteered at the Special Olympics, rescued a kitten from a tree, and beat the dog snot out of some guy who was mugging a little old lady coming out of the Social Security office. Big deal on all counts because I liked doing every one of those things and did none of them because it was the right thing to do.

Anyway, where was I? Oh right. You might wonder about the safety of a bunch of high school girls alone at a campgrounds site. Like, what horror movie reenactment could happen there? I suggest you just follow Maria's dad's lead on this. Her dad stopped worrying about her safety a long time ago. Not only is she a powerful fire elemental, she's also a Class 3 physically and doesn't need anyone else to fight her battles. Her dad figured it out when Maria was three years old when she wandered into the street chasing the neighbor's dog. The dog made it across the street, but Maria didn't and was hit by an SUV doing 45 in a 25 mile per hour zone.

Her dad tried to get to her before she made it into the street, but was too late as he just missed swiping her up as she went between the cars. When the SUV hit her, she was thrown fifty feet down the road. Her dad was right there and had a front row seat to see his little girl get run over.

Thinking he was going to see his baby girl dead in the street, he came around the cars parked along the curb to see Maria standing in the middle of the road where she had landed; covered in flames, saying "doggy" over and over, and opening and closing her little hands at the dog that had stopped running to come back and check on her. The entire front of the SUV was engulfed in flames. Her dad has fire powers as well and ran up and picked up his bonfire of a little girl. From then on he stopped being afraid for his little girl and started being more concerned with the wellbeing of any driver, or boy, who gets in her way.

My great dilemma in choosing the life path is a little like my wanting both Tess and Maria. Each fills a want for me. Both are incredibly strong girls, but Tess is good, representing the life I've watched my parents have: a stable, loving home, and a fulfilled life. Maria represents the opposite: She's all risk, and excitement, and chaos, and living by your own rules.

I want my life to be both. Some of Tess and some of Maria, but not all of either. I love the life I had growing up. I love the idea of having a loving family of my own and raising my own kids like my parents. But I also have certain ambitions that may not be attainable to a hero. They are also ambitions that do not typically lead to the sedate and secure life my parents have. It would be a simple thing for me to become a supervillain and chase that life of excitement and chaos. Where would it end, though? I'm a smart guy: super genius; mad scientist; inventor; and competitor. I might become a supervillain. Or, I could become a superhero. Superhero is more likely to require I live a life like the life I see Tess having, once she finds that right guy. But it will be a lot less of what I see in Maria. I'm not sure yet which one is the bigger draw for me. It will be one or the other because the excitement, adventure, and brutal competition of the world of supers are the keys in the future I am planning. Whichever it is, hero or villain, order or chaos, discipline or absolute freedom, it has to be something I can wrap my entire existence around and give everything too willingly.

Chapter 3

This year I'm the only one going to Nova Academy for Advanced Superhuman Studies in my school. There are a number from my school going to other colleges for supers, just not Nova Academy. It's the top advanced sciences academy for supers. And it is an open campus that has no requirements of being a hero, or a villain.

Although, Missy Parks from next door started at the Academy last year, and I'm not looking forward to seeing her. She's as mean as a wolverine, and I have no doubt she will make a fine super something one day. She busted my lip in second grade after I let a door close on her because she was taking too long to leave class. It wasn't my fault! I didn't have all day to wait; she was messing with me.

It was lunch time, and Mrs. Froshe made me hold the door open while everyone filed out of class. It's because our classroom door had a really strong door closer on it that smacked into one of the other kids in the first week of school. After that one of us had to hold the door every day while everyone else filed out. Today was my turn and I didn't want to be the last one in the lunch line because I liked to go out in the field and ball after eating. If you were late getting on the field, you didn't get to play.

Well, little Missy decided she was going to take her sweet time. I know she was doing it on purpose because she liked to mess with everyone and she knew I wanted to get in line early to play. She's mean, I'm telling you. She always has been. So I got tired of waiting and let the door go so I could take off to catch up with everyone. Of course, the door smacked her as it slammed shut. It didn't hurt her a bit, as one of her many powers is Class 3 toughness and strength, like Maria. Honestly, I could have dropped the entire building the door was attached to on her and it wouldn't hurt her. She's also a lightning elemental, but I was fortunate that power didn't manifest until we were in junior high. Anyway, when she caught up with me, I was at the head of the line and just about to hand the checker my lunch card. That's when she grabbed me by the hair and popped me one right in the mouth. I've stayed out of her way ever since.

That was also the day I vowed to make my armor super suit so no one could ever hit me in the mouth again. Or, so it doesn't hurt as much when I do get hit. I'm a problem solver, and getting hit in the mouth is a problem for me.

I've mentioned "Class" level a couple times now, so let me explain. A Class 3, in any superpower, and especially in physical strength and toughness, is all the rage in the genetic breeding program. It has been for the last twenty years since FTL space drives were invented and NASA put the word out that the only people who will qualify to go on an FTL spaceship is required to be a Class 3 or above physically. That's so they can handle a constant acceleration of 30Gs. A Class 3 can bench press a couple tons and, like I said, you could drop a building on them and they won't be hurt.

If your parents do not have the genetics to pass on a power, there is still hope. It's an expensive genetic modification because such a complex string of genetic code has to be spliced into your DNA. Attaching superpowered molecular strands to human DNA is tricky.

When my parents were "designing" me, they didn't include Class 3 strength in their little bag of genetic goodies. If they had, they would have had to give up on most of the other genetic mods they wanted me to have. So they settled for me inheriting the Class 2 physical strength and durability that both of them have. Fortunately, inheriting Class 2 strength from both parents actually resulted in my having the high end of Class 2. I'm just going to have to get stronger another way.

What I inherited in strength and toughness doesn't qualify as Class 3, but it does go well with my Class 3 speed. Class 3 speed means I top out around 160 mph. It's pretty rare, but I have met people faster than me. What I have never seen is anyone who can match my acceleration and quickness. By the way, when you punch someone, how fast your fist is moving can make up a good bit for not having as much strength in your punch.

There are a huge number of superpowers with a wide range of strengths. Take Ernie's power making bubbles. It is not strong enough to be useful as a super. But, if he had more power in his bubbles so they could take damage, or resist being broken, then his Class level would be higher. If his power was Class 3 or higher, it would qualify as a bubble shield, and could even stop bullets. Class 4 or 5 bubbles? Who knows? I've never seen them.

Chapter 4

There are a few people in my neighborhood, that I know of anyway, who have the super class levels needed to get into Nova Academy. My best friend, Ernie "Bubble-E" Beck won't get in, not with his only real power making Class 1 bubbles and his borderline Class 2 strength. I really feel for Ernie. He's the ultimate superhero in his soul. We both grew up wanting to be superheroes. I sort of grew out of it, while Ernie never gave up the dream.

We met on the playground when we ran into each other. Literally. He was running, holding a blanket cape behind him, and I was zipping around pretending I had a cape. We ran into each other and then we were fighting over who was the better superhero and who got the blanket cape. Yes, I tried to steal his cape. It was the first day of second grade. I won the fight but gave him the cape after one of the playground monitors glared at me and headed over to take it away. I figured it was better for Ernie to have it than have it taken away from both of us. We've been best friends ever since.

A lot of kids, like Ernie, do not have enough power to be called super and refuse to play Superheroes. I think it is because they know other kids that really have superpowers can get to be superheroes and it just sucks that they can't. Those kids who do have superpowers also like to pick on the kids trying to be superheroes who are only enhanced, or god forbid, baselines. Ernie got away with it because we were always a duo and other kids knew any fight they had with Ernie would also be a fight they had with me.

Not to say I was the toughest super in the neighborhood, but I was one of the fastest. I was also the most willing to get into a fight to defend my friend, and everyone knew it. It happened more than Ernie ever knew.

Bubble-E and I are the best crime fighters in our neighborhood, but Marcus, the "Dragon," Shelby and his sidekick, Ken, the "Animal," McGee, still managed to kick our butts behind the community center last year.

They don't technically live in our neighborhood, but they do go to our school. Or, they did. They were seniors when they kicked our junior butts, which is my excuse for losing. No, really that's the only reason they won. They were older than us. That and the Dragon is a Class 3 that you'd have to hit with a truck to take him down. Animal is the weaker of the two, but not by much, so I had Bubble-E take him while I took on the Dragon.

Yes, that's right; we were playing "superheroes" in the eleventh grade. You can do that when you really do have superpowers because you're not actually pretending. Bubble-E was kind of pretending, but still came up with some rather original uses for his bubbles to fight crime. Just for the record, Animal was given his name when his dad yelled at him, calling him an animal, for fighting after school. From then on, Animal was his name. It has nothing to do with Animal's power to actually shape shift into a werewolf looking thing with giant claws.

Anyway, our fight with the Dragon and Animal was epic. All of us considered ourselves superheroes, but fights between superhero teams are not unknown. They tend to be territorial with egos as big as you might expect. When there are no supervillain teams running around the neighborhood, you fight who you can if you want to play the game. Supervillains tend to keep a low profile when they're kids and claim to be superheroes. Otherwise, they might end up in therapy sessions they really don't want. That's my theory.

Everything was going great for a while. The Dragon and I were pretty evenly matched and at an impasse. I couldn't hurt him, and he couldn't touch me. I ran around and smacked him upside the head a couple dozen times as he stood there, arms waving in the wind. He was trying to grab me, which would have been the end of me, but I wasn't going to let that happen. Eventually, I figured out I couldn't hurt him and just stood about ten feet away from him and glared back. I had a few other options, but if I use any of my inventions on the neighborhood kids, my dad will give me a thrashing.

The Dragon knew he wasn't going to touch me unless he could find something to throw, and so did I, which is why I had made sure there wasn't anything to throw when I picked this location to have our fight. Thankfully he didn't decide to pick up a glob of dirt and paste me with it. The guy has no imagination. So we finally called a time out for our fight so we could watch Bubble-E and Animal go at it. The Dragon and I decided whoever won between them would win the battle for their team.

Those bubbles sting your eyes like crazy and can even knock you back a bit. They make me cry so I can't see anything. Nobody likes to fight Bubble-E because you look like you're crying and bawling your eyes out when you fight him, while all he is doing is shooting bubbles into your eyes so you can't see him to hit him back. Animal was putting up a good fight, though, trying to chase down Bubbles as he got smacked in the face and tripped up by thousands of soapy bubbles. Eventually, Animal gave up trying to see and closed his eyes, lowered his head, and just charged in whatever direction he thought the bubbles were coming from.

Thinking back on it, he may have been using sound or smell to locate him as well. I'm not completely sure how "animal" Animal becomes. Bubbles was backing up as fast as he could and moving all over the field; barely avoiding Animal's charges. This went on for a while to the hooting and hollering of both the Dragon and me encouraging our respective teammates. Animal finally caught up with Bubbles and was about to close the final gap when Bubbles stopped shooting bubbles and tried to sidestep Animal's charge. I had seen him do it before and he was hoping Animal would lose track of him when the bubbles stopped. It worked for a second, but as soon as Animal realized Bubbles had stopped shooting bubbles, he popped open his eyes enough to see where Bubbles had dodged and changed direction right into him at the last moment. Both of them went down hard, with Bubbles taking the worst of it, landing hard on his back in the grass and Animal landing on top of him.

Animal smacked his face into the grass as he almost over flew Bubble's body in an endo, but managed to somehow use his own face to push himself back on top of Bubbles enough that he wasn't able to scoot out from under Animal and make his escape. Too bad it was grass and not cement. It would have been lights out and a smashed face for Animal if it was. We would have won the fight. Or, at least that is what the Dragon and I had agreed when I voiced my opinion on the matter. Anyway, it was just grass and so Animal pops back up with a mouth full of grassroots only to receive a face full of bubbles. Bubbles was blasting everywhere at this point in a panicked, last ditch effort to get Animal off of him, squirming the entire time and trying to push him off. There was a cloud of bubbles and it was becoming hard to see the two fighting.

This is where Animal could finally use his power. He doesn't have super strength any more than Bubble-E, but he's a lot bigger and has him pinned to the ground, so Bubbles isn't going anywhere.

I was laughing and joking around with the Dragon ever since we called our truce because our fight wasn't going anywhere anyway, and so we could watch the "Animal and Bubble-E Show." Not anymore. Animal was pissed and was starting to transform into his werewolf form. I watched in slow motion as Animal drew his arm back. No, it really looked like it was in slow motion as I think Animal needed to take some time to transform. Animal's power is to grow claws on his hands and feet like some kind of werewolf, and that's what he was doing. His face changes too, but that doesn't matter here. It only takes him a few seconds to grow claws on all four limbs. Later, I found out Animal does not like to grow his claws while he is wearing shoes because it tears apart his shoes as his feet change. I guess he wasn't committed enough while chasing Bubbles around that he sacrificed his shoes.

Once they were on the ground, though, Animal kicked his shoes off just before he started drawing his arm back. Growing massive claws on his hands as he drew back, I knew things had gotten dangerous from a little rivalry fight we could all fondly remember in twenty years, to death by evisceration all of us would regret forever. Especially Bubble-E.

The Dragon and I both yelled, "NO!" at the same time and started for the two on the ground. Ernie's face drained of all color; throwing his arms across his face to protect himself. His bubbles stopped shooting out and it had just become the Animal Slaughters a Sheep Show, with Bubbles as the sheep. Ernie's arms were not going to help much as they would just get shredded by Animal's claws. But, getting his arms shredded was not his biggest problem. Not when Animal slid down from sitting on Bubble's stomach to sitting on his legs, exposing his stomach. This wasn't a case of Animal just being pissed and a little out of control; the guy was thinking, targeting, and intending to gut my best friend like a pig.

Uh-uh. No, that's not going to happen. I got there first. The Dragon took his first two steps, which his being slow is why he couldn't touch me when we were fighting. I grabbed Animal's arm before he could follow through and rip Ernie's guts out. When I did, Animal spun on me and tried to take me out with the claws on his other hand, but I caught it too and just held him there. I was a lot stronger than him. Not by a full class, but plenty to hold him. So, he wasn't going to get me with his massive claws.

I was holding them about eighteen inches from my face as his claw-hands opened and closed in a way that was starting to make me nauseous. Did I mention the claws on Animal's feet? Animal used my holding his arms up like he was holding a bar to do a pull up on, crunched his stomach muscles, and thrust his clawed feet at my stomach. I yelled, dropped him, and jumped back just in time to avoid his claws shredding me, and backed straight into the Dragon coming up behind me.

The sorry cheating bastard, Dragon, grabbed me into a full nelson while Bubbles scrambled away from Animal.

Animal's head started snapping back and forth between Ernie and me like some cartoon character trying to look at two things at once.

He was unable to decide which of us he wanted to turn into shredded kibbles first. It must have been too much for his little bundle of brain cells to compute. That's when I said, "We're done! We're done!" before Animal could make up his mind. I didn't like the Dragon, but at least he wasn't a deranged psychopath like Animal, and he called it.

The Dragon yelled at Animal, "That's it, we won! Animal, that's it! We won!" Animal snapped his head back and forth another dozen times before he finally looked at the Dragon, grinned like a banshee, and said to Ernie and me, "Who's my bitch?"

I lost it long enough to figure out I couldn't break free of the Dragon and rip the arms off Animal. And, for the first time in his life, Bubbles kept his mouth shut and didn't step up to answer the question.

Chapter 5

I'm not sure I want to become a super crime fighter or even a supervillain. It is only partly because I still think about that fight; imagining my best friend shredded into a bloody mess, and I can't get there in time to save him. Would I get nightmares after every battle if I were a superhero? Would I do that to someone if I become a supervillain?

I'm not that gung-ho. And, my idea of right and wrong doesn't mesh very well with the strict justice codes for supers, but I'm not a bloodthirsty murderer, either. I'm more the "professional" type. Keep it impersonal. Do the job. Get what I want. I don't need to gut a guy that pisses me off when simple, blunt force trauma, or an ice pick, will end them just as well. Dude, what did you expect? Being a super is life and death. It's pure. Fierce. And ends badly for one side or the other nearly every time they meet.

That's my problem in making up my mind to be a hero, or villain, or whatever. I'm a little more flexible in the right and wrong department than most, but there is a right and wrong there. Maybe I am overthinking things. I don't know; I'm quite flexible in what constitutes right and wrong in the super community.

There are a lot of superheroes who push the limits, though. Heroes use every dirty trick they can think of to win and rarely take a vicious villain alive. If everyone is going all out, why would I even put that limitation on myself? It's a good way to die. And that will be enough about career choices.

My parents spent a solid year and a ridiculous amount of money at The Gene Center going over my genetic code before I was born. I really do have some pretty cool powers.

I was one of five eggs my parents created by harvesting Mom's eggs and fertilizing them in a test tube with Dad's little army of love. That's what Dad calls them, not me. I'm just happy they selected my embryo to be the one they decided to stick back in Mom. As for the rest of the embryos, my parents tell me I'm not an only child and I still have four other brothers and sisters. It just happens they're currently frozen and made up of about twenty cells each. Dad says they are "backups" for me in case I screw up.

Only eighteen percent of the population has no "enhancements," or "powers." An enhancement could be anything from having eagle eyes to having an eidetic memory or sensitivity to someone's emotional state through telepathy. They are not quite "powers." Enhancements become powers when they are strong enough to give what the government considers a "significant competitive advantage" over the "average" person.

Almost everyone has some enhancements. There are literally thousands of them. About thirty percent of the population have full-on powers, and twenty percent of those have powers that are physical in nature.

Baselines are what people whose genetics have none of the extra "long" molecules, or what scientists call "Nova DNA," that makes supers super. They come from "The Event" that happened in 1852 when the Earth was bombarded with massive levels of gamma rays and debris from an exploding star. The Event was the near extinction of all life on earth when the directed energy emitted from one of the poles of the star when it exploded. Remnants of the star had a "near miss" with the Solar System. Which means we caught the edge of the energy beam and debris, just not quite enough to turn the Earth into a lifeless husk.

That was nearly two hundred years ago. The Event didn't just give us superpowers; it caused a mass extinction of earth's biosphere. Most of the survivors of the initial gamma radiation exposure had their DNA altered in ways that can only be described as causing the rapid evolution of "super" dominant life forms on earth. Now most humans, and nearly every other life form has something going on with their DNA that makes them stronger and more capable of surviving than they were able to before The Event.

Fortunately for the human masses who managed to live through The Event, but lack Nova DNA, a life of being average does not have to be the life you pass onto your children. And, they have the super advanced minds of some of those who were altered to thank for it.

Today, a baseline couple can create a test tube embryo and have it genetically enhanced with any number of powers. They can make their child super by going to a lab similar to The Gene Center. That is if they have the money. And, they're willing to have their baby start life in a petri dish, like me. By the way, the government limits any DNA alterations to give no more than a Class 3 level in whatever ability is being altered. They do not want to be responsible for creating a supervillain they can't stop.

Today it is considered a better investment to pay for enhancements and powers than it is to save up and pay for your kid's college. If you give them the right powers, they will be able to pay for their own college. Which is what my parents did, and I'm paying for my college with the money I've made from my inventions.

Most people consider how much damage a person can deal out and take to be the most important factor in determining a person's ability to survive or dominate as a super. That may be if you're a Class 5 strongman, also called an Atlas. (There are only a couple hundred on the entire planet, and they inherited their powers as they passed down generation to generation from the original victims of The Event.) An Atlas can shrug off being hit by artillery. But, when it comes to dominance and survival, that's not how my parents think. They've always taught me any power can be defeated, if you're smart enough to figure out how. True to their own advanced intellects, they believe it's intelligence that is humanity's greatest power.

Whenever I get cocky about my awesome powers and how much smarter I am than everyone else in my school, Dad reminds me of my embryo brothers and sisters and tells me it's not too late for me to be replaced. He says they already have a plan ready to go. The man is a genius and, quite frankly, the closest thing to a mad scientist I've ever known. He may not be joking. Honestly, I'm not sure they're kidding. So, I try not to get too cocky just because I'm the smartest kid in a school that has over two hundred geniuses.

I am also smart enough to know that if I want to be a super, I'm going to need a super suit, like an armored super suit, because I've seen what supers with my physical powers can do by themselves, and it's not a lot. And, I've also seen what a good set of super armor can do when used by a baseline, which is also not a lot. They tend to be bashed into paste inside their suit. But, I figure I can multiply what I can achieve if I combine my Class 2 physical abilities with super armor. Unfortunately, super armor costs a lot of money. This is, besides seeing graphic images of pulped supers in their pristine armor on T.V., why you almost never see a superhero wearing super armor.

Chapter 6

Summer is awesome. I'm two for two, sort of, with Tess and Maria. Tess caught onto me pretty quick, and we're "just friends" now. Which is cool. We still do things together and go horseback riding. It's good to have a friend like Tess. She reminds me of why it is good to be good. Fortunately, she didn't hold it against me when she figured out I had another love interest, which took her about an hour. We were not at the point that she considered us exclusive.

When I am not doing things with Tess, Maria and I are dating and see each other at least a few times per week. Tess knows I am seeing someone, but doesn't know it's Maria. I'm not going to tell her. I'm sure they'll eventually meet each other, but we'll cross those live wires when we get to them. Tess won't be a problem for me, but I'm not sure if she will take it well that someone like Maria is the other woman.

Maria is a different story. When she finds out, she will definitely introduce me to her pleasure (to give me pain). I don't think she believes in being exclusive, but I also don't think she gives a damn what she believes when she's pissed off. I'm a little scared, but that's what I signed up for.

Breaking away from my day dreaming, I answer my buzzing cellphone, "Hey, what's up?" Ernie says as I answer.

"On my way," I tell Ernie, realizing I'm late, and head for the door. I know why he is calling. "Mom! I'm leaving!" I yell to what looks like an empty house, but I know she's here somewhere.

"Dude, that's my ear!" I hear through the phone.

"Sorry, be there in thirty seconds." I hang up and haul out the door without waiting to hear Mom's answer. She'll figure it out.

Ernie only lives a few blocks from my house, on the next street over, and I cut the distance by going through the playground. I'm running pretty fast, but take the time to look around the park as I cut through as I'm already falling into superhero patrol mode.

It's interesting that no one ever messes with people's party stuff when it sits out overnight. Not around here, they don't. My sociology professor says that petty crimes have mostly been wiped out ever since The Event as the stakes of messing with someone who is as likely as not to have superpowers makes the potential conflicts so much more serious that people avoid meaningless conflict.

Before, when everyone was a baseline, the most that would happen is you might have a little scuffle or fist fight. Now, you could end up with an entire neighborhood demolished and multiple people dead. Piss the wrong person off, and they may cave your skull in with a flick of their finger. You just can't tell how powerful a person is by how they look. The opposite has happened with major crimes though, as a lot more people believe they have the power to do whatever they want and no one can stop them.

Ernie and I do hero patrols and cruise this park a few nights a week, which I like to think is the real reason everyone's party stuff is safe, but today I'm heading over to his house so we can head out to the county fairgrounds later. The county fair is this week and, as with every year, there are hotheads, would-be supervillains, and general purpose wannabes stirring up trouble at the fair. Alcohol and superpowers make for poor life choices.

I'm about to knock on Ernie's door when it opens. "I'm ready, let's go," he says.

"Wait. Do you have it?"

"No, I'm not bringing it," he declares.

"Why not?"

"It's deadly force, man. I don't want to kill some schmuck because he snatched a purse. Besides, I don't want to go to prison."

"It's not for schmucks. It's for people who are too powerful for you and are trying to kill you," I come back at him annoyed and frustrated. After watching him almost be killed by Animal, I was sure as hell not going to go to college without him having a real way to defend himself against supers. I know the superhero-maniac isn't going to stop going super hero every chance he gets just because he has to go solo. He will get himself killed if he doesn't have better defenses. I won't be there to back him up. "What are you going to do when you get into it with the next Animal you have to fight?" I'm swinging my arms from up high and spread apart to show Animal's size, to down low and close together pointing at the ground to show where Ernie ended up when Animal got hold of him. "You have mad hand-to-hand combat skills. For having Class 1 strength, you're deadly. But, that won't be enough even against a Level 2. Your only defense will be to run."

"No, I'm not using it. And, thanks for being a dick." I've hurt his feelings. Never call Ernie on not having enough power to be a superhero. Stubborn and sensitive.

"Sorry. I'll tell you what. Wear it for the rest of the summer when we go out. Chances are you'll never even turn it on. Just have it on you. Just in case." If I can just get him to use it once, he'll never leave without it again. "I know when you saw me test it out I blew a chunk out of that tree. That's deadly, I know. But, I was using my full strength to attack. You know you're not going to hit that hard, and you can hold back when you use it until you get it dialed in on how much damage you do. Or, just use it for defense. C'mon, man, I can't leave at the end of the summer knowing you're going out without me. Use this, and it'll be like I'm there." Ernie doesn't really have a heart string, but I'm trying to pull it anyway.

"You know what, I'll carry it on missions when I've mastered using it on inanimate objects and can control the damage I do."

"It does a lot more than damage things. It'll keep you alive nearly as well as being a Class 3," I can tell he doesn't want to argue anymore, "All right, fine, we'll work on it tonight and every day until you're a freaking ninja with it." I'll have him totally in love with this thing in a day. "Now, let's quit screwing around and hit the fairgrounds."

Chapter 7

We drive to the fair in Ernie's car as it is farther than either of us want to walk. The county fairground is a huge fenced in field just out of the south side of town. The fair is made up of a handful of warehouse buildings scattered about the grounds for housing the arts & crafts exhibits and two open barns for the Four-H livestock. The rest of the structures, food stands, games, and rides were all trucked in and set up last week.

"Go ahead and park in the fairgrounds parking lot. I'll pay for the parking," I tell Ernie. "If we park on the side of the road farther out we'll just get your car vandalized or stolen." Which would be ironic and hard to explain since our reason for being here is to patrol for criminal activity.

I get out and look around as Ernie is stripping off the civvies he is wearing over his superhero costume. We have to hide Ernie's costume from the parking attendants, otherwise they will tell the local rent-a-cops about us. We don't need the hassle as rent-a-cops tend to be wannabes just like the villains at the fair. I'm wearing black and grey camo pants and a long-sleeve black shirt I got from my uncle's hunting and military surplus store. Not exactly superhero clothing, but pretty good for working in the dark.

"You ready?" I ask.

"Yeah, let's go." Ernie walks around the car to my side as we head away from the fair entrance to patrol the perimeter of the parking lot. "How long do you think it'll take to do a full circuit?" We always do the perimeter as there is already security inside the fair and we would just get thrown out if we tried to patrol there anyway.

I look around and reply, "We're not going to be able to go all the way around, so we're going to have to double back and make a second patrol to get back to the entrance." Ernie is looking at me with a "what for" look on his face, so I clue him in to my thinking, "If we try to go all the way around, we will have to walk by the rent-a-cops at the entrance to get back to the car." Now he gets it. I don't know why, but the parking lot rent-a-cops tend to be uptight about superheroes and can harass the hell out of us. "I'm figuring a couple hours."

Skirting the parking lot is uneventful. No one is hanging out around the edges of the fair; it looks like a slow night, for crime, anyway. The parking lot only extends to one edge of the fairgrounds, and the rest of our patrol is going to be along the fence line around the perimeter. On our right is a pitch black grassy field and we can't see anything as there is a thick overcast of low clouds and no moon out. It affects Ernie more than it does me as I have low light vision and am seeing everything in black, white, and grays even out in the field. We'll get a little more light and be able to see inside the fence when we're walking due to the lights from the fair. I hope it doesn't rain, but we're sure to get a pea soup fog around midnight. The fair closes at eleven, so most people will be home before it fully sets in and we'll be long gone.

On our left is the fair with all the noise and lights. We can't see much of anything going on in the park as the view is blocked by the big trailers and tents that are put up around the perimeter of the fairgrounds. We're taking our time and trying not to make much noise. Part of doing a good patrol is not letting the bad guy know you're there before you can get a look at what they are doing. We're pretty well backlit by the fair to anyone on the outside, so I'm expecting any action to come from our left. The only way we're going to surprise anyone is by catching them going in or out of the fence.

I spot a single car a few hundred yards out, but don't see any people. There's a back road over there that runs parallel to the main road heading into and past the fair that will take you to Emeryville and it's not uncommon to find abandoned cars on this side of town. I don't see anyone out there, so I'm not going to worry about it.

"Hold up," Ernie says, putting his arm out across my chest.

I stop looking out at the empty field to look back at the fence line. Ernie's been watching the fence as that's about the only thing he can clearly see. There is a little light to see by from the glow of fair lights reflecting from the low cloud cover. I spot cut fence about ten feet in front of us, which must be what Ernie is having us stop for. No one is there right now, but we have no way of knowing if that piece of fence has been cut for an hour or a month. All I know is it wasn't cut at last year's fair. "You want to do a stake out?" I ask him.

"Yeah, let's give it some time and see what happens," is Ernie's reply.

There's no place to hide, so we back off and go prone about twenty yards out in the field, and away from the fence, so we're not being backlit by the fair. Time to wait.

It doesn't take long. Someone in the park yells, "Stop! Stop!" and is then drown out by yells and the stomping and pounding of feet from people scattering just on the other side of the two big rides that are placed up against this part of the back fence. Ernie smacks my arm and points at the large canvas tent flaps between the two rides that are being used to give a solid appearance and keep people from wandering behind the rides. The flaps blow out like they were hit by a strong wind and three people come running out through the opening. They're all pretty big, dressed in dark colors, and wearing Halloween masks. The one in the back is wearing green camo pants and a black t-shirt and is yelling, "Go, go, go!" at the top of his lungs through his rubber Frankenstein mask.

I'm pretty sure one of them is a super because the flaps on the tents didn't blow themselves out. "I think one of them is a super," I say, "Maybe an ele." Then I bounce up into a crouch. "Bubble, can you snipe until we know what kind of power these guys have?" I don't want to see a repeat of the Bubble-E and Animal Show.

Elementals are some of the most dangerous supers there are and my mentioning there could be one was all Ernie needed to overcome his eagerness to get in the fight. At least a little. "I'll stay back as far as I can and still use my power, but I'm not going to stay out of it while you go it alone."

That's fair. "We do it together, but we do it smart. Try to work from the field and stay away from the fence. I don't want us to be backlit by the fair." The three masked men had to have lost their night vision while they were in the brightly lit fair and I want to take advantage of using the night for cover as long as we can. Bubble will be hitting them with his bubbles, so I pull my goggles up from around my neck so I won't get any bubble goop in my eyes. Ernie moves out into the field in front of the fence then turns back to our three villains, soon to be victims of our vigilante justice. I head for the cut in the fence. Having him stay at range will help me focus on what I need to be doing without worrying about him.

"What are you going to do?" I hear Ernie shout-whisper from behind me. Fortunately, there is so much commotion going on from the three men and all the people yelling and trampling around on the other side of the two rides that no one else hears him.

I turn back to Ernie and reply in my own shout-whisper, "I'm going to peck them to death." That's what I call it when I do hit and runs to avoid getting hit myself. I can't hit them as hard, but it is much more effective at keeping me protected from taking a hit by someone when I don't know what their powers are. Ernie and I have used this tactic before, but this'll be the first time we did it in the dark where blinding them with bubbles won't have much more of an effect on them as the darkness will on Ernie. The stinging eyes and bubbles will have a better chance of confusing them, though, as they're not going to know what's happening to them. I can use that.

The first guy to reach the fence is wearing black pants with a hoodie and is wearing a green alien mask. He stops suddenly about six feet from the fence and, like the Three Stooges, the other two guys smash into the back of him. Both fall down, but the guy they ran into, wasn't pushed forward even a step. It seems our little green alien is at least a Class 1 in strength.

"What the hell! Why'd you stop?" One of them yells while the other is rubbing his face after running into the back of the first guy in what I'm betting felt like a brick wall.

A muffled, "Ow," comes from the guy who is now holding his nose. You can bet he's a baseline, at least physically.

"Quiet!" Green Alien Guy says.

All three of them freeze where they are. I think he heard us. They're not looking my way, though, so it doesn't look like they have infrared or night vision. I concentrate on my mind for a second to see if I can detect someone attempting to probe my thoughts. Nothing, they're probably not telepaths.

The two on the ground get back up without making any noise; all of them looking around in a half-crouch. I'm not too worried if they haven't spotted me yet. I just need to be quiet and still until they get through the fence.

They start moving towards the hole in the fence again; they're having a hard time seeing where they are going as the second and third guy are holding their arms out to keep from running into Green Alien Guy again. Green Alien Guy holds open the fence for the other two as they duck through. "Get to the car," he tells them.

I wait until they start running away from the fence and then give my best pissed-off-dad voice, shouting, "Freeze! Hands up in the air! You're all under arrest!" The words are different, but that voice always works on me when my Dad uses it on me.

All three freeze and start looking around.

"I said get your hands up. Now!" I yelled, "If I have to tell you again I'm going to shoot!"

The three would be thieves stand still; putting their hands in the air. Two of them start to go down on their knees without being told. Apparently, they've done this before. The guy in the green alien mask stays standing and keeps looking around.

"You're not cops." He says. "You don't have flashlights."

Flashlights? Are cops required to carry flashlights? "Shut up and get your hands up!" I shout back.

Green Alien Guy drops his hands; zeroing in on the sound of my voice. I start sliding to my right. This is about to go south, but as a hero, I can't be the first to attack as long as they're just standing there. There are rules to being a superhero. They're annoying rules.

Dropping into a crouch and ripping off his mask, Green Alien Guy shouts, "Get moving!" to the other two guys and leaps right at where I was standing.

Instead of turning and facing now unmasked Green Alien Guy, I make a speed move to the opposite side of him to his friends, looping around to put them between us, and rush the nearest of the two who is no longer on his knees and is now up and running toward the car I saw earlier. I punch him twice, once in his ribs above his kidneys where I feel the crunch of his ribs, then once again in the kidney, and he drops screaming to the ground. For a moment I feel a rush of air all around me, but it stops when he drops. The guy either forgot to use his powers, or they were not all that powerful to begin with. Amateurs.

The other guy that was kneeling is now making pretty good speed toward the car. He must have at least enhanced speed. I break toward him and look back to Green Alien Guy and see he's batting at something in front of his face and yelling obscenities continuously. Bubble-E is laying it on him.

That gives me time to go after the second guy running to the car. He's got a twenty yard head start on me now, and I need to get him down before I can take on Green Alien Guy. It takes me about two seconds to catch up with the guy running and as I'm about to repeat the ribs and kidney shots I gave to the other guy, he must sense me and turns to take a swing at me. When he turns, it places his solar plexus right in line with my punch, and I drive home a sharp punch. His guts seize up and air whooshes out of his mouth. I can tell he is Class 2 strength as he resists the hit pretty well. I'll need to hit him a lot harder if I want to take him down. He's like The Dragon, but he would have laughed at me. It is clear this guy is not as good of a fighter as he lets me draw back again and put everything I have into a second punch into his gut.

He buckles under my punch. I jump back as he crumples to the ground with a choked on gasp of breath. "Stay down," I tell him.

Green Alien Guy is about to plow into me when I hear Ernie's shout, "Look out!"

I jump straight up like a startled cat as that is the fastest move I have from a dead stop standing and Green Alien Guy passes directly beneath me. He manages to hit my foot on the way by and I start spinning and hit the ground pretty hard. It doesn't hurt me when I land on my shoulder, but it is disorienting, which is not good for staying out of the guy's way.

I shake my head and have just enough time to see Green Alien Guy has swung around for another pass. He's going to try to use his whole body as a weapon like Class 4 and 5 strong men would do. I know there's no way a punk at a fair is a Class 5. Although, I think his freight train style attack is going to work for him in taking out a Class 2 like me, even if he's a measly Class 3. I do something I never thought I would need to do until I really do go pro. I activate a similar device to the one I was trying to get Ernie to wear and my body takes on a blue glow.

Bubble-E sees I'm in trouble and is running towards us screaming at the top of his lungs things I can't understand and Green Alien Guy is just about to run me over, so I make like an Armadillo, drop to the ground, and curl into a ball to protect myself.

Green Alien Guy turns his last step into a kick and drives his foot into my side. I can feel the kick through the repeller field and I go flying. It's not like the rib crunching blast it could have been; more like I'm being kicked through a couch cushion or blocking pad. Green Alien Guy's foot bounces back and literally makes him do a forward one-and-a-half flip and plowing his face into the ground. It didn't hurt him, but the humiliation factor is monumental. Around eighty percent of the force from the kick was sent back into his foot by the repeller field.

I jump back to my feet as Green Alien Guy stands up slowly, confusion showing all over his face under the dirt pie he just ate. Even in the dark, I can see the scowl.

"Nice trick. You're going to pay for that."

With the repeller field, I am about an even match for Green Alien Guy in toughness. Strength works a little differently, however. I can hit him just as hard as he can hit me because of the field, but I won't win any weightlifting contests. That is so long as the custom made, five minute, ionic battery holds out. I also have my usual speed advantage; so long as he does not get his hands on me.

I say, "You're not going to win this before help arrives and your buddies aren't going anywhere. Why don't you just go get in your car and drive away while you can?" I can feel a vacuum created when Ernie's mouth drops open from him sucking in air. I have just committed an unforgivable sin.

Green Alien Guy says, "Yeah, you gonna do me a favor, eh?" as starts walking towards me. "How 'bout I just see how long that shield of yours lasts before I can crush your skull?"

I zip around the guy faster than he can follow in the dark to a place between him and Ernie. Behind my back, I wave at Ernie to get back. "Because you're never going to get another shot on my shield," I say. That got his attention.

Realizing he's dealing with someone a good deal faster than he is and not just a shield buffed squishy, Green Alien Guy stops his advance. He says, "You're lucky I don't have time for you, punk," then turns around, runs to his buddies on the ground. One retching his guts up from the shots to the solar plexus I gave him and the other is nursing broken ribs and a ruptured kidney. Green Alien Guy grabs the guys and throws them over his shoulder as he runs for their car.

"You let him go," is Ernie's statement in the form of an accusation.

"That's right, I did."

"Why?" He's getting angry.

"Because we couldn't win," I say as I turn off my device while still watching Green Alien Guy running away with his buddies bouncing around over his shoulder. "It would have taken too long to take him down, and the rent-a-cops will be here in any second. Somebody could get killed."

"But you let him get away," was Ernie's defeated response as he turned back toward the hole in the fence to meet the approaching flashlights of the fair's security people.

Right then I remember a line I heard in an old movie, "A good man always knows his limitations." Ernie knows his, he just doesn't accept them. That's good and bad. Right now, it would be bad.

Chapter 8

The summer goes about as well as I can ask; Ernie starts using the repeller device I made for him. Tess and Maria find out about each other, or rather I find out they already know about each other. Neither says a word about it until I say my goodbye to Maria and she punches me in the gut and tells me I'm not as smart as I think I am, to which I silently disagree — Saying it out loud will just mean I have to pick myself up off the ground a second time. Silence is golden. Besides, at the moment I can't breathe well enough to use words. Then she hauls me up and gives me a kiss, slaps me, and tells me not to screw it up. I think she means college, but I'm not going to ask. Mom and Dad are not making the trip out to Nova Academy to get me settled as they know I'm pretty independent and really don't want them getting in the way. So instead I get a teary hug from Mom and a backslapping hug from Dad when they drop me off at the airport.

Nova Academy, in North Chicago, is located at a former Navy training center the government sold off fifty years ago. It is a huge campus that is spread out over the entirety of the former base to give enough room for all of the supers to be as super as they can be, without having to hold back because there's a squishy nearby.

After we land and debark at Terminal 3 of Chicago O'Hare, I make my way to the Shuttle Bus Center next to the Lot A Parking structure to catch the bus to the academy. The bus looks like it used to be one of the rental car shuttles with its green and white stripe paint, except that "Nova Academy" is painted over it in big red lettering. "Hi. You heading for Nova Academy?" I ask the driver, who is a little Italian guy with a pot belly and receding hairline.

He stands up from his seat and steps out of the bus into me in response, so I take a step back. His bus; his rules. "Sure is," he says, "Let's put your bags in the back and get you loaded." We walk to the back and he grabs my bags; throwing them over the lip of the back gate onto the floor of the shuttle along with several other bags as I cringe at the thought of how many of my tools and equipment he just threw out of alignment.

"Could you go easy on the bags? I have some pretty expensive stuff in there and I don't want it broken," I ask him.

He throws my other large bag in the same way, "Sure," is his only response as he heads back to the door to board the bus, "You're the last one, get in."

You know, some days I feel like being a supervillain could have merit. Open up my options in explaining to people how I want things. I board the bus.

Three other people my age are already on the bus, scattered about in the seats, so that none are within two rows of another. If I want to maintain the spacing standard they've established, I'll need to sit in the front row across from the driver, so I do just that to avoid disturbing the trend. None of them look up to see me come on the bus. Two have their faces shoved in their phones and the third is looking out the window and rockin' out to whatever music is coming through his earbuds.

We drive north along the coast and arrive at the campus gates, which still have the guard shack between the lanes from the old Navy base. We pass through and drive by what looks like the administration building, which is the first sign I've had that Nova Academy is actually a prestigious school for supers, rather than a rundown old military base. I'm wondering if they're trying to keep a low profile, and why they would want to. Tuition is through the roof, so it can't be they don't have the money.

The admin building is a styled early American, three story, stone building with a dome tower in the middle like you'd see if you visit most state capitols. This is the first quality building I have seen; there's nothing rundown about it. As the bus goes further into the campus, more buildings are popping up. The campus itself is huge with a mixture of early American and modern design buildings scattered throughout its ten square miles. I can see as we drive through en route to the dorm areas that a lot of money was spent. Some of the buildings qualify as architectural phenomena. Each group of dorms is clumped together surrounding a central common building that houses the student lounges, study halls, and food courts.

The campus is busy with cars, kids, and parents walking around and getting checked in for the new school year. Bags and luggage are being hauled out of cars over to the dorms while kids who arrived earlier are going in all different directions in search of their first adventure on campus. The energy in the air feels great; I'm even more excited about being here.

The bus driver looks up into his mirror, "Tesla Quad coming up. Anyone staying in the Tesla dorms?"

"Yeah," says the earphones wearing guy, and starts to climb out of his seat. I see a spark jump from his finger to the metal back of one of the seats as he stands while the bus is still doing forty. I guess bus drivers who haul around supers all day don't worry about them getting hurt if they don't stay in their seats until the bus comes to a complete stop. High school is over. Or, maybe that ended in grade school and I didn't notice. The bus stops and the driver pushes the door release, "Welcome to Nova Academy. Let's get your stuff."

Tesla Quad is the area supers with elemental powers live. It's a mix of edgy modern design and 1920s style retro lighting with giant insulators and high wires. There are giant Tesla coils operating near the entrance to the Commons that are shooting huge arcs of electricity between them. That's just cool. This isn't my area though, and I won't be spending much time here. Maria will if she comes here next year.

The next group of buildings will be my stop unless the map I memorized from the student union website is outdated. "Atlas Quad, next stop. Anyone?" says the driver.

"That's me," I say, and stand as the bus comes to a stop. Looking back at the two remaining riders on the bus, I see they both have their faces scrunched up in distaste as they look out the windows. Huh. Then I turn and exit the bus with the driver to unload my bags and the driver points to the nearest building, "That's Atlas-2 over there. Are you a speed or power guy?"

"Little of both," I reply looking at the building he's pointed at, and scrunching my face up in distaste.

"Nice. Three? Four?" he prods.

He's pretty nosey for a bus driver, so I ignore him. The Academy tries to place like powers together in the quads, then further splits them up by levels in the same dorm so as to minimize opportunities for bullying and mayhem. Atlas Quad houses students with primarily strength and speed-based powers. The next group of buildings after this one houses the students with mental powers like telepaths, and the last building on this side of campus, Oppenheimer Tower, is a single building that provides dorms for the geniuses and mad scientist wannabes. It's a single building with a Commons next to it. Behind them is a large, modern, white building set a couple hundred yards back that is full of labs, machine shops, and even a foundry that the students can use.

I should have housed with the science students but decided last spring to go with speed as my primary power when I applied to go to Nova. It was a safety decision as much as anything as I can't imagine that many super geniuses being in one place without one, or more, eventually blowing them all up. That and they tend to be the most paranoid and anti-social bunch of idea thieving bastards you'll ever see.

Mad scientists stealing ideas? No! Really? Yeah, really. The only thing mad scientists like doing better than inventing new things is taking someone else's new thing and going one better. Because you can't reach the top of the scientific heap by inventing the "next step" off of technologies everyone already knows about. You would be just like everyone else if you did that. Nope, you have to invent the step-after-the-step-after-the-next-step if you want to really make something no one else has already made. And who better to get an extra step from than another mad scientist?

"Sure," I say and grab my two bags from the back. It's none of his business what my class is, and although he tried to make it seem like he was being helpful, he was actually being nosey as I heard him asking the same things to the guy we dropped at Tesla. I wouldn't be surprised if someone was paying him to collect information on the students that ride on his bus. Call me paranoid.

    The driver looks at me and sees I'm not cooperating with his little information gathering, so goes for the low blow, "Atlas-1 will most likely be where they put you. It's over there on the other side of two." He starts heading back to get on the bus and says, "Good luck, kid." I watch the bus for a minute as it heads off to the rest of the campus to make stops at the dozen or so other quads housing all the kids with different power types. It is pretty amazing to bring this much talent all together into one place.

Chapter 9

I may need some luck, but not as much as the bus driver thinks. I throw my bags over my shoulder and head for Atlas-2. The driver could have been right with Atlas-1 if I wasn't also a Class 3 speedster. Atlas-1 is for Class 2s, and Atlas-2 is for Class 3s, and so on. Baselines and Class 1's don't get a number at Atlas because they would never be placed here to begin with. My speed could almost qualify me for Atlas-3 just because of the rarity of speedsters compared to strong men, but they gave me the option. Being stronger than the other guy begins to become less important if all your punches look like they're moving in slow motion to the guy you're trying to hit.

Atlas-2, like all the buildings in the Atlas Quad, is a three story white building with all the styling of an inner city project, although a better comparison might be to project housing in the former Soviet Union. Tesla has very modern styling with sweeping glass lines and tall I-Beams with heavy cabling holding up canvas sheeting, it looks like modern art.

I'm not sure if the appearance of Atlas Quad is due to alumni being cheap, or if muscle and speed types are just naturally a bunch of slobs who don't care about appearances. Or, if they're paying homage to the old Soviet Union Olympic power lifters. For my purposes, living in a dorm where people only pay attention to big muscles, and who are more entertained by punching holes in walls than creating a laser, is perfect. No mad scientist would ever think to sneak into these dorms. What would they steal? Barbells? And, the native population doesn't have any more curiosity than Farmer John's cow and won't go snooping around my projects.

I walk into the lobby of my dorm where people are coming and going from the wide stairwells and echoes of dozens of students talking all at once are bouncing off the walls. In the middle of the lobby are half a dozen strongmen types: muscle bound apes, and an ape-ette that's buff enough that you have to wonder if she doesn't have gorilla DNA. The apes are making a lot of noise and harassing other students that walk by while poking each other's pecs and bragging about how much they can lift. One of them has a "Welcoming Committee" sign he's shoving into student's faces and pushing them around.

Taking a detour around the Welcoming Committee, I head over to the Dorm Master's desk to check-in and see it is crowded with students all talking at the same time to get their dorm keys. Waiting my turn, I keep watching the Welcoming Committee. Everyone has started giving them a wide berth, so now they are moving in a herd back and forth across the lobby toward whoever is closest they can mess with. I can't believe these apes are from this dorm. They musts be Class 3 or 4, or there would have been multiple fights by now. A Class 2 can tell if someone is a Class 3 or higher the first time they bump into them. It's like running into a walking, talking, fortress. Just before I get my key, the herd moves over by the entrance to the stairwell and takes up station as the best place to mess with the most people.

My dorm room is on the third floor. I have my bags with my duffel bag of clothes and basics in my right hand, my backpack on and cinched down, and my bag with all my equipment in my left, farthest away from where I'll be passing the herd on my right. Heading towards the stairs, two of them have already noticed me, the first of whom starts off with, "Hey, fresh-meat," with a smile like he's greeting me with all sincerity and open arms. I want no part.

I'm just out of their reach when I make my move, throwing my duffel bag of clothes to the top of the first flight of stairs onto the landing, and all of their heads snap around to watch it fly up and hit another student right in the chest as he rounds the corner. My "Look, a bird!" shout provides a distraction that works a little bit better than I intended.

"Nice shot!" one of them shouts.

I don't wait to see who says it and before they have their heads turned back to congratulate my aim, I'm at the top of the stairs with my duffel bag. "Sorry, man. You all right?" I ask my victim.

"I'm fine. Didn't appreciate taking your bag in the face, but have to give you cred for getting past those assholes."

Of course, I smacked a guy who is cool and laid back while trying to get past the a'holes. "Thanks. Really, sorry about hitting you."

He's looking down at the Welcoming Committee, "You think you can throw me past those guys?" He asks all serious.

"Uh, no. I don't think that's going to work twice," I reply as I look back. The welcoming committee has moved around to block the entire entrance to the stairwell. "You may want to go out a window."

He looks at me like I just showed him where to find the Secret Door to his favorite RPG game then turns and runs back up the stairs and onto the second floor. Shrugging, I grab my bags and start the climb up to the third floor.

Chapter 10

My dorm room is dark and empty, except for the pile of bags thrown on the bed by the window, so I move to the other side and stake my claim on the remaining bed.

"Hey, roomie," My roommate comes in about the same time I finish putting my clothes in the dresser on my side of the room and start surveying the wall to decide what I might want to put up for decorations. There are nail holes and tape all over the wall, and I'm thinking the first thing I'm going to put up might be spackle and paint.

I give him a chin nod and say, "That you?" and point to the bags across the room.

"Yeah, Carlos. Carlos Jones," he replies, and steps over to me shake hands. Carlos looks latino, but I'm going to assume with the last name Jones, it's on his mom's side. He's a little taller than my 6'2", and broad shouldered like pretty much everyone in this dorm. Thick black hair and a friendly smile, he looks like he'll be okay for a roommate.

Normally I avoid contact with strangers as part of my policy of not giving anyone any more information about me than I absolutely have to. But if he's going to be my roommate, there's no reason to hide the basics and offend him for something he'll know within a couple days anyway. I reach back and we shake. Carlos does not have what I would call a "firm" grip, but I can feel the toughness in the skin and muscles of his hand, he's definitely a Class 2 or higher body type.

"I'm a 3-2," he offers, noticing that I noticed his grip. "What are you, a 2-2?"

"2-3," I reply. Body and speed, when it is offered, are always given in two numbers with body type first, and speed last. Carlos offers up that he's a Class 3 body type, which makes him among the strongest who will be living in this dorm. But, he's not as fast as me, and that's my edge. For most people, body type or strength go hand-in-hand and rarely do you see someone with them more than one class level apart. It's a natural consequence when someone is so strong they tear their own body apart, or you're strong enough to get yourself into trouble, but not tough enough to take the damage. A wide variation is not the most successful in the Darwinian world humans have been living in since the Event. Add in services like The Gene Store, the few families that have wide variations go out of their way to boost their children up to a more survivable class level match their other traits. Carlos is fast enough, though, which with his strength is deadly. The exception is with the Class 5 strongmen. Most are no more than Class 2 speed; presumably, all those high density muscles get in the way of freedom of movement, or twitchiness of the muscles, or something. New genetic research has it the same genetic sequences involved in giving Class 5 strength are also involved in higher class levels of speed. So, if you're the lucky one in a hundred million or so to get Class 5 strength and toughness, it is not as simple as getting lucky another one in another ten million times to also get higher than Class 3 speed.

"Nice balance," he smiles back at me, "Just don't get caught, right?"

"No crap, huh." He'd never touch me.

Carlos and I get to know each other as he starts and I continue to unpack. He's from Miami and his mom's Cuban while his dad is a transplant from Ohio who decided to move off the farm and go live the life of sun and surf. We don't talk about our powers any more, which is pretty common to not give much information about what you're capable of to people you only casually know.

Once I finish unpacking I ask Carlos, "Hey, feel like hitting the quad?"

"Yeah, there's supposed to be an Atlas only party in the Commons. You ready?"

"Bump to that. Just a sec," I say as I turn and put my lock on the double wide locker I shoved my bag with my equipment into and slap my padlock on it. It'll have to do for now, until I can get a more secure place to store my stuff. "Let's go."

We skip taking the stairs, and running into the Welcoming Committee again and just jump out our window to exit the building.

Carlos is about to snap his neck trying to check out every hot chick that he can see in the Commons Lounge. The music is blasting and everyone is still wearing their hot weather minimal clothing and summer tans. This could be a great year for my social life, but I've got to keep that under control so I can focus on more important things this semester. Another reason I worked so hard to date both Tera and Maria this summer was so I could get it out of my system and focus on work when school starts. I'm beginning to think that could be a problem, though as, at nineteen, hot college girls don't really get out of your system no matter how much time you've had with them over the summer.

The women in the Commons were coming in two flavors, Amazon Goddesses, and Russian power weight lifters. There was no middle ground, and the Amazonians outnumbered the Comrade Helgas three to one. It is pretty well accepted that the ratio of good looks to not so good looks reverses the higher physical class level you go in power. "Supers" magazine makes it clear in their photo spreads every issue, without actually saying it in print. When it comes to strength and toughness, the more you have, the uglier you look. I'm not sure why that is, I'm just glad I'm not a Class 5 because I've yet to see one that wasn't ugly as a baboon's butt. It's not worth it.

People are up doing some low key partying and just hanging out far longer than I can handle. Carlos and I lose track of each other, so I am on my own. He was trying to put his best detail on a blonde from Atlas-2, and I am not interested in being the third wheel. I wander around for a while before heading back to the dorm room. When I get back to the room, Carlos is already there, with his blonde, so I head down to the lounge on the first floor. The Welcoming Committee is gone. They were wandering around in their herd on the quad for a while before I saw them going off toward Atlas-3. Some of them were bragging about being Class 3 and 4 strength, which is pretty pathetic they wasted their time harassing Class 2s and 3s. That's a waste of an existence if ever there was one and I'm fairly certain the Welcoming Committee's futures will be as human construction equipment where their brains will be secondary to their brawn.

Chapter 11

It's Monday, the first day of school. Carlos is racked out and sleeping off a second night of partying. It's only 5:30am, and the sun is just beginning to light the eastern sky out our window. I love this time of morning, but usually only when I am up to work on a project. Today is an exception, but only because I need to go over to the science lab to grab a locker before they are all gone. Showered, dressed, and out the door, I'm off for some much needed breakfast. The food court is already fully staffed, but only a few students are here, some still in their pajamas.

I eat a lot and, fortunately, the Atlas Commons is set up to feed the biggest appetites in the super community. Class 3 and higher speedsters have high metabolisms and eating a big meal is a must. I hurry and mow my five eggs and country fried steak and gravy and hash browns. Thankfully, I will never have to worry about cholesterol or clogged arteries or getting fat, and can eat anything I want.

It is three hours before my first class, and it gives me just enough time to tour the labs before class. They were locked up over the weekend, so I wasn't able to reserve one of the larger secure storage lab lockers for my equipment. It's first come, first serve, for getting lockers and I'm sure they will go fast as the only ones that will be open are the ones that were vacated last year by graduating seniors.

My first class is Superpowers 101 in the Liberal Arts building, located on the other side of the campus from the science labs. I have to run to get there in time and nearly take out a crotchety old professor on the way. The only reason I am late is because of the near fight I got into with another student over the last large locker available; it was a fight I lost as the other guy was a junior and buddies with the lab clerk who assigns the lockers. I settled for a mid-sized locker that will have to do. Fortunately, it is located in the back of the labs across from the Metalworks Lab and near the back entrance, so I'll be able to come and go without too much attention.

    I enter and take a back seat in the auditorium style classroom just as the instructor enters the class from a side door at the front, "Good morning, my name is Professor Blake, and I will be your instructor for the next three weeks to help you familiarize yourselves with the wide range of enhancements and superpowers that exist so you can learn the first lesson in any super conflict: know when to run." That gets laughs around the classroom. "This is a mandatory class for all incoming students, but as you know, it is only a three week course. After this, many of you will move on to the advanced class, Superpowers 301, or you can go straight into whatever late starting courses there are available," the professor said as he walked along the front of the class, sizing up each person he looked at as if he could tell exactly what power set they have just by looking at them. "I would advise anyone who has not thoroughly researched their specialty to take 301 first as you may find there is another path you want to take. This could save you taking a class you don't need and wasting a lot of money." He's definitely not speaking to me.

    The professor finally gets to the back row of the class in his tour of student faces and I feel, rather than see, him looking at me. The SOB is trying to mindprobe me. Not that he can get through my natural defenses, but that's just rude, and unethical. I raise my eyebrows at him to let him know I notice what he is doing. I'm not a telepath, and I'm sure he knows exactly who the telepaths are in the room even before he entered. He apparently did not know I have sensitivity and a strong mental defense. It is pretty rare for non-telepaths.

"Interesting," he says, taking a last look at me, "Well, let's get started."

"That was rude," I say in a low voice as I shift in my seat and give my head a shake to recover from what amounts to a dump truck running into the iron gates of my mind.

"Wasn't it though," comes from my left out of a very attractive mouth, which is attached to an even more attractive face, which is framed by a mane of beautiful long curly brown hair. "The man has the finesse of a sledge hammer," she adds.

"He do it to you, too?" I ask the newfound object of my attention.

"Oh, no. He was very careful to avoid the active telepaths," pointing with a wave of her fingers over to our right in a very general manner, "there are several over there; he avoided every one of them."

"You could feel him doing it?" I'm surprised to hear.

"Sure. Not a lot of people can, but I can."

I realize I have been focused on her mouth the whole time and pull back to take her in fully. She just told me she could do something I have never heard of before. Sure, a telepath can often tell when another telepath is using their power, and all of them know if another telepath is using their powers on them, but to be able to tell exactly who another person was using their telepathic powers on in a crowd, is pretty amazing. She is able to tell who the professor was using his powers on, and who he wasn't. I need to take a closer look at this girl.

The brown curly hair that frames her face surrounds a smooth, perfect face with high cheekbones, a straight sharp nose, and beautiful gold flecked, green eyes. Those would be hazel, I think? Her chin has a slight dimple that must mean a strong chin in the men in her family, but for her adds just the right amount of strength in her feminine beauty to place her in my personally preferred category of Warrior Goddess.

"Hi – Theo," are the only words I can manage now that I've fully taken her in, and I stick out my hand. The professor is background noise I no longer care about.

"Carly," she responds and takes my hand with a smile. "You've got a strong mind - and I like that it stays in your head," she tells me, "Kind of refreshing to meet someone who isn't either broadcasting every thought or trying to break into my head." She's still holding my hand. I noticed, but am avoiding doing anything to make her notice hoping she doesn't pull her hand away, "You know, it's always one or the other. But, you're different. Huh," she is looking at my forehead as if looking through it into my brain.

"You can sense what other telepaths are doing?" I ask, even though she has already said she can. She pulls her hand away to my disappointment.

"Yeah. There are half a dozen telepaths in this auditorium; they've sifted through the minds of every non-telepath in the room. Except yours," she replies, briefly pointing at my forehead.

"So why didn't I feel them like I did the professors?"

She looks at the professor like he's some kind of eyesore, "Because the professor is a bull in a china shop. You don't have to beat on a wall to know it's a wall, and yours is definitely a wall."

Carly and I have a whispered conversation for the rest of the class, with the occasional annoyed look from the professor, which I return in kind. At the end of class I ask, "Hey, would you like to get lunch later?"

"Sure, that'd be fun. What's your schedule?"

"I'm in the science building in a specialty class right after this until one o'clock. How about you?"

"What is that, a five hour class?" She doesn't wait for an answer and continues, "I've got algebra until ten, and then I have my specialty class from eleven to three. When's your last class?"

"I get out of my last class at six," I say, and then explain, "I'm carrying twenty units this semester."

"Wow, you sure you have time to eat?" Once again not waiting for an answer from me, she continues, "Okay, what about meeting at your commons later and we can get dinner?"

"Okay. Do you know where Atlas Quad is?"

"You're in the monkey house!" She laughs, amused and shocked at my admission.

Is my quad that bad? Well, yeah. Maybe. *That is a fitting name for dorms full of the super strong - and the not too bright,* I think, the "Welcoming Committee" coming to mind.

"Yeah, I guess I am," is my almost, but not quite embarrassed, response.

"Wow, never would have guessed," she says, letting me off the hook.

I'm taking that as a compliment to my intelligence, rather than a knock on my physique. This has been a great conversation, though, so I'm going to stick with the positive. "So, seven o'clock?"

"Sure, I'll see you then. I have to go! Bye, Theo!" She waves and turns to go; I see her long wavy brown hair bouncing half way down to her very attractive, athletic, backside as she rushes out of the auditorium.

Shaking off the warm blob of goodness I'm feeling, I grab my bag and head out for my science class. It doesn't start for an hour, but it is half way across campus in the science department's specialty buildings, and I want to check out the lay of the land in that part of campus as I will be spending most of my time there.

Chapter 12

My specialty class is Engineering for Advanced Minds 301, located in Hoover Building. I took every advanced science and math class there was at my high school and two mechanical drafting classes and a basic engineering class at the local community college during my senior year to qualify for this class, but it was worth it so I can get the most out of what Nova has to offer.

By the time I get to the large auditorium where the class is scheduled, it's mostly full, and I'm stuck taking a seat in the front row. I hate sitting in the front. It's annoying to have so many people sitting behind me, where I can't see them. Especially a mob of potential mad scientists.

There are easily sixty people here, but the room is mostly quiet with only a couple conversations that I can see. That's about what I expect in an advanced science class full of super genius science geeks. You could win a bet on there being less than ten of them having any more social skills than a door stop.

Walking into the class late, the instructor starts before he reaches his podium, "Good morning. My name is Dr. Manning, and I will be your instructor for this class. All work is to be completed in the lab, using lab equipment." He goes on with the usual spiel professors give on the first day of class that students need to listen to so they know what needs to be done to pass the class, but find mind numbingly boring.

I turn and look back at the room. Everyone's attention is hanging on every word, except one person in the back of the class who turns and looks right at me. Except that his eyes are closed. It's creepy as I am pretty sure he can see me even with his eyes closed and I can feel what can only be described as tentacles touching the walls around my mind. It is unusual in the extreme to have a super genius that is also a telepath. The powers use different parts of the brain, so it's possible, but generally, the more overdeveloped with superpowers one part of the brain is, the more normal developed the rest of the brain. Jet black hair, sharp features, and a nose like an eagle's beak. He has a creepy feeling telepathic ability. I take care to remember the face as a person to keep mindful of.

Pulling my attention back, the professor continues, "I take roll at the beginning of every class and expect you to attend every lecture. Lab time can be difficult to get...." I start tuning out Dr. Manning as he walks behind the lab table that extends the width of the room in front of the white board and grabs a huge stack of papers, continuing his syllabus lecture. He handles the stack of papers as if they have no weight; giving away he is at least a Class 1 super.

Carrying them to the front row of the class, he begins handing smaller stacks of what are thick, stapled syllabi to the people along the front row and says, "Pass these back. Everyone take one and pass the rest," the droning continues and I only start listening again when he brings up cheating, "Trust me when I say that if any of you tries to plagiarize someone else's work, I will know about it and you will find yourself expelled not just from this class, but from this institution." Dr. Manning gives us a minute to let that sink in, but I would be astonished to hear that someone that qualifies to be in this class would be willing to put their name on someone else's work. Having super science ability is a badge of honor and the level of arrogance that goes with it leaves no room for stooping low enough to be willing to cheat. Secretly steal their designs to use to advance their own research? Sure. Cheat on assignments with a possibility of being exposed as being so stupid as to need to steal someone else's work? No way.

"The room next door is our drafting lab. We will be spending the next two hours in there where you will do your first draft assignment so I can assess your skills. The last hour we will spend in the lab going over the safe operation of the machinery. Are there any questions?" Half a dozen hands go up, "Good. Make your way into the drafting lab and let's get going." Dr. Manning walks out of the room without acknowledging the now falling hands that were up. The first assignment isn't just to show how good at drafting we are, it is for us to design and draft schematics for our first project for manufacture.

My final two classes on Monday are required for my major, Advanced Chemistry and Advanced Logic Algorithms. Both are thankfully subjects I'm familiar with from my personal studies, but they will go much further and still take up a good amount of my time. My Monday and Wednesday schedules are the same and make up the bulk of the classes I'm taking this semester. Tuesday and Thursday I have two classes in the morning, Metallurgy followed by Robotics, with those afternoons and my Fridays free.

On my free afternoons and Fridays, I will be mostly working on my own projects in the Student Labs. At least that's the plan. This will allow me, for the first time, to have access to real custom manufacturing and prototyping machinery. I will finally be able to build my own inventions with the quality and materials I've always wanted and not have to send off projects to custom shops for manufacture like I had to do back home.

Chapter 13

It's 6:30pm by the time I make it back to my dorm room. I can see Carlos has already been here as the backpack he uses for school is hanging half on, half off, his bed. The guy from class with the jet black hair who was looking at me while his eyes were closed is still creeping me, but I don't have time for crazy. Carly is meeting me in the CL Commons in thirty minutes and I need to get ready. I'm feeling a little giddy.

Getting ready for a date, that isn't supposed to be a date, but you want to lead to a date, is a delicate process. You want to look good without looking like you tried to look good and you definitely can't dress like you're going on a date. I start to go with my new pair of khaki knee length shorts, but they look like I just took the tags off of them, which I did. Then I go for my blue jeans because you can't go wrong with blue jeans, but it's like a hundred degrees out with ninety percent humidity. Definitely shorts. Going with a print tee shirt and sports shorts wouldn't give a good impression to a trailer park manager, so I finally decide to go with my desert camo cargo shorts and a red pullover from a *Bone Diggers* concert I went to last year. Spending this much time to get ready makes me think I'm into this chick way too deep, which is nuts. Why would I spend this much time worrying about how I look? I didn't spend this much time getting ready for my prom.

Then it hits me. Did Carly mess with my head? Something doesn't seem right, so I sit on the side of my bed, close my eyes, and settle my mind to try to figure out what is going on. This is another one of my powers. One that I inherited from my mom that she made me practice religiously. I focus my conscious thoughts into my subconscious mind, which in my mind's eye looks like a fortress with eyes within a mountain with feet, and start my search. My power is the ability to see the organization of my mind as a construct and to track how it changes and what influences made the changes. I don't need to look at everything right now, just what I'm suspicious of, which is Carly, so I skip past the usual walk-thru my mind I normally take when doing this. I review my memories of our entire conversation and can't find anything, but something is not right, so I start looking for triggers, which my mom taught me are external stimuli that activate body chemistry in order to illicit a desired reaction. The only way to really test a trigger is by activating it, which I had not planned on doing as it can take forever to go through all the possible things that can be used as a trigger. Since this seems to be all about Carly, I can focus on only the triggers that could be related to her.

I've never known of anyone getting past my mental defenses, and I'm a little spooked - and getting a little pissed, which is not the emotional mindset I normally have when rummaging around in my own head. I go through the various ways I can think of that could be used for a trigger in this case: Carly's face, her smell, her voice, even the cute little way she scrunched her nose up a couple times when we were talking. Nothing was happening. I'm beginning to wonder if I'm not fabricating something out of nothing and I let the spooked feeling and anger subside. Relief floods through me and I think about seeing Carly in the CL Commons for dinner - and POW, my brain gets flooded with endorphins. I can see it in my brain like you would the lights in a high rise at night all coming on at once.

Whoa! That's pretty cool what she was able to do, except now I'm going to have to kill her. I easily identify and sever the connections to the endorphin trigger Carly installed as they are very simple and do not have the complexity of a naturally created trigger.

Without another thought about my appearance, I grab my keys and head for the Commons.

Chapter 14

I walk in looking for Carly. The Commons is packed with students, most of who live in the Atlas dorms, which mean they're loud, boisterous, and completely oblivious. Bobbing and weaving I look around the chaotic flow of bodies in hopes of spotting Carly before she spots me. I finally spot what looks like Carly's mane of curly brown hair; she turns like she knows I'm here, looks right at me, and gives me a smile topped with those golden green eyes. I'm not smiling, but that does not seem to stop her smile. Her eyes, I realize, have a far more predatory look than they did when I was talking to her this morning. Or, that could be just me projecting.

Making a "T" with her hands like she's calling time out in a football game, Carly gives her head a jerk toward the double "Emergency Exit" door she's standing next to and walks out the door. I'm still standing where I first saw her staring at the emergency exit as it swings closed until some ape playing catch with a Nerf football slams into me while going for a long pass and knocks me on my ass.

I pick myself up and dodge out of the way of the ape that ran into me and see he's the same guy that was holding the "Welcoming Committee" sign when I checked into my dorm.

Your time is coming pal, keep it up. I think to myself. Turning away, I look back to the exit Carly went out and it hits me. She knew where I was when I spotted her. She knew that I spotted her. And that I knew what she had done. She had to; otherwise, why make the "T"? Why duck out? Should I follow her?

By the time I finish asking myself if I should follow her; I'm already at the exit and pushing through. I brace my mental shields as I go through the exit, sidestepping as soon as I'm through. Carly is facing me, ten yards away, with her hands held out away from her sides, palms out where I can see she is not holding anything. She's trying to show me she's unarmed and means me no harm, but the stance she takes is the same one an energy projector could take to throw lightning, or fire, or a dozen other types of energy. My body jerks as I stop myself from diving to the side to avoid the attack and I start toward her.

Giving a head jerk at me again, this time toward the grassy quad that is mostly vacant, Carly heads out into the open space. I follow and pick up the pace to close the distance but not enough to look like I'm chasing her. Just before I get within reach of grabbing her arm and spinning her around, she spins around on her own and says, "Wait."

Pulling up short, I'm about to start yelling, but managing to keep it down and ask her what the hell she thought she was doing messing around in my head. After that I snap my mouth shut with a toothy 'clack' and just stand there looking at her, trying not to go into a rant. Tess says the best conversations she has with me start with me shutting up, so I give it a try, raise my eyebrows at her, and just look into those big golden green eyes.

"It was a test." Carly raises her hands, which I look down at before she drops them back down and takes a step back. "It was a test. I'm sorry, but I had to do it. I needed to know."

"Needed to know what?"

"I needed to know that you can control your own mind. That you can protect yourself from a telepath."

Confusion is setting in if it wasn't before. "Why the hell would you need to know that? Isn't it obvious? You were in my head! How the...how did you even get in my head?" I'm rapidly moving past my confusion and into anger. Unlike confusion, anger for me isn't really asking questions to get answers as much as it is to justify being angry. "How is that okay?"

"I can explain!" Carly shouts as I start to open my mouth to vent more anger in the form of a question.

I step back, take a deep breath, and let it out too fast to be of any help calming me down, "Explain."

"I really liked talking to you in class and ... and I want to get to know you more." Carly takes a step toward me, "But I don't want to know just anyone. I want to be careful, and pick friends who can take care of themselves. Take care of themselves around telepaths, I mean."

That gets a surprised look from me, "Why? Why would I need protection from telepaths? Wait, wait. I know why I need to be able to protect myself from telepaths, but why does that matter for you? You're a telepath. Do you want me to be able to protect myself from you?"

"No. Well, I mean, yes. Yes, you should be able to protect yourself from me. But it's not me I'm concerned about." Carly turns and spreads her arms out, "Have you looked around? Do you have any idea how many telepaths are on this campus?"

"There is a whole quad full of students with mental powers, I'd say a lot."

"Yeah, a lot. Hundreds of them." Turning back to me she says, "Do you have any idea what they're doing?"

"You mean other than planting crap in my brain?"

"No, I mean reading thoughts and messing with the heads of every baseline brain they can get away with poking into. Did you know that some of our instructors actually give out assignments to control other students? They say it's the only way you will really learn to control your powers."

That stops me in my tracks and I step back and turn to look around the quad. I'm in Atlas Quad, home of the biggest bunch of muscle bound apes with weak minds on campus. Could a telepath walk in here and own this place inside of a day? "They can't do that to me," I say, less certain than I would have been if I had said it this morning.

"I could," Carly says with a little regret in her voice. "At least I was able to up until you came out of that exit," and points back at the Commons. "I needed to test you to see if I could allow you to be a friend of mine. All the muscle around here are toys to a telepath, but they're boring. Now, the friends of another telepath? Them? Friends that can't protect themselves? They're fun. Messing with them is like messing with another telepath when they can't do anything about it."

"What you did was wrong. You don't get to go in my head. Nobody does." I'm glaring at Carly, but as she is telling me this, I'm becoming less confused and angry. "That's messed up. What telepaths do," I start into a new rant, and then realize, "Even the professor was doing it!"

"That's the way it is here. This is a university for 'higher learning.' How do you think telepaths learn? They can do whatever they want here and nobody will say a thing. Because nobody has anything they can do about it, except another telepath. It's become a game to them, and most baselines don't even know they're being messed with or even outright controlled." Carly is getting annoyed and starts pacing in front of me, "And, it's dangerous. Out in the real world, the only way telepaths stay safe is to be anonymous and don't attract attention. They claim to be all neutral and above the petty existence of the rest of the world. They claim to not meddle with other's heads. But, that's not true. They don't have to limit themselves here as far as they are concerned. No one dies; no one gets turned into a pet human — at least not for more than a few weeks at a time. And, no one is going to hold them accountable. Not when they control as much as they do here."

I'm doing fish face motions, not quite knowing what to say.

Carly turns to me, "I'm sorry. I really am. But, I can't let that happen to one of my friends. So I have to be careful who I let be my friend. It's sad, but that's the way it is."

She's looking at me, and I'm not seeing red any more. I'm seeing someone who wants to be my friend and has the brass balls to take a shot at me to test my powers. But now she is afraid she may have screwed it up? I'm not sure, so I leave it alone and instead ask, "So tell me what you did to my head and how you got around my defenses." The whole time we've been talking I've been giving half my attention to trying to detect if she's trying to get into my head again. I don't feel anything, but until I'm able to sit down and focus, I won't know for sure.

"My telepathy works a little different from most people because of a recessive gene that activated before I was born. Only about one in six million telepaths have it."

"Okay and...."

"And, it lets me see mental walls and defenses... All mental defenses, like a blue print. That lets me find ways in that a normal telepath can't usually see."

"You mean I have a hole in my head you can just walk right through?"

Carly looks away and sucks on her bottom lip, almost laughing, but also nervous, "No, I mean you have a very tiny hole that I was able get through just enough to set the trigger that amped up your endorphins when you thought about meeting me tonight. Your mental defenses are phenomenal."

I'm trying to process everything she's just told me and every time I try to think about what she did, I start thinking about all the other telepaths on this campus that are messing with people's minds; it's scary as hell. "How do I close the hole?" I ask her.

Perking up, Carly says, "Oh, that's easy! I can teach you in about thirty minutes how to fix it and even make you stronger!"

I'm still pissed, but it's quickly being redirected toward what telepaths are doing to the other students. If it's true, Nova Academy is not the place I think it is.

"I can prove it. I can prove what they're doing," she says, seemingly reading my mind, "I won't be able to show you what I see as they're doing it, but I can take you someplace that inside of five minutes a hundred telepaths will be pounding on your mental barriers and you can feel that."

This morning I was confident enough in my mental defenses that the idea of a hundred telepaths trying to break into my head would have made me laugh. "Not until I close that hole, you won't."

"Okay. Do you forgive me? I'm really sorry." She's sincere when she says it, but I can see a hardness in her that won't be hurt if I don't.

"Yeah, I forgive you. For now. This better not be a bunch of bullcrap, though. If I find out it's not true…." I let the rest remain unsaid because I frankly don't know what I'll do if she's lying to me other than stay the hell away from her. "I'm gonna be pissed."

Putting my hands in my pockets, I look around at anyone but Carly. I need a reset from this whole conversation if I want to let this go and get back to the fun I had talking to her in class this morning.

Is that what I want to do? She's like a double edged sword. One edge cuts with the grain. That was this morning. She's a telepathic Maria.

I finally look back at her, we're both feeling a little uncomfortable after what just happened. I smile to try and change the mood, "I'm starving. Are you hungry?"

Carly gets a big smile and we head for the food court in the Commons.

Chapter 15

As we walk through the entrance area and over to the food court, neither of us is so much as brushed past by another person. No one runs into me, over me, or through me, which has been the norm for me in the Atlas Commons since the first night I came here with Carlos three days ago. It's a little creepy that people are flowing around us without even taking notice we're here. I swear the Welcoming Committee apes that were playing Nerf football started all moving to the other side of the entrance area as soon as we came in the door.

"Are you doing this?" I ask Carly.

The only answer I get is she looks back at me with a quick smile. I could get used to this if it weren't so incredibly creepy. Looking around at all the super strong and fast students in the room are just a small portion of the hundreds that make up the population of Atlas Quad, I realize that all the alpha males may as well all be sheep. Until now I have looked at these same people as being the apex predators of humanity. Hercules incarnate. But, nearly all of them are completely vulnerable to being controlled by a telepath. Carly could tell the strongest person in the Quad to pound me into powder; I bet they would do it.

So, why did Carly just let me see this? Is this her peace offering? I've never even heard a whisper of telepaths being able to control people like she is doing. Tess has some ability, but nothing like this. And I could never see her doing this. She would think it is an abuse of her powers.

I wasn't paying half attention to getting my food or going to sit down; it wasn't until Carly spoke to me again when I realized we had sat down in the back corner of the seating area of the food court. No one was within two tables of us even though the place was pretty crowded. I'm guessing she is responsible for that as well.

"Theo?" Sorry, Theo is currently on another planet. "Hey, Theo!"

Finally resurfacing from my thoughts, I look down, "I ordered a tuna sandwich? How did I get a tuna sandwich for dinner?"

"Uh, well, you didn't really order it," she tells me, "You just took someone else's order from the counter when the cook put it up. I started to say something, but you were kind of lost there for a bit. You looked right at it when you took it, so I thought it was what you wanted."

"What level telepath are you? What class I mean?"

"Telepaths are hard to categorize in into the class system. Our powers are so diverse; telepaths are really only as good as they train to be. Unlike all the muscle in here, telepaths have to seriously train their minds to control their powers. A well trained telepath is much more powerful than what the class system says they are. At least up to a point. Raw power can be hard to deal with too."

I can relate to that, "That applies to the people here, too. Don't sell the "muscle" as you call them short on the need to train. Most of them just don't know how much difference it would make. It's easy to not work on your skills when you're already stronger than everyone else in your school; most of these guys have never worked out a day in their lives outside of gym class. But the ones that do train up in martial arts, or have done fighting leagues, can sometimes beat a guy a full class above them if they haven't been training. There are just too many weak points on the human body to take advantage of. If you don't know how to protect them, you're going to be in trouble."

"Have you trained to fight?"

"Yeah, I was in an under-18 free form fight league for almost ten years and then learned to really put it together working for a couple years with a pretty serious mixed martial arts instructor. I still have a lot to learn though. I'm going to look into joining a fight gym here if I can find one."

"So are you a badass?" She asks, teasing me with a smile.

I'm not quite ready for the witty banter, but this makes me laugh, "No, more like a running shoes wearing survivor. I never seem to meet up against guys my own strength, and you seriously want to be careful grappling with a guy ten times stronger than you if you can help it."

"Running shoes wearing survivor, huh. So you're fast? What class are you?"

"I'm pretty fast." I've got a goofy grin on my face, "It's about the only thing that keeps me out of trouble."

"You're cute. Funny, but I'd bet your smarts are what keep you out of trouble more than your speed. I can't read your thoughts like everyone else in this place; that alone tells me you have a pretty well developed mind, but I also watch your eyes. They never stop moving. It's like you need to know everything that's going on around you."

Just like I didn't tell her my speed class, I'm not going to tell her that I have the brains to be a mad scientist. "Yeah, well, Atlas Quad can be a dangerous place if you're not paying attention."

Carly and I start eating our dinner. She wouldn't trade me plates, so I'm stuck eating the tuna, which wouldn't be bad if I had made it at home - using real mayo, and not this salad-dressing-mayo-wannabe-dressing crap, with pickle relish in it. Instead of being a big baby and giving away how little I like this sandwich, I keep it to myself and just pick at it.

"So where are you from?" I ask, wanting to shift the conversation to her.

"I was born in Boston, but we moved to Richmond when I was little. My dad worked for the Corp of Engineers; they have a big installation outside of Richmond he worked at until he retired a few years ago."

"What about your mom, did she work?" I ask. Both my parents worked, and I spent a lot of time after school hanging out with friends.

"Yeah, but only part time. She's a telepath too and a psychologist. She actually is a therapist who works with other telepaths. She told me once she could do an entire day of therapy without anyone ever saying a word out loud." Carly laughs, but for me, it is just adding to my very limited understanding of telepaths.

Neither of my parents were telepaths, but both are in the top one-tenth of one percent of intelligence in the country, and both have some telepath like abilities. My mom can block out telepaths from being able to read her mind or control her. Which is where I inherited the ability. My dad can't shut a telepath out of his mind but can feel when he is being mindprobed and has my ability to organize and inventory his mind. I also get my eidetic memory from my dad. But they never warned me about telepaths.

A shadow appears over my plate, and I look up. Standing next to our table is a mousy looking girl with stringy hair done up in pigtails. She looks at me for a second and frowns before looking at Carly and saying, "Would you mind turning it down a bit?"

Carly sits up straight and looks around the seating area, "Oh, sorry. Sure."

"Thanks." Mousy Girl looks at me again and stares long enough to make me want to ask her who she is staring at. Instead, I raise my eyebrows at her and stare back until she finally tilts her head to one side, then spins around and walks away.

"What was that about?"

"Oh, nothing. I was affecting her boyfriend; she didn't like it." We look back over Carly's shoulder and Mousy Girl is holding hands with a blond haired, beach bum, looking Ken Doll who is wearing a wife beater tank top. He's totally ripped and has muscles everywhere; her hands are all over him.

"Is she a telepath too?"

"Yeah. I don't think she was able to sense it was me, but it was pretty obvious with everyone flowing around us like running water. That, and no one is sitting within three tables of us. Did you notice how she looked at you?"

"Yeah, I could feel her. What was that about?"

"She was trying to read your mind. I don't think she's ever been totally blocked before."

"Wow, is it that big a deal?"

"For you, yeah. You're like looking at a wall. Even most telepaths can be read unless they are actively trying to block you out. But they have a spongier feel. Like looking through a fogged mirror. You, you're just a solid wall, and you just don't see that."

"Cool. Wait, my hole is gone now, right? No one can sneak in my head again?"

"No, it's still there. But I wouldn't worry about anyone else being able to get through it. Not many have my ability."

"Okay. Good. Will you help me close the hole?"

"Sure. It won't take long to fix. But, do you have a couple hours to sit around and let me try to crack open your head afterwards?"

"No, not right now. But, I might take you up on it later." Letting her try to crack open my head doesn't sound like something I want to do, but how else am I going to learn to protect myself?

Carly's finished eating, and I'm not going to try to eat any more of that tuna sandwich. It would make me barf all over Carly if I did. "Hey, you want to get out of here? Go for a walk around the quad?"

She gets a big smile like she's surprised I asked her, "Sure."

I grab both of our trays and dump them on the way out. Once again people just seem to flow around us as we make our way out of the Commons. It's after seven, the sun is low on the horizon; lighting up the underside of some high clouds and giving them an orange color backed by the first stars starting to come out. It's still warm out as the sidewalk is bleeding off heat from the day, but there is a light cool breeze that feels really good. Carly and I start heading across the quad to the outer walkway that runs between the parking lots and dorms and loops around the entire quad. Other than the occasional student walking across our path from their car to the dorms, there is no one around us. All the hormone induced activities that seem to dominate Atlas Quad socializing tends to happen back at the Commons, so there is very little going on out here.

"Thanks for clueing me in on telepaths." I'm still a little stunned about it and don't know what else to say.

"You deserve to know. I wish everyone could know."

We walk around the quad making small talk, getting to know each other like a normal guy and girl would do when they first meet. I'm feeling that great feeling you get when meeting a girl that rings all your bells and my anger from earlier is gone. She's got everything Tess has for smarts and strength of personality. And, she's got everything Maria has for being powerful and brazen, but she's doesn't seem full of anger. At least that's how I'm choosing to read her. Right now she's the perfect girl; I'm feeling pretty good about the unexpected opportunity for a new girlfriend. We'll see how long it lasts.

Chapter 16

Classes in the first week are easy with the exception of all the reading that has been assigned for the second week. Nova Academy has some of the best advanced sciences instructors; none of them disappoint, at least academically. Professor Blake is a telepath, so I really don't think of him as one of my instructors like I do my science professors. And there is no way I would consider him "one of the best." We're doing a lot of case studies, which are pretty wild. And, he seems to have stopped trying to break into my skull. He has started digging into the minutiae of superpowers, how the superpower classes really break down over different types of powers, and especially that relying on a power ranking to judge how dangerous someone is will get you killed. He's also an arrogant prig, but I can live with that as long as he's teaching me stuff I want to know. Even so, I still think he's phoning in his lectures. Maybe I'm biased against him because he tried to get into my mind.

All of my science and math classes are tough, but I've taken less intense versions of some of this stuff before. It seems the Academy feels like the only people who will take science and math classes are borderline or better geniuses anyway, so the classes need to be challenging on a whole other level from the classes you find at a traditional college. I've almost bitten off more than I can chew with all the classes I'm taking; it's cutting into my time in the student lab. I'm going to have to work on making an efficiency plan for getting all my work done because use of the student labs is half the reason I came to Nova.

Advanced Engineering starts out with teaching us to calculate the structural integrity requirements for devices we'll be making later in the semester. The last thing you want is for something to fall apart from its own stresses while you're using it. I've studied machine structural engineering on my own for the devices I have built and sold, but mostly I just over-engineered projects and let whoever I sold the devices to make any changes they wanted to save weight. This is way cooler.

Carly and I get dinner together every night. We visit a different quad commons each time for variety and entertainment. Last night was the elemental commons at Tesla Quad. Those guys are pretty cool, except it's not really safe to go out on the open areas around the quad as there are people all over the place causing the earth to move, animating golems, or what one girl did when she made an armor outfit out of grass, roots and all. Carly said she wasn't really controlling the grass so much as the top layer of soil the grass was growing in. There were also lightning strikes hitting these towering lightning rods that were placed all around the quad. It's scary but really cool, so we're going back there again next week.

Tonight I'm going to beg off dinner with Carly so I can spend as long as I can in the student lab and start work on the subsystems of my Big Project. I've been working on plans to make a combat super armored suit for four years and never had access to the equipment I need to make one. The student labs have tons of equipment. Carly seemed like she had other things to do, too, so I don't think she was upset about my taking a night off. She's not the needy type.

Chapter 17

When I walk into the student labs, the place is buzzing with people talking in little groups. Some are huddled up like they wish they had a Cone of Silence covering them so no one can hear what they're saying, while others are as loud as the apes over at Atlas Quad having an argument over some power amplifier technology I tinkered with, and passed on, a few years ago. By the time I'm half way across the Lab Lounge heading for the hall that leads back to the lockers and private labs most of them have turned and are staring at me. A few of the ones staring are in my Advanced Engineering class, so I'm not sure what the big surprise is about. For the rest, I'm guessing they're wondering who the hell I am and what am I doing in their labs. Most have never seen me before as I'm not living in the Oppenheimer Quad where all the rest of the science students live. I'm pretty happy with that decision, by the way. Even with all the stares. Because there have already been two evacuations of the dorm at Oppenheimer Quad due to out-of-control experiments, and we're only in the first week. Mad scientists are freaking dangerous when they get around each other. It's like they each have to top the others on a daily basis.

I ignore the stares and continue down the hall to my locker. When I get there, I pull out my tablet and interface it with my lock. Three people have tried to tamper with the lock, without success, and their fingerprints are being downloaded to my tablet. This particular lock looks like a common hardened key lock used by the military to secure arms lockers, which is what it started out as when I purchased it in a lot auction of army surplus a few years ago. After some minor modifications, it is now a hybrid electronic/key lock that looks like a key lock. I type my password into my tablet that reactivates the key lock's mechanism and proceed to unlock my locker.

My first project is to build a number of very strong, but very flexible, power distribution systems with amplifiers and cabling that I will need for the armor suit. I already have the computer language instructions to download into the school's robotic prototyping 3D lathes to make all of the parts; I just need to cut the various small blocks of the superconducting composite I developed. After that, it is a matter of wrapping the coils and adding the electronic components, which I had made over the summer. The last step will be calibrations, but that won't happen until they are installed into the suit and connected.

Access to a private lab is strictly scheduled; they are so in demand you can only get a few hours per week in one. For the rest of the time, you have to use the machines in the common lab, which are just as good as the private lab equipment, they're just first-come first-serve and you have to stay with the machine or someone will junk your stuff because they want to use the machine. It seems to be a pretty common thing for super genius types to be completely oblivious to the fact someone else may be using the equipment they want to use and not even notice they're trashing someone else's production run. It's amazing they (we) can be so oblivious while being so brilliant.

My time in the private lab is scheduled for 4:00 AM on Sunday. I scheduled it then because you can get an extra hour of lab time if you're willing to work the least demand times. I'm not sure if Carly and I will be going out Saturday night. I'm hoping we are, but we've both been assuming the other was available all week and not planning anything until the day of for anything we do. Maybe if we do dinner and a movie I can get back early enough to get a decent amount of sleep before going to the lab.

I grab my memory stick and tool box from my locker, lock it back up, and head over to the first-come, first-serve machine shop. All of the advanced robotic lathes are in use, but I can see one guy running a batch of casings for something that looks most of the way done as he has a big stack of completed casings and only a couple metal blocks left he is cutting them from. The guy, actually the girl, doing the production run is sitting beside it reading the same textbook I'm using for Advanced Engineering.

"Excuse me. Hi. Are you the one using this machine?" I ask.

She looks up from her textbook and pushes her protective goggles up her nose, "What? Oh, yeah, that's mine."

"Are those two the last ones you have to do? If they are, I'd like to use the machine when you're done if no one else has claimed it."

"Uh, yeah. Sure. I'm almost done." She looks around like she is seeing if anyone else wants her machine before me, then says, "Are you supposed to be here? I've never seen you before; the labs are only for use by the science students."

I don't bother correcting her that the common science labs and machine shops here, and every other department's public spaces, have unrestricted access for all students. The only restrictions are on the private labs that are restricted by major. It doesn't matter anyway, I'm a science student. I point at her textbook, "I'm taking the same class you are. Are you in Dr. Manning's afternoon class? I have him in the morning."

"Really? I haven't seen you around. What dorm are you in?"

"I'm not staying in Oppenheimer. I can't do all science all the time. When I'm not working, I need to be able to turn it off and do other things."

She looks at me like I'd just spoken a blasphemy to her religion. "Are you being rude to me?"

"No!" I smile and start to laugh at such an odd question, but catch myself. This is what it's like talking to super science types; it's hard to carry on a regular conversation without it going sideways. "Anyway, I hope to see you around the science buildings some time. I'm going to wait over here until you're finished." I point to the lathe, "By the way, it looks like your piece just finished."

As soon as I mention her part being completed, she forgets I exist and turns away to open up the plexiglass cabinet of the 3D lathe to swap out the casing for the next metal block.

Her last two parts take another ten minutes to complete; I use the time to look at the plans on my tablet for the flexible joint pieces of my suit. I have another formula for the synthetic material of the actual suit worked out, but I'm still deciding on the how-to to produce it into a material I can use to construct the best combination of flexibility and protection. It either has to be made into sheets or into a woven armor cloth.

With armor suits, it's all about finding the right combination of protection strength, weight, flexibility, and durability that you can. That also fits in your budget. This is one of the coolest things about Nova Academy. The facilities I have access to here will allow me to make my suit for about one percent of the cost it would take me to build it if I had to contract out all the manufacturing, which I would have to do if I wasn't going to the Academy. Even with the huge cost of tuition here, I'll come out a hundred grand ahead in savings in the suit cost. It would be millions if I was buying the technology and designs instead of making them myself. The only things I have to outsource are the prototype microprocessors I designed, and the optics and display systems that will be in my heads-up display. If there's a drawback, it's that building it here might take all year.

I get the machine after the girl finishes her last part and dissuade some clown that just walked in of the notion he's next. The guy is an ass and actually threatens me when he leaves. Anyway, I'm on the machine and have about three hours of lathe time before I'm finished. I can't leave, not just because I need to protect my job. I also have to change out the pieces each time one finishes. This machine isn't quite as advanced as some of the others in the room that have a feeder that automatically loads new raw materials and custom programming when the last job finishes.

I'm going to be spending a lot of time sitting next to these machines this year as I make most of the parts I need, so I come prepared with the plans for the suit to study on my tablet. I stick with working on my suit designs while the robotic lathes do their thing, but don't have an answer to my joint pieces issue yet. What I do have is a bunch of research to do to get my answer. After that, I move to the project I'll be working on when I get to use the private lab.

I reserved the lab set up for working with armor plates where you can do metallurgical and ceramics. This lab is awesome with high temperature furnaces for forging extremely high melting point materials, ovens for controlled cooling, and centrifuges for working with ceramics, and a dozen different types of fabrication machines that will let you pour and shape armor plates or even weave armor cloth. I can even make my own ballistic cloth here if I want, that is if I didn't already have a vastly improved material to use for flexible ballistic armor. The armor plates I designed are on par with the depleted uranium used in main battle tanks, without the need for creating it from a toxic radioactive element. It has just as much strength as DU, but can be tempered to different rigidities. I can't wait for Sunday.

I look up to see two guys standing next to my machine. Both are skinny and wearing Arena Robot T-shirts, but one is about a foot taller than the other and has a white band around his forearm that extends from his wrist almost to his elbow. I can't tell what it is for as there is nothing on the surface showing. It either has a lid covering the controls, or it's operated in some other manner. There is an optical pickup on the end of the device, near his wrist. It could be anything from a camera to a laser, there's no telling from what I can see.

The shorter one has his nose pressed against the glass looking at my lathe cut out the power couplings I'm making I had just put in a few minutes ago. I know it still looks more like a block of metal than a casing, so he's not getting much from the view.

"Can I help you?" I ask, not in the friendliest manner.

The taller one's looking at my completed couplings sitting on the cart beside the lathe. He turns to me and says, "What are you making."

"Matchbox cars."

"Really," looking back to the stack of casings, "Not sure they look like cars."

"That's odd," I respond and go back to working on my tablet while keeping one eye on the two nosey bastards.

Peeling his nose off the glass cover of the lathe, the shorter one steps over to the cart and reaches for one of the finished couplings.

"Don't. Don't touch the casings," I tell him, adding a "Please," at the end. He's got my full attention and I set my tablet down on the cart with the blocks waiting to be run through the lathe. My body language and tone are in conflict. The tone I use is flat, almost disinterested. However, my body language says I'm about to jump him if he touches my stuff.

He keeps reaching for a casing but stops his hand a few inches from the casing when his buddy elbows him. At least one of them can read body language. The short one goes, "What? I'm just looking at it."

"Leave his stuff alone," he says, then to me, "You about done with the machine?"

He can see I have several blocks left to run through the machine, so I'm thinking this is a poor attempt at intimidation. "I'll be done in a little bit."

"Sure, we'll see you around."

I reply with raised eyebrows. That was a little odd for a couple science supers. Most would just come up and pick up a casing and start looking at it without even noticing me. I watch them leave the lab and catch a look at them speaking to the guy who threatened me through the door of the machine shop. They're standing in the hall outside the shop; the guy who threatened me getting in their face. That could be trouble. I'll have to keep an eye out for that guy, or maybe I'll just pound the crap out of him until he decides he doesn't want to threaten me anymore.

It takes me until near midnight to finish making the various parts I need. When I'm done, I gather them up and head back to my locker to collect what I'll need to assemble them in the dorm tomorrow, and I head back to my dorm.

Chapter 18

We're three weeks into the semester and both Carly and I have just finished our first round of tests in our specialties. Carly aced her telepathy tests, which makes complete sense with what she was tested on, "Passive Redirection of a non-Telepathic Subject," which is basically what she does on a mass scale every time we have lunch in the Commons of Atlas Quad. My test wasn't difficult, either. I created a housing for a jack hammer. The only trick to it is you have to reinforce the stress points and make it robust enough to handle the constant hammering of the piston.

By the way, there is not a mad scientist alive who ever made a housing for a "jack hammer." But, there are countless mad scientists who have made housings for heavy machine guns and light auto-cannons that have been mounted on a wide variety of vehicles, robots, battle suits, and hidden base guard towers.

It is simply amazing how similar a housing for a jack hammer and one for a mounted weapon are in construction, even while being complete opposites in public perception of their suitability for teaching how to build to advanced engineering students in an advanced engineering class at a nationally recognized university, even if it is a private school.

After our exams, I meet Carly at the Valderen Quad. Armando Valderen is the most famous shape shifter in history who lived about a hundred years ago. Carly and I get a table after getting our food, the selection of which is almost exclusively protein based.

We're enjoying watching Nova Academy's version of the Westminster Dog Show when Carly says to me, "You know, there is more than one reason I want to get to know you. And, I am very glad I'm getting to know you, by the way. The first is that I like you and want to get to know you is because you're cute and I like you, but there is a second reason that is just as important to me."

That sounds like a prepared speech. I guess my assuming she just wants me for my body is wrong. "Really? You mean there's something more important than girl-likes-boy, boy-likes-girl?"

"I don't know about MORE important, but maybe just as important. Don't get me wrong, I'm digging the G-L-B, B-L-G, thing we have going."

I'm not sure where this is going, but I do agree with the boy-likes-girl part and wait for her to continue.

Carly gets that same unsure look she had the night she explained why she was poking around in my head. "But, seriously. I don't want to…. Okay, look. I want you to be my partner. We could make a great team; I think I can rely on you to have my back." I'm staring at her with that stupid look people give me when I try to explain to them how one of my inventions works.

"Like for doing super things with," she tries to explain to me. I'm getting nothing. "Like for doing superhero things with."

Ding! The freight elevator has arrived.

Carly is biting on her bottom lip, or more like scratching her bottom lip with her teeth. I'm learning she does that when she's uncertain of something or afraid of an answer. "What do you think of teaming up?"

I look at her and am surprised at what I'm hearing. Not so surprised that it doesn't make sense. It actually does. I already know Carly digs the idea of being a super and even did some of it in high school similar to what I used to do with Bubble-E. But, we haven't spoken about anything even closely related to superhero work. "Wow. Uh, that could be really cool, but…." I pause.

"But what?"

"But we haven't even gotten to the point where we trust each other enough to share what all of our powers are. Or, what our goals are. I know you're a telepath. And a pretty powerful one at that. But you haven't told me what all you can to with your mental powers or what other powers you have. You haven't told me you're at least a Class 2 body type. Even though I can feel that for myself just by holding your hand, you've never actually told it to me. Actually, you're not a baseline in any way that I can tell." I raise my eyebrows when I look up at her, "Are you willing to share your secrets?"

"Are you? I know you're fast. I know you're strong. And, I know you're about the most intelligent person I've ever met anywhere. What I don't know is how fast, how strong, or how your smarts stack up against, say, a mad scientist. God only knows what else you have going on. You seem to avoid the muscle in your quad, but I'm not sure if you avoid them because they're idiots and can hurt you, or if it's because you're too smart to want to be around a bunch of walking construction equipment." Carly crosses her arms and I realize this is one of those times that my social skills can sometimes be a little too clinical – and clueless. And, I might have hurt her feelings when I immediately started poking holes in the idea. Not much I can do about it at this point, though.

I take a deep breath and give a little twinge around my eyes like I'm feeling pain. "Sure. Mostly. I mean – maybe not right away for everything. But, eventually. At least for what we're likely to be doing, yes. Honestly, there are a few things I have not even shared with my best friend back home. My plan is to use the time I'm here at Nova Academy to become someone that can take on anything that comes at me and, as much as I'm able," I hedge, "to do it without anyone knowing what I'm doing."

Carly isn't sure what I just said, so she cuts to the chase, "Are you saying you want to partner? Because it sounds to me like you're going to need a lot of practice if you're going to be a super."

"I'm not sure I want to be hero," I tell her, anxious to see her reaction.

Carly looks startled for a minute before asking, "You want to be a villain?"

"Not necessarily. I want to be me. Free to do what is right for me," I tell her.

"You want to be a supervillain." This time she says it as a statement; I can't tell if the new look on her face is disapproval or not.

"Like I said, not necessarily." I am not that black and white, but I'm not going to get into it with her if she disapproves.

Carly might be starting to get a little testy with me. I can't be certain. I am certain I'm not doing a good job of expressing myself at the moment, and I'm okay with that. I want to see her reaction first, which she gives, "When you come out as a super, and declare your name, it's a big deal. From that moment on you're fair game – you're a target for whichever side you don't choose. You're not choosing either side is going to have everyone after you."

"When I come out I'm not going to announce it to anyone. And I'll have a plan. But, right now I'm going to do what I want and see where it leads me." I might be the one getting testy.

"Okaaay," She says in a drawn out statement that translates to, "What the hell are you talking about?"

I'm not doing a good job of communication here, but it's not the first time we've had trouble communicating. Carly is used to grabbing whatever she needs to understand what someone is saying to her right from their mind. One of the perks of being a telepath is you always understand what someone is trying to tell you. No matter how poorly they're saying it. Because a telepath can pull it directly out of their minds exactly the way they're thinking it; the rest of us try to explain thoughts by translating them into words. But, Carly can't use the advantage due to my mental defenses; she doesn't have a lifetime of experience saying what she is thinking.

"I'm a long way from going pro. And, I'm a long way from being a goody, goody, superhero," I tell her.

"Well, you're no villain, either," Carly retorts. She's not saying it like she's trying to convince me. She's just stating the facts.

I don't like that she says it like it's some kind of obvious conclusion, "You sure about that? Being a supervillain doesn't mean you have to take over the world or blow up the moon."

"You like people. You care about the little people. What are you going to do that will make you a supervillain?"

"Fine. I won't argue that. But, I don't plan on spending much time with the little people. And if I decide to do something heroic, it will be because I want to and not because everyone expects me to do it."

"From the start? You're going to play in the big leagues day one? Are you kidding?"

I smile at her in my way that tells people they just don't understand the things I understand. Some see it as condescending, but Carly just crosses her arms and throws it back at me with an arms crossed, "You're full of it," look.

She keeps going, "Have you looked at the statistics for hero and villain deaths? Most who die do it in their first year. And very few of them start out playing in the big leagues. You think you're that good?"

I'm honest, "Not yet. But, I will be." No one. Not Carly, not my parents, and not even Ernie knows what I plan, or what I can be. I can't explain it to them. "All right," I say, "I get what you're saying. I've seen the same numbers, too, and I get it. But, I'm a little further out than two standard deviations in brainpower."

"All right, fine." Carly concedes so she can move the conversation back to us teaming up, "We would both have to go in with a significant amount of our abilities and a significant amount of trust to make this work. I would need a real commitment. You have to bring a significant part of what you can do to the table, but I can handle you keeping a few tricks up your sleeve. Are you in?"

It takes me a minute to respond. The whole time I'm staring at Carly, but not seeing her as I mull the whole idea over in my head, "Yeah, I'm in," I finally say, without actually coming to a conscious decision, "I was planning on doing some low-key solo work anyway so I can assess myself. With you, I can do real patrols; it'll be a thousand times better. But, honestly, I may not always want to be on the 'hero' side of things."

"Yay!" Carly claps and throws her arms around my neck and squealing in my ear, "We are going to kick some ass!" She doesn't acknowledge that I just told her there may be times I'm the villain. I take that as a good sign. After all, villains never talk about being villains. And since she's not talking about it, it can only mean she's okay with it.

Chapter 19

It's Saturday by the time Carly and I get an opportunity to go someplace private to do a "show and tell" of our powers to each other. We head over to a local rancher who will let you rent his horses for the day to get off campus to someplace secluded. I show them I know how to ride my horse, Ranger, while Carly just gets on her horse, Frida, and challenges anyone to be able to spook the horse while she's on it. I swear you could fire a gun next to Frida's ear and it wouldn't twitch. I didn't have a gun, but I did clap really loud.

"How did you do that to keep the horse from spooking?" I ask, "I didn't think telepathy extended to animals."

"For some people it does, but most telepaths can't control animals. I have a more limited ability in that I can keep domestic animals calm, but that's all I can do." Carly starts laughing, "I used to practice on my mom's Chihuahua. That little rat dog was so high strung it was perfect to practice on. I'm pretty good at it now. I could walk in the room with it yapping its little fiend head off; it'd just stop yapping and sit down. I could even clap hands in front of its face and it would just look at me. It takes a lot more concentration than it does with humans."

I didn't even want to think about her keeping humans "calm." So I asked, "Does it hurt it? To be controlled like that?"

Carly was horrified by the idea, "No! I wouldn't hurt an animal. As soon as I left the room, it would go back to being a little fiend for whoever was left in the room."

"Okay, good. I love dogs. Not so much little rat dogs, but still, I don't like to see them hurt."

"Me too! I have a Basenji back home. She's the best, but she won't mind anyone but me, and I think even when I'm using my powers on her, she's only calm because I bribe her with treats."

We walk the horses for a while and head out to some trails that go into a wooded area and on to a lake a couple miles from the ranch. I'm hoping we can find a secluded spot by the lake to stop and do our show and tell.

"Have you thought about how much of your powers you're going to share?" Carly asks.

"Yes, I have, and I think most of what I hold back will be related to technology and not so much my actual powers. I also have something for you that I think you will like."

"Really? You mean like something I can use when we're patrolling?"

"More like something I hope you never have to use while patrolling."

Frida stops, and Carly looks at me. "What does that mean?" Then she looks at her horse like she doesn't know why it stopped, "Frida, keep going," and Frida starts plodding along again.

"You'll see," I say smiling at the way she is communicating with the horse like she's talking to a person.

Fall in the Illinois countryside is as beautiful as any place you'll find, once you get away from the blight of urban Chicago. There is a chill in the air, just enough we can see our breath. The fall colors of the trees, the brilliant scarlets of the red maple and dogwood trees and the bronzes, oranges, and yellows of beech, oak, and poplar trees, are glorious and stunning to behold. It takes us a couple hours to get out to the lake and scout a grassy clearing that is secluded enough we can show off our powers a little without being seen or accidentally hurting someone.

We dismount and tie our horses off on a sapling that has already lost all its leaves.

"It's beautiful. Everything is beautiful out here." Carly grabs me into a hug, "This is amazing," and she pulls me down and gives me a slow and wet kiss that is its own kind of wonderful.

I come up for air, "This is pretty cool, isn't it. I really didn't know it would be like this."

Grabbing the blankets, water, and lunches-in-a-box we brought that you can get in the Commons food courts, I lay things out in a nice spot under a huge oak tree. "I think you get credit for being the last to disclose a power with your horse-on-valium mind trick, which is pretty cool by the way. There have been a few times I could have used that trick on my neighbor's Great Danes."

"You were attacked by a Great Dane?"

"No! They're the friendliest dogs you'll ever know. But, they're a year old and think they're lap dogs and have the same energy as your mom's Chihuahua." I walk out into the open grass and turn around, "Okay, you showed me yours, my turn to show you mine," and I jump forty feet straight up. When I come down, I try to do the superhero kneel down landing you see in the movies; mostly pulling it off.

"Oh, wow! No crap, you can jump over buildings?"

"Little buildings. Mostly I land on top of them."

"Okay, my turn." Carly grabs a big black backpack she brought along and pulls out a handful of what look like little balls. Tossing them up in the air, they all freeze in place and then move into a four-by-four pattern.

"Are those steel ball bearings?"

"Yeah," she replies, concentration on her face, "I have these and I have ones made out of dense rubber that are a little bigger." The bearings start moving around in synchronous patterns until Carly has them space themselves out about three feet from her body in a dome shape. "I can do twice this many in a combat situation, but I wouldn't be able to talk - it takes too much concentration."

It dawns on me, "You're telekinetic!"

Carly gets a big smile, "Ya think?"

"No way! I had no idea." Accusingly, "I'm not the only one keeping secrets, now am I? Ha! I love it!"

She's a little smug this time, "No. No, you're not."

"All right, fine." I take off at a full sprint for a giant spruce tree near the lake shore. The tree must be a couple hundred years old as the trunk is huge. The tree is about forty yards from me when I start. I'm full speed well before I get there, run straight up the side of the tree until I'm half way up and grab a branch to keep from pushing off from the trunk. Standing on a big branch, I look down at Carly.

"You told me you were Class 3 speed! That was way faster than Class 3!"

I drop off the branch and grab a branch to swing from to slow my descent before walking back to where Carly is standing. "I am Class 3 for my top speed. But, I'm closer to Class 4 in acceleration and quickness."

"I thought Class 4s had trouble with traction? They always slip when they take off because they can't get traction. I've seen it! They look like they're in a cartoon!"

"They only have trouble if they are unprepared for the surface they're running on. They get into trouble when they get on variable surfaces or something they're not prepared for. Even for baselines, if you wear shoes good for paved surfaces, you'll slip if you go on grass or dirt."

"I don't have that problem, because I designed my own combat boots." I pull up the leg of my pants to show Carly a dull black, form fitting, low boot, with a wide, thick sole. "My boots are variable surface. When I press down to run they feel the resistance and slip and adjust to the surface. If I'm on grass and dirt like we are here, they feel the earth give and any slip and react. The harder I press or more I slip, the more the shoes will extend cleat spikes that dig into the surface and give more traction. If they're feeling a hard surface, like asphalt, they keep more of a surface like a jogging shoe, but better. It all happens on the fly; the pressure on my feet provides the power for extending the cleat spikes."

Carly grabs my foot and twists it upside down so she can see the bottom of the sole. "Spikes come out of the bottom? Oh! I see them!" Dropping my foot, "And that lets you run all out without slipping? Because I've seen so many supers on Super Bloopers slip slide into walls and people and – I saw one guy slide off a cliff that was hilarious."

"I saw that one! In fact, that's the show that made me realize I needed better traction if I wanted to use my speed."

"That's funny. So, you see a problem and go create something to fix it, just like that? That's mad scientist territory."

"You know, there are a lot of up and coming mad scientists at Nova Academy," I say, without acknowledging I am one of them.

"So, you just invent something on a whim? Whatever you want?" She's impressed, and my chest may be starting to puff out. My head definitely is feeling a little larger.

"Actually, almost every one of the science students has invented at least one thing. Submitting your inventions is one of the things you have to do to when you apply for admission and want to take any science courses."

"Oh, well, that makes sense. I had to be tested for my telepathy and telekinesis. What'd you submit?"

"I submitted a process for bonding ceramics and metals in armor plating. Then they asked for something else, so I submitted a process for amplifying the power in chemical lasers."

"Have you made a chemical laser?"

"When I was a kid, but they can't be reduced in size enough for me for how I want to use them. I prefer electron beam or plasma for energy projection as I already have a power generator design more suited to them that will fit in a suit."

"You mean a combat suit? Like the one Kinetose uses?"

"Not like his, but yeah. A combat suit."

"You've got a combat suit?"

"Not yet, but I'm working on it."

"My boyfriend is going to wear super armor," Carly says, and I can tell she's like most people and thinks super armor is for wannabes.

With my best, you-have-no-idea, voice I tell her, "You won't be thinking that way when you see what it can do."

Carly steps back, "Okay. Fine. You're going to have to show me then." Turning her shoulder to me, she says, "Here, I have one more thing to show you. Punch me. As hard as you can, punch me."

I'm staring at her like I have no idea what she just said, except that she can tell I do know what she said by my mouth hanging open. "No way!"

Indignant, she shoves me, "Hey! I can take a punch!"

"I have no doubt. But, I'm not hitting you." My mom would kick my butt if I ever hit a girl.

"You guessed I'm a Class 2 body, but what you don't know is I can take a punch from a Class 3 like he was some wimp punk."

"Seriously?"

"Yeah, seriously. Just punch me in the arm if you're worried about it."

"Okey, here it comes." I step up and take a full swing, but I'm aiming to just graze her arm and not to hit her square, but instead of grazing her, I feel a force on my fist as I get close to hitting her and my punch is deflected.

"Is that your telekinesis?"

"Yeah, you felt it?"

"It's strong, and I just grazed it. That's awesome. Wait, that reminds me. I've got something for you. Although, now I'm not sure you need it." I get a field generator out that's like the one I gave to Bubble-E, and hand it to Carly. "I want you to carry this; it hooks on your belt."

"What is it?"

"It's a repeller field generator. It will protect you from taking a hit and amplify your punches, but it doesn't look like you need it." I was a little disappointed, which is odd because I was completely relieved to find Carly can take a major hit without being wiped out. I show how it works and clip it to her belt. "Go punch that oak."

Carly walks over to the tree and gives it a punch, doing about as much damage as you'd expect from a low Class 2 with the field generator on. The oak has a pretty good gash. Carly steps back from the tree, squares up, and punches the ground. I feel the punch in the soles of my feet moving through the earth, and look down at the foot deep hole Carly just put in the ground.

"What was that?" I ask.

"I didn't want to kill the tree," is all she says.

"No, what'd you do?"

"I added my telekinetic ability to the punch. It works great with the repeller field."

"That's awesome. But, you can't use the field in combat. It only has a five minute charge. You're supposed to use it to help you escape if you get in over your head."

"Oh cool, but I might use it to finish the fight, instead." I've never heard Carly snort laugh before. It's hilarious, and a little gross, but I don't tell her she blew a booger on my shirt when she did it.

After we finish laughing, her at her joke, and me at her, I ask, "I'm hungry, you ready to eat something?"

"Yeah, I'm starving."

The lunches-in-a-box are nothing special, but they do the job. We're not noticing though, and spend the next hour talking about our powers and some of the fights we have had when we patrolled back home. Carly describes a fight she had with another telepath and, for a fight that neither person ever moved or threw a punch, it was pretty brutal. Telepaths are vicious fighters when fighting each other. Carly says it's because both of you know if you lose, the other person can just climb right into your psyche and do whatever they want to your mind. If they get the upper hand and want to turn you into a quivering lump of neurological jello, they will.

We pack up and ride back to the ranch in the afternoon; both of us looking forward to our first patrol together.

Chapter 20

We try patrolling the campus and actually catch someone breaking into one of the science buildings, but campus security gets pissed off at us and reports us to the Dean of Students, Mr. Raith. The next day we both receive a form letter telling us it is against campus rules to conduct superhero activities on campus. So, naturally, we move our operation to Marston, the little town next to campus, Population: 7,248. That lasts one patrol. We don't break up any crimes, this time and we see at least three other teams patrolling and two people soloing. But, we do find an industrial technology complex that is far too busy in the middle of the night to be doing anything legal. The next day we receive another form letter from Mr. Raith, titled "Second Notice." Apparently, the town is off limits too. That puts us out of business. For the moment anyway.

I'm having dinner with Carly over at Oppenheimer Quad; it's our first time having dinner there as I've been making excuses not to have dinner there for the past couple weeks. The last thing I want to do is have dinner with a bunch of semi-hostile, mad scientists. Half of them are assholes. The other half are so socially inept as to believe being rude is actually just a polite way of getting to the point and not wasting other people's time.

Usually, I'm the one being stared at when I come over to Oppenheimer to use the science labs. Tonight, no one seems to even notice me. However, by the time we sit down with our food, several of them are staring at Carly and it's starting to make me nervous.

I lean across the table and whisper, "Why are they staring at you?"

"I was scanning people when we came in; I think some of them are able to detect it," she says, without the least bit of concern.

"Stop scanning them! Now!" I say it a little too loud and look around. A couple people may have heard me, but there are enough people looking at us that it doesn't matter, we already have their attention.

Giving me the hand, she replies, "I already did. Geez, I wasn't expecting it to be a problem. The ones staring at me all have something blocking my telepathy, anyway."

"I think we need to go." These science students are literally capable of anything, and I have no idea if they will escalate having their minds probed.

Carly stands up and starts to pick up her tray.

I say, "Leave it," grab her arm, and head for the emergency exit that is the closest way to get out of the building short of breaking a window. I have a feeling of dread when a couple people hold up their smart phones and take pictures.

We both break into a run when we get out of the exit and I point toward the nearest dorm, "That way! And don't scan anyone!" Carly may not be as fast as me, but she can run faster than any Class 1 I've ever seen. We get to the dorm and run through the lobby and out the rear entrance to put a building between the Oppenheimer Commons and us. No one is following when I look back, so we slow down to a jog, then a walk as there is no sign of anyone coming after us.

"Why did we run?" Carly asks me, in confusion.

"Mad scientists are unpredictable and, in that environment, if one of them decided to do something about you scanning him, we'd never see it coming."

"How many mad scientists were in there!?!" She exclaims.

I tell her, "Two that I saw have been giving me the creeps every time I see them, but I couldn't tell you how many there were. It could be all of them for all I know. What did you do in there?"

Carly seems confused by their reaction, "I did what I always do -- gave the room a surface scan to see if anyone was having feelings of hostility. I can tell you, it was most of them. But, it was weird. I couldn't scan several of them. I could feel them, but they had a metallic flavor to them. Those are the ones that started staring at me. They had to be using some kind of technology for it to feel like it did. And, for them to detect me scanning them? On top of blocking me? That's some pretty serious tech!"

"Really? They all felt the same?" I ask.

She scrunches up her face, "Yeah, I can still taste the flavor of their minds in my mouth. It's nasty."

Skipping past my curiosity of how telepathy has flavors, I start thinking out loud, "They're probably using the same tech. How many did you feel? I saw six that I can clearly remember. Two of them I've seen before."

Carly says, "There were five of them that tasted like metal. The sixth one was a telepath."

A mad scientist telepath? That can't be good, I think, "Which one was the telepath?"

"There were two on the left that were carrying their trays towards us. One was already looking at us, the one with him was the telepath," she tells me, pointing back to the building we just fled as if she was going to point them out.

"The one that was looking at us I've seen in one of my classes. He's creepy," I say as I keep us moving.

"What the hell is with this place? Why do I feel like I'm in danger on my own campus? I mean, I can deal with the telepaths digging around in everyone's heads, but they're not going to hurt anyone," Carly says.

I briefly struggle with Carly's trusting perception of her fellow telepaths. Telepaths are not going to hurt anyone? No. "I can't. Telepaths are scary as hell," I finally say.

She looks at me like I've just declared the sky is not blue, "Yeah. Well, I hate to tell you this, but telepaths do that everywhere you go," she says it like it's a fact of life, "I'm talking about the hostility I feel here. I don't feel it from everyone, but there have been some really strong emotions of hatred directed - not just at me, I've felt it towards others too. I couldn't feel it from those guys back there, but I could see it in their faces. Did you see it?"

"I did, that's why we ran." Cutting across campus, we walk back to Carly's dorm. "I think I'm going to start keeping my repeller field on me around campus. I think you should too."

Carly laughs, "You need to come up with a name for that thing. Something catchy, because 'repeller field device' is lame." Then, "Do you really think you need it?"

I consider her question before replying, "I don't know. It's small though, so it's not like it's hard to carry. I know you're strong and can take a hit from a Mack Truck and not get hurt, but with the device, you don't need to be concentrating on protecting yourself for it to work. Just think about it."

"All right. More is better." Stepping up to me and putting her arms around my waist, Carly says, "I like it when you're looking out for me. It makes me feel safe."

We take our time kissing good night. I'm not going to stay over tonight. Besides having school in the morning, Carly's roommate, Imelda, doesn't like me. I'm sure it is because she can't dig through my brain like a bum goes through a dumpster. Carly says Imelda's boyfriend isn't telepathic and she has him do things and put on shows for her friends and he has no idea.

"I'll see you in the morning," I tell her as I leave her room.

Smiling at me, she replies, "Let's stay at your place tomorrow."

Now she's talking.

Chapter 21

Superpowers class has been a letdown. I've already read the book; the professor isn't deviating from it at all. Carly has the repeller field device, which I've decided to officially call it a McCleary Repulser Field Projector. If that's still too long for you, I'm okay if you call it a repeller field, because that's what I'll be calling it most of the time. Carly laughs when I tell her the name and Professor Blake gets mad that we are disrupting his class. For a minute I thought he was going to make us leave. Anyway, Carly said she liked McCleary being in the name, especially since I'm the one who invented it. Yeah, it made sense to me too.

It's Friday and I have time scheduled in one of the private labs. I already told Carly; she's cool with it because tomorrow we're going to drive into Chicago and stay the night so we can do a patrol downtown on Saturday night. We'll be together all weekend.

Chicago's a decent sized city, but it's about as blue collar as it gets outside of the downtown area. High society commutes from the city to the suburbs and leaves the crime ridden city neighborhoods to the filthy masses. The supers that are protecting the city are as blue collar as the villains. It's one of those places a young villain can hone their skills and have a reasonably good chance of pulling off a job here and get away with it. Because of that, Chicago has one of the highest supervillain crime rates in the nation. They're a bunch of bush league villains who are still working their way up, or who peaked too soon to be able to make it on the Coasts.

They'd get stomped and hung out to dry in New York or LA, but not here. For Carly and me, bush league villains are major league and about as tough as I want to take on.

As soon as my last class is over, I grab a bite from the nearest food court on the way to the student labs. I've brought what I need for tonight when I left my dorm this morning and have been hauling my big bag with me all day so I won't waste time going back to pick it up. I have to get three things done before we leave tomorrow. Two of them I'm going to take with me, and the other is for the suit.

Thankfully, I don't run into any of the guys I've been having problems with when I get to the lab, but my relief from that goes to crap when I discover my lock has been changed. That is, it's been changed with another lock that looks exactly like my lock and even works with my key. What's missing is the custom electronic locking mechanism that was on my lock. Whoever cut my lock off and replaced it didn't realize it had it. I tear open my locker and go through everything, but nothing is missing. Someone has been through my bags, but they didn't take anything. I reach back into the back of my locker to see if they detected the false wall I installed the second week of school. I put it in to create a secret storage compartment for some of the more sensitive items I keep in the locker. It doesn't appear they found it and all my stuff is still here. I check the memory sticks; none of them show marks on the insertion slots. I use an ultraviolet coating on the outside of the slots that easily wipes off whenever the stick is inserted, so I'll know if my data is ever compromised.

I have work to do so I will deal with this later. Grabbing my bags, I relock the cage with the new lock so it looks like I don't notice anyone has broken into the locker, and head for Private Lab Six. The first thing I do is get the kiln going to its maximum temperature, which will be barely hot enough to soften the bonds of the many layers of graphene and my own nickel-iron-aluminum-graphene alloy enough for me to form the various armor plates I'll need to make up my suit.

The helmet pieces will be the hardest to shape, but I have all the forms I need, but it should go pretty fast once I'm able to heat up the sheets to the proper temperature and run a six-phase current through the molten material to bring it up to the energy state needed for creating the alloy. The cool down will be the tricky part, but that's actually done by the computer controlled oven, and all I have to do is load the sequence for tempering the alloy. There will be twenty layers to each armor plate made up of three different profiles that all have to be tempered.

Once all the pieces are made, I'll be able to compress them together into the plates. I sort of ripped off the multi-layer, multi-characteristic alloy idea from a documentary I saw about the multi-layered, Chobham armor composites used on the old main battle tanks. The formulas for the alloys and tempering, however, are all mine.

It takes an hour to heat the oven to the right temperature and another two hours of heating and mixing before I can combine the molten components into an alloy. I'm also making a shield I designed after the large round hoplon shields used in ancient times by Greek Spartans that will make a huge difference in being able to defend myself from a wide variety of attacks: ranged, melee, and even elemental powers. While the oven is heating, I finish work on a weapon I've been working on to increase my hitting power so I can have a chance of hurting a Class 4 body type if I ever have the need. Hurting a Class 4 being the best I can hope for without a plasma beam projector or a nuke.

For all intents and purposes, I've gone Medieval and made myself a war hammer. It's a leather wrapped, thirty-six inch long shaft, with a six pound head and spike. The war hammer is a lot simpler to construct than the armor will be as i didn't do the layered design with multiple temper alloy like I did with the plates and shield. It's just a single solid piece with middle of the road hardness to flexibility temper on the shaft to prevent bending when it hits something at an off angle, and an extremely hard temper with flexible core on the hammer head. I estimate I can get the head speed of the war hammer up to at least a few hundred miles per hour with a full swing. If you want to know how much force that is, square the head speed and multiply it by half the weight of the head of the hammer, which comes out to about 120,000 pounds of force, if I hit you at full power and cleanly, in an area less two square inches. That'll put a major hurt on a Class 4 and seriously piss off a Class 5. The really, really cool thing is the war hammer which, like my shield, is compatible with my repeller field. So when I energize the repeller field, it will encompass the war hammer and amplify the amount of force I can hit with.

I finish up and get all my stuff in the ovens, then start on the tempering process. I finish and get everything into the ovens with about five minutes to spare before they kick me out of the lab. The ovens are reserved for private lab use but are not included in the lab time limit for this type of work. It's going to take twenty hours for the tempering process to complete and there is no way of making it go faster. I move my little operation over by the ovens and start work on the optic cabling control harness for my weapon systems for the suit as I wait for the ovens to do their work. I will have to put a lock on it later as staying in front of the oven for twenty hours is not happening. Until then, I can do the cabling without any machines, so it lets me stand guard over the ovens while I work since I don't trust the other science students to not mess with the oven settings.

      Once the tempering is completed, I do a hot application of a carbon coating to the surface of the hammer and shield that gives it a flat black finish. Most of the patrols I've ever done have been at night, and I like the idea of being hard to see more than I care about looking like a bright shiny superhero. I know, it's not very superhero like, but I've always preferred practicality over appearance.

Chapter 22

While I'm pulling an all-nighter playing the mad scientist over at the lab, Carly gets a full night's sleep and is up early Saturday morning to rent us a car at the Rent-A-Reck just outside the campus gates. She loads her stuff up into the Chevy Volt I reserved for us under a fake corporation I set up some time ago. I set dummy entity up for purchasing restricted materials for my projects. Since I have not been arrested, I think it will hold up under scrutiny should someone try to trace it back to me.

When I leave the lab, I make sure to re-use the replacement lock that was left on my locker to make it look like I don't know it isn't the original. I prefer they think I never discovered my locker was broken into. Grabbing my bag with the equipment I only keep stored in my dorm, and the big case of my now ready to use, fully tempered and layered, armor plates, shield, and war hammer, I head back for the dorm to meet Carly. I'm only an hour late, so I'm doing pretty well.

I spot Carly coming out of the Commons, and watch as she comes over to meet me. "Sorry I'm late," I say.

"That's okay. How'd it go at the lab?"

"C'mon, I'll tell you upstairs. I'm beat." We head up to my dorm. I don't tell her about the lab because we're both asleep five minutes after we get to my room.

We only get four hours sleep before I'm up and about the room getting my stuff ready to leave on our trip. Securing my equipment and armor plates in my locker, I grab the bag I packed yesterday, and the bag holding my new shield and war hammer, and we head out.

I'm a little worried about my stuff in my dorm locker, but the lockers in the dorms of Atlas Quad are built to withstand the strength of the super strong students that live in the dorms and are far more secure in design than the Oppenheimer Quad student labs. I don't really have a choice but to trust my stuff will be okay. In reality, it is far safer in the dorms than in the lockers in the labs. Carlos is asleep in the room and smells like he went on a bender last night, so I try not to wake him.

Once we are on the road, Carly asks, "So what happened at the lab?"

"Someone broke into my locker." I have to point back to the road to stop her staring at me. "They were slick about it, too. They replaced my lock with an exact duplicate, and I could barely tell my stuff was moved."

"Wait. So how do you know they broke in if they didn't disturb anything and it was the same lock?"

"It wasn't the same lock. My lock looks like a Drake Heavy Duty Security Lock, but it's not. I modified it so it has an electronic key as well as the regular key and you can't see the electronic key from the outside of the lock. I'm guessing they cut off the lock and didn't notice when they put on the replacement."

"So, what did you do?"

"Nothing. The stuff I keep in the locker isn't unique enough for a mad scientist to want to steal. I think they were looking for my designs or something I created." Pointing at the road again for both our benefit, I continued, "I don't want them to know that I know they got into it. So, I'm just going to use their lock like it was mine." I blow out an annoyed breath to relieve a little stress, "There's nothing I can do about right now, anyway."

"Who do you think did it?"

"I don't know, but I'd bet it was those same guys I've been having problems with. There's something not right about them – more than just being weird." It feels relevant to distinguish. "They went to some trouble to hide that they broke in. If they were just being jerks, they would have just trashed my locker and everything in it. So, I don't know."

"Well, what if they come back? Are you going to report it?"

"It doesn't matter, and no."

I'm watching Carly trying to solve the mystery; she's going to have more questions. She knows I'm not going to report it so that only leaves the two of us to break the case. Fortunately, she's not into 'what if' questions. They don't really fit her style. But, sometimes she'll just keep asking me questions when we're talking; this feels like it's about to be one of those times. I'm beginning to wonder if it's a telepath problem she has communicating with me since she can't read my thoughts. Carly has never had a boyfriend whose thoughts she couldn't read, or who was not a telepath themselves. I'm the first, and it's one of the reasons she likes me. She used to hear every disgusting, perverted, lying, cheating thought her baseline boyfriends ever had, along with everything else they were thinking, and never had to ask questions before. She was always fully informed before anything was said. Even the one telepath she tried to date would broadcast his thoughts all over the place. Even more than the baselines. It turned out his parents believed telepaths should all share their every thought and live in harmony, which sounds great except that just about every open society telepath commune there has ever been, has ended up in the nightly news for a mass murder for one reason or another.

I can see her continue to struggle with how to continue the conversation, so I decide to help her move on, "Let's not talk about it anymore. They'll still be there when we get back. Today, I want to have some fun, and tonight, bust some bad guy heads."

"Okay," Carly says, but I can still see she has unformed questions she's working on.

It's interesting to watch. She doesn't want to know everything I'm thinking, but she is so used to knowing everything other people think, that it's uncomfortable for her. "You okay?"

"Yeah. I'm just – you know." She's talked to me about it before and is well adjusted enough to not want to hide it.

"Yeah. I know. It's okay. We'll deal with what happened when we get back."

"All right! I'll stop. So what's the plan?"

"We'll be in Evanston in about thirty minutes. We can have a late breakfast there. I found a local greasy spoon not far from the high tech park our target is located at that has five stars on Yelp. It's about a mile north of Northwestern University, and we can eat there. Then, we'll scout around the tech park and make our plan. We need to identify some good observation points for the buildings used by Henderson Robotics. I read about them in Advanced Robotics Monthly as having a new product demonstration tomorrow. It is just the kind of tech a mad scientist like me would want to steal to integrate into their own design for an armored suit. Kind of a coincidence I know," I admit, smiling, "We also have to plan exit routes in case we need to get out of there fast if the police show up."

"What's the product?" Carly is stoked to go on patrol, but I'm not sure how convinced she it at my wanting to stake out some technology park.

"It's a revolutionary, direct mind link, neural interface for communicating with just about any advanced electronics. They're mostly promoting it for use with the military, but it could be used for just about any kind of system interface. The versions available for civilian use are nowhere near as capable as the military version, that's why I think someone interested in the technology wants to steal the military versions or designs. The location is their main R&D headquarters so it will be the most likely target. And, the product demonstration they have scheduled for tomorrow will be with several of the military versions, so there should be some on site. You should know, if I get a chance to get a sample of one of those neural interfaces, I'm going to take it."

"Oh, really? Planning on go all villain on me?"

"Maybe. But, I'm hoping we will get lucky, and someone else will break in to steal it. Then we can put a beat down on them and take it. You know, spoils of war and all. It's not really stealing then, is it?"

"Kinda, yeah. Still stealing," is Carly's laughing reply.

"It's better than breaking in there myself. By the way, that's what I am going to do if I have to. I need that device. It will save me a year of research on my suit."

Carly takes a second before replying, "Okay. Then let's hope someone breaks in the place." She says it matter-of-fact like she does not have the slightest problem.

"You're okay with that?" I ask, giving her a chance to put up a protest. Partly because I don't want her to do something she is uncomfortable with, but more because I don't want to have this conversation when I'm trying to break into the place.

"Sure."

That's all I get for an answer. She's not worried about it. Well, okay then. "We'll be done scouting by two or three o'clock. The room should be ready by then, we can check in."

"What're we going to do for the rest of the day?" Carly asks with a smile.

I give Carly my biggest smile, lean over, and whisper my plan for the rest of our day.

Chapter 23

The hotel room is great. It has a separate living room and bedroom, and a huge bathroom with a walk-in shower big enough to have a party; with multiple shower heads — and a Jacuzzi bathtub. The shower is our first stop and also our last in our exploration and breaking in of the room, and it's an incredible afternoon – our first ever where there was no concern of a roommate walking in on us.

Carly is beautiful and amazing, and we melt into each other in a way that is more than physical. I can feel our minds touching in a way I've never felt before; it's like falling softly into a warm pool of ecstasy. It's almost seven o'clock when we finish our second shower and start pulling ourselves together. We haven't spoken a word since our first kiss.

Still feeling Carly's soft touch on my mind, I check the clock. It's time, so I get up from the bed and grab my 'hero' bag to pull out the clothes and equipment I'm going to wear on patrol tonight, "You ready to get going?" I ask Carly, who is still in bed and showing no signs of wanting to do anything else.

I look back to my bag to finish unpacking, still waiting for Carly to give an answer when her naked body slams into me and we wrap around each other into a long kiss where we land on the carpet. Finally breaking the kiss, she says, "Yeah, I'm ready," then breaks free from me and I look up and down her gorgeous body as she bounces in her steps over to her own hero bag.

If we don't get ourselves killed tonight, this may be the best weekend of my life.

The tech park is backed up against a small river running into Wilmette Harbor, north of the bridge we have to take to get back to our hotel just on the other side. The plan is to get on top of an office building next door to the park and use it as our observation point. It has a commanding view of the tech park and the front and back of the long industrial building where Henderson Robotics does most of their prototyping.

We park the car in the lot of a restaurant in a retail center next to the office building we will be using to observe the tech park. It's a three story, white building, with zero architectural styling that was common for buildings built in the 1970s. In other words, it was an incredibly boring, tall box with windows.

We scale the outside of the building. "Nice job scaling that drain pipe." I grin at Carly after watching her scamper up the drain pipe. She can still see my smile as my makeshift hero mask is still shoved up off my face.

Carly just smiles back at me and does me a solid by not mentioning how I almost slipped and fell two stories when I broke one of the brackets that holds the pipe to the wall. Carly went first, and I was shocked how she went up the pipe like a spider monkey. So naturally, I tried to do the same. I'm faster than her, but also heavier - and, oddly, maybe not quite as coordinated.

It's fully dark; there are no lights on the roof. This office building has a bank on the first floor, so we need to make sure we don't set off any roof alarms, if there are any, so I pull out a broad spectrum energy detector, a little device I made, and sold, for a nice chunk of change that is paying for part of my education. I use the detector to scan the roof for energy sources and don't find anything. There is nothing on the roof that is monitoring us or that we could trip an alarm on, except by the roof access hatch. It looks like they weren't expecting anyone to scale the outside of the building to get at the bank.

"Here, put one of these on each corner." I'm speaking in a normal voice and feel pretty calm, it's just like patrolling with Bubble-E back home.

Carly looks pretty relaxed herself, which confirms for me she's done this kind of thing before as well. "Are these the detectors?" she asks.

"Yeah. Number one goes there, on the North corner," and I point to one of the corners. "Then go clockwise with two, three, and four. They're just motion detectors. I'll get a signal in my earpiece," I tap my left ear, "The signal will be a different pitch for each...."

Moving off without any further need for my explanation, Carly heads over to put out the detectors while I go over to the side that faces the tech park to set up. I pull out the tripod for the mini recorder and mount the recorder. The two 3D goggles I brought are plugged in. They will let us both control what we see independently.

"You brought chairs?" I'm looking at two compact folding chairs for camping like you can buy at an Outdoorsman supply store.

"What? Were you planning on standing there all night?"

"No. I...." The practicality of the chairs settles in for me asI think how much more comfortable I'm going to be if I have a place to sit that's not rock covered composite roof. "That was smart," I say, and hold out a hand for a high-five. I think of myself as a mad scientist; yet I don't even think outside the mission enough to bring a chair so I'm comfortable on an all-night stake out.

Chapter 24

After five hours of watching we knew three things: first, the police patrol the office building every hour, on the hour; second, the only security at the tech park is a big kid who spends most of his time in his beater, a dinged up Fiesta, because he's only wearing a windbreaker and it's forty degrees outside; and third, the entire history of each other's childhood as we've been trading stories to pass the time.

I get the motion detector double beep in my ear of the hourly police patrol car entering the parking lot, and three more pairs of double beeps in differing tones as it drives around the building. Neither of us looks over the edge as we learned the first time it came through the patrol officers are using a spot light on the building, looking for anything out of the ordinary. *Nope, nothing unusual here. Nothing but us night owls*, I think to myself.

Twenty minutes later, the first patrol of the night enters through the main entrance of the tech park. It's a rent-a-cop, in a car marked to look like a State Trooper's cruiser. Only it's without the blue lights that are restricted for police use. The car drives around the empty-of-life tech park and pulls in next to the security guard who's still sitting in his beater.

The driver of the patrol car gets out, and I zoom in with my 3D goggles to get a better look at the driver. His head is on a pivot looking in all directions as he moves around the back of the car and over to the driver's side window where the kid's sitting and I get a chill. Something is not right about the guy. He seems jumpy, and way too alert for a routine patrol.

The big kid is sitting in his Fiesta and isn't moving or looking at the approach of the rent-a-cop and the hairs on the back of my neck prickle even more. The hair on my neck standing up is always a good indicator of something about to happen for me, so I turn on the camera's recorder and pull down my 3D goggles so I can check the monitor to make sure the camera is recording.

Carly touches my arm, "The new guy is a telepath."

I pull off my goggles and look at her. Her head is bent down; her hands are up, massaging her temples. I can't tell if she's about to pull off her goggles or just concentrating.

"Can he...."

Holding her hand up, "Wait, I need to concentrate."

I shut up, look around the roof to make sure we're still alone, and put my goggles back on. The kid in the car still hasn't moved, he has his hands on the steering wheel, and he's looking straight ahead like he's driving. The rent-a-cop has the driver door open and is leaning in the car, then steps back and closes the door. He looks around again then steps into the driveway of the parking lot behind his car and turns slowly in a complete circle. When he looks toward our building, I can feel...something...on my consciousness, like the little pressure I get when I push on my eyes with the palms of my hands after working on the computer for hours. I put my hand out to touch Carly just for the comfort of confirming she's still there and she intercepts my hand.

"Wait," She says, squeezing my wrist tighter.

Turning my attention back to the rent-a-cop slash telepath, he has his phone up to his ear and is speaking to someone. I snap several still photos zoomed in all the way on his face. Part of his face is always cast in shadow from the high collar that is flipped up on his jacket, so I can't get a good look at him, but that won't matter if I can get several shots at various angles and run it through my image compiler program back home.

"He's pretty powerful," Carly drops her fingers from her temples and tells me, "I got a trickle of him when he used his power on the kid. I'm guessing by the looks of it, the kid was given a hallucination of driving somewhere. It's odd because the guy could have just knocked him out. Anyway, when he walked behind the car, he did a full scan in all directions. I could feel his focus move around like a lighthouse beam."

"I saw him turning and wondered if that's what he was doing."

"Yeah, that's another thing, he's got a good bit of power, but his control isn't very good. If he was, he wouldn't have to turn to face the direction he wants to scan or move out in the open like he did. He's undisciplined and has some erroneous preconceived notions about how his power works."

"What does that mean?"

"It means he's still in training and I can hide from him pretty easily — now, anyway."

The telepath hangs up his phone and leans against the trunk of his patrol vehicle, seemingly to wait.

"What do you mean, 'now?' " I ask as I zoom the camera back to wide view so I can see the whole tech park.

"I've been scanning all night while we've been sitting here, but I was watching all around and wasn't projecting nearly as much power as him. When he started his scan, I had to shut off my mind to keep him from detecting me; it's not like turning off a switch after you've been broadcasting for several hours straight." Then Carly adds, "That's why I had to have you wait – so I could focus on closing up my mind."

"Wow," I respond in a moment of high insight. I'm beginning to feel a little inadequate in the mental department, which is new for me.

Carly, now well ahead of me in the mental department, says, "He called someone, and he's waiting for them to arrive. Let's get ready to move if we need to," and starts stuffing our gear back into the bags.

I join in and we pack up, so the only things out are the tripod with camera and goggles and my shield and hammer. The only other thing out is a rope coiled and ready to throw over the side of the building into a shadowy nook on the side where the light from the parking lot is blocked. It's both a quick escape route and our path to advance on the tech park if it's needed.

Chapter 25

A few minutes after we're packed up and we are ready for action. It's not long before a forty foot semi-tractor trailer, followed by a black SUV, rolls into the park and makes its way to the buildings in the back of the park. It backs up to the loading dock for Henderson Robotics. Three men jump out of the semi's cab and run to the rear of the trailer. They're wearing blue jeans and jackets and, I'm guessing, are the worker bees. The SUV pulls up alongside the semi and three more people step out, one wearing far too much bling on his fingers and around his neck. The other two look like the muscle, in black leather jackets, one a huge guy in jeans, and the other's a tall skinny guy, in black slacks.

I recognize the huge one who got out of the SUV. He's the Welcoming Committee sign holder from Atlas Quad, and I know he's at least a Class 3 body type. "The guy in the jeans. The big one that got out of the SUV. You see him?"

"Yeah, got him," Carly replies after a few seconds, "He looks familiar."

"He should. He goes to Nova."

"Really?" she says, looking over to me, "Okay, I recognize him now. He lives in Atlas Quad, doesn't he? He was at the commons cafeteria there the first night we met." She's taking it all in, and I wonder if she's scanning them until I see the telepath walk around the building from where he was waiting with the kid.

Eventually, Carly asks, "What do you think?"

"I think they're up to no good. But there's too many for us, and I don't think they've actually committed a crime yet."

"Should we call the police?" She asks and starts pulling her mask down over her face.

I say, "Good idea," and pull out a disposable phone I picked up while we were driving around today and dial 911. It took a lot longer to get through than I thought it would on what looks like a pretty sleepy night, at least that we can see. "Hi, I'd like a report a break-in in progress...." I pass on all of the information, except for giving a fake name for myself, I tell them exactly what we see, and the operator tells me they're sending a "unit." *Yeah, good luck with that,* I think and pull down my own mask.

We wait and watch Mr. Welcoming Committee go up on the loading platform for the roll-up door next to the one the trailer is backed up to where he shoves his fists through the steel door and rips open a large hole. A skinny guy ducks under and enters the building. A few seconds later the roll-up door where the trailer is parked starts to open.

"Well, that's breaking and entering. We've got our cover if we want to take them down," Carly points out, "But, I think we should wait for the police."

"Agree."

The three men who were riding in the semi are inside the building making a racket with what sounds like power saws, while bling guy and his two goons, and the telepath, stand out on the loading dock. Bling guy keeps looking through the roll-up door and rubbing his ears; he must not like the noise. After a couple minutes, he throws up his hands, points to the tall muscle guy wearing the slacks, and motions him to follow. They start to get into the SUV and Welcoming Committee shouts something and starts to come over. Bling points at the telepath and says something back, while Welcoming Committee stops trying to get in the SUV. Bling gets in the SUV by himself, and they drive off.

We continue to watch and wait. The three that were inside are now making trips back and forth between the warehouse and the semi-trailer. They're loading boxes and equipment. It's a full twenty minutes later when the police patrol shows up. Carly notices him first, pointing to the entrance to the tech park and I see a single police patrol car, without lights flashing, enter the tech park. "Oh, that's not good," I say, "I hope they have backup on the way."

Carly stands up, "I think we're the backup. Let's go!" and she's running for the rope. My shield and hammer are strapped to my back, so I grab our bags and drop them again, remembering we're not leaving yet, and I follow. We can get them later.

Grabbing the coiled rope up off the roof, Carly throws it over the side and jumps over with it, which shocks the hell out of me, but not enough to stop me jumping right after her. Carly more or less does a controlled fall with one hand on the rope, using it to slow her fall, and lands in a three point superhero landing like a pro. I follow right behind and am about to land on top of her when she rolls away just in time for me to land only slightly better than a toddler jumping off a bed.

I pick up my dignity, and we're both up and running across the parking lot. The office building and tech park are both surrounded by waist high hedges, with the two rows separated by about thirty feet and trees in a row between. The trees are full grown and provide shade from the parking lot lights. Hopping the first row of the hedges that run along this side of the tech park, we make our way across the separation by running crouched down and kneel down behind the second row of hedges. The semi is about two hundred feet away from us on our right, and I'm praying none of those guys has enhanced hearing. Most people don't, so it's a reasonable risk to take.

The police patrol car is going up and down the first couple rows of buildings of the park, finds the security guard and calls it in. We can't see it from where we're at, but the officer turns on the blue and reds on top of his vehicle, which is SOP when stopping to investigate an unknown vehicle, and we can see the lights flashing on the next building over.

Spinning around from watching the three in the building work, the telepath, who wasn't paying attention before, realizes someone else is in the tech park.

I see him give the Welcoming Committee a hit on the arm. "Someone's here, let's go," he says as they jump off the ramp and head across the parking lot toward the end of the building between them and where the cop and security guard are parked.

I pat Carly on the shoulder, and we start low running along the hedges to get in position to see what happens and intervene, if needed. Giving a quick look back, I can hear the three working in the building, still going at it. They either do not know what is going on or are not concerned.

Chapter 26

We are ahead of Welcoming Committee and the telepath and get in position a few seconds before they come around the building. The police officer is standing next to the security guard's car with the door open and speaking into his walkie-talkie velcroed to his shoulder. We can see perfectly Welcoming Committee and the telepath, maybe sixty feet away, edge up to the end of the building and peek around. Welcoming Committee motions a, "Let's go," but telepath pulls him back and steps forward. He looks around the building; that's when I see the first movement from the kid since he arrived.

The kid wakes up and gets out of the car. The cop starts talking to him, backing up as the kid keeps coming at him.

"Time to go," Carly hisses, "He's using the kid." Carly stands up and...nothing, she just stands there.

I look at her, then to the telepath, and I can see him physically smack into the wall. Then it dawns on me – Carly's not just standing there. Welcoming Committee is looking at his telepath partner and reaches out and gives him a push. He gets no reaction. Thinking the attack on the telepath is coming from the police officer, he steps out from behind the building and starts looking for who's doing the attack on the telepath. The officer is still stepping back from the kid and commanding him to stop, to no effect, and he starts to draw his gun.

Whoa! It's time for me to act. I ready my shield and hammer and jump over the hedge, running at a sprint toward Welcoming Committee. "Hey!" I shout and, as he turns to face me, I kneecap him with the hammer. I don't take a full swing as I don't know exactly how much damage the hammer can do, or that he can take. It turns out I hit him pretty good, though, as he does a heels over head flip with a loud "Augh!"

I keep going and grab the kid out of the line of fire of the cop and shove him to the ground and shout, "The kid's under mind control! I'm here to help!" This does exactly squat to stop the cop from shooting at me.

Fortunately, the guy seems to be a baseline without any real power. I don't stop running; holding my shield between us while ducking and dodging. "Stop!" I shout again as I feel another bullet ping off my shield. The cop empties his gun into the air behind me, just missing with each shot, as I run circles around him. He clip empty, he backs away to reload. I can see the panic building on his face; he has never been up against someone with my speed. With the black suit I'm wearing, you can bet he also thinks I'm a supervillain.

Closing the circle I'm running, I run to the cop and use my shield to bat his gun away and give him a sharp shove with the shield to knock him off his feet. Which is also when I realize I've made a terrible mistake.

Welcoming Committee is up and appears to have had no problem shaking off my hit to his knee. I don't care who you are, or how tough. Getting kneecapped with a hammer hard enough to drive in a nail hurts like hell. I swing my shield back just in time to catch Welcoming Committee's fist and I'm lifted off the ground from the impact and blown thirty feet to the other side of the driveway where I just knocked down the cop.

The shield does exactly what I meant it to do and absorbs most of the hit, which is to say, it absorbs just enough that the hit didn't kill me and I didn't break anything. That hit was at least Class 3 strength. I'm on my back, looking at the sky, lying on the grass strip between the parking spaces and the front door of the building. The police car's red and blue lights are still flashing, which is doing all kinds of messed up things to my eyes that are still rattling in my head. I give my head a shake and roll away from Welcoming Committee, putting my shield up again in case he's already on top of me. Either he's stupid and taking his time thinking I'm finished, or he's not as fast as he is strong. Being both is less likely, but more welcome.

I'm up and running as Welcoming Committee steps up to the cop and draws back his fist; if he hits the guy, he'll kill him. I reach full speed with my shield up in a bull rush. It does not matter how strong or tough you are, if you weigh less than five hundred pounds I'm going to launch you into the air when I do a bull rush. It's all about force versus mass and leverage, so unless he latches onto me, and let's hope he doesn't, I'll be fine.

I'm taking a big risk with this move, but there's no choice if I want to save the cop. I hit Welcoming Committee just as he punches down toward the cop and I knock him about half as far as he blasted me. The difference is, he also went vertical as I hit him full body, coming in at an up angle and negating all of his leverage. Hitting him hurt, and my face feels like I'd just been the one blasted. I watch him flying through the air and his face looks like he's just been pissed off, without so much as a hair out of place. He just glares death threats at me as he flies through the air. Well, I've got his attention.

Sparing a moment to check on Carly, I see the two telepaths now facing each other and just staring. I have no way of knowing who is winning or if Carly needs my help, so I pull out the baseball I keep in a pouch on my hip and throw it as hard as I can at the telepath. *Try keeping your concentration when that hits!* I think.

The ball stops in mid-air, two feet from the telepath's head, and my eyes bulge. The telepath hasn't even moved and I think we're in trouble. Then I look to Carly and her hand is up toward me in a motion to stop. Carly stopped the ball. If that's the case, then Carly has her guy under control. I hope that's the case.

Out of time for sightseeing, I look back to Welcoming Committee as he's standing up. He's pissed and completely unhurt from the looks of him. The guy must be a Class 4. I do not have any doubts at this point. I briefly consider if he's a Class 5, but throw that out as they're so rare and powerful I would not have survived his first punch even if he was holding back. He also wouldn't be chumping around with this crew if he was a Class 5. He'd be big time.

I think I can take a Class 4. If I'm lucky and he's not too fast. Welcoming Committee looks slow. I should be able to work him down as long as I can avoid taking a solid hit. I'll have to use my usual hit-and-run tactic on him. It's too early to activate my repeller field and try to go toe-to-toe, but maybe I could use it another way….

"I'm gonna kill you, you little maggot." Welcoming Committee is in a rage. I can see veins popping up on his head and neck, and his arms are starting to bulge even more than they already were.

Definitely a Class 4, they're always calling people 'little maggots' on television, it's kind of a signature card for a Class 4 to remind everyone else we're inferior.

"Shut up, stupid," is my standard reply to anyone trying to dialog, which has pissed off every guy I've ever had words with during a fight. It has the same effect here.

He's coming at me, but I don't wait. I rush him and sidestep just before I come in range as he reaches out to grab me. Stepping to the side, I spin to pick up momentum in my swing and, once again, drive the hammer into his knee. Only this time it's into the back of his knee, and I swear I get two full revolutions out of him as he flies up and slams back into the pavement. "Boo-Yah!" I yell.

Okay, that was stupid sounding. *Be a pro, Theo, and shut up yourself.* I tell myself.

He's not hurt, and I know it, so I step back to let him pick himself up. I have a policy: don't ever rush a guy who is a hundred times stronger than you while their legs are bunched under them when they're getting up. He'll launch himself right at you if you do. It's suicide. I keep running around him about twenty feet away, trying to avoid giving him a spot to line up to jump at me. "So, where you from, Cupcake?" I say. It's better than saying "boo-yah." That just sounds stupid. Taunting, however, is canon.

"C'mere, dead man," is his only reply.

He's not very nice.

Welcoming Committee finally thinks he has me lined up and pushes off with a thrust of both legs and flies at me. I'm ready for it as it's one of the most common moves there are for a strong man, and sidestep to give him a smack with my shield as he goes by. I use the shield's wide surface area to smack him so he has nothing to grab onto. It's heavy and knocks him away at a forty-five degree angle from the direction he jumped at me and he lands in a heap.

He starts snarling and I get worried.

I'm really not trying to toy with him, but that's what I'm doing. I just don't have much ability to do more than that. I have my war hammer, but I don't know its full damage potential. I decide to get a better idea of Welcoming Committee's limits before I risk hitting him in the head. Hopefully, he doesn't surprise me. I really can't afford that.

As he's picking himself up from smacking into the security guard's car, I steal a glance over to Carly and see they're still in the same position, only this time the telepath is on his knees and one of the guys who was in the semi is laying on the ground about fifty feet away. Criminy, I'm getting tunnel vision on this Welcoming Committee guy while Carly is taking on multiple opponents!

Welcoming Committee decides at that moment to reassert himself and bull rushes me. I hear him approaching and spin around. I'm dead stopped and flat footed; he's right on top of me. The big muscle monkey is on my shield side, but that's not going to help me once he gets hold of me, so I panic, flip on my repeller field as it is the only thing that has a chance to stop him, and swing my hammer. The head is now glowing blue, energized from the repeller field. I do the fastest overhand swing I can and crash my hammer into the top of Welcoming Committee's head as he comes in. The sound is sickening; I think I crushed his skull.

Instantly regretting I hit him like that, I watch as his head smashes face first into the asphalt parking lot, busting the asphalt. The fear in me I've killed him wells up inside me before I even finish swinging the hammer.

I've killed him. He's not moving; his face is imbedded in the asphalt, literally. I'll say it right now, if he gets up from that hit, I'm finding another profession.

De-energizing my field generator, I push his head with my hammer. It's still intact; there is not much blood. None of it was pooling, anyway. I push his head with the head of my war hammer so his face lifts out of the depression it has made. Rolled to the side, I can see his face. He's breathing. The back of his head is bloody, but his skull isn't caved in, which is freaking incredible. I'm not sure in this case the field generator didn't provide a bigger surface area than the hammer head would; spreading the force of the impact more when it hit his skull. His face looks like hamburger, a bloody mess with a smashed nose not even a mother would recognize. Fortunately, he's unconscious.

The cop is standing up and looking at me. His mouth's hanging open and he keeps trying to pull his gun from his empty holster, so I go over to him. "You okay?" I get no answer and I realize the cop wasn't looking at me, but past me at Welcoming Committee's body still lying on the ground. He's in shock, so I just leave him to it and head over to Carly and her telepath in case she needs help.

I think calling the telepath Carly is fighting as getting "owned" might be an understatement. The guy is on his knees and dribbling saliva out of his mouth like a broken faucet. His eyes are completely vacant and out of focus and his hand is twitching. He's wet himself and maybe more. Holy crap, I've never seen a guy this messed up. Not even on television.

Carly is looking at me and isn't even paying attention to the telepath, so I jerk a questioning thumb back towards him as I walk up to her.

"He'll live," she says, without much in the way of concern in her voice. "He'll be in therapy for a long time, and he doesn't know he's a telepath anymore, but he'll live." She's trying to put on a show of nonchalance, but I can see she's exhausted.

"Damn, that's incredible," I say and give her a short-lived hug. I hear the semi's engine revving, followed by gears grinding. Someone's in a hurry. I can hear it pulling out and heading for the exit on the other side of the building we've been fighting next to, "I've got this," I say. I grab my war hammer and run to cut off the fleeing truck loaded with at least some of what they had come to steal.

The driver of the semi isn't holding anything back and is driving the rig like it's a race car. It beats me to the corner and turns up the main drive to the exit.

I could run it down, but I've had enough screwing around tonight and instead throw my war hammer at the engine compartment of the semi. The hammer hits the sheet metal cover of the engine housing and punches right through it and into the engine block. I hear a loud crunch and the engine explodes. The engine compartment cover is ripped off and thrown into the air and the truck starts to slow.

Walking up to the semi, I reach into the mess of the engine and pull out my war hammer. The leather wrap on the shaft is torn up a bit. Other than that, it's not even dinged; I feel a twinge of pride at my creation.

The two guys riding in the semi are still sitting in the cab, too scared to move. The driver is peering out the window and down at me with a terrified look on his face. "Both of you, out! This side, and don't pull anything or I'll rip your heads off!" That should work, and it does.

I put zip ties that I keep on me for just this sort of occasion on them to secure their hands and walk them back to the area of the fight. I stop them in front of Welcoming Committee, who still isn't moving and I'm not sure if he's alive or not, and kneel them down in front of him to show them the futility of trying anything. "What were you stealing?"

Both of them snap their heads from staring at the unconscious Class 4 in front of them and look at me, a different type of fear comes over them now. Instead of looking like they're about to die a horrible death, they look like they're imagining someone giving them a horrible death in the near future. At least that's what I'm imagining they're imagining. They don't say anything and just stare at me.

I'm looking back at them, waiting patiently for a response, when the one on the left's eyes go all out of focus and become glassy. I look to Carly, she's looking at the guy like a curiosity in a museum. After a minute his eyes come back into focus and he shakes his head while the one on the right becomes the one with unfocused, glassy eyes. "I've got everything they can give us. We need to go," She tells me.

That reminds me and I look over to the police officer. He's still trying to pull his gun out and staring off into space. "Are you doing that?"

"Not at first, but I've kind of kept it going to keep him out of trouble." She walks over to him, "You want him back now?"

"Yeah." I walk over to him and he starts to come out of his…condition. Grabbing his walkie-talkie off his shoulder, I ask him, "You okay?"

His eyes come into focus and he looks at me and smiles, which raises my eyebrows.

Stepping up next to him Carly says, "He knows we're the good guys," and puts her hand on his arm, smiles, and looks at me like she's introducing me to her new boyfriend.

"Well, that's good to know." I look to the officer and say, "Do you know what's happened here?"

He starts looking around and I can tell he doesn't, so I go to Plan B. "Listen, I have video of everything that happened, including before you arrived. Here's my card," I hand him a business card that's solid black on both sides and blank except for a website address, user name, and password, "Everything that happened here tonight, along with our statements, will be on this website by 10 AM tomorrow. Do you understand?" The officer does a slow nod. I assume he's got it, and he can figure it out later if he doesn't. "Just login to the website and you'll have everything." I thought of the idea of using a dropbox to get files to the authorities anonymously over the summer and set this location up a couple months ago.

The officer nods and takes my card. He's still staring at it when I key the mike on his walkie-talkie and talk to dispatch, "Dispatch, this is Officer Michaels at the Sheridan Tech Park, over."

"This is a police frequency, identify yourself," Immediately comes back and it's obvious they know I'm not Michaels.

"All right, listen up. My name doesn't matter, you're not getting it. I'm a super who just saved Officer Michaels from being killed. He's over at the Sheridan Tech Park and needs backup right now, so quit screwing around and get over here." I look over at Welcoming Committee and add, "You better send an ambulance too."

Putting the walkie-talkie back on its velcro strip on his shoulder, I tell him, "Help's on the way. We're going to leave now. Don't forget to get the evidence from the website." Looking over to Carly, "You sure he's going to be okay?"

"He's fine. Just still in shock. I didn't want to mess with his head any more than I have to; he needs to process what happened on his own."

Which reminds me of the telepath and I look over to where he's still kneeling on the ground, drooling. I'm not going to ask again if he's going to be all right, it's obvious he's not. "Okay, we're out of here," I say as the distant sounds of sirens start to fill the air.

We both run back to the office building. I want to detour and see if I can steal from them what they were stealing from Henderson Robotics, but there's no time and I keep going. I really, really, want that tech now that I know it is worth the effort to the guys we just took out. Thirty seconds later I'm coming back down off the roof with our stuff and retrieving my rope and heading in the opposite direction of the tech park to get to the retail strip center on the other side where we parked the car. It's parked in front of a Smokey's BBQ restaurant, which reminds me I'm pretty hungry right now. Carly ditches her mask and puts on a bright yellow jacket she's carrying in her bag and walks around to the car as casual as a customer. If anyone saw her that's not a telepath, they won't remember her, which gives her a lot more confidence than I'm feeling of getting away clean. She gets in the car and pulls over to the side of the building and I put our gear in the trunk and get in.

"Let's follow the plan and circle South around town and cross at the bridge on the other side of town. We'll just make a big loop back to the hotel." It takes us an hour to get back to our hotel that's only a mile and a half away as the crow flies.

Chapter 27

When wee get back to the room, we're both still amped about what happened. We didn't talk even once during the ride back, and I wonder if Carly was walking through her mind everything that happened like I was. Dropping our bags in the entry to the room, we turn to each other and grab each other in a hug.

"You were incredible tonight," I say into her hair I have my face buried in.

"So were you," she replies into my chest. We're both pretty sweaty and break away the hug a little sooner than we would like to spare our noses.

"Come on," I take Carly's hand and we walk into the bathroom for a long, hot, shower. We repeat our afternoon, except slower, less rushed, and with a lot more emotion. We easily outdid our afternoon session, which I didn't think was possible and fell asleep in each other's arms.

In the morning I call for room service and order half the breakfast menu, then sit down at the office desk in the room and start writing out our statements. I want to make sure I meet the time I gave the officer for uploading the files to the dropbox and I'm going to need some time to get out to a Starbucks to use their Wi-Fi so the authorities can't track where I'm sending from and who I am.

After breakfast, we pack up and head out. Stopping at a Starbucks, I make the upload without actually going inside the coffee shop in case they have cameras, then we drive back to Nova Academy. Our weekend was a success so far as we are concerned, although I'm not very happy about not acquiring one of Henderson's neural interfaces. We will have to wait and see how it is reported in the news. We have not heard anything on the television this morning or on the local AM news talk radio shows.

By Monday morning, nothing has been reported on the news channel, so I check the website to see if the files have been downloaded, and they have. However, when I check the URL the files were copied to with a tracking program, I discover it wasn't a government website in Evanston that accessed the files, it was some website in Russia, which makes no sense. Unless whoever accessed the files was routing their connection through multiple servers to hide their location. That makes a lot more sense than the villains being Russians – in Russia. After all, I have just done the same thing and routed my computer through a server in Iceland and a dozen other countries to check to see if the files have been accessed. It also means the files were not accessed by the police. I have my doubts now of ever seeing anything on the news.

I tell Carly about the Russian URL and we're both stumped as to what to do next.

There's not much we can do about the story not making the news, so we decide to just keep an eye out and get back into our weekly routine. I'll keep checking the drop box to see if anything comes back, not that it matters. After dinner Monday, we go back to my dorm room. Carlos is working tonight at the Commons, so we have the room to ourselves.

"Hey, come 'ere," I say, grabbing Carly by the waist and pulling her to me.

Putting her arms around my neck, she gives me a nice slow kiss, then pushes me away and says, "Behave. We need to go over what happened."

Instead of getting wild and passionate, we spend the next three hours going over every detail of our stake out and battle on Saturday and watch different parts of the video taken by the camera we left on the roof.

I ask Carly, "Are all telepath duels like that?"

"Yeah. Pretty much," is her response.

"Seriously, you just stand there and look at each other?"

"Physically, yeah. Well, most of the time. But that's not the duel. The duel is in our heads and is just as violent as the fight you had with…what did you call him again? 'Welcoming Committee?' It's all in our minds, though. I don't know if you can imagine what it's like. He was trying to force his way into my consciousness with brute force. It was all violence and anger and willpower. The only thing I could do was deflect it over and over and over -- he was stronger than me but didn't have any finesse. I've never had someone try to smash into my mind as brutally as that. He was trying to kill me," shuddering, she continues, "I could see what he was trying to do. He was going to reach into my mind and just rip the whole thing out." Carly got a distant look. Like she was reliving the fight; taking deep breaths and beginning to hyperventilate.

Adrenaline flushes into me in a fear response and ice fills my chest then descends into my stomach as I realize she may not have won her fight with the telepath as easily as she made it look. What if she were killed? Or turned into a vegetable? I don't know what I would do. I'd have killed the guy. Just smashed his head like a pumpkin in the same way I put down Welcoming Committee. Only he wasn't a Class 4 who could take that kind of hit. Wow, I realize I'm getting angry just thinking about it.

Letting go of the thought, I say to Carly, "But you beat him. How'd you do that if you had to constantly deflect his attacks?"

"Men don't multi-task worth a damn," Smiling at me with the insinuated jab, Carly goes on, "Deflecting him was hard, but he was doing the same attack over and over in the same way and I would deflect the attack a different way all the time to keep him mentally off balance. He had his own defenses up, so while he was pounding on my mind, I was poking his defenses. Only I was poking all over the place. Not too hard, but in several different parts of his brain simultaneously. I kept doing the same four attacks over and over and he started predicting my next poke, which wouldn't have mattered, except he started predicting my next poke to limit how much concentration he needed to put into countering me."

I was showing my standard response whenever Carly tells me about telepathy stuff, my mouth was half open, my eyebrows were trying to climb up on top of my head, and I stared at her, in awe of her every word. I've never had a problem visualizing anything. No matter how complicated. But, trying to get an understanding of telepathy is beyond me.

"He quit protecting everything except the next thing he thought I was going to attack so he could put more effort into his attack on me. It's a pretty simple trick I pulled on him."

My mouth starts to move like I'm going to ask a question, but Carly cuts me off before I could formulate the words.

"I just went through the attacks, 1-2-3-4, 1-2-3-4, over and over until I felt he was defending before I started. Then I just changed up the order, and he was wide open. My first attack to get through tripped his mind into REM sleep; I gave him a pretty vicious nightmare. Once I did that his mind was there for the taking, so I went through his memories. That guy is messed up. He hurt a lot of people from when he was in grade school on."

"Wait, what? You went through his memories?"

"Yes, I did. What do you want to know?" The I-know-something-you-don't-know look Carly's giving me gets a frown back from me. She's been holding out on me!

"You've been holding out on me!"

"No, I haven't!" Carly gets excited and throws it right back at me, "You said in the hotel room, we would go over everything that happens later! Well, it's later." My frown of disapproval was met with a matter-of-fact, tough-crap, deal-with-it, stare; she put her hands on her hips for effect.

Bowing to her will, I reply, "All right! You're right." I hate arguing with Carly — because it turns out she is usually right, which is really hard for a super genius to admit.

Looking at me like she's trying to judge if I'm going to start arguing again, Carly tells me what I want to know, "They were trying to steal the neural interface, just like you thought. The telepath, Tim Johnson was his name. He didn't know much about it other than it was a neural interface and it was going to be used to improve a piece of equipment his boss is working on. His boss was the guy with all the bling, which is what we thought; only he didn't know his real name. He was just told to call him, 'Mr. Newton'. He wasn't able to read his mind. The one time he tried, he woke up a few hours later with a major headache. I accessed his memory of when he tried; they were all smudged and nonsensical. That's what happens when someone does a down and dirty, sloppy job of wiping your memories."

We finish putting everything we can together on the guys who did the break-in, then spend twice as long going over our teamwork and what we are each capable of doing and how to work together better. Carly isn't as vulnerable as she looked after the first minute of the fight, which is how long it took for her to break the guy's defense and only a few seconds before I threw the baseball at him. Once she broke him, she was able to pay attention around her and use her telekinesis to stop the ball. She was actually protecting the guy to keep him from getting hurt any more than the hurt she was already putting on him.

It's important that I know when she's vulnerable in those situations, and also when she can start defending herself again or needs to call for my help, which is tricky as she won't always be able to call me for help if what happened to the other telepath had happened to her. Still, Carly can take care of herself, which is a nice improvement over Bubble-E.

Chapter 28

It's been a week and nothing has been reported about the break-in at Henderson Robotics. Then on Sunday, a local news channel makes a report about the robotics company being broken into and some prototype robotics equipment that was stolen the night before, which, I'm thinking, is a week later than it actually happened. And they didn't get away with anything the way the news report says. That's until I see a reporter's camera pan over to the roll-up doors at the tech park and there is a forklift stuck into the door used to force it open. What the hell? There was no forklift. What happened to our break-in?

Were they able to cover-up the first break-in? Was this a second break-in? They may not have had a strongman (thanks to me) for tearing a hole in the door the second time, so they had to use a forklift? I haven't seen Welcoming Committee around the Atlas Quad this week. He's usually hard to miss.

I call Carly and she comes over to my dorm room so we can watch the news channel's website and watch the news report again, this time together.

Carly asks me, "What do you think?"

"I think these guys are seriously connected, is what I think. To be able to suppress the first break-in. And they've got resources and manpower," I reply, mulling over what it all means. "I'm also wondering why Henderson Robotics didn't move the stuff out of there before the place was hit again.

That's if it was hit again." I didn't voice that it could have been an inside job or a repackaging of the earlier job.

"You're assuming they knew about the first time the place was hit — It hasn't been on the news, maybe they didn't know."

I start to ask why they wouldn't know, but it's pretty obvious, "Right, telepaths. They could have changed everyone's memories of what happened. Right?"

"It's not that simple, but yes. We don't know if anyone else knows about it, or maybe they know it, but don't want it reported. Corporations have their own telepaths. Even small ones contract out to services to do regular employee scans. The cops sure as hell have their own telepaths – and their own super teams. You can't tell me they didn't go through Officer Michaels head with a spaghetti strainer."

I don't have anything to say to that. I was not aware telepaths are being used as much as Carly is describing. I browse through the news channel's articles online and don't say anything. I'm not finding anything closely related to what happened last week. It's frustrating the bejeezus out of me that nothing has been reported – I want credit for taking that guy out, even if they just say unknown supers took them down. Just put on the news that a Class 4 was found unconscious at the scene with his face smashed. I smile at the thought of that, then have an idea, "Why don't we just send the video footage and our statements to everyone: police, FBI, local and national news organizations, — Hell, let's send it to Super Slammers!" I'm suddenly stoked about the whole thing. Super Slammers is a bloopers TV show for super humans being hit, smashed, and bruised in ways that would kill a normal human. It's hilarious.

"Really? Super Slammers?" Carly looks at me, smiling at the ridiculousness of sending our video to the show. "We can't."

"Why not?"

"Because no one will be able to tell you didn't kill the guy, and Super Slammers won't put on videos where someone looks like they've been killed."

My newfound bubble of happiness is popped, "Aww, man."

"We can send it to everyone else, though." Carly is trying to cheer me up with the consolation prize. "You sure you want to?"

"Damn right," I say, starting to feel a little indignant nobody reported the biggest win of my super career in the first place. "I'll set up a dummy email and send it to everyone I can think of. Then, I'm done with this damn thing."

Nothing ever was reported on the news or online. Whatever.

Chapter 29

Neither of us brings up doing another weekend in Chicago for the next few weeks. I'm pretty sure it isn't because we're getting into our first round of major exams, which is taking up a lot of our time. It's more like we both got a pretty good shock that our first time out we get into a pair of death matches that could have easily ended in both of us being killed. For me, it's not that I'm not scared to go out again; it's that I'm preparing to go out again. If Welcoming Committee was a little faster, he might have hold of me. I still have my field generator, which could have broken his grip if he had, but I'm not sure it would be strong enough to break it if he really latched on. That means I have more work to do to be better protected and make sure the heavy hitters don't get to latch on. It would be the end of me.

It's Friday morning, my free day, and Carly is in class. This is my favorite day because it's all about what I want to do. This also means I'm at the Student Lab working on my projects. The Suit is coming along, all of the armor plates are done, and I've finally put together the flexible armored joints for my knees and elbows. At some point, I'll have to upgrade my boots to get some armor into them, but that really won't be until I can get someone to manufacture, shape, and sew the armor cloth into the pieces I need. I have the formula for the cloth, and I can make a batch of the stuff any time, but I don't have an extruder to turn it into the heavy thread I need. The Student Lab doesn't have machinery for weaving anything, no less nearly indestructible materials. But I do find a small ballistic tech company in Richmond that makes Kevlar cloth and bullet proof vests that can make it for me. And they have laser cutters that'll be able to cut out the patterns. I'm still negotiating the terms and pricing so they can't steal my formula — not legally, anyway.

Today I'm casting the helmet and face shield, which is a little premature since I won't have the electronics suite ready for it for a few more weeks. I get the molds out of my locker as they are too big to be humping around campus and I'm not worrying about them being stolen since they're just shapes with no tech, and head to the common foundry to see if I can get a station to melt down the alloy bricks I brought. I create the bricks to have the extra alloy ready to go when I make the rest of the parts I need. By leaving out a final step in the process I am able to keep its melting point low enough to use in the school foundries. If I had finished the process like I did with my shield and war hammer, I never would have been able to melt them down again. At least not without getting access to a Cartwright Carbon Industrial Blast Furnace.

I walk into the common lounge area and, as usual, there are twenty students in there talking science. Only today all but one of them is wearing a hat. It's cold outside, but not that cold. Some are wearing snow beanies, but most are wearing a light cap, with a few *Super Nova Academy* ball caps thrown in. The oddest one is a guy wearing a headband that it looks like he took from a 1980s Morning Workout show. He's just missing the leg warmers.

About the time I ask myself, *Why are they all wearing hats?* Every one of them turns to look at me walking in. It's pretty creepy. I try to keep a neutral face and pass through like I don't notice; they seem satisfied to just stare at me walking across the room to the hall leading to the foundries. I can't imagine what living in Oppenheimer Quad would be like, but it can't be good.

There's no waiting at the foundries. Two of the three stations are vacant, the third being used by a guy I have in my metallurgy class. He doesn't have a hat on, thankfully. "Hey, Jimmy."

"Hey, Theo. What'cha gonna work on?"

"Molding some pieces. How 'bout you?"

"Oh, making parts for a mag-launcher. We're going to enter the pumpkin-chunkin competition over in Waynesboro over Thanksgiving break."

"Cool! Let me know when you have it finished, I want to see it." Wouldn't that be great to use my creative genius for making toys to play with instead of a suit to get myself killed in fighting supers? Nope, I guess fighting supers is how I play.

"Right 'O."

"Hey, what's with everyone wearing hats lately?"

Jimmy looks to the hallway door leading back to the common area, "I have no idea, but more and more people are wearing them over at the Oppenheimer Dorms. Even my roommate is wearing a ball cap all the time now."

"Wow, maybe I'll have to get one." There's a fat chance of that. I hate wearing a hat and will hate even more having to wear this helmet I'm building. Except it has all kinds of really cool features and it will most definitely save my life.

I get to work as it's going to take several hours to make the helmet, plus a few pieces I'm planning on putting into an overpowered fist Taser. Most of today will either be heating metal or slow cooling and reheating to add the temper, so I settle in on my laptop and work on my power supply design while the foundry does its job. I had originally planned on not powering the suit in any way, and for movement, that's what it'll be. For me to make a powered suit, I would have to add way too much weight, which would affect my speed. Instead, I am planning for lighter weight with fewer bells and whistles. But, now I'm beginning to see the need for more firepower, which either means something like a gun that uses individual stored power rounds or an energy weapon that does not use ammo.

I just don't have the strength to get the armor to where I want if it isn't powered in some way. It will be too heavy. So, if I'm not going to power the armor, I need to power the weapons and repeller field. The question is whether I can make a power supply that can power an energy weapon that is strong enough to play in the big leagues and is still light enough for a Class 2 to carry without being weighed down.

Decent amounts of power can come from one of two places: stored power or generated power. For what I need a strong enough battery is going to weigh so much that I may as well just make a power generator, which is exactly what I'm doing in designing a mini-nuclear power supply.

I'm using Promethium-147, which normally isn't used for this sort of application, but it has the power potential, safety, and stability I require in a nuclear generator that will be operating within a few inches of my skin.

Did I mention one of the really, really cool things about Nova Academy? If you are able to provide the Science Department Oversight Committee a safe and viable design for an invention, they'll let you build it – even if it is nuclear powered. The Academy actually loves when you bring them new inventions because they have a clause built into your admissions paperwork that they are permitted to study your designs and make derivatives of the invention that they can sell. Fortunately, the student does also get a healthy commission of every sale.

Well, I'm about to give them a doozy. A high energy, nuclear powered, hundred year power supply — with no moving parts.   Right now I'm putting the final touches on my presentation to the Committee for our meeting tomorrow; I'll hopefully have full approval by next week. They'll make millions off of it, which I can live with so long as I get to build it in their facilities.

It is late afternoon when I finish making my helmet and the other parts. I am also able to finish my presentation and practice it a couple times, so I head over to my dorm to clean up for my date with Carly tonight. We're going to see the new *Commander Khan* movie that just came out and then have a late dinner at our favorite restaurant, Power Pizza.

Chapter 30

"So, Mr. McCleary, let me see if I understand this correctly. This device of yours, you plan on encasing a seven hundred gram plate of a...," Professor Manstein stops for a moment to hold up the pair of glasses he has hanging from a chain around his neck, as if he were actually reading from my paper, "...an alloy of Aluminum, Potassium-40, and Promethium-147 contained within a proprietary alloy you have created, but which does not have a name."

"Yes, sir," I reply, "The chemical composition of the alloys for both the power source and shielding and protective case are included in the Appendix."

"And you believe this will give you a thirty amp continuous power supply that will last roughly a hundred years?"

The disbelief he is putting into his voice is annoying me, but I suck it up. "Yes, sir. All of the calculations and proofs are included in my paper." I look over to Carly who is attending the meeting with the Oversight Committee more for her own curiosity than any moral support she thinks I need. She seems to be completely absorbed in the Committee members and does not notice me. Something has her attention, and I'm guessing she's poking around in one, or all, of their brains.

"Very well, Mr. McCleary, you seem to have submitted all the required documents for us to make our decision. I only have one final question. Can you assure this committee that the materials to make this device will all be acquired legally? Specifically the radioactive materials?"

"Yes, sir." I'm becoming annoyed, but keep it to myself, "In fact, the radioactive materials will be created here at the school under Science Department supervision." That got him to shut up.

Pursing his lips and raising his eyebrows, Professor Manstein conceded, "Very well, Mr. McCleary, you'll have the Committee's answer by midweek."

"Thank you, sir," I reply, in the respectful demeanor I've maintained throughout the meeting. You can't be too respectful to someone who has the ability to completely crush your dreams.

Carly and I exit the Committee's conference room located in the staff offices of the Science Department, "What'd you think?"

"The professor on the left, Reynolds. He was wearing one of the devices that blocked my telepathy."

"But he wasn't wearing a hat?

"No, but he was wearing a hair piece. I think it was imbedded in his rug. The rest of them I could read; they were all drooling over your invention, except for Professor Manstein."

"What was his problem?"

"His specialty is nuclear engineering. He was thinking he can make a better version of your design than you can; he was annoyed you submitted the design."

"Bullcrap! I engineered the crap out of that thing. No way he can make it better."

"He was thinking you should have put a feedback loop and power cutoff into the design so you can interrupt power generation if you want to."

"Well, yeah, I could have. But that defeats the entire design concept of not having any moving parts that can break during a super fight. His idea could work on less intensive uses...in fact, it's a pretty good idea. I should have thought of it, and likely would have if my intended use called for it." I've stopped being defensive and started thinking about it, but in the end, I refuse to give Manstein credit for having a better idea.

"Yeah, well, you never told them you intended to install the thing into your combat suit, so don't be surprised if they try to make you install one," Carly says.

I laugh, "They don't need to know it's for my suit, and they can demand all they want of any changes to improve the design. And, what they don't know about the final build won't hurt 'em. I may need to build two of them, so there's going to be some sleight of hand going on anyway."

Looking thoughtful, Carly replies, "You want to try having lunch at Oppenheimer Quad? I want to check something."

"Why?" I'm suspicious, because the last time we ate at Oppenheimer Quad, we had to make a hasty exit.

"Nothing I want to talk about just yet. After we have lunch, I might know more."

"Okay, back into the lair of the mad scientists. Great." I hate Oppenheimer Quad and every one of those unpredictable mad scientist wannabes who live there.

Chapter 31

We get to the Oppenheimer Commons and the place is not only packed, a full half of the students are wearing hats of one sort or another. "Again with the hats," I mutter. "Hey, you're not scanning anyone are you?" I don't want a repeat of last time. It was creepy. And a little scary.

"No, I'm completely closed up and keeping my brain to myself," Carly replies, keeping her voice low.

Some of the students look at us, but there are just too many people in the food court for us to stand out. We have to walk one behind the other to get through; I lead Carly over to the counter to get in line. The people in here may be a bunch of science geeks, but don't let that fool you as nearly all of them are physically super in some way or other. Pushing through the crowd is as much about asking nicely to pass as it is pushing through people.

"What are you going to get?" I ask Carly, but she's not paying attention to me, or the menu board behind the counter. Instead, she is looking all around at everyone she can see. No one's paying attention to us, so I don't think she's scanning anyone. "What do you see?"

She grabs my hand and pulls me out of line, "Let's go."

This is her scouting mission, and I'm clueless as to what's going on, so I follow. She has my hand in a vice until we get to the same double door exit we left from last time.

I'm looking around when Carly stops and pulls me to the side of the door so other people can pass. "Okay, listen," Carly pulls me close and I bend down so she can speak into my ear. "I'm going to do a quick scan. Just long enough to confirm something, so be ready. As soon as I finish we get out of here."

Nodding in response, I reassure myself of the grip I have on her hand and make sure no one gets between us and the door.

Banging into me, Carly says, "Go, go, go," and pushes me toward the doors and we make our exit.

On the way out, I look back and at least half of the people are looking at us. I wait until we're on the other side of the dorms in the quad before I ask, "What did you see?"

"Most of the people with hats on were blocking me; every one snapped their head up and looked at me when I scanned them. I don't think they could pick me out with all the people there, though." Carly is agitated and starts walking faster, "They all had that same metallic flavor, like last time, and there's no way that it's natural. No one's mind tastes like metal."

"Somebody's distributing the hats." It is a conclusion I am giving, not a question. "The question is, 'Why?' "

Carly's not responding, doesn't look at me, and speeds up even more.

"Carly, what's going on? You know something." I'm not always slow on the uptake.

"Not here," is her short reply.

We head over to Carly's dorm; it's not the first time I've been here and I don't particularly like the people here. Every person we get close to stares at me until we pass and I'm beginning to understand why Carly never wants us to hang out in her dorm. She did say my ability to block telepaths was rare, and they all seem to know it whenever I get close to them.

The lights are out and curtains pulled when we walk in Carly's dorm room, but the room's not empty. A rather average looking girl with brown hair is sitting cross-legged in the middle of the floor. She ignores us as Carly crosses the room and works the lock on her personal locker. I gave her the lock at the beginning of semester, anyone wanting to break in may as well tear a hole in the side wall as try to cut the lock. Carly is only in her locker for a few seconds and comes out with a large leather-bound journal with an old brass buckle strap holding it closed.

"Imelda. I'm sorry to bother you right now." Looking down at Imelda on the floor, Carly continues, "Can I ask you a question?"

Imelda takes a deep breath and lets it out slowly, with just a touch of annoyance on her face, "What do you want?"

I'm guessing they're not best buds.

"I'm sorry to bother you, I know how much you hate being disturbed when you're mind walking."

"Why is he here?" Imelda ignores Carly and is looking at me with.

"I'm with her."

"Okay, why are you here?"

Thinking Carly is looking to ask her a question; I better give her an answer, so I tell her again, "Like I said, I'm with her," and try to give her my imitation of a friendly-harmless smile.

She stares at me for another twenty seconds without saying anything; I can feel her trying to pry open my brain. It doesn't hurt, but I'm getting annoyed that she's trying.

"Imelda," Carly takes a step forward, "Could you not. I just need to ask you a question."

"What?" Imelda never takes her eyes off me.

"Have you scanned any people lately, maybe some of the science majors, and felt anything strange?"

"Well, yeah. Everyone has. They're trying to free themselves of our 'oppression,' " she replies, saying it in a sneer.

My head nearly explodes as the meaning of that statement hits me like a hammer.

Carly looks down at her and doesn't say anything, but I'm pretty sure they're communicating telepathically. Then, after a full minute of silence has passed, with both of them just staring at each other, Carly says, "Let's go."

Imelda and I stare at each other as we make our exit. Me with a smile, and her with a look like she's having a hard time opening a pickle jar.

I'm not having a hard time keeping up with Carly, but I would be if I were a baseline. She's making good time heading out of her dorm building. We're halfway to the parking lot before I realize that's where she is going. "Hold on. Are...where are we going?" It's my first question since we left the dorm.

"We need to go off campus to talk."

Now, that surprises me. Nova Academy is freaking huge and has open fields and private areas all over the place. "Okay," I reply, not understanding, but going along.

Carly's only response is to get in the car and open the lock so I can get in.

Chapter 32

Carly is staring straight ahead, not saying anything, so I keep the burning questions I have to myself for a while longer. We're just coming into town when Carly turns onto a road named, "20 Mile Road," that from the map I remember goes exactly nowhere for at least twenty miles. Which I'm wondering at this point if that is how far Carly is going to take me before she starts talking to me again.

In actuality, it was only eleven miles before she turns off onto an unmarked dirt road we are passing.

Now standing in the middle of the woods on a dirt road, I'm ready for some answers. "Now can you tell me what's going on?"

Taking a deep breath and slowly blowing it out, Carly says, "Yes. I'm sorry. I got spooked back there. We didn't need to come out here, but I wasn't feeling safe on campus and I need to be somewhere where I can't detect anyone else."

I lean back against the front fender of the car and cross my arms, indicating I'm waiting for her to go on.

Carly starts out, "I don't know where to start on this. I…. It's…. There's a lot of history you don't know. It could matter to what's going on, or it may not. But, I think it is time to tell you before things go any further."

"From the beginning, then?" I offer.

"Yeah, okay. You know what 'The Event' was," she not quite asks, "Of course, everyone does." You can see she's grasping at how to explain whatever it is she is trying to get out.

The 'Event,' as it is commonly known, was a near death experience for the entire human race, when, nearly three hundred years ago, a beam of gamma radiation and other materials that were ejected from a Hyper Nova in near the core of the galaxy, reached Earth. The beam barely missed, or rather, barely hit, the Solar System and the Earth was bathed with a massive dose of gamma radiation and ejected high mass materials from the core of the exploding star. The gamma radiation is not what created super humans, it instead killed nearly half of the world's population. And for a large portion of the remaining life, the gamma radiation disrupted and fragmented their DNA. During the Event, Earth was bombarded with heavy elements and fractured long molecules the super nova's core ejected from its center in the wake of the gamma radiation. These pieces of long strand molecules were similar to the long strand molecules which fell into earth's primordial soup billions of years ago that evolved into life. Nearly every person on earth was affected to some degree as the fragments managed to bond to their own fragmented DNA during the bombardment and from ingesting the molecules that contaminated the planet's ecosystem. A billion years of evolution happened in about a year.

Evolution is a messy process. Only the fit survive. The unfit die either from being eaten, killed, or from starvation. Or they die from an inability to procreate. Or, for some evolutionary changes that are not viable and are labeled deformities, diseases, or aberrations.

Of the half of the population that survived the initial gamma radiation bombardment and the weeks after of slowly dying of radiation poisoning, they were "gifted" with hyper intensive evolutionary change. Many were extremely fortunate and developed superior traits, or their children did. But even more people, who thought they had survived the gamma radiation bombardment, soon found out they were no less doomed than the dead.

Over the next year after The Event, after the gamma radiation victims quickly died, another nearly billion people died because their DNA was altered in ways that were not viable to survival. For the next fifty years after, life on earth thrived like never before, died unable to compete, or found they could no longer survive because of the changes to their bodies. Only a small percentage suffered no changes, and most of them interbred with those who were changed over the next several generations.

This all happened nearly three hundred years ago; changing the course of Earth's history in a way no one could have predicted. Once all the bodies were cleaned up, and humanity went through a famine for nearly three years after the Event, we pulled it back together and started getting back on our feet. But there was nothing normal about the world. Not anymore. People, animals, and even plants began to show radical changes. The real changes, however, occurred in the children conceived after The Event. Real superpowers began to emerge as well as unimaginable deformities. Miscarriages went up to over seventy percent of all pregnancies in the first generation after The Event.

Over a period of nearly fifty years humanity worked out its new condition as successful mutations were able to survive and procreate at accelerated rates and the undesirable and unviable mutations were weeded out of the population. Genetic screening had become the norm once the early super geniuses began to rapidly accelerate technological achievements. By the time the twenty year mark hit after the Event, humanity was on an upward population growth rate, unlike anything ever been seen before. Food and resources were plentiful, and the world economy was booming. The average family size shot up to over 8.2 persons per household in nearly every nation.

One other thing happened during that time, humanity became a much more conservative place where people were expected to help themselves. Social services were limited to the truly needy, and even some of them were left to their own devices if they were deemed to be sound of body and mind. There would be no free rides in post-Event society. The struggles were too difficult. Sympathy for those unwilling to help themselves disappeared. Survival of the fittest extended into society only marginally less than it existed in the natural selection of wild animals.

"Well, for the last three hundred years there have been telepaths, or advanced minds, that were created out of what happened during The Event."

I didn't bother correcting her that advanced minds include super geniuses.

"About fifteen years after the event people began to realize that telepaths exist, but no one thought anything of it for many years. That is until a second generation super; a super genius, who happened to also be a telepath, came along. His name was Malcolm Beaumont, and he was the most powerful telepath of that age. He was also the first known Mad Scientist. And he was totally insane. He managed to take over the federal government by bending dozens, or possibly hundreds, of elected officials to his will. He was controlling all of them and setting the US up as his own personal kingdom."

I have never heard any of this before, and I took three years of honors history on American History, The Event, and The Awakening that came after.

"Beaumont took over just about everything and started to change society at his whim by presidential fiat. After nearly three years of his rule, a young telepath was able to kill Beaumont with a sniper rifle from a distance of over two miles. It took telepaths banding together to figure out how to undo the changes that were made to the minds of the most powerful men in the country whose minds Beaumont had enslaved. He was advanced in his powers beyond any other telepaths in that age.

"I've never heard any of this before," I reply, shocked.

"No one has," she explains. "At least no one today who isn't a telepath. Telepaths at the time did not recognize the dangers that Beaumont represented to them. They were not nearly as intrusive in what other people were thinking at that time; it went unnoticed for a long time. After Beaumont, there was in inquiry; that's when the world figured out how powerful telepaths can be. The government blew what happened out of proportion; people panicked. Not that Beaumont didn't do a lot of harm, he did. But they took it to another level in a propaganda campaign to turn people against telepaths."

Carly was becoming upset. I can tell she believes to her core everything she is saying. "What happened?" I ask.

"The worldwide reaction was immediate and nearly unanimous. Telepaths were caught completely off guard. They were rounded up. At first, the telepaths were ordered to register themselves with the government. Once they thought they had most telepaths identified, every known telepath was sent to an internment camp or just killed. There was no due process. Not a single trial. Not a single charge against anyone who was put in a camp. Any they suspected of being involved with Beaumont or was suspected of having used their powers against another human, were summarily shot." Carly pauses, turns away from me and runs her hands through her hair, "That's when telepaths had to learn to fight back. And, when they did, they were angry, and they were scared. As far as telepaths were concerned, they had just saved the world from a mad man. But instead of being thanked they were being rounded up and exterminated. It was genocide."

Taking a minute to breathe out some stress, Carly then continues, "Telepaths known from any government records were rounded up. That was most of the telepathic population as at that time no one tried to hide their powers. Being a telepath was a badge of honor to them. The handful of telepaths who were not rounded up began to fight back. First by freeing as many captive telepaths as they could, then by wiping the memories of anyone who knew they were telepaths. It took years to overcome and take control of the very government programs that were meant to round them up and imprison them. Most telepaths went underground, and there were literally millions of them. When they were finished, they had altered the memories of nearly the entire population of the world. As far as baselines were concerned, telepaths were harmless and rare; that's what telepaths made them believe."

Carly is becoming agitated like it was her who lived through those times, "But, the telepaths weren't happy about having to hide their powers while everyone else was openly using theirs, so they took action. They wiped the whole history of Malcolm Beaumont from the public consciousness and purged all records of his existence. Every telepath alive was part of the 'Cleanup.' That's what they called it. "

Carly is pacing back and forth in front of me by now. She's staring at the ground as she tells the story and her arms are waving around for effect, "It didn't end with Beaumont. Two other Class 5 telepaths have tried to take over since then. Only those times the telepathic community reacted much faster and the fallout was controlled. Today there is a telepathic protection service that guards our public officials and every telepath is taught from an early age not to be ambitious. Not to want to control other people. Not to be a leader. They're taught to remove bias against telepaths from anyone's mind whenever it's found, but other than that, stay out of the way. Stick with your own kind. Can you imagine that? Being told that?"

I'm completely stunned and what she's telling me is ridiculous like the wildest conspiracy theory ever invented. Except that from what I've been learning about telepaths since coming to Nova Academy, they could do everything she's talking about. They are that powerful and there are a lot of them, three percent of the population is considered to have advanced telepathic, or telekinetic, minds of a level that is considered a 'power.' The number does not break down between telepath and telekinetic.

This is all incredible, but I am not one to stray too far from the subject, "So what does that have to do with all the hats?"

"It's not the hats, it's the neural neutralizer. That's what Isabel said they're calling it. The hats are covering up the devices. I assume to hide them."

"Okay, but what does it mean? Why are a bunch of advanced mind science students wearing neural neutralizers?" I'm trying to absorb what she's just told me.

She gives a short laugh, "That part's simple. To stop anyone from scanning their minds or to know what they're thinking."

"That doesn't sound bad to me." If I didn't already have that ability, I'd sure want it with what I know now.

"There's another reason to want to protect a person's thoughts." Carly says, this time without the laugh, "If a telepath were to change someone's mind, they could hide what they've done by using the neural neutralizers. To be able to change what they're thinking without another telepath being able to see what has been done and change it back."

I don't want anyone mucking around in my brain and changing what I believe. Not that anyone could, but I understand how everyone else would want it, too. "And, how is that a bad thing? Not the part about having your mind changed. The part about no one being able to see your mind and change anything in it?"

"Neither case is good news for telepaths. The very existence of neural neutralizers is a threat to our survival. Even if the only motivation of everyone wearing them is to stop people from reading their minds, it's a threat to our survival."

"What do you mean, 'only motivation?' "

"All right, here's the deal," Carly says, "Somebody created this device, and somebody is distributing it. And they're able to do it without telepaths stopping them. At least no telepaths seem to have made an attempt to stop them yet. You have to realize, normally if someone were to create such a device and decide to build one, any telepath that scans them will know it and wipe it from their memory. Then the creation of the device is stifled. It never gets made. More importantly, any scientist that thought of building such a device would have it wiped from their memory before they could even have it on paper."

I'm stunned. "Do telepaths pay that close of attention? To what scientists are doing, I mean?"

"Absolutely. Keeping an eye on scientists is a first line of defense for telepaths. Every science lab and every school of advanced science in the world has telepaths working there."

I absorb that for a minute before asking, "You said they're calling it a 'neural neutralizer'?"

"Yeah, that's what Isabel called it."

"You remember the break-in at the robotics factory; do you remember why I wanted to watch that place when we went to Chicago?" I have a feeling there is a relation here.

"You mentioned they came out with some kind of neural interface so someone could communicate with a power suit," she replies.

"That's right. But, I'm wondering now if it can do more than that,"

Carly is not seeing the connection, "How do you get to thinking that? How do you know these are related?"

Carly has no real understanding of technology. It just isn't what she's studied, and I don't have the words to explain the concepts to a layman. So instead of trying to explain it to her, I just look back at her. She's got to learn to trust me on these things. Besides, I hate being questioned about my deductions. I don't need as many, or as obvious of links, as most people. And, to have to explain my reasoning to people who are not going to get it anyway is just annoying. "You're going to have to trust me here, the technology is similar enough, and I don't think it is a coincidence it is in close proximity to Nova Academy. Especially with that welcoming committee guy involved. There's a connection."

Chapter 33

"Welcoming Committee, the guy I fought, he's from here. His dorm was in Building 4 of Atlas Quad, so there's a connection with the college. The nature of the device, a neural interface versus a neural neutralizer, I can imagine some similarities of those devices because I've been trying to design one for my suit. And, they are both incredibly advanced tech that are both making their debut around the same time. Add it together; you can make the beginnings of the case of the two being related. At least enough to want to look into it."

Carly runs with that train of thought, "So what do we have altogether. The devices are being rapidly distributed to the science students, at least that we know so far. The person, or persons, has enough powerful connections to suppress a news story of our fight at the tech park. And they are able to avoid the telepathic community's interference."

"And they're willing to break-in and steal what they need," I add, encouraging her to follow my thinking. "What we don't have is why they're being distributed, and why the science students. We don't have the end goal. And, there is an end goal. There's always an end goal, but it isn't the wellbeing of those students. You don't do everything that's happening just to protect people you don't know. There has to be a selfish reason underneath all of this."

"I don't know, either. But, I know the telepaths on campus will eventually step in to shut the whole thing down." Carly has more faith in her fellow telepaths than I do.

"I'm having a hard time feeling any sympathy for the telepaths to make me want to stop whoever is sending out the neural neutralizers. They're messing with millions of people's minds on a daily basis." I say, thinking I might incite some anger in Carly to protect her fellow telepaths.

"Billions." Turning to look at me she says, "They're doing it to billions, and they have been for over a hundred years."

I'm starting to get a little queasy. "You're not helping me be sympathetic to your side."

"It's not just my side. Don't think you're not benefitting from what they're doing. You've got an advanced mind too."

"Yeah, but my advanced mind is in the sciences and nobody can see into it anyway."

"Don't be too sure about the security of your mind. Besides, your ability to block out telepaths is definitely on the telepath side of advanced brain abilities. Both hemispheres of your brain are advanced. Damn, you're lucky you're not insane."

Click. A piece of the puzzle might have just fallen into place. "What if there is a Beaumont wannabe behind this? You said there were two other times after Beaumont that a telepath tried to take over. What if it's happening again?"

"First off, you're reaching. Second, what good would it do to make people immune to a telepath's power? If you're a telepath trying to control everyone's mind, why would you? Wait, we already know why."

Right. That firms up the thought whoever is doing this must be trying to defend the science students from other telepaths because their minds have already been altered. "What if there are telepaths doing this and they have already gotten to the students and put them under their control BEFORE they have them wear the devices?"

Carly is taking her time chewing on the idea, "But why the science students? Why not politicians in Washington?" Whirling on me, she continues, "If this is a telepath that's doing this, I can tell you, they're not going small time. All the telepaths who have attempted to control large numbers of people have one thing in common, they think they're strong enough to do it; telepaths don't think like that if they're not actually extraordinary in their abilities. It just doesn't happen. They are constantly testing each other. And they're the most self-analyzing people you'll ever meet. Just about all telepaths collect other peoples' opinions of them like they're collecting baseball cards."

"Every science student at Nova is genius level, or above," I say, "He could do just about anything with them. Death ray, armageddon bomb, zombie apocalypse virus. Anything," I start laughing at how much he could do, "Hell, he could do all three at the same time. I'm wondering if he's one of them."

Carly blanches at the thought, "Now that's just scary." We look at each other in silence; each imagining their own horror of what it could all mean.

We decide we need to find out a lot more information about what is going on and who is behind it, then it's time to head back to campus.

Chapter 34

On the way back to campus, I ask Carly, "Why would I side with the telepaths on this? I mean, don't people have a right to not have telepaths messing around with their heads?"

"Telepaths do a lot more in people's heads than protect themselves. We haven't had a major war in over a hundred years. Racism, bigotry, religious intolerance, they've all been largely removed from our society."

"You're saying telepaths did that?"

"Yes, they did. Telepaths have been using their power as a stabilizing force in international relations and on societal issues for generations. We're taught as kids by our parents to make a better world, so we do — the only way we know how. And, they are expected to do it one person at a time."

"And who polices the telepaths? Who stops them from going beyond keeping wars from happening and stamping out bigotry?"

"Peer pressure for one. For another, it's fairly easy for a telepath to see if someone's mind has been changed and what was done to it. It also doesn't normally take more than a beating or two for your parents to knock the idea you can freely mess around with other people's minds out of you. That's all it took for me.

"So, we're all under the control and whim of telepaths who can turn us into drooling idiots with a snap of their fingers, and the only thing keeping them in line is peer pressure and a couple beatings when they were children?" I state, more than ask.

"Yeah. It's a good thing you have an advanced mind and will never have to worry about it."

"Ya think? But, I do have to worry about it. According to you, telepaths could take over the whole world if they want to and the only thing stopping them is some shared values that you'll limit yourselves to only controlling free will for stuff that's really bad. How's that work? Is there a Universal Standard Guide Book of Acceptable Behavior for Normal People?"

"We do limit ourselves! I know! I've seen it! People are not being controlled in their everyday lives; no one is directing them like some puppet!"

I begin to wonder if Carly is trying too hard to defend herself, "What about all the supervillains? Why don't you stop those criminals?"

"For one, they're dangerous," she says.

"I'm sorry, what?" That's just absurd, and I can't believe I just heard it.

"Telepaths are no more heroic than anyone else. Actually, less so, the way we're taught. Besides, supervillains give superheroes something to do with all that super-ness. So, we're supposed to stay out of it."

"What about the telepaths on campus using Atlas Quad students as playthings?" I don't really care about dumb jocks being controlled like puppets, other than it is a sign of a larger issue. I've seen enough jocks out of control to be okay with someone slapping a leash on them.

"As much as anything, they're practicing their skills. Nova is kind of a 'suspended rules' zone so telepaths can practice their skills. They're free to do what they want, within reason."

"Okay, say I accept that, in an oddly practical, and totally twisted, way." It takes me a second or two to wrap my head around the idea of supposedly pacifist telepaths doing whatever they want playing with the most aggressive, super brutes and bullies of society. "Say I accept that generally speaking, telepaths are not power hungry puppet masters. Instead, you want me to believe they're benevolent overlords gently nudging humanity along in a peaceful manner. I'll give it to you, for the sake of argument only. But, who is setting the limits? Who is overseeing the overseers? At what point do our benevolent overlords get tired of nursemaiding the masses with lesser minds, full of ugly thoughts and inadequate brains, and decide to become a little less benevolent and a little more overlord? Who is going to stop them?"

"We police each other! When a telepath goes too far, other telepaths are able to see what they do and undo it. They talk to the one that's going too far and they make him stop."

"Yeah, but what's the standard? Who sets that?"

"Every community of telepaths sets their own standards. There is no central place that sets the rules. It's just a matter of what works best for that community." Carly raises a finger in the air to highlight a point, "But! We live in an age where everyone is interconnected with international travel and trade, and the internet. People all over the world are talking to each other all the time. My dad says there is a lot more uniformity in how telepaths do things than there was a hundred years ago. Back then there were entire countries under the control of powerful groups of telepaths. The world has changed a lot — for the better! And telepaths are part of the reason the world is a better place."

I can tell Carly is committed to her beliefs; I'm not going to change her mind. I'm not sure I want to change it as there is an argument they are providing huge benefits to society to have people that quietly prevent wars and fix messed up people who may become mass murderers. I can see that. And, they don't have power over me, so it's a lot easier to accept. "If telepaths prevent wars and stop people from doing things like becoming murderers, why don't you stop all crime?"

"It's too much work to stop all crime. And, it would take much greater control. More than can be justified. Most telepaths scan surface thoughts – things people are actively thinking, and that's where you can easily see the worst from people that have fixations with committing an act. For us to go deeper into another person's conscious can be extremely unpleasant because you're getting into all the things that motivate them and a lot of it was traumatic for them. It's just, yuck." Carly is wringing her hands and making a face like she just took a full bite of a lemon.

"I take it you don't like going deep into a person's psyche?"

"No telepath does. If they do, it's because they're as messed up in the head as the guy whose head they're in.

Look, do you like the world you live in? I mean, really. Is this world one you would raise a family in?"

"Yeah, I would. But, you know what else I would do? I would make sure every one of my kids inherits my ability to block telepaths. And, if they didn't, I'd get them one of those neural neutralizers."

"Well, that's just because you know you need one," she replies, slamming home a point.

"You're damn right I know…. Well, I know now." Letting it settle in and start to process in my brain, I turn from Carly and start walking down the dirt road with my hands on my hips and head tilted back, looking at the sky. I do my best big picture thinking like this. Carly stays where she is with her arms now across her chest in a self-hug.

I get two hundred yards down the dirt road before I start coming to conclusions and turn to Carly…who is still standing by the car, watching me. I start back to the car and organize my thoughts on the way.

Chapter 35

"Theo. Hear me out for a minute. Will you do that?"

Running my hands through my hair, I let out a deep breath, "Yeah, I'll listen to you." What else can I do?

Carly explains, "There is absolutely nothing you and I can do to stop telepaths from doing what they're doing. These neural neutralizers, they might be able to change that. And, I'm actually glad someone figured out how to build them, but I'm even more surprised a telepath didn't wipe the idea from the maker's brain as soon as the light went off in their head. I mean, really surprised to the point that I don't think it was possible for someone who doesn't have an advanced telepathic mind themselves to create these devices without being stopped before they even got going. The only exception would be if you did it."

"I didn't do it." I need answers, "So who could have built them? They're all over the science wing of campus, we've seen them. They may have something to do with the break-in at Henderson Robotics, which could mean this is some kind of illegal operation. How much super-villainy do telepaths do?"

"Normally, I'd say none. Their parents tend to fix their kids as they grow up when they're prone to criminal conduct. So, let's just start with the easiest thing. Where are the science department students getting them? And, why are they being given to them? How can we answer those questions?"

Once I finish shuddering at the thought of my parents telepathically digging in my head and rearranging the chairs of my own personal Titanic, I get back on track, "There are only two ways. We watch them until we see how they do it. Or, you pull it out of one of their heads."

"Watching them will take too long. We'll have to get one of them alone and pull the device off his head long enough for me to go digging." Carly has gone into problem solving mode and is running scenarios through her head. I know. I did the same thing when I took my walk, so I give her a minute to work it through and come up with an idea. Who knows, it could be better than the plan I came up with.

"Wherever we do it, it needs to be isolated."

I go along, "Right, we'll need to get one of them by themselves with no chance of being disturbed. How long will it take you to read their mind?"

"Probably only a few minutes. If I can follow their thoughts about the device, it should lead me right to the memories associated with it pretty quickly. Memories are like big libraries, except they don't have search engines for people to come in and look for things in a nice, neat cross-referenced catalog. Instead, you follow thoughts or stimuli associated with a memory and they'll take you where you want to go like following a trail of crumbs to everything that has to do with that thought, or that stimuli. In this, we'll have the device to use as a stimulus to activate his memory; I can follow that."

"Wow, but okay. I can work with it only taking a few minutes. Then the only other thing will be we need a place that we have a good chance of escape if we are caught in the act, which means it can't be anywhere there are a lot of people. Definitely not at Oppenheimer Commons. And, we need to pick a target who won't put up a fight, or who we can take down fast enough they don't have time to put up a fight."

"Okay, who? And where?"

"I know the where, the who is going to depend on the when, though. For the where I think our best bet is to take someone down who is using a private lab at the student labs. The rooms are private and secure, and we'll be able to find someone working alone. The private labs are in use 24/7, so the when should be when the labs have the least number of people there, which is usually between three and four AM."

"And what about the 'who?' "

"The private labs have to be reserved in advance and are always booked several days in advance. We can pick anyone we want on the signup list."

Chapter 36

We decide to make the grab this coming weekend, which gives us three to four days to decide who on the private lab signup list will be the best one to take. Stopping by the student lab the next morning after our talk out in the woods, I make a list of all the people who have reserved the lab for Friday, Saturday, and Sunday nights anywhere from midnight to five AM. There is a little more risk of students still being in the building at midnight, and some early risers, but I want to make sure I find someone who, first and foremost, is wearing a hat and Carly can't scan them. Next, and most important, is how much of a fight I think they'll be able to put up, which is as much situational as individual. A guy using a grinder with hearing protection on, or who is head to foot in bulky protective gear because they're working in one of the private foundries, will be easier to sneak up on, but I don't want them to be a Class 3 or Class 4 no matter what they're wearing, or doing.

I go over the list, one name sticks out, "Hajiro Sukimaki." Hajiro is in my Engineering for Advanced Minds class; I've seen him trying to lift an eighty pound mounting bracket for a rocket motor during lab. He's definitely baseline strength as people were laughing at him trying to muscle that thing into place. He's also been wearing a hat to class for the past few weeks. I just need Carly to try and scan him, just in case he just happens to like hats.

The next day is Wednesday, one of the days I have my engineering class, and I have Carly standing behind one of the pillars outside the exit to the lab so she can give Hajiro a quick scan on the way out. The only thing she knows about him is he's a Japanese guy with a hat and always walks with his head down, which kind of precludes her seeing his face to know if he's Japanese or not. She'll figure it out.

When I come out, she falls in step with me, "He's blocked. Same feeling as all the others, only he didn't react when I scanned him."

"That's not surprising, the guy is pretty meek. I doubt he would have reacted if you smacked him in the head."

"He sounds perfect."

Chapter 37

I go in the front entrance to the student lab, just like I always do, and head for my locker. A couple people are down one of the halls to the public labs, otherwise the place is pretty deserted, which is normal for this time of night. I know because I'm in here at this time at least a couple times per week to work on my suit or some other thing that pops into my head. Currently, I have six projects going, besides all the stuff I'm making for my suit. Some of it is more or less research to test out if the concept will work, like my 'Polyphase Neural Scrambler,' which like it sounds, is based on some fantasy I'm having of how a neural inhibitor might work. This is to say it's a knockoff based on what I know about telepathy and a total guess as to how to disrupt the power. It is not as easy as just disrupting brainwaves like it is with a baseline mind.

Rummaging around in my locker, I find the Loop Recorder I created, which has two pieces, one of which I'm going to place on the ceiling next to the security camera, and the other is a projector that fits over the security camera lens. The piece next to the camera will record for thirty seconds and then transmit it in a loop to the receiver/projector covering the lens. I made it out of an old junk digital camera on the cheap this morning and I'm hoping it works long enough for us to get in and out of the building. The hall I have it projecting down is the same hall as my locker, and the same hall the private lab Hajiro is using tonight. Once the recorder is set up, I head down to the end of the hall and go to the left down another hall that goes to the back emergency exit. This hall has a security camera as well, but where they have it placed all I will need to do is flip the camera around in the other direction as both directions look the same. No one is around using the hall, so it's unlikely they'll notice they have two cameras looking down the same hall.

I make quick work of the subterfuge and get to the back emergency exit where I open the door and drop a wedge into the opening to keep the door from closing. Carly is standing just outside the door when I see her.

"I'll be right back," I tell her, and head back down the hall and out the front door that I came in. I want the security cameras in the front to see me leaving just in case something goes wrong and we are not able to make our escape undetected, or if there is an investigation.

Keeping an eye out that no one is around and I'm unobserved, I make my way around to the back of the building, and Carly. She's already in the same outfit she wore when we did the stakeout in Chicago, and mine is in the bag at her feet. I switch into mine and am very aware I am without my shield and hammer tonight. I couldn't afford to bring them here as this is where I made them; I can't be sure no one here has seen them before. I am wearing the new gloves I made with the bar taser on the knuckles, which will definitely rattle anyone's cage if I hit them with it. I don't have my new power supply yet as I'm still enriching the fuel for it, but I did hook up an extra battery pack that I have for my field generator, so the taser maxes out at a short, five thousand watt jolt, rather than the sustained, twenty thousand watt jolt it could do. It'll have to do.

Head to toe now in my stealth black suit, albeit without the armor pieces, I'm ready to go in. Carly and I head in after checking the hall is clear. It's empty, and I don't hear anyone, so we make our way down the corridor to Hajiro's private lab. The door has a magnetic key card, which isn't an obstacle since I made a copy of it back when I used this lab for making my armor pieces. Listening at the door, I swipe the key card and crack the door to peek inside. Hajiro is standing at the foundry in full protective clothing, including a big helmet with blast shield over the face. He's holding what looks like a glass pipe into the furnace and spinning it around.

When we enter the room, Hajiro is not wearing his neural neutralizer while working in the protective suit he is wearing. And, Carly is able to make him go to sleep almost instantly. I grab the glass blower before it hits the ground to save the guy's work. She gets to work and soon gives me an update on her progress as I finish crafting his glass, "He doesn't know where he got the hat or the neural neutralizer. He only knows it's the coolest thing there ever was and he wants to wear it all the time. He's even sleeping with the damn thing on. His memory has been erased of everything else related to it – how he got it, who gave it to him, it's all gone. I'm going to have to go deeper in his mind and start kicking over things to see if I can find something."

"How long do you need?" I ask her.

"How long do I have?"

"Two hours until his lab time is over, but we need to be out of here by four-thirty."

"Why's that?"

"The early crowd is here by five, and we want to be long gone by then." Super science majors tend to be early risers.

"All right, then. I'll see what I can do." She turns back to Hajiro, "Watch the door, I've got him. Oh, and break that thing he was working on."

I look at the glass, then back to Carly with a question mark lighting up my face, she lets me in on her plan and says, "I'm going to plant it in his head that he broke it and needs to start over to cover the time we're here."

I feel bad because I know what it is he's making; I was hopeing to finish it for him. It's a 'focus' for advanced optics and they are really hard to make. The crystal alone is few hundred dollars. *Sorry, Hajiro.*

I hang out by the door listening and we catch a break no one bothers us for the forty minutes Carly is digging around in Hajiro's head. The hall is clear when we're ready to leave; I grab my gadget off the security camera on my way past and we make our way out the back door.

"What did you find out?" I ask her on the way back to the dorm.

"He has no memory of anything about the neural neutralizer or anything associated with it. But, I think I might have something else. Every couple days after classes, at 5:30, he has a compulsion to meet a bus in the back of the Oppenheimer student parking lot to go work at a 'part-time job.' The thing is, it's not associated with any other memories. There's no memory of getting a part-time job, and there's no memory of him working at his part-time job, even though he has memories of riding on the bus — which means the compulsion was planted in his mind. He may have other things buried deeper, but that's what I could get in the time you gave me."

"When's the next time he's meeting the bus?"

"Tonight."

Chapter 38

"Look, is that the bus coming?" I ask.

"It looks the same as the one in his memory."

Carly and I are standing at the front entrance of the parking lot for the Oppenheimer Quad, which is on a dead end street that backs up to a forested area. The other entrance is a one way street, so no matter which entrance the bus uses, it's going to have to pass where we're standing when it leaves. "Good. I'm going to pass behind it as it comes out of the parking lot and put on the tracker."

We wait and watch as students come walking from the different dorm buildings in the quad and approach the bus. All of them are wearing hats, but not everyone out on the quad wearing hats is heading for the bus. "You think they have them going in shifts?"

"Could be. We can check tomorrow and — Look there! That's Hajiro going to the bus."

"You called it. Nice work." Carly's telepathic abilities are incredible to me. Scary and incredible.

"Are we going to follow them?"

"No. The tracker will record its position and tell me where it's been in about ten hours from now by sending a file to a dropbox I setup online."

Carly is laughing as she says, "You are so Cloak & Dagger."

I shrug back at her and say, "Maybe I should call myself, 'The Shadow.' "

"Sorry, it's been done."

"How about — Wait, they're leaving. Hold on." I walk over like I'm going to cross the driveway to the parking lot on the sidewalk and wave the bus to go ahead. Doing like I always do passing behind a moving car, I time it so I pass just behind the vehicle. As it passes, I reach under the bumper and stick the tracker to the inside of it and keep going.

Catching up to me, Carly declares, "Well, that's it until we get a file from your tracker, right?"

"Yup. I'll check it in the morning and we can look at it in Superpowers class." Not passing up an opportunity to create quality time, I add, "Carlos told me he was going to see a movie tonight with some friends."

"Do you want to go?"

"No, I was thinking more along the lines of my dorm room is free tonight." I didn't have to let that idea hang out there very long.

"Let's go," she says and grabs my hand to pull me along.

Chapter 39

Carly makes it to class ahead of me and has staked out a mostly empty section at the back of Superpowers 301's auditorium classroom. "Hey," I say and sit beside her. The professor's not here yet, but it's normal for him to be five to ten minutes late for class. I'm pretty sure he has tenure because he's mailing in his lectures and should have been fired a long time ago.

"Hey, yourself."

"They found the tracker last night about forty-five minutes after they left."

"How? And, how do you know they found it?"

"When I check the dropbox this morning, the file was there, but the time stamp was 5:58 PM. Someone had set off the anti-tampering trigger; it sent its packet early."

"Does that mean they have your tracker?"

"No, if it was able to send the file, then it would have also self-destructed right after. They have a melted glob of metal and plastic. What it did tell me is they were on the highway heading towards Chicago. The last recorded location was that big truck stop; do you remember the one? It had a huge red neon sign that says 'Stellas Truck Stop & BBQ' with that giant pig on it?"

"I remember. You wanted to stop there."

"Man, don't ask me to pass up BBQ," is my response as I'm starting to salivate at the thought.

"So, are we going to go down there?"

"I don't think so, not yet anyway. I don't think that was their destination. I'm thinking I need to use a little smarter tracker, but it's going to take me a week to get the parts I need." I'm also thinking that my new combat suit shipped yesterday from the ballistic tech company I contracted it out to, and it should be here tomorrow.

The next day the suit is delivered to the lobby of my dorm; I pick it up when I get back from classes and take it up to my room. I pull it out, hold it up, and I want to cry. It's beautiful, with a soft sheen on the jet black finish. The texture is like you find on the really expensive, light armor super suits, but thicker and not as much stretch. I practically rip my clothes off to try it on and I'm thinking it's just a little too big in all the limbs and way too big in the chest before I remember the extra space is for the armor plates, which reminds me to open my locker and pull out all the armor parts stored in there. I strip out of the suit to start putting the armor pieces in, which takes a while as everything is fitted really tight and getting everything just right is a pain.

Carlos walks in and stops, with the door standing open and kids passing by in the corridor. "Wha...."

"Shut the door," I tell him, just before I kick it closed myself.

"Is that your suit?" He asks as he jumps out of the way of the slamming door. Carlos knows what I've been building as I am doing too much work on it in the room and storing all the parts for it in here instead of my locker at the student lab.

"Yeah, just came in today. Trying to get all the armor segments installed on it," I tell him as I go back to work and begin to ignore him as he goes through the pile of parts laying on my bed.

"You have shoulder pads on this thing?" I hate when he touches my projects.

"They're not shoulder pads, they're pauldrons. They protect my shoulders, upper arms, and back," I say, snatching the armor piece from his hands, "They will attach to the chest piece and back pieces and help give me full protection. It's going to be a real trick getting them together just right, so quit bugging me."

Ignoring my last comment and asks, "Why is the chest piece so flimsy?"

I'm used to him ignoring me when I tell him to stop bugging me. It's not flimsy. You could hit me with a bat full in the chest when I'm wearing this; I'd barely feel it. If you could hit hard enough to crush the bat, I might get a bruise from it, but that's about it. "It's not 'flimsy,' it's flexible. I'm using combination armor with a hybrid plate, scale, and solidifying reactive armor design for the chest."

"Dude! That's awesome! Buuut, nobody wears armor; people are going to laugh at you, bro." It's funny how Carlos' very proper English takes on a Latino flavor when he's putting something down. He even gets in big arm motions to emphasize his points. He says he gets it from his cousins.

"They'll laugh right up until my Class 2 butt takes a full hit from a Class 3 and I'm still standing. Here, look it," I show him how the pieces go together, "The plate and layered armor pieces are backed by the solidifying reactive armor lining. The whole thing is designed to take a hit in a small area and spread it throughout the armor. The reactive gel stiffens only on impact so it is already in the shape of my chest at the time of impact. It distributes the force better that way." Knocking on the armor with my knuckles, I continue, "If I take a massive blow it'll still protect me by going rigid and holding my body tight in whatever shape my body is in when I take the hit." The armor by itself should let me go toe-to-toe with at least a Class 3 — at least so far as taking a hit, and he doesn't wrap me up in a bear hug.

What I don't tell Carlos is that once I add in the nuclear power supply I'm almost finished building, to power a beefed up repeller field generator that I still need to build, I might have a chance of taking a hit from a Class 4 without being turned into a shattered mass of pulped meat. But Carlos doesn't know about my repeller field generator, and I'm not going to tell him.

"Now leave me alone, I'm working here," I tell him.

"You're always 'working here.' You've turned our room into a factory assembly line."

I ignore him, which is my way of winning all of our arguments about the messes I make when I work in our room.

"You need to get out and have some fun, bro. All you do is work all the time."

"Have you seen my girlfriend? I'm sure as hell having more fun than you out trying to find a one night stand every weekend."

"Hey, screw you, man. I've dated half the girls in this quad. Beat that."

I go back to ignoring him with the full knowledge Carly was "beating that" without even trying. Then, I wish I hadn't let him suck me into responding to him in the first place.

"I'm out of here." Throwing a chin toss at all my suit parts on the bed, Carlos tell me, "I want to see it when you're done."

Yeah, he won't be laughing when I'm finished with the suit, he'll be asking me to build him one. And, for a few hundred grand, I'd consider it.

I finish installing the armor plates in the legs and arms and start on the knees and elbows, which take a while longer to get the flex pieces installed correctly. When I get to the pauldrons and chest piece, I manage to get it installed but will have to adjust it with the suit on, which I can't do alone.

Chapter 40

"Hey, you busy?" I make a quick call to Carly for the rescue.

"Can you come over?"

"Yeah"

"Cool. I'm going to blow your mind." I hang up before she can ask me how I plan on doing that and get back to working on my suit.

I hear Carly's footsteps coming down the hall and shout, "It's open!" when she gets to the door.

She comes in and gives me a kiss that ends in a head butt as she looks at the suit in my lap, "Hey, I'm here for my mind blowing. Oh! Wow! It's here!"

I'm smiling like a kid showing off his first BB gun to his friends. "It's awesome, just like I thought it would be! Hey, I need your help when I get this on." I stand up and start putting on the suit.

Carly moves around behind me while I struggle with it. It's still hard to get into with the pauldrons and chest piece not quite right. I finally stand up all the way and turn around to show Carly.

"It has shoulder...."

I cut her off, "They're pauldons; it's armor, they're called pauldrons."

Carly, being a little more attentive, and actually caring about my sensitivities, concedes, "Okay, 'pauldrons.' Whatever those are."

Starting to push and shove on the shoulder...pauldrons, I say, "Help me with this."

I get the help I need to finish getting the pauldrons and chest pieces in place and seal up the suit.

"You look insane in that thing. It's all black and sleek, and you look like you have muscles everywhere. And your stomach is all rippled. What is that?" She asks and starts running her hands over the armor on my stomach.

Taking a deep breath to keep from getting excited, I tell her it's scale armor so it can be flexible and she starts pushing on my stomach.

Carly has a huge grin on her face when I look up. I watch her draw back and give me a punch in the stomach that would have crushed a baseline, and I barely feel it. She was smiling the whole time. Damn, she's hot.

"That all you got?" I come back at her.

She steps back and gets a wicked look in her eye I've never seen before, and drives a perfect side kick into my chest. It lifts me off the ground and throws me into the locker door.

Leaning against the locker door, I look down at myself and see the dusty footprint in the shape of Carly's shoe on my chest. "You want to try that again?" I challenge and receive another kick into my abdomen for my trouble. This time she completely leaves the ground in a flying kick.

I take the full blow as I'm thrown back against the locker and I can still barely feel the kick. This suit is so awesome.

"That suit is awesome," says Carly, and I'm beginning to wonder if she can read my mind after all.

"Here, wait," I say and grab my helmet and boots from my locker. I get them both on and stand up again for her to see. The helmet is black like the armor and has a single full face, unbreakable, visor that is integrated into the helmet. It's a full-faced, enclosed helmet with wide eye slits for better visibility and respirator to filter contaminants. She can't see the heads-up-display, but I can. The electronics are packed into the back of the the helmet where there is a small bulge toward the base of the skull. "Intimidating," is how I would describe it.

"You look like one of the 'enforcer' guys from the 'Chaos' movies."

I like the sound of that and remind her, "They're villains."

"I know. They look bad ass."

I can work with that. I wave Carly back and start some martial arts moves to test out how restrictive the suit is and am happy to feel it's not restricting my movements at all.

"Looks like we're ready to kick ass," Carly says, with a big smile, "When are we going to try to track the bus again?"

"The parts for the tracker are backordered, so it's going to be another couple weeks."

"That's going to take us into Thanksgiving break," she almost pouts.

"I know, but I'm pretty sure we're going to need the new tracker to be able to find out where they're going." That and I'm excited about the design of my new tracker and want to use it as much as I want to find out where the bus is taking the kids.

"Okay," Not sounding pleased, Carly accepts the delay.

"Hey! I've got something for you!" I almost shout it out and start digging into the bottom of the box the suit came in. Pulling out a smaller suit, I hold it up for Carly to see, along with a scale armor flexible piece that will cover her from neck to crotch. "What do you think?" It is a lot lighter, and easier to make than my armor, but she doesn't fight close quarters as much as I do.

Carly is hopping up and down and clapping as I hold it out to her. She has to strip out of her civvies to get into the suit, which just makes me even happier I made her a suit. The most fun is when I help her fit the chest piece and get everything tucked into place before I seal up the suit and step back to take a look at her.

"Oh, you are so getting laid for this!" Carly promises as she tries to look at herself all over at once.

"Are you ready?" This time I'm the one with the wicked look in my eye.

She gets the "For" out of the "For what?" she's wants to say before my side kick takes her off her feet and throws her into Carlos' locker across the room.

"Bastard!" Is her response before she starts laughing uncontrollably, "Oh! You are so going to pay for that!"

Sure I am.

Bouncing back up onto her feet, Carly looks like a beautiful assassin from a video game as the sleek all black suit covers her from ankles to neck and her long curly brown hair flows around her face and shoulders. Maybe we can get in some Cosplay action tonight? I'm all for it and thinking Carly may be game for just about anything right now.

As if in acknowledgement, she leaps at me and wraps her arms and legs around me and starts trying to kiss me through my face plate. I think she's pretty happy I made her the suit.

Chapter 41

I get the notice the parts for my tracker have shipped on the day I'm leaving to go home for Thanksgiving. This means I won't get to work on it until I get back next week. My power supply is completed though, so I'll be able to advance the work on my suit during break. I'm not too distraught about not being able to complete the tracker. Honestly, I'm glad for the delay in getting the tracker parts as it's given me the time to exponentially increase my abilities and I think I'm going to need it when we find out where they're taking the science students on the bus.

Carly's family lives in Upstate New York, so we said our goodbyes last night before she had to take an early flight this morning. We won't be seeing each other through the holiday, which blows. I'm already missing her and have her smell on the shirt I'm still wearing from last night because I didn't want to change it for the trip home. What are the odds the person sitting next to me on the plane has a super smell and complains about my BO? Sucks for them if they do.

Dad picks me up at the airport for the forty minute drive home. I want to talk to him about what's been going on, but can't bring myself to ruin the good feeling of just being home. It might be better if I wait until after Thanksgiving. Mom is waiting in the kitchen, which is not really like her to spend any time in there, but she's putting together a late lunch for us, and it's really good to see her. It's short lived though, when she tells me she invited Tess over for Thanksgiving dinner. Tess' parents are going to be out of town, and Mom ran into her when she was out shopping and decided to invite her without asking me. Great.

    Not that I don't want to see Tess, she's great. I just don't feel comfortable with her around my parents...because she's a telepath, which is something I've never thought of before. Tess is actually a great person; I can't beleive she would ever hurt my parents. Except now I know telepaths read people's minds all the time and will change a person's mind if they see something they don't like when reading your mind. It's like Mom's asked a really nice person over to supper, but the person will be carrying around a big carving knife the whole time they're here. It also means I have no choice but to wait until after Thanksgiving to talk to Dad. Actually, I think I will talk to Mom and Dad on this one.

    I have to go see Maria first because she'll break my leg and roast me on a spit if I don't. I'm hoping it's not going to be awkward. When I get there, it takes her about two minutes to figure me out and ask me what my girlfriend at school's name is, which is a little faster than I gave her credit for to figure it out. She takes it pretty well and lets me know to tell Carly that if she doesn't learn to share by the time she gets there next year, she'll roast her. Next year could be interesting. But then again, Carly might just make Maria not remember who I am. Elemental powers just don't seem as powerful as I used to think they were.

Chapter 42

When I get back home, Dad is watching a shootout between what looks like superpowered villains and the city's super police team. At least one of them is an elemental, and he's tearing up the pavement and pushing up earthworks around the bank building they've holed up in. I sit down to watch it with him and the shooting dies off as both sides stop shooting at each other. Less than a minute after the shooting stops, an opening appears in the earthworks and a man steps out into the street and looks around, then he turns and waves at someone in the building. A mother and two children come running out; the telepath directs them off to the side. He looks around again, nods to a Police Observer who is standing in plain sight, and then just walks off in the same direction as the woman and child. The Observer ignores them after that. And, when I look closer, I can see he is wearing the All Seeing Eye patch. He's a telepath.

"Did you see that?" I ask my Dad.

"You mean the three people that came out?" He replies, never taking his eyes off the TV.

"Yeah." My voice is starting to rise. Everything I have been learning about from Carly is right there in front of me. It's in front of everyone watching a television.

"Oh, yeah. That happens in a lot of these shootouts. Sometimes the villains just don't want to hold all of the hostages and will let some of them go."

"You don't think that's kind of odd? I mean, the police are not even acting like the people coming out are even there. Look! Three cops just ran right past them!"

"Why would it be odd? It makes sense for them to send out hostages they don't need."

My dad is smarter than that, "Okay, but shouldn't they be escorting them? Or, helping them get to cover? Look, they're just running off into the crowd."

"Why would they? The police need to focus on the gunmen." There is confusion directed at me in his voice. As if he has to point out the obvious and the problem is with the question.

It makes sense all right: if the guy was a telepath and didn't feel like being a hostage, then it makes total sense. But if he can do what I just watched him do, he could stop the whole shootout. That's when it really hits me what Carly said about telepaths only doing what they need to do to protect themselves. She was serious because that guy didn't care about anyone but himself and that family.

The sound of shooting on the television starts back up and pulls my attention back to the shootout starting to pick up again. The camera angle changes to an overhead view from what must be a helicopter and I'm able to see on Dad's 140" Ultra HD TV, the mom and child that came out of the building. She's wearing a red jacket and dragging the kids along by their arms. The telepath is not with them. Looking around on the screen I finally see what looks like him heading away from the shootout on his way to the parking garage beside the bank. That wasn't his family. Did he know them? So, maybe the guy isn't completely self-serving. But he could have done a lot more than he did. He could have stopped the whole thing. The Police Observer may be able to do the same. So, why don't they?

Dad starts giving his take on the shootout and says, "They're not going to be able to get them out with that elemental in there. The super team will not want to go in with all the damage he could do to the building." He is rubbing his chin with one hand, and pointing at the TV with the other. It is a common position for him when he is trying to give me an impromptu education, "In a lot of ways, the elemental supers have the most powerful abilities among all supers," he lectures, "I bet they end up negotiating a surrender."

He sounds confident and matter of fact, "Last week they had to let some supers go over in Valencia. They had to; they would have torn up half the town if they tried to fight them. It was reported after that they got away with almost twenty-million dollars in rare gems that were stored in a private vault." I can almost see the glazing over of his eyes as he gives into fantasizing what it would be like to get hold of that much money. Dad and I are a lot alike.

My dad, the genius, never misses a car chase, shoot out, or any other "crime in progress" breaking newscast that comes on TV. And, I don't think my dad, the genius, has a clue the guy who came out of the building in the shootout had to have been a telepath. I have always hated watching these things, unless I could see a super versus super fight. There are better things to be doing with my time.

Can I afford to talk to him about what telepaths are doing? It is clear he does not know. And, he is too smart not to have figured it out. If I do tell him, will some telepath just erase the memories, or will they do more than that? Will they come after me because I know too much? Carly doesn't think so, but Carly also said every telepath does what they think is right and every community is different on how far they think they should go in protecting themselves. I can't take that risk with his life, or his mind, which means I can't talk to my dad.

"Theo," my mom calls from the kitchen. "Can you give me a hand in here?"

"Sure," Giving my dad a last look of disappointment for something that's not his fault, I go help Mom.

I go into the kitchen and Mom is leaning against the sink; I can't see that she needs anything. "What you got?" I ask her.

"I was listening to you and Dad talking. About the shootout." Her voice is soft. Softer than she usually speaks.

"Did you see what happened?" I ask her, not keeping my voice down at all.

She puts her hand on my arm in a calming touch, "You mean about the man walking out of the building in the middle of the shootout? Yes. I saw it. I've seen it and things like it a lot in my lifetime."

I am a little slow on the uptake and do not get the message in the message she is giving, "But, why would that happen? That guy should have been shot, or at least running!" I'm pointing back at the swinging door going into the den, my voice is starting to rise from the frustration of not being able to talk about why I think it really happened.

Mom presses her hand more firmly on my arm, "Now, keep it down," she tells me, chastising my being so loud, "You've seen things like that happen before, haven't you? What did you think about it the other times?"

"I've seen things like that, yes, but I don't think I was really paying attention before. It's weird. I mean, it's not right. The absurdity of it is just crazy." Oh yeah, I'm just a well of reasoned thought put into words, I am.

Mom looks at me with those loving Mom eyes. Her head tilts to the side just a little and a half smile on her face that she gives me when she sees me learn something new. She also looks at me like that when she is trying to figure out if I'm lying, but I do not think that is the case here. "Yeah, it can be, can't it," she agrees. Then, she changes the subject, "Can you get me down my big blue mixing bowl from the top shelf? I'm going to need it for the mashed potatoes."

I get the bowl down for her. She keeps it on the top shelf, and at her 5'4", she never can get it without the stool, "Thanks, honey."

What was that? Mom just...I'm not sure what Mom just did. Maybe it's not Dad I need to talk to. I decide I can be a little more direct as long as I don't say anything that would get a telepath's attention. "What do you know about telepaths?" How's that? If she doesn't know anything, because her memory was altered, then she won't say anything that could get her in trouble.

This time it is Mom who looks to the door to the den. Dad is still watching the shootout that is still in progress according to the local news announcer sounds coming from the TV. "Theo, let's talk about this later when it's just the two of us."

"You know, don't you?" My heart rate is speeding up; my anxiety building to match.

"Later dear," glancing at the door for a moment she adds, "and yes." Giving me a tight smile, she changes the subject once again, and asks, "Have you confirmed with Tess that she's coming over tomorrow for Thanksgiving supper?"

Actually, I'm not sure she is changing the subject. That can just as easily be a warning, "Yeah, she texted me this morning that she's still coming. I'm also going to meet her tonight over at *Benny's Lobster Shack* to catch up." Mom knows how fast my metabolism is and does not bat an eye that I am saying we are going out to a restaurant after dinner.

"That's nice," is Mom's reply in what has become a very neutral voice and seems to be struggling with saying something.

Tess being a telepath is not something I was even thinking about. I reassure Mom, "I'm sure we'll just catch up on what's been going on since I left for school. Don't worry, I'll be home early." We are so tap dancing around this, which makes me certain now Mom and I need to have a talk about telepaths.

Meeting up with Tess is pretty uneventful. At first I felt like a moth flying too close to a flame and all I could think about is what she can do to people with her telepathic powers, but then I relax after a couple minutes because, if she could read my thoughts, then she would know what I was thinking and it would be too late, but since she can't, it doesn't matter and I can relax already. She has been my friend for years. Why am I doing this with Tess? I know her. Then I realize that I didn't know her before, and what I know about her now is what's bothering me. I just need to not care about what she can do; like I used to. Like when I thought it was cool she has telepathic powers, but I don't think of them as part of an unspoken worldwide conspiracy among telepaths. She's my friend. Why didn't she tell me like Carly was willing to tell me?

We hang out and I finally have fun catching up; once I let go of my paranoia. Tess never asks about my having a girlfriend, unlike Maria, which is what you would expect from Tess. I give her a ride home, and she gives me a hug and kiss when I drop her off. We see each other a couple more times over break. It is nice. No expectations, no demands. We both give and take what is offered. I don't ask about who she is seeing, and she does the same.

Thanksgiving is good and uneventful. My mom's two sisters and my cousins come over, and my dad's brother and his family. I'm the oldest, which is nice when you have a girl come over to spend thanksgiving dinner with us, and there is no one older that tries to embarrass me in front of Tess. All that wrestling in the back yard with my cousins when we were growing up is paying off. They all know I'll turn them into a pretzel if they mess with me while Tess is here. Really, they know. Because that's what I told them I'd do. Tess and I do our familial duties and have a great meal with the family, then excuse ourselves to the back patio.

Later, when Mom and Dad go up to bed, Mom asks me, "I'm going out to Henderson Ranch tomorrow morning to buy some of those brown eggs your dad likes so much. You want to go?"

"Sure," I reply, hoping this is Mom setting up our private conversation.

Chapter 43

The car ride out to Henderson Ranch takes about thirty minutes and is several miles past the fairgrounds out in the country. Mom waits until we get out of town before speaking. "You know, I think I like the car ride more than I like the eggs. It's so beautiful out here."

"It is, isn't it." I'm looking out the window at the forest of trees along the two lane country road. The fall colors have been in full bloom for a month, and the trees are starting to lose their leaves to take on that skeletal winter look that reminds me of haunted houses out in the woods you see in scary movies on Halloween. "Mom, I want to ask you about...."

"Telepaths," she finishes for me. "Before we start, I have a single question, "Has anyone ever read your mind? Not that you would know, necessarily."

"No. Telepaths can't read my mind. Mom, I'm dating a telepath at school. Her name's Carly."

Mom's giving me this look that is clearly asking, "And, why didn't you tell me you had a girlfriend sooner?" But instead, she says, "You know you don't call me enough. You've maybe called six times, and you've been gone for three months."

This conversations NOT on the topic I want it to be on, "Sorry, I'll call more. I promise. Right now, though, I need to talk to you. Can telepaths read your mind?"

"No, they can't. And that seems to be why they can't read yours, either. I was hoping your ability to protect your mind was strong enough but didn't know for certain. It's not like I can go ask a telepath to test it out for me. The less you bring to their attention, the better."

"Are you afraid of telepaths?"

"Let's just say telepathy is the most powerful ability there is, and they don't like feeling threatened about anything."

A few months ago I would have argued with her about which power is the most powerful, but not anymore. "Does Dad know?"

"No. Not anymore. I tried to talk to him about it when we were dating, a long time ago, but within a couple days he would forget I ever told him anything. Several times I tried," she starts to explain, "Back then we lived in Rosemont, but I moved us out of there as soon as we became engaged. It got so I felt like I was being watched all the time, and I think it was because everything I told your dad was being read by telepaths and then erased from his mind. They were finding out what I know from what I was telling him." Her hands are spending as much time waving around while she is communicating with me as they are on the steering wheel.

"They thought I was a threat or something, I don't know. It felt like I was in one of those movies where a couple moves to a small town run by a cult. And, I was born there!" She exclaimed at the end, hitting the steering wheel with both hands. I can see tears starting to build up in her eyes.

I'm stunned and horrified that could even happen. "Carly's told me what they do, and it all sounds so," I search for a word, "antiseptic. Like they think they are doing the world a service. That there's nothing wrong with what they're doing."

This time it's Mom that's stunned, "She told you? About telepaths — what they do? Oh my god, that's amazing!" She reminisces her experience, "I have been looked at strange by telepaths my whole life, but not one has ever bothered to talk to me. Not about them, not about my powers."

I put my hand on the dashboard, "Could you pull over? Stop the car – before you run into a tree?" Mom's driving isn't doing a good job staying straight, but at least she lets off the gas pedal; we probably won't die when she hits a tree.

With a loud, "Oh!" Mom straightens her driving and pulls off onto a dirt siding just before a big curve in the road coming up.

"Tell me," are Mom's next words and I realize that she may get more questions answered than me in this conversation.

I tell her everything Carly has told me, even about Malcolm Beaumont, and what I have seen at Nova Academy. I answer all her questions. I tell her what is happening with the neural neutralizers and the "investigation" Carly and I are doing into what's been happening. It seems like the more I tell her, the bigger her eyes get, and I see big tears beginning to well up even more than before.

"So, you decided to do it. You're going to be a superhero."

Wait! What? Where did she get that? Too stunned to talk, I just stare at her.

"And, the first thing you take on is the biggest secret there has ever been." She looks out the front window; I can see her beginning to shake. She's scared.

Damn. I should have just talked to Dad. "No, Mom. I have not decided to be a superhero. But, someone needs to find out what is going on and no one else seems to know to even look. We are going to give whatever we find to the police and let them handle it. I promise."

Mom mulls it over, and I am not sure she believes anything I have said by the look on her face. "Why did she tell you?" She finally asks.

Taking a moment to sift through all the reasons, I can't find a single thing, "I don't think she likes that that's what telepaths do very much. She's not trying to change it, or anything, it's just that I think she sees in me someone who she can tell her secrets without worrying about someone else being able to take them out of my head. I'm someone she can trust who is not a telepath, but who can protect their thoughts."

"She must trust you very much."

"She does, Mom. And, I trust her."

"You still need to be careful with her. No matter what she says, she's still a telepath. She's one of them. And you're about to poke a hornet's nest."

"That's just it; I'm not trying to expose telepaths. I've thought that through and even if I could expose them, it would just go back the way it was within a few days. The only way to stop it from becoming secret again would be to kill all the telepaths, and that's so far beyond wrong there's no way. They're not Evil Overlords, they're people." I didn't add my concerns about hoping they stay that way.

"I didn't have as much information as you, but I came to the same conclusion twenty years ago when I wanted to tell everyone about what I was seeing telepaths do. You've made the right choice. Besides, there isn't another option." She's looking out the windshield, working out what we've been saying, "But, what are you doing then? With these 'neural neutralizer' people? How can you stand in the way of them being able to protect their memories?"

"That's not what's happening, though, Mom. They're being controlled. Somebody is making them wear the neural neutralizers AFTER they change their minds. Not the students. They're not changing their own minds. The telepaths behind this are changing the minds of the students, and then putting a neural neutralizer on their heads to stop them from being discovered. I assume to hide it from other telepaths."

"And you're sure of this?" Mom asks, still skeptical.

"Yes. I think the neutralizer is being used to keep other telepaths from changing their memories back, or knowing what is being done to them. Carly said one of the ways telepaths police each other is if one telepath sees something changed in a person they don't agree with, they can change it back, or fix the change, so it doesn't affect the person. We were able to get a neural neutralizer off of one of the science students and Carly scanned him. He'd been given compulsions to do stuff and to never take off the hat his neutralizer was hidden in. He's being made to get on some bus; they take him somewhere like three times a week, and he thinks it's a job."

"Who do you think is behind it?" Mom asks the obvious question. She knows I don't know. She's only asking because she does not want to let go of her objections to me being involved.

"We don't know." What I don't tell her, is what my gut's telling me: there is a powerful telepath behind this who wants to be the next Malcolm Beaumont.

I think Mom has finally had enough. She is restarting the car and just says, "You WILL call me every day from now on. Right?"

"Yes." Because "No" is not an option for me to say to my mom.

"By the way, we can't speak about any of this to your dad."

"I know." But, I wish I could.

The rest of the week after Thanksgiving gives me a break I didn't realize I needed and it's good to be home. The only thing I'm not thrilled with in being back is my lab in the basement. It's barren compared to the student labs, which makes me think that now I know why mad scientists like to break into corporate labs all the time, steal equipment, and build lairs. I know a website that tracks all the major corporate laboratories in the nation. I might need to check it out.

Chapter 44

The airport shuttle pulls into Atlas Quad, and I pick up my package for my parts at the lobby desk. I break open the box when I get up to my dorm room and pull out the five sets of Dragonfly wings I ordered. Two sets of little ones for the tracker with a backup pair, and three large sets for a much larger, support version of the Dragon Tracker, that I'm calling my Black Dragon. I built it at the same time as the Tracker and mounted a simple compressed air gun with an automatic targeting system that can hurl a 7/8" steel bearing out at two hundred miles per hour at a designated target. Carly's flight is not due in for a few hours, so I take the time to assemble the wings onto the bodies of the Dragons and do some test flights around the room. We're in business.

Neither of us feels like we can wait any longer, so we choose the first day back from break to attach the Dragon Tracker to the bus that's due this evening. We do everything the same as we did before, except I don't have to approach the bus this time. Instead, I toss the dragon up as the bus goes by on the road to turn into the parking lot and the Dragon Tracker unfolds itself in the air and buzzes over to the bus to attach itself to the roof of the vehicle. I am having a hard time following it as it is silent and well camouflaged to match the background color of a blue-gray sky.

I wait to see that it's working right and, just like I designed it, the Dragon Tracker takes off and hovers a thousand feet over the bus when it comes to a stop, and then lands on it again when it starts to drive away with the science students on board. Unless you're searching the bus while it's moving, good luck trying to find the tracker.

Once the bus drives away, Carly and I high-five and head over to the Tesla Quad Commons to get some dinner as we've worn out the menu at Atlas and it would be nice to have something different for a change of pace.

We meet again for breakfast in the morning because we don't have any classes together on Tuesdays. "We got it," is my greeting to Carly and I sit down across from her in the little cafe next to the Liberal Arts buildings. Reaching into my bag, I pull out my tablet and say, "Have a look," and open up my maps program. "I've input the tracker data to my maps app. Look here, they did the same stop as last time where they found the first tracker." I get some satisfaction in saying that for the unspoken fact that they did not find the Dragon Tracker. "Guess where they ended up?"

Carly takes over control of my maps app and pushes the map down until it comes to a stop at a place the track line indicates they spent the next nine hours. "That's on the other side of Chicago," she says. Switching the road map to the satellite map, Carly zooms into a top-down view of a big industrial building. "Do you know what that place is?"

"Yeah," I say and spin the tablet around and minimize the map app to bring up the video app. I start the paused video that comes up on the screen, "Look, they went into the back door of this building and, look there, on the door. Below where it says 'Deliveries,' can you see what it says?"

"Henderson Robotics. You're kidding?" She looks at me, mouth open.

"Nope. It's another one of their production facilities. They have now taken over the company they broke into, twice. Either that or they were breaking into their own company. In either case, we have our target."

"We'll have to wait until this weekend."

"We can leave after your morning class on Friday."

I spend the rest of the week maintaining my equipment and make time to finish installing the HUD to the face shield for my suit.

Chapter 45

We're on the road for Chicago by 11:30 AM Friday morning and make good time. The place we decide to stay is a campground with rental cabins. It is the offseason and only a few of the cabins are being used. Our cabin is well off the main road down a dirt road marked with a huge sign carved in the side of a giant tree that looks like it had fallen over in that very spot some hundred years before. The Tree Fall Cabins gives us the privacy and out of the way location we may need at the end of the mission.

Carly takes a walk around the cabins and scans all the other guests. There are only eight of them, and she makes everyone think we're the most boring and irrelevant people ever, and nothing we do would be interesting in the slightest. I can't say I'm happy about her using her powers on them, but this is a mission and the mission comes first. Practical, that's what I am.

There's a single porch light outside of the cabin that doesn't have a switch, so just before we leave, I unscrew the bulb so when we come back no one will see us reenter the cabin in our super suits. My suit is a little bulky to fit in the driver's seat, so Carly does the driving. When we're close, she turns out on the two-lane road toward the Henderson Robotics production facility.

It is only 4:30 PM when we get the car parked in a little glade in the woods that will give the car good cover. I put on my helmet and grab my shield and hammer to attach them to the harness on my back as we make our way to a place we can observe at the rear of the facility, which is where my tracker showed the bus stopped. No vehicles are at the location; it looks deserted, which is odd. The work day isn't over, even if it is a Friday. I'm beginning to doubt the building is being used during the day.

"What do you think," I ask Carly.

"Looks deserted."

"It does. Think we should go take a look before they get here?"

"If we don't, we'll have to wait all night or do it while they're in there."

I say, "Okay, let's do it," and move over to one of the fence poles of the chain link fence. I look up at the top of the ten foot fence and jump straight up, grab the top cap of the fence pole and swing myself over the top of the fence without touching the chain links.

"Showoff," Carly says, grinning, then scrambles up the same pole by grabbing and scaling the chain links like a spider monkey, flips herself over the top using a similar, but infinitely more stylish, acrobatic flip and lands beside me.

"Showoff," I counter, and we run for the building. "Over here," I say, and point at an enclosure built to the side of the building with a lower roof than the thirty foot roof of the main building. I'm hoping we can go up there and find a way in through a skylight. Making our way onto the flat roof, I see there are skylights evenly spaced across the building, just as I suspected there would be. Most big industrial buildings use skylights to provide light into the warehouse during the day, and vent hot-air built up in the warehouse, so the business doesn't have to spend as much money on energy for lighting and air conditioning.

I don't know the layout of the building, so I head toward the front of the building as it's the most likely to have offices built there. I'm hoping they have built a mezzanine on top of the first floor offices that we can use to lower ourselves down onto rather than having to drop thirty feet to the warehouse floor if we try to enter through one of the skylights above the warehouse. I pick a skylight that looks like it's in a good place for what I'm planning and pop the locks off the cover and pull it off. Setting it aside, I'm looking at a second cover that has hinges on one side, so I know it opens, but whatever releases it is on the inside. Not letting that stop me I bend the louvers on the side of the skylight that let hot air out of the building and find a crank for opening the skylight. Taking another thirty seconds, I crank open the skylight and am rewarded with seeing the top of a drop ceiling for a second floor mezzanine offices about two feet from the top of the roof. Jackpot, we're in.

Carly and I stick our heads down into the skylight and listen. There are no sounds, and I do not see any wiring for alarms or motion detectors, so we decide to make the entry. I pop open the ceiling tile and set it gently aside so I can put it back in place later and drop down into what looks like an office training room and almost snag my large utility bag on the ceiling grid. I brought the bag for whatever evidence, or interesting tech, we find. Henderson Robotics seems to be rotten with illegal activity, and I'm not going to feel much guilt for taking their stuff. Not that I would feel much guilt anyway.

While I'm adjusting my bag, Carly drops in beside me then we make our way out into the hall to start our snooping. I have three things I'm looking for: the server room so I can connect a Snoop that will let me break into their network; the production facility so I can see what they're making; and a finished goods storage so I can steal a couple of whatever it is they are making, especially the neural neutralizers. I find the server room, but it's locked; I don't want to force the door. I settle for connecting a remote dial in router to the back of one of the executive's computers in their office.

When I come out, I see Carly finishing her sweep of the upstairs. She's looking for anything that could provide us with useful information she can either takes a picture of or steal if she thinks it is important and won't be noticed.

We head downstairs together and stop at the bottom of the stairs to listen. I still do not hear any sounds in the building, so we each head in different directions with the assumption the building is empty. Carly goes to the front offices, and I look for the lab and production areas. I go downstairs and enter the lab where I find upwards of fifty workstations for doing electronics assembly. Neural neutralizers and some other electronic pieces of equipment in various stages of assembly are laid out on two assembly lines. All of the bins marked "Completed" are empty and nothing else in the room stands out until I see several pages of wiring and assembly diagrams on one of the tables. They won't tell me nearly as much as a blueprint will, but it will give me a lot I can use towards figuring it out myself.

I quickly take pictures of the diagrams and head out the back double doors to the lab that I'm sure leads to the warehouse. The warehouse opens up into various areas for storage, shipping and receiving, and a locked cage holding what look to be hundreds of completed neural neutralizers and other inventory. Some of which I recognize, and some of which I have no clue what they are, which makes me very happy, as I want to see what the brainchild of these devices has created.

Whoever is running this operation is well on their way to building themselves a private work force of mind altered super geniuses. And that can only spell trouble with a capital "Mad Scientist."

I look up and see whoever installed the cage was sloppy, it doesn't have a top on the cage and doesn't extend all the way to the roof, so I jump up and grab one of the cast iron sprinkler pipes and swing myself over the fence and into the cage. That's when I hear it, the sharp sound of air rapidly released from the other side of the warehouse roll-up doors. The same sound I heard the bus making when it stopped in the parking lot to pick up the science students to bring them down here. They're here an hour early.

I doubt Carly can hear the sound from in the offices, and she doesn't have enhanced hearing like I do, so I jump back over the fence and run for the offices to find Carly. When I find her, she's still going through offices. She seems to have found some things of worth as I see the bag she brought for collecting things has a bit of a bulge to it just as she ducks into another room.

"We've got a problem," I say as I poke my head into the office after her.

Chapter 46

As I pull my head back out of the room and run down the hall, I call back to Carly, "They're here! We have to go!" I don't wait to see her a moment later; she's flying out of the same door and running toward me. I drop my helmet's face shield into place and lead her back through the lab I was in before. From there I head for the double doors going back into the warehouse and look through the window only to see a light in the shape of a door open in the back of the warehouse.

"Come on, we need to get back upstairs," I say, and go back the way we came. Just as I'm about to come around the corner to the hall leading to the stairs, I hear voices and skid to a halt. I almost clothesline Carly as I hold my arm up to stop her. "Too late," I whisper.

Someone is in the hall talking, "Get them going, I want to put out another fifty units tonight." Then I hear the tromping of heavy footsteps going up the stairs. A door clicks and the footsteps recede up the stairs.

I risk a look around the corner and see at the end of the hall a second way out to the warehouse that I didn't notice before.

Turning back to Carly, I say, "We didn't put the ceiling tile back in place." The plan was to put it back as we made our exit and not get caught inside the building, so I didn't worry about it. "I don't think we can risk trying to hide."

Carly is looking at my face shield, but can't see my face. Her eyes are also blocked with the wrap around goggles I gave her to use. Both her goggles and my face shield are providing light enhancement (I can't wait to get my HUD upgrades installed so I can see in multiple wavelengths). It seems like the hall is fully lit when only a couple lights in the hallways have been left on, one in the back by the exit to the warehouse and the other at the opposite end...which would be located near the front entrance to the building. "That way," I run down the hall and into the reception area, only to find the front doors are industrial steal fire doors, and they've been locked closed with a heavy chain.

"Aww, man. Screw these guys." I'm getting pissed and feeling like I'm being backed into a corner. Putting my hands on my hips and staring at the lock I tell Carly, "We may have to fight our way out of here."

I look over as she doesn't say anything and I see her adjusting her gloves and goggles and looking back at me. *She's waiting for me to take the lead,* I tell myself, *It's up to me to get us out of here.*

I take a deep breath and turn my back on the chained and locked door. I could bust through it, but it would make hella racket; they'd be on us in moments – in a room with only one exit. I whisper to Carly, "If we have to fight, I want it to be in the warehouse. From there can make our way outside. And I'll need the room to fight." Looking at the ceiling and the closed in walls, I'm suddenly feeling claustrophobic. One of the most important aspects of my superpowers is my speed, and I won't be able to use it trapped in here.

Continuing to whisper, I say, "Okay, let's give them a few minutes to get all the students into the lab and out of the way. Then we'll make our way out the door to the warehouse by the stairs."

I get a nod of agreement, and Carly pulls her goggles off long enough to put her full hood mask on then puts the goggles back on. Being recognized would not be good, and I unlimber my shield and hammer. "I'll go first to clear the way. Anyone not wearing a neural neutralizer gets put to sleep. Be ready though, I'm betting they have at least one telepath."

Carly is tight lipped, but I don't see any fear, only determination, so I continue. "If you're able, tell me which ones are telepaths; I'll try to hit them with a fast ball. If anyone gets near you, rip off their hat."

Her mouth curls up in a smile, and I can tell by her head tilt she's amused by my instructions. "Will you go already? You're starting to make me nervous."

Okay, I guess that's my queue. I switch my war hammer into my left hand with my shield so I can have a hand free to reach into the big utility bag on my belt and pull out what looks like an Ostrich egg. Carly starts to ask me a question, but I think she remembers that she just got me to shut up, and decides to let it go. The "egg" has an indent on one end I press, making an audible click.

No one comes to investigate the noise, so I start moving quickly for the door to the warehouse. Half way there the door opens and in walks two men. The first is looking back, talking to the other, and they don't take notice of me until I speed up my walk in to a run. By the time they notice, it's too late. I use the shield as a battering ram to knock them back out into the warehouse. The first one is sprawled out and starting to roll over with a groan while the second one bursts into flames, which makes him my second ever elemental I'll have had to fight.

Fortunately, bursting into flame seems to be bad for neural neutralizers as his hat bursts into flames along with the rest of him. He's just about to throw a ball of fire he was building in his hand when his flames go out and he falls back to the floor, unconscious; courtesy of Carly's telepathy. This then reminds me to reach down and pull the hat off the first guy before he clears his head. I'm past him and scanning the warehouse when he joins the fire elemental in sleepy land.

A shout of, "Hey!" comes from the middle of the warehouse where five men and a very tall Amazonian looking woman are standing around one of the students. The student, the amazon, and one of the men wearing a long coat are not wearing hats.

I don't know how well Carly can do against two telepaths, so I throw the egg up in the air, grab my baseball and throw a fastball at the closest of the two not wearing a hat, which would be the guy in the long coat. I'm rewarded with the sickening thud and crunch of bone of the baseball impacting his face, followed by the sound of his body hitting the floor. This is major league.

This seems to provide the motivation necessary for the woman and the remaining five men to scatter, but the student just stands there like nothing was happening. A second later, he turns to look at Carly; his eyes going wide before he turns and runs toward the lab. The time Carly spends saving the student with a telepathic inducement to run leaves her open to attack from the Amazonian, who stretches her arm out to Carly with her fingers spread out like you see vampires in the movies do when they're trying to mind control their next victim. Only this time it's not mind control and Carly is thrown against the fence surrounding the finished goods.

Carly reacts instantly by swiping her arm across herself and seems to be released from whatever it was pressing her up against the fence, then brings her other arm around and holds it up toward the Amazonian and clenches her fist. I've never seen telekinetics fight before, and I'm surprised to see them waving their arms around.

That's the last thing I see before something slams into me from behind, and I'm thrown across the room and slam into a pile of shipping pallets stacked up by one of the roll-up doors. Dumb, dumb, dumb. I let myself be distracted while gawking.

I can feel whoever hit me still has a grip on my shoulder with one hand and gripping my forearm with the other. He's a lot stronger than me and about to crush my arm and shoulder in one go, so I activate my field generator and whip my shield back; the edge catching him in the chest.

The strongman is thrown back, and I hear an audible "crack" of ribs breaking. It sounds more like the crack of a rifle shot than ribs, followed by a loud "Oof!" of air bursting out of his lungs. I don't think he is a Class 4 like Welcoming Committee. I'm figuring he's more of a Class 3, based on the pain I'm feeling in my shoulder. If he were a Class 4, I wouldn't have a shoulder.

The sound of cracking ribs is satisfying to hear; I bet he's never broken a bone in his life. The suit does its job perfectly, and I react instantly after slamming into the pallets rather than the normal head shaking and clearing of cobwebs I would have had without armor. That and my shoulder and arm would have been mush without the protection of my armor plates.

I'm up and spinning around to face the guy with the now cracked ribs. He is standing, but bent over, holding his chest in front of me. So I sweep his legs with my hammer to get him out of my way and leave him to his pain. I turn off the field generator as it's messing with my face shield's display (something I didn't test for before the mission). There are still at least four more people in the room who may want a piece of me, and I take the time to do a quick sweep of the room. The light amplification in my face shield leaves no shadows in the warehouse. I'm wishing for my upgraded HUD as it would display red targeting cursors over the five people spread around the room I now have to identify as targets manually. As it is, the feed from the Black Dragon is only putting a targeting dot on one of them. It helps, but not a lot.

One of the three is running straight at me while two others are circling me and the fourth is standing still and pointing something at me. I break toward the guy running at me, hoping to get him in the line of fire; kneecapping him as I go past. Only his knee isn't there and I miss. "Speedster?" I ask myself and feel three strong hits to my chest. The hits knock me around a little, but my armor continues doing its job.

I keep running and pull the shield up to protect myself from the guy who I now know was pointing an assault rifle at me, which he is unloading at me through the barrel. I give a command to Black Dragon to target lock and fire a volley of steel bearing at him while I do a quick scan around the room to find Carly. The booming staccato of the assault rifle is silenced, and I catch a glimpse of the owner jerking from the hits of the steel bearings impacting his torso.

Carly, standing up against the fence, cries out. No one is near her, and I'm worried the speedster got to her while I was distracted.

Then I remember Carly told me that when a telepath in a telepathic duel cries out, they're in trouble, so I scan back to where the Amazonian woman was standing – she's still standing there, now with a look of sheer pleasure on her face, so I re-target Black Dragon and have it unload all of his ball bearings on her. I'm amazed she's able to stop the first two bearings as they stop in mid-air, then she drops like a stone to the ground as the next four bearings pummel her to the ground. In great pain and her concentration broken, she screams and grabs at her temples. The bearings had all hit center mass, so I'm pretty certain Carly was able to recover and is now tap dancing in the amazon's pain clouded mind.

I go back to worrying about the guy with the assault rifle as he's once again shooting at me and make a rush at him with my shield up, blocking the bullets. When I reach him, I flip my shield up into a backhand shield bash that shatters his gun and sends him flying. I'm not too concerned whether he is a baseline and don't hold back when I use the edge of my shield to punch him in the throat.

Changing direction to swing back by Carly, I feel a "whoosh" go past me. The speedster just misses me as a blur goes past the right side of my head, just in my view. He's faster than me.

But, the odds are a bit more even now, and I'm feeling a little more like we have a chance to escape. I am also counting on my armor and equipment giving me the edge I need to beat the speedster. I continue to try to track him and the last guy who hasn't committed himself yet.

The speedster has settled into doing drive-bys; I'm having a hard time keeping my shield in position to take the hits. He's at least a Class 2 strength and may be a Class 4 speed, but I'm not sure as I've never a met a Class 4 speedster, I'm just certain he's a lot faster than me. He makes several passes on me and finally gets a hit on my shoulder that spins me around. I'm up in a flash, but not before he hits me again and flips me back into a storage rack. At least now I am pretty sure he is Class 2 strength as he is not hitting me hard enough to be anything more than that.

I roll under the rack and into the next aisle and ready myself. Between racks, he can only approach me from the two directions, so I'm able to see which way he's coming from and get turned toward him. This time I don't try to get my shield up to block him; instead, I do the opposite and open my shield to pull him in close. He smashes his fist right in my chest at the exact same moment I punch him in the kidney. I was still holding my war hammer but had a choked up grip as I didn't have room to swing it in the narrow aisle. The added weight of the war hammer with my kidney punch had to have hurt, but the results are far more than what you would expect from just being punched.

I go flying when he hits me as I did not re-energize my repeller field generator. Instead of re-energizing the field, I focused on hitting him first and activated the Taser in the bar across the knuckles of my gauntlet. I'm not the only one who goes flying.

We both hit the ground hard, but my armor did its job. I'm barely shaken up, while he's still down. The speedster made the mistake of hitting me in the strongest part of my armor, the chest. I stand back up and look over to see him spread eagle on the floor, his body is bent in the middle. He's groaning and trying to get back up, which is surprising. Carly pins him to the ground using her telekinetic powers, then he stops moving.

I've got a few cobwebs in my head and try to get myself re-oriented when I hear a growl and something heavy coming from behind me. Spinning around and swinging wildly with my shield, I miss my last assailant as he bowls me over in a mass of hair and claws and teeth. This guy, this monster, is a mass of hairy claws and teeth and he's seriously testing the material of my suit as he is raking them across my chest and stomach. I try to bring up my shield; he bats it away, landing on my chest. He is trying to shred my suit. It is holding up, but I am not confident enough to keep from panicking. I try to swing my hammer up into him, but he's too close; I can't get any leverage. I try again to punch him with my weapon hand. He blocks it again, and this time brings his foot up and grips my arm with it like he has an opposable thumb, or toe, to hold onto me with. My suit is holding up, but the panic I'm feeling is increasing as the sheer violence of his attack has me in full defensive mode. I drop my shield; it's not doing me any good anyway, and use grappling techniques to break his foot's grip on my arm so I can reach for his head that is all gnashing teeth and fangs. I feel him try to bite my head as I break his grip; his teeth are scraping against my helmet. I can see the back of his mouth, surrounded by teeth, through my face shield.

I grab him on either side of his head. He thinks I'm trying to hold his head back from biting my neck and face and he's pressing down with all he has to get to me. I make him pay for it, though, as I pull the neural neutralizer off his head. I'm expecting Carly to put the monster to sleep, but he just keeps trying to get to my face. I can't see Carly but can feel the monster being pushed off of me. She must have resorted to her telekinesis; I'm wondering why her telepathy didn't just put the thing to sleep.

The monster slash werewolf slash hound of hell, whatever it is, is thrown off by Carly and I'm surprised to find I'm going with him as he doesn't let go with any of his four limbs gripping different parts of my body; my neck being the most concerning part.

We land with me on top, though, and I use the momentum to aid my switch from trying to push his gnashing teeth away, which hadn't stopped their gnashing as we flew through the air, away from me to jerking him in for a head butt. His snout full of teeth smashes into the front of my helmet; my vision blocked by the blood and teeth splattering on my face shield. We roll again and the monster sits up on my chest with a blank stare and his arms drop to his sides. Mary mother of god, this monster is scary.

Rather than wait for him to snap out of his stupor, I charge the Tasers in both fists and bring them up together on both sides of its head; he's thrown across the room. Carly finishes him off; his body limp and flopping like a rag doll when he hits the ground.

Carly runs over to me and helps me to my feet, and we look around to see if anyone else is around. As I look toward the offices, I see one of Black Dragon's target designators pop up in my HUD, marking a person standing in a large observation window on the second floor of the offices. The figure is looking down at us through the window. He looks familiar, but I can't place him. Whoever he is, he's well over six foot and has an impressive build. I have the feeling of someone trying to pry open my brain just before I hear Carly catch her breath and begin to gurgle a cry that sounds far worse than the one I heard her make earlier, then I'm lifted off the ground.

I'm flailing around and can feel him trying to push into my mind and grit my teeth and try to throw my baseball at him, but I don't have any leverage hanging in the air and can't aim my throw. The ball hits the ceiling and falls to the ground. The pressing on my mind is becoming painful and, not knowing how to push back telepathically, I'm mostly just tightening all the muscles in my face and neck, and I can feel the blood pressure in my head rising from my straining, making the pressure worse. Carly has stopped making sounds; I hear her fighting back, doing what sounds like Lamaze breathing exercises. She's still fighting him, but doesn't sound like she can last much longer. Using my helmet comms, I do the last thing I can do and order Black Dragon to suicide into the plate glass the figure is standing behind, and detonate.

Turning toward the window, the drone accelerates and detonates just as it impacts the glass, sending a shockwave of glass shards at the figure where he disappears from view in the explosion. We're released and drop to the ground.

I lift Carly back onto her feet, "Are you okay?"

She pushes me away, screaming, "Let me go!" She's visibly shaking and seething with rage.

Rage that we don't have the luxury of indulging, "Come on, we have to get those kids out of here!" I shout and run to the lab doors, "Everybody back on the bus! It's time to go! Now! Drop what you're doing! GO!" Either everyone was brainwashed to take orders from people in black super-suits, or I scared the hell out of them. Because every one of them jumps up and starts running. Carly finishes getting everyone out of the building and on the bus while I do a smash and grab for a handful of completed neural neutralizers in the security cage and grab our bags from in the hall of the offices, then we get the hell out of there by taking the bus they came in on.

We spend the rest of the night parked behind our cabin trying to undo, or at least patch, the changes that were made to the science student's minds. It takes a while to explain to them what is happening and to get them to accept we actually saved them from mind control; and we weren't abducting them from the facility. We are going in circles arguing semantics until one of them asks how he ever came to work for someone without being paid. From there we are able to let them hash it out between themselves, which goes on for most of the ride back to the campus. At least they leave me alone to drive the bus. Carly is giving nudges to the ideas that explain correctly what happened and suppresses the wild claims coming from the students as they talk about what had happened to them.

It is a full hour after we get back to campus that we remember we left Carly's car behind and hit up Carlos to borrow his car. On the way back to the cabin we are exhausted, but the thrill and excitement of the fight is starting to surge through our veins again as we talk about the fight. Something we did not feel we could do with the kids on the bus. We go back and forth about what we did, and why. And how we could have helped each other more. I do not think there is much to critique, but Carly tears down the whole thing in detail as I drive and try to absorb everything she is saying.

The last thing we discuss is the telepath we fought at the end. We know nothing about the man other than he was incredibly powerful. Far beyond Carly's power to fight telepathically. And, he was telekinetic. He scares me. A lot. I was helpless to stop him; we would have died or been captured if not for the Black Dragon.

On the way home we drive in separate cars, and I spend most of the time thinking about what could have happened, and how I can stop it from happening next time.

Chapter 47

Freeing the rest of the students from mind control turns out to be time consuming, but not difficult. We keep the bus and simply show up every evening at 5:30 to pick up the next group of kids who come to get a ride to the facility and take them for a different kind of ride instead. The Henderson Robotics people did not reappear to continue their abductions. On the fourth day, no one shows up; we figure we got everyone. I do not see any other science students on the campus with the hats on, and those we do see we pull their hats off and Carly quickly scans their minds. None of them complain as Carly also takes care of any objections they have to having their hat snatched off their heads. A couple days later we ditch the bus in town because we don't know what else to do with it. All told, we freed 132 students from mind control.

Things go back to normal after that, and we are able to go through semester finals in December without any surprises. Although my engineering professor tries to fail all of us with a surprise final project that counts as half of our final exam. I do the final without any problem, even if I am cussing the professor the entire time I build the project that turns out to be a manufacturing run for a device the professor is using students to build what he is selling on the eNgineers.com auction site. Thinking back, several of our projects were just the type of thing you could sell on that auction site.

The neural neutralizers are a mix of two mad scientist designs, the first being the neural network design of Henderson Robotics and the second being adapting it into a neutralizer by whoever is behind this whole thing. It takes a while to figure it out and reverse engineer, but I am finally able to figure out the principals involved and implement elements of both scientist's work into my suit. What? You didn't think I'd use someone else's work? That somehow I am too proud to think something someone else made could be useful to me? Get real. First, there are plenty of advanced science minds out there just as good as mine, and second, no one else could have adapted the device to work with my HUD and suit. So, shut up.

I replace my HUD with instantaneous neural imaging and communications using the neural interface and upgrade the neural neutralizer into my field generator. Next, I am working on Carly's.

We're in one of the private labs I reserved earlier in the week; Carly is leaning over my shoulder, watching me work, all curiosity as she tries to figure out what you get when you combine a neural neutralizer with a field generator, "Will this make my shield stronger? It's already pretty strong," she asks.

"This won't make it stronger, I'm just giving it a new feature you can use," I reply, teasing her along.

"Really! What's it do?" I love it when she gets excited about my inventions.

"It should block mind powers from being used on you."

Frowning, Carly asks, "What about my powers? Will it block my powers when it's activated?

"Yes, it'll block the neural energy going in both directions. Nothing I can do about that." Before she can protest, I continue, "But! I have two settings for you: one that uses the same field it's always used, and the other that routes the power through the neuro-frequency modulator."

"The what?" She shakes her head, "Nevermind. But why would I need it?"

"I need it to keep from being lifted up in the air like a helpless rag doll. And you need it because I need it, which means I don't know why you need it since you can fight that kind of power, but just in case you do need it, we have it." The truth is I know why she would need it, but I'm going to keep that to myself rather than offend her.

Carly looks at me like, *WTF kind of logic is that?* but there's not much to be done about it, because if she wants to have the field generator, she's going to have to take it the way I give it to her.

Finishing making the upgrade to the generator, I put it on and energize it, "Okay, hit me."

I didn't have to ask her twice, and she punches me in the gut. I could feel the punch, but her fist never touches me.

"Nice shot," I say, "Now use your telekinetic power on me," and I turn on the modulator.

I can see her trying to do something to me with her powers, but nothing is happening. This goes on for a minute before she resorts to a different tactic and picks up an iron bar on the table and hits me with it. I can say I wasn't expecting it, and the results are more me jumping in surprise than the bar smashing into my shield.

Carly helps me back to my feet, "Well, it definitely works, but it's not a perfect defense. I couldn't touch you with either my telepathy or telekinesis. And, there is no feel to your mind like I usually can. But, it didn't stop me from hitting you with that bar."

"Yeah, thanks for that. Point made, by the way. But, I'm not trying to stop the powers completely, just stop them from working directly on me." Although, that just gave me an idea. What if I could project the field onto another person?

"Is this what it's like to be a mad scientist?" Carly breaks my line of reasoning with her question.

"Pretty much. A little bit, anyway. Except I didn't build in a world ending super bomb or weather control device."

Chapter 48

I hear someone running in the hall outside my dorm room just before the door flies open and Carlos bowls his way into the room. "It's you! Isn't it! You and Carly!"

My stomach sinks as I know exactly what he's talking about, "Close the door, would you. And, what are you talking about?"

"Man, I saw the pictures, I know it's you," Carlos continues as is his annoyingly persistent habit.

"Come on, Carlos, we both know you don't know anything."

"No, huh-uh! This I know, smart ass. I've seen your suit!"

I could kill him. Stuff him in his locker. And no one would know until the end of the year. "What are you talking about?" I say instead.

"The fight in the warehouse in Chicago, it's online! You were seen in your costume on that bus on campus for like a week after the date stamp on the video! That was you! I've seen your suit, bro. You're working on that thing all the time!"

"How is that me? I wasn't anywhere near that bus!" I'm not above lying to a nosey roommate.

"Yeah, sure. YOU weren't near the bus, but that suit you been working on sure as hell was! I've got a picture – Look!" Carlos shoves his smart phone into my face and, sure enough, there is a picture of me, in my suit, standing on the first step of the bus.

He's got me, and he knows it. I may be doing his homework for the next four years. "That's not me. You don't know crap. And, if you say anything to anybody about me, the guy in that picture is going to pay you a visit."

"No, man. Your secret's safe with me." Carlos says. The smug bastard is not capable of being as sincere as he's trying to make himself sound.

"Just don't. Really. Don't," I warn him.

HA! My roomie's a superhero!" Carlos yells at the top of his lungs and leaves as fast as he arrived. I can hear him laughing his fool head off all the way down the hall.

My day is officially ruined, so I see no reason not to take care of anything else I can that could ruin tomorrow and call Carly to let her know about Carlos. The call goes something like this: "Hey - Carlos knows - video - yeah, me on the bus - How are you going to take care of it? - Oh! Right, of course. Wait! - But! - All right. - No. Go ahead." And, now I'm not concerned Carlos will be able to expose our identities. And, I'm glad I never gave Carlos one of the neural neutralizers I took from the facility or I would have to snatch it off his head for Carly to do her magic.

With Carlos "fixed," (I know, it sounds like he's been neutered, which is kind of the case) things go back to normal, and Carly and I are able to continue to enjoy our anonymity. The new semester has started, which doesn't mean anything to me as most of my classes are just continuations of first semester. With the exception that I no longer have a class together with Carly, which sucks. We make up for it by having lunch together every day.

That's how things go up until Christmas break. Classes, work on suit, more classes, create something new, even more classes, and lots of Carly in between, during, and after.

We talk about meeting each other's parents during Christmas break, but the entirety of that conversation lasts about three sentences; I guess we're not ready for it yet. The holidays are a lot like Thanksgiving and it is great seeing my family and friends, but I miss having access to the student lab a lot more than I miss my parents. By the way, it would be better if you didn't tell my mom I said that.

Speaking of my mom, I am able to have a couple more conversations with her and let her know all was quiet on that front at school. Her advice of being careful messing with telepaths is reinforced, and my (unspoken) refusal to listen to good advice is foremost in my opinion on the matter. Villain telepaths are no more dangerous than villains of every other stripe; they just have a different way of operating. Instead of hiring henchmen, they control their minds. Instead of beating you into a pulp, they turn your brain into mush. Instead of monologues about how ingenious their plans are, they just put it in your mind how brilliant they are.

Chapter 49

It's my first day back at Nova Academy after Christmas break, and I only want to do two things: see Carly and go to the student labs. I'm not sure which one I want to do more. Carly's first as she calls me before I can grab my stuff I need for the lab, and we meet at the Commons to catch up and hang out. It doesn't take her long to figure out I'm fiending for some lab time and she cuts me a break to go to the labs, but only if she can come along, which is fine by me as there is usually a lot of idle time while using the machines.

I spend Christmas break coming up with some new designs since I can't actually make anything at home. So I have a large number of G-Codes ready to go for loading into the CNC Machines in the student lab as well as a circuit diagram for several unique microchips and circuit boards I'm going to need. I only took the first three days of break to come up with these new designs, the rest of the two week break was spent writing the machine codes and schematics needed to have the machines in the lab make the parts for assembly.

We grab some To-Go boxes from the Commons food court and head over to the labs. When we get there, no one is in the lounge area. Classes won't start again until tomorrow, and I'm pleasantly surprised to see the open use machine shop is empty. Now I can run multiple jobs at a time and be finished with the machining in a quarter of the time it usually takes.

I get all of the lathes going on producing one part or another and then settle in for some quality time hanging out with Carly. It's like the best of both worlds; I'm building my inventions at the same time as I'm hanging with my best friend, lover, and partner in crime fighting.

"What are you making?" Carly asks.

"When I went home over break, I couldn't build anything, so I spent most of my time coming up with new equipment we might need. What I'm building right now is an upgraded Black Dragon design. I put a better weapon on it that has a larger magazine for the ammo, which we could have used during the fight. And, I put on a pod that'll allow me to customize the weapon or other gear it's carrying, depending on the mission. The other thing is for a replacement for my baseballs. I love 'em, but they're just not a serious weapon. So, I am making a variation on a bolo. Except, on my bolo the three balls will have Tasers that should disable just about anyone other than a lightning elemental. The last thing I'm making, for myself anyway, is to make more of the nuclear power supplies like the ones for our field generators. They take so long to make, I need to get ahead of the demand. There is no doubt I'll invent something else that needs one, and where would I be if I don't have one?" The question isn't a question.

"I like the bolo idea. And, you may not have had to sacrifice the Black Dragon if it hadn't run out of ammo. I was thinking I could use a couple things, too…maybe?" Carly is lobbying for some new toys.

Short of saying, "Hey, what about me?" And knocking on my head, Carly could not have dropped a bigger hint that I am neglecting making a shiny new (deadly) toy for her.

"You're right," I acknowledge her unspoken complaint; "I need to make some more equipment for you. I came up with a couple ideas on break, but want to ask you what you want first."

"I'm not sure what I need. The armor and field generator are a great defense, so I was thinking something I can use on offense."

"That's what I was thinking, too. You have your telepathy and telekinetic abilities for ranged attacks. I think you need something for up close and personal. I built in the secondary neural field generator for defense; you may want something so you can still fight without your powers if it's ever activated."

"What about a hand gun, or better yet, dual handguns?" she asks, not knowing the idea of using handguns, for a mad scientist, is one of the most offensive suggestions you could ever make.

I decide not to be offended, "Guns are boring. And overdone. Every baseline in the country owns one."

"That's because there isn't anything that gives a better bang-for-the-buck," Carly argues, "and, baselines have to have them to have any chance at all of beating even low level supers."

"All right. I'm going to have to work on the ranged weapon concept. I've got a mental picture that I think you'll love, but need to work out some technical issues on it before I can finish the design."

"You're not going to tell me what it is, are you?"

"Nope."

"That's rude."

"Yep."

"Alright, fine. I can wait. Do your thang, baby." Carly is pretty happy now with hanging out in the student labs with me since now she knows some of that time is going to be for her benefit.

"Doing my 'thang,' is right. What about fighting sticks for close in?"

"They're cool, but...," trailing off I can tell she's not thrilled with fighting sticks. She has the sad puppy dog eyes going.

Let's see if this changes her mind, "The fighting sticks will be energized with your field generator and your striking power will be amplified about a hundred times, give or take. Is that a little cooler for you?"

Perking up, she says, "That's a lot cooler. Okay." She has that predatory gleam back in her eye.

I think to myself, *You want cool, wait until you see the blasters I'm going to make you*...just as soon as I figure out how to stabilize the power conversion.

Finishing up in the machine shop, we head back to my dorm to store my stuff. The student labs are still quiet so I might come back later to work on the battle management control system for my suit. It's not anywhere close to being an AI, but it will be someday. For now, it's mostly going to control power distribution and the HUD display and targeting.

Monday mornings this semester start with my speed class, Advanced Speed Control, which really gets me jazzed and burns off a lot of energy for the rest of the day. After that is my second semester of Engineering for Advanced Minds, which is completely empty of people when I walk in. I sit down and start looking through my syllabus to see if there hasn't been a room change, then do the same on my phone by accessing the professor's website he maintains for his classes. I'm in the right place, according to the website, so I sit tight.

Dr. Manning walks in the class and sets down his bag, "Ah, good morning, Theo. How was your holidays?"

Looking around, I'm like a deer in the headlights as Dr. Manning has never addressed me about anything personal before. "It was good. Umm, thanks for asking."

"Great. Well, let's get started, the last time we met, we discussed...." And Dr. Manning picks up right where we left off on the last day of class before Christmas break.

I let him go on for a couple minutes because I'm not sure what is going on. My need for an answer gets the better of me, and I finally interrupt the lecture by saying, "Excuse me, Dr. Manning. Where are the rest of the students?"

"Well, like I told you at the end of last semester, none of the other students did well enough to advance to this class. It's rather unfortunate, I know, but that just means we'll be able to cover more material without the less capable students slowing us down."

What are you talking about? is very nearly my response as what he just said is total rubbish. I was in the top ten percent of the class, but there were at least four other students who outscored me on the exams last semester, and NO ONE failed the class that I know of. Besides, this is the seventh meeting we've had for this class and all the ones before Christmas were full of the same students from first semester. "Uh, right," is the best response I can give Dr. Manning. Something is so not right here.

I sit through the entire class and have to give credit to what Dr. Manning said, one-on-one does let us get through a lot more material than we ever did with a full classroom, but something is messed up here. After class, I head over to the Admin Building and have the clerk look up my class. According to the school records, I'm the only student registered to take Engineering for Advanced Minds at 10 AM, Mondays and Wednesdays.

I'm starting to get a pit in my stomach.

Chapter 50

I walk into Advanced Chemistry and find the class has about half the usual number of students. The ones that are here are either Biology majors or some other major other than the physics and engineering sciences. I'm beyond concerned now and having a hard time sitting still through the class. Algorithms class is nearly as bad as Engineering for Advanced Minds as the only two other students in the class are studying neurology, which puts me over the top and I leave the class five minutes after it starts. Where is everybody today?

Carly's in class right now, so I text her and ask her to meet me at my dorm later, then start taking a walk around the Science Department only to find class after class either empty or nearly empty. I don't know which lecture halls have classes scheduled in them at this time, but it can't be all of them. I pull up the course catalog on my phone and see several classes scheduled for this day and time, but the catalog does not have the room numbers listed, so I head back over to the Admin Building and start playing twenty questions with the clerk again. None of the classes have been cancelled, but several that are listed as active do not have any students registered as taking the class.

Carly gets to my dorm after class, and I fill her in on everything. Afterwards, we decide to go check out the Oppenheimer Quad to see who is there. What I'm afraid of most, that no one will be there, is exactly what we find, with the exception of the Commons staff who are all still there and carrying on as if they were feeding a few hundred people. We go next to the dorm, and I can't find anyone I know to be in the physical sciences. The buildings are nearly empty of students with many of the dorm room doors standing open. There not being many kids makes sense, as it is in the middle of a school day, but doors standing open that obviously look lived in doesn't make sense at all.

Carly and I try to report the missing people, but no one in Admin will listen, they all think we were put up to some kind of fraternity initiation prank, and when we try to report it to the local police, they call the people in Admin, who say no one is missing. That almost gets us arrested for making a false police report.

"What do we do?" Carly asks. We are sitting in her car in the parking lot outside my dorm.

"Who is left?" is my best response.

"The only people who can't be fooled by this type of thing, at least as a group, are the telepaths. We need to talk to Imelda."

"Great. You know your roommate is kind of creepy, right?"

"If you have a better idea of who to talk to, tell me who it is, and we'll talk to them instead."

"What about Professor Blake? He's a telepath."

"Professor Blake is more likely to be a villain than he is to be someone who stops a villain. The man is creepier than Imelda by far; trust me.' "

"All right, fine. We talk to Imelda."

We leave the car as it will just slow us down and run over to Carly's dorm. When we get there, Carly stops before entering her building and announces, "There's a lot of tension here."

I ask her, "What do you mean?"

"I can feel a lot of anxiety, it's not normal for this place. Telepaths are generally the most confident and laid back crowd you'll ever meet."

Well, that makes sense, I think. Telepaths always know where everyone stands.

"Let's go. Stay alert." Carly grabs my arm and pulls me into the building to go to her dorm room. "She's not here," she announces as we're walking down the corridor to her room.

"Do you want to wait?"

"No, let's go over to the Commons and see who's there," Carly says. The Erikson Quad Commons is always an adventure. I hate Erikson Quad, and the Commons is the worst part, "Great. I get to be stared at by a hundred people. Lovely."

"Oh, stop. They're starting to get used to you. Most don't even stare at you anymore." This earns Carly a scoff from me. As if.

"That's not because they've stopped trying to break into my head. It's like my head is a window and a hundred people are tapping on the glass with their finger."

"Yeah, well try having a hundred people talking to each other through an open window that you can't close, and you'll know what I'm feeling. Why do you think we always meet at your quad for dinner?"

Point taken. That would be worse, so I shut up and follow her to the lounge in the Commons.

The room is full of people and, as soon as we walk in, the tap-tap-tapping starts in my head. Which, since I'm already annoyed, causes me to shout, "Hey! Knock it off! Have some freakin' manners and leave my head alone!" I stare around the room as even more people stare at me. At least the tap-tap-tapping has died down to a tolerable level. "Thank you."

"Really?" Carly says, shaking her head, "How do you get away with that?"

I guess she can tell they stopped, so I just shrug and smile and motion her to lead on. Instead of moving further into the student lounge, Carly starts scanning the room. I'm assuming she must be doing something telepathic, and it's confirmed when I see someone in the back of the room look up at Carly wave us over.

"Hey, Spencer."

"Hey, Carly, what's up?"

I'm pretty sure they're speaking out loud for my benefit as when I look around the room just about everyone is engaged with others, but no one is saying a word. It's the quietest gathering of a hundred plus students you'll ever see in the known universe in here. I can even see a classic case of a boyfriend being chewed out by his girlfriend. The body language from one to the other is unmistakable. He's getting his butt chewed on like he's being yelled at by his mom for breaking the window when he was six, yet neither one is saying a word out loud.

"Theo," Carly tries to grab my attention, "Theo! This is Spencer." Carly pulls me back from my gawking at the freak show.

"Oh, sorry. Hi, nice to meet you. Spencer, right?" is my recovery response.

"Yeah, you too. This your first time here?" He asks.

"No. Couple times," I reply.

"Nice ability you have. That might make you the only non-telepath on campus that can survive being here."

Without smiling, I reply, "I think the jury is still out on that one."

Spencer's laughing, "I bet. Carly tells me something's up over at Oppenheimer. Want to fill me in?"

I tell him everything, from Henderson Robotics to the missing students today and have to give Spencer credit for listening the entire time without asking a question. It took Carly a month together with me before she could listen to more than a few sentences from me without asking me to clarify something.

Getting more and more apprehensive, Spencer finally asks in a tight voice, "What do you want from us?"

It is pretty clear Spencer is not eager to even know what I've just told him, but the telepaths are the only source of information we can think of right now, "It's on us to find them. No one else seems to even know they're gone. We need some help."

"Well, I can tell you you're not the only ones who know they're gone. A couple telepaths who have minors in science saw some of it. There were at least three busses loading students on Sunday, but they didn't know what it was as everyone they saw seemed to want to be there. Are you sure the science students didn't voluntarily leave?"

"I've already had this conversation with Carly. Having someone make you want to do something isn't the same as you wanting to do it. That's what happened before, and I have no reason to believe it's not happening again." I'm starting to get annoyed, "Let me cut through the crap here, I know what telepaths can do. I'm immune to it and have serious problems with it, but I'm not trying to change the status quo. I don't think I could change anything even if I wanted to. What I can do, is try to help these students, if for no other reason than there is no one else who will."

Spencer turns to Carly, "You told him?"

"Yes, everything. And, before you start, know that I'll defend telling him. And I'll win. He has an advanced mind, and he has a right to know."

Spencer does not seem concerned, but continues to try to warn Carly, "I think you could make that argument under normal circumstances, but if this gets out of hand, I doubt very much your argument will stand. You're taking a risk, you know."

Carly doesn't back down, "I know, it's my risk to take. I don't know who the telepath is behind these kidnappings, but he's powerful, and he's ambitious. Two traits you know don't belong together. Not in a telepath."

"That's true. All right, I'll put the word out to keep an eye out for these guys," he concedes and offers to help.

I say, "Honestly, I doubt it if any of the students will be in public. Try looking for people who you can't read their minds."

"Actually, it'll feel mushy and have a metallic flavor to it. Like licking aluminum." Carly offers.

Spencer looks at Carly with a frown, clearly not understanding what she's trying to describe, "Show me," he says.

Carly and Spencer stare at each other for a few seconds before Spencer says, "Icky," and shudders. "Okay, words going out now, but don't expect to hear anything for a while."

"That's okay, at least someone is looking," I volunteer. We take our leave and I'm not disappointed to feel several of them take a crack at breaking into my mind as we exit the room. Bunch of jerks.

Chapter 51

It's been nearly two weeks without a word from Spencer or any other telepath. Carly speaks with Imelda about what happened and is happy to know Spencer kept his promise and is spreading the word about who we are looking for. She also finds out the telepath network is actually nationwide, which she didn't know before, and which raises our hopes of them finding something.

With all the one-on-one class work I'm getting, my studies are advancing rapidly; I'm able to spend a huge amount of time in the student labs. They're empty, so I have multiple projects going at once and use the private lab any time I want. The same goes for the campus nuclear reactor. I'm the only one using it, so I do a major upgrade to my power source design and more than quintuple the power output as well as crank out a couple extra units. The Academy has a Budget Expenditures Board to show how much money for each field is available for student projects. I'm proud to say, I'm putting a pretty good dent in the budget all by myself.

"Hey, these are for you," I tell Carly. We're hanging out in one of the private labs as they have become our own private hangout over the past two weeks.

Carly accepts the two long sticks I hand her and starts feeling them for weight and balance. The sticks are a little shorter than the standard length as Carly is a little shorter and they'll work better for her if they're matched to her size. They are made of rattan escrima, with an added 1/16th inch outer shell made of the same composite as my shield. The 7/8" thick sticks are heavy and pack a hell of an impact when used by an expert. Carly takes the sticks and steps into an open area of the lab and starts doing a routine that tells me she has worked with fighting sticks before, a lot. She's incredibly fast, even with the heavier sticks, and knows how to use them. I've got a big stupid grin on my face as I am relieved from my concern they wouldn't be right for her.

"They're awesome," Carly calls out without breaking her routine.

"When you're running your repeller field generator, they'll power up the sticks, too, so keep that in mind." There is a contact surface in either end of the sticks that will complete the circuit through the new gloves I've also made for her. When she hits someone while the sticks are powered with the repeller field, it should amplify her impact power by a couple orders of magnitude.

I go back to working on my other two projects I have going, one is an advanced scout/attack drone that will use one of the nuke power supplies, so it has unlimited endurance. It is powerful enough that I have added a harness so I can be a passenger if I want. The other is going to be the ranged attack weapon I'm making for Carly, which I'm also going to make for myself since I figured out how powerful it will be.

Finishing her routine, Carly comes over, "What are you working on?"

"Well, that's going to be the drone I was telling you about," I tell her as I point to the drone, then, "If we get something from your community, it may not be specific, so I want to be able to put it out on a search if we need to. And these," I say pointing at the four heavy forearm gauntlets laying on the table in front of me, "These are going to be force blasters."

"You made force blasters? Isn't that tech pretty common?"

"Hey! Don't knock a good knockoff. And yes, the tech is pretty common. However! These are not. Not when they operate off the repeller field generator." I'm bragging a bit at this point as I love these things, "These will absorb a portion of the field generated in the suit's repeller field and align all the energy in a pulse through the gloves. It'll hit whatever you're pointing your lower arm and hand at when you trigger the discharge. If you point your hand, it'll discharge a narrow pulse. Or you can point with your fist, and it will discharge in a cone."

"Wow, how powerful is it?"

"Up to a full discharge of the field. You can control the amount of force you put into it through the suit's neural network."

"Okay, but how powerful is that?

"Oh, with our current power supply, a hundred percent, focused pulse, will hit about as hard as I hit that Class 4 with my hammer, maybe more." I'm really guessing as they've never been tested, but it's probably a pretty good guess, "At ten percent, I'm not sure, but I expect it'll take someone off their feet and throw them back. With the new power supplies and increase in the strength of the repeller field generator, I still need to test it, but it's going to be epic." I'm smiling from ear to ear, and happy as a new daddy holding his first born son.

"Holy," Carly's mouth falls open, "you could kill somebody with that."

Losing my smile, "Well, yeah, that's kind of the point. We can't be playing bush league with these guys, or we'll be the ones who get killed." She is looking at me like she's just been told something completely new and profound. "Carly, they're real supervillains when they kidnap a couple hundred students. Don't think for a moment they won't kill us if given the chance."

Setting her jaw, Carly is not happy to hear what I'm saying. I'm sure she already knows it, deep down, anyway. My saying it makes it real and I'm a little concerned, "Carly, can you do this? If you can't, it's okay."

"No, I'm fine," Shaking her head, "I mean, yes! Yes! I can do this. It's exactly what I signed up for: to compete with the best. Good or bad, I want to play hardball, not soft pitch." Setting her shoulders, she looks at me; she's committed. Just like me.

Carly and I haven't spoken much about whether we want to be superheroes or supervillains. Right now it's clear we're the good guys, but that's not because I'm all gung ho to stamp out evil in the world. It's more that something I consider mine has been messed with and I don't like it.

Wrapping Carly in my arms, I say, "Good, because we're a great team and we can do a lot together."

Chapter 52

If I were the leader of a rescue mission, I would start today's entry with, "Two months and no word on the fate of the missing science students. Doubts are beginning to creep in, and the crew is getting restless." We've gone back to Carly's roommate, Imelda, and Spencer and the only thing they can do is shrug and say, "Nothing yet. It takes time."

Keeping busy is the only way keep from thinking about it as I've kind of become a little obsessed. Fortunately, I have plenty to do. The new scout/attack drone is finished; it's a two hundred pound beast capable of flying for months on the smaller nuclear power supply I installed. I've also completed and tested the blasters. Yesterday I installed them in both of our suits. Carly made me dial the default setting on her blaster's power level back to ten percent to satisfy her she wasn't going to kill anyone, but she can adjust the power level with a twist dial on the wrist of the blasters any time. She doesn't want it connected to the neural net in her suit, which is odd for a telepath. She says it is because she does not trust herself to not accidentally max the power output if she gets in a tight situation. I think we're ready to take down some bad guys. If only we knew where to look.

We're sitting in the Oppenheimer Commons when Carly's phone rings, "Hello?"

Motioning me for a pen and paper, "Where were they seen?" Carly starts writing, "How long?"

Hanging up her phone, Carly looks to me, "Two men with the 'metal feel on their mind' have been seen off and on for the past three months in a little hole in the wall town called 'Van,' in West Virginia. Apparently, there's only one telepath in the town; he only heard about us looking because he took a trip up to a bigger small town called 'Danville.' I guess small town folk in West Virginia don't get around much."

Looking up the town on my smart phone, I ask, "Was there anything else?"

"Yes, they said he has no idea where they are staying, but said just before they showed up there was a construction gang in vehicles that went through town back in December and all of the people there had the metal feel to them."

"What could they be building?" I'm looking at the map; there is not much in the way of civilization for fifty miles in any direction. I see a couple tiny communities that can't really be called towns. The rest is forest land and rolling hills. "What did they do, build their own compound?"

Looking over my shoulder at the map, Carly agrees, "Kind of looks like they would have to, doesn't it."

"Well, okay then. We have a starting point. I can work with that." I can feel my mind accelerate into action putting together a plan.

Waiting for me to expand on how I'm planning on "working with that," Carly asks me, "So, what's the plan?"

"I'm going to send 'Dragon Tracker II' to West Virginia and get it going on a search for some place big enough to hold all of the students that looks newly built in the area around

Van." I look at Carly for some acknowledgement that it's a great idea, but get nothing back, "Until we hear something more, that's all we can do," I argue, mostly with myself. Carly finally gives me a head-tilt nod with a quick "eh, okay," look. I'll take that as an endorsement.

Carly asks, "When do you want to make a trip out there? We're going to need to take the drone up."

"Oh, we're not going anywhere," I tell her, "I'm going to launch the drone from here."

"Really? That's awfully far," I can hear the skepticism in her voice. Ye of little faith.

I check the map, "Uhh, it looks like it's about four hundred and...forty miles. As the crow flies, or Dragon in this case."

"Your drone can do that?"

Scoffing as if there isn't a question in the world that it can, I reply, "Sure. I can control it on my laptop through the satellite data service I bought for it. Actually, I can control it anywhere in the world."

Carly leans over and give me a kiss, "You're amazing. I love it."

"Can you ask Spencer to ask the telepath community to do some searching around that area to see if they can find them?"

"Yeah, I'll ask him," she replies.

Planning out the drone's itinerary, I let Carly know, "The drone will be on its way by tonight; it will be there in around eleven hours." Then, looking online at the National Weather Service website, I add, "I may have to ground it once it gets there. There's a storm coming that looks like it's going to hit West Virginia some time tomorrow. Once it's past, we're in business."

Ten hours later I put the final touches on the search plan, and explain to Carly, "I put Dragon Tracker II on a custom search pattern. He's following every road mapped in a fifty mile radius, but it can only search during daylight hours. If it finds any structures, It'll take a series of pictures, then continue searching, so we will need to go through the aerial photographs it takes every day."

"No worries, we'll get it done," Carly replies while I wonder how long it will be until our brains turn to mush from looking at rundown buildings in rural West Virginia. Dragon Tracker isn't able to distinguish old from new, so we are going to have to do it when we look at the photographs it sends.

Switching gears, I tell Carly, "Oh, hey! I found a combat range and training center up in Waukegan that we can use. I called them this morning; they'll allow us to use force blasters and just about anything else on their advanced weapons range." Once we find the students, we are going to have to free them, and I want to get some work in with our new equipment.

"Good job, because I need to spend some time with the blasters and field generator you put in my suit if I want to have any chance of using them in battle. I was going to ask you about getting some practice time in, but you're already ahead of me."

"For once!" I claim, knowing that's not true.

"Ha!"

We spend the next three weeks looking at thousands of photographs every night and going to the combat range every chance we can get. Along with doing all the work from our classes. It's a great time as nothing else seems to matter except us being together and working to be heroes who battle the evil villain and rescue the student hostages. Yeah, okay. Why not. It's pretty clear we've romanticized the whole thing. I just hope we don't get a rude awakening when it comes time to save the day.

Carly is sitting on one of the big chairs in the lounge of the student labs; one leg kicked over the arm, swinging up and down, while she browses the images downloaded onto my laptop from the Dragon Tracker earlier this evening. I'm sitting across from her, using a second laptop, doing the same thing, except tonight Carly is distracting me as I find myself just staring at her while she searches. She's making pops and smacking sounds with chewing gum, and I'm just mesmerized watching her mouth move. With the exception of classes, we've spent all of our time together, and I would have thought we would start annoying each other by now. But, we haven't. It's actually as good a period of time as I've ever had in my life; so much so that I'm starting to wonder if Carly could be "The One." It's actually scary even thinking about that kind of commitment. I'm not even through my first year of college, and I have a huge distance to go to get where I want to be in five years. I have it all planned out and having a committed relationship is not in any part of the plan.

Thinking about it, though, the adventures Carly and I are caught up in have actually helped me to move my plan forward and are responsible for at least two major advancements in my super suit: the blasters that operate with my field generator; the defense field that blocks telepathic (and telekinetic) powers; and, now that I'm thinking about it, the nuclear power supply I'm powering it all with. Although, I've been kicking that idea around for years, but didn't pursue it because I didn't have access to a facility where I could make it. I've been toying with the Dragon concepts in the back of my mind for a long time, so I won't count them, other than what we have been doing that took them off the drawing board and into the air.

Carly has also exposed me to an entire underground society of telepaths. Their potential power is more dangerous than any group of supervillains I've ever heard of in history. Just knowing about it completely changes my understanding of the world in a way that will have a huge impact on how I make decisions on just about everything. Without Carly, I would still be just another clueless Neanderthal walking around oblivious as to the ways of the world. I won't even go into how amazing she looks. I mean, that's another topic altogether. Really. Her looks are not going to be what captures my heart, as I can have looks any time. Maria and Tess are both beautiful. And, they're great, each in their own way. But, neither of them is able to match up with me like Carly.

"What?" She catches me staring; I do not even realize it until she says something.

"Nothing. Thinking is all," is my startled response.

"About what?"

"You," I say, coming around.

Smiling, "What about me?"

My face begins to flush red, but it's not an embarrassment I'm ashamed of, it's a feeling of warmth, "How good you are for me. How good you've been for me."

Still making popping sounds with her gum, Carly sets aside the laptop and comes over to me, and climbs in my lap, "Tell me all about it," she says and starts kissing me in a long, warm, kiss.

It's two hours later, one hour later than when we started searching pictures again, and an eternity after the first time we ever did it in a public place. Except, now I'm the one chewing Carly's gum and making popping noises; I don't care the gum has gone stale.

"Hey, check this out." Flipping her laptop around, Carly shows me an aerial photograph of a group of wooden buildings and next to one of them are three big yellow busses.

I'm getting excited already, "Are there more pictures?" I move over to sit on the arm of her chair.

Bringing up the folder on her laptop showing the thumbnail image files, Carly says, "Yeah, there are a bunch of them. Look, here's one of some people standing outside."

"I don't recognize them."

"Me either." Flipping through several more pictures of the buildings, Carly stops at another photo with people in it, "How about this one?"

"Him, I know. He's in my algorithms class, or at least he used to be. I think we found them." Looking at the location and time stamp on the photo, I see the picture was taken yesterday afternoon. "Can you plug the coordinates into the mapping program?"

"Hold on," she replies and tabs out of the images. "Look here, they're forty miles southeast of Van, West Virginia. Where's the road?"

Looking at the map, I see there isn't a road leading to their location and tell Carly to switch the map to satellite view. "Zoom in all the way," I say.

Carly zooms; there's a dirt road leading to the buildings. "No wonder. Draw back some." After drawing back, it's clear they are located down a barely-there dirt road that connects to another dirt road, that connects to a little two lane road that is an unstriped road well off the main road running through the area. "We were lucky. The Dragon Tracker wouldn't have followed this dirt road; at least I don't think it would. It looks like it was transiting over to this other state highway and overflew the property. It's no wonder it's taken so long to find them. They don't want to be found." Satisfied with knowing where they are, I tell her, "Okay, let's go back to the pictures. I want confirmation and to get the layout of the place. See if we can spot any security."

We spend the next three hours going over the images, zooming in and finding there are a number of people patrolling the perimeter of the compound. None of them look to be carrying guns, so I'm betting they're all supers. I've seen a number of kids I recognize from school moving in and out of the buildings. All of them are wearing hats of one sort or another. It's pretty clear we are going to need help.

"Let's talk to Spencer," I ask Carly, "and, can you have Imelda there as well?" A group of telepaths and telekinetecs could waltz through that place with no trouble, so that's where I think we should start.

"I'll set it up," she confirms, then asks, "We're going to need help, aren't we?"

"I think so," I reply, not hiding the concern in my voice.

Chapter 53

Spencer and Imelda both make it clear that this isn't a telepath problem, and refuse to provide any help. Spencer makes it sound like telepaths wouldn't get involved unless we could prove conclusively they were being led by a telepath. And, he tells us, they would have to take over at least a mid-sized city before they would even consider getting involved. Imelda is a little better. She says they might get involved if we can't defeat them, and considers that a generous offer as she normally would require a known super team to fail to defeat them before anyone she knows would even consider getting involved.

We're up in my dorm room where I'm pissed off and trying to pace it off, "That's pretty messed up," I tell Carly.

Carlos is in the room, being quiet for once. Since I usually kick him out when Carly is here, I think he's curious to know what we're up to and doesn't want to draw attention to himself.

"Yes, it is. But, I told you they don't get involved." Carly replies, looking at me and pointing with her eyes at Carlos, "Show some discretion if you don't want his mind wiped again," she tells me, without bothering to keep Carlos from hearing.

My mouth drops open, she said it right in front of him like he's not even in the room! Carlos looks at her, alarm starting to show on his face as he realizes she's talking about him. He stays like that a few seconds while Carly looks at him.

Then, his shocked look fades, and he goes back to listening like he was before.

"Really?" I tell her.

"Well...sorry. It was easier just to say it."

I now have being incredulous added to my anger. Giving a grunt of a laugh, I say, "Okay, whatever. So, if they're out, what are we going to do? We need help."

"I don't know. No one believes us, and I don't think any super group will throw in unless we have someone in authority vouching for us."

"What are you guys doing?" Carlos finally chips in.

Looking at him, I decide we may as well have another brain working on the problem. Starting with a clean slate like he is, maybe he'll see something we've missed. I can't help but smile as I fill him in, "We need to put together a super team strong enough to take down a supervillain crime ring." That's the best explanation I can give him, without going into details he doesn't need.

"Oh." Carlos has always been helpful like that.

Carly and I go back to not coming up with a solution until Carlos chimes in again, "Why don't you put it up on the Bulletin Board?"

Blink. Blink. The idea is completely...what? "Can we do that?" I look to Carly as I rub my eyes for a moment; wondering where the hell the blink-pause came from.

Blink. Blink. Carly seems to have the same blinking problem. "Umm, why not?" she replies.

I continue to stare at Carly; you can almost see the gears churning in her brain. "There are a lot of people on this campus with ambitions to be supers. You wouldn't believe how many I can hear thinking about it every day." Carly stops and looks at Carlos, shrugs, and continues. "Most of them won't be powerful enough. Or, they don't have any combat training. Or, they are some out-of-control egomaniac. We'd have to interview and do some kind of tryouts so we don't bring someone who will just get themselves, or us, killed."

Looking at Carlos, I wonder, briefly, if he's going to remember any of this an hour from now. "Okay, let's think about it, and if we don't have a better idea by tomorrow, we'll put it up on the Board."

Well, no one has a better idea, and it's now tomorrow. Well actually, now it's today, but we really don't need to go there. Carly stops in to my dorm on the way to class, and asks the obvious question, "So what should we say?"

I say, "How about this," and spin my laptop around for Carly to see. On it is my idea for an ad to be placed on the Bulletin Board, an online posting site for jobs offered and for students to exchange information, seek each other out, or post anything else they want other students to know.

SUPERHERO TEAM FORMING FOR SINGLE MISSION!

STUDENT SUPERHEROES NEEDED!

Two member, student led, superhero team has an immediate need to form a multi-member, superhero rescue team. Mission is the rescue of over 200 students under mind control from a supervillain gang. Villains are suspected to be CLASS 3 or higher and extremely dangerous! At least one member of the gang is known to be a powerful telepath! (Protection from mind control will be provided to all members of the team.) Chance of deadly combat is HIGH and possibly unavoidable.

If you are a Nova Academy Student, with the drive, experience, and training to become a full-fledged superhero - AND you are ready to take on a REAL mission - You MUST take advantage of this incredible opportunity to make a difference!

Recruitment Meeting: March 28th at 6:00 PM at the Oppenheimer Quad Open Field Area

ALL APPLICANTS ARE REQUIRED TO DISPLAY THEIR POWERS AND SKILLS - COME PREPARED!

(Supers with Class 3 or better primary power preferred)

(APPLICANTS ACCEPTED ONTO THE TEAM ARE REQUIRED TO COMMIT TO A MINIMUM OF TWO WEEKS TO PREPARE FOR THE MISSION)

MISSION WILL TAKE UP TO THREE DAYS AND REQUIRE TRAVEL!

(mission to be conducted on a weekend within the next four weeks -- transportation will be provided)

PROTECT YOUR IDENTITY! WEAR YOUR SUPERHERO MASK TO THE MEETING!

"I like that you're stressing it's a dangerous mission and that we want people with experience and training. But, we should hold back the details and only brief the chosen team with them later."

"Why is that?" I ask, without thinking about it.

"If I were to kidnap a couple hundred people from a campus and wipe everyone's mind to cover up the crime, I'd still want to have someone keeping an eye out make sure no one figures out what I've done. Anyone who knows what happened will see that ad," Carly points at the laptop's screen, "and immediately know it's the missing students that are the target of the rescue."

"Well, damn. Okay, I got this. We'll just drop it is to be a rescue and drop that there's a telepath, then just say it's a mission to take down a criminal gang." Typing on my laptop as I say this, I'm already making the edits.

"That should work. Once we have the team put together, we can fully brief them on the mission. Now, what about us? We can't go into a recruitment meeting saying we're a superhero team and not have names. We'll be in our suits, so our identities are safe."

I'm not liking where this is going as my plan is to not pick a super name until I graduate from Nova Academy. "Do you have a name?"

Carly gives me a big smile, "Yes, I do. 'Dreamweaver.' "

Okay, that's a cool name for a telepath, especially a totally hot one anyone would like to have dreams about. "Nice. I like it. On multiple levels."

"I thought you would. What about you?"

I frown, "I've avoided even thinking about a super name for the last nine years. You know why."

"Yeah, well, it's time to think about one. Even if it's temporary."

"No way, I'm only going to pick a name one time."

Giving me an amused expression, Carly says, "And...."

"And, give me a minute." Aw, man. Do I name myself after my suit, after my skills as a mad scientist, or after...what? My speed? "What about 'Anvil?' It kind of relates to my armor and anvils are used in crafting."

"Mmm, it's not working for me. A speed guy named 'Anvil' doesn't really make sense. Just do something temporary and don't worry about getting the perfect name right now."

I look at Carly with skepticism, "What, so I have to cover everything? Just make up some crap name?" I'm not liking this naming party one bit.

"No, but what you use shouldn't clash with another part of who you are. You could call yourself 'The Brain.' It could work; at least it doesn't clash with the suit or your speed."

"That name's taken. Besides, that's a name for a lab rat scientist. I'm more the inventor, slash engineering genius, slash mad scientist, slash armored warrior, slash, slash, slash."

"Why don't you call yourself the 'Engineer?' " she offers.

"Will I have to wear a railroad conductor hat? No. Not feeling that one."

Carly bails from this naming train, "Okay, you can figure it out and let me know."

Frowning, I know I'm going to have to waste way too much time figuring out what to call myself, "Yeah."

We get the ad posted on the Bulletin Board and, over the next several days before the meeting, Carly tells me she's felt several people thinking about applying, and even more who want to show up to see the "spectacle." Great.

Chapter 54

"How many do you think?" Carly asks.

"One hundred and two are wearing costumes, and there are another two hundred forty behind them in civvies. None of them brought popcorn." My HUD is providing the head count through its targeting and tracking system; it's showing how much potential my upgrade has. Even now, it is processing threat assessments; tagging perceived non-combatants.

Excited, Carly says, "A hundred and two is incredible. That's a lot. Do we have enough applications?

I pull out a large stack of 5"x8" cards that are printed with a short "application" list of boxes to fill out: Super Name; Power(s); Experience; Combat Skills; Support Skills, and a few other things I could think of. "Barely," I answer, "Hopefully no one screws up their app and asks for another."

We're standing next to each other, in full costume, on a portable platform I borrowed from the student labs. Gathered all around us are our "applicants," with the looki-loos behind them. Carly's wearing the suit I made for her, with the new blasters installed, and a new half-mask with upgraded HUD I made for her. She doesn't want to go with the full helmet and face shield because she says it's too closed in and distracts her when using her telepathic powers.

I'm in my full armor, with all my recent upgrades, and have my war hammer strapped to my back with the head over my right shoulder. My large round shield is affixed to my back as well, covering the handle of the war hammer. Both of us are wearing solid black, without a single spot of color on our costumes, which has garnered a few whispers in the crowd that we look more like supervillains. They're going to have to deal with it, though, because the red, white, and blue shield has been done and I refuse to follow in anyone else's footsteps.

Stepping to the front of the platform, I shout, "Listen up! I want to thank all of you for coming today. My name is Nova," then turning and raising my hand to indicate Carly, who is laughing through my earpiece at hearing my super name for the first time. She knows how long I've been pulling my hair out trying to think of a decent name that isn't already being used by another super. Nova is a good name for a super; no supers are using the name and I'm not worried about the Academy suing me.

I ignore Carly's laughing and continue, "And this is my partner, Dreamweaver. We placed the ad on the Bulletin Board because of a serious threat to our common good. A supervillain gang, who has avoided the attention of the authorities, and other super teams, needs to be stopped and we are the only people who can do it. All the details of the gang and the mission will be briefed to the people here who we select for the team." I turn and walk to the other side of the platform to give some face time to them, not that they can see my face, or have a hard time hearing my amplified voice coming from my helmet, but to use decent public speaking skills I learned in high school. These are all college kids; there are plenty of the smart ones I want to attract that will notice. "Anyone interested in applying to join the team and learning more about who we are, please approach the platform and take an application." I split the stack of applications I'm holding and hand half to Carly as two people out of the more than three hundred here start to make their way to the platform. None of the others move.

"What are your qualifications to lead a super team!" is shouted from the crowd.

I stop looking for people in the crowd to hand applications to and answer the obvious question I knew was coming, "We're a new team, less than a year old," I feel like it's time to brag a little, without looking like I'm bragging, "The two of us have had two engagements together, along with solo work and work with other supers over the past five years as junior superheroes. The two engagements were both close combats. One engagement included a Class 4 - which we won decisively; and the other versus eight supervillains, in which we took down seven of the eight, and ended in a draw. Neither of us was severely injured during the engagements, and both of the engagements were against the same supervillain gang we will be facing on the coming mission." I switch to my suit comm channel and whisper, "How was that?"

"Good, I think we have a few more coming over now." Optimist. Five out of three hundred isn't what I would call, "good."

From the audience, a deep rumbling shout comes, "You're going to have to do better than talk if you want me to join your team!"

I knew this might happen, and I switch back to external speakers, "Feel free to leave if you don't want to be here. Nobody's stopping you."

The speaker starts clearing his path of anyone too slow to get out of his way as he approaches the platform and shouts, "How about I feel free to come up there and kick your ass!"

I recognize my new adversary as he's not wearing a costume. He lives in Atlas Quad in Dorm 4, which should mean he's at least a Class 4 strong man. Once again I switch to my suit comm channel, "What can you tell me about this guy?"

Carly breaks into his head as easily as breaking open an egg, "His name's Derek Strong, he thinks he's a Class 4. Wait, yeah, he's a Class 4. He doesn't think he can be hurt. I'm not seeing much else, oh, he's a Class 2 speed."

"So, a classic strong man. You have anything on combat skills and experience? Does he think he's a hero or villain?"

"He's been in a number of brawls, but none with someone his own strength and I don't see any memories of fighting against exotic powers. I'm not getting anything on any particular loyalty to heroes, but don't see any villainy, either."

"You see any reason I should hold back on him?"

"Are you going to fight him?"

"I'm seriously considering it."

"You didn't kill that other Class 4 when you hit him in the head with your hammer. Besides, I don't think you can afford to hold back with a Class 4."

Correcting her, I say, "War hammer. It's a war hammer. And, I won't be using it." I hop off the platform and put my arm out, palm up, and switch back to external speakers, "Hold on a second, let these people move back. What name do you go by?"

He stops and looks around at the same people he has just been shoving out of his way; as if it is the first time he's seeing them. Crossing his arms, he turns back to give me the fighter's stare, "Call me 'Anvil.'" If this guy wasn't already beginning to annoy me, and I wasn't concerned he might kill me with one punch, I'd be rolling on the grass laughing. But, if he's a Class 4, we might be able to use him. I flip on my field generator and start my force blasters charging. I need to put this guy down, fast and hard, so I set up an alpha strike by setting my force blasters at sixty percent discharge. I'm a little afraid of going a hundred percent as I haven't tested the full powers of the weapons yet. They might kill him. Or, they might blow up.

People have backed up as far as they seem to care to, and Anvil unfolds his arms and starts his approach again, "You ready, tin can?"

Real original, "tin can" has been a nickname strong men have used as an insult to supers in armor for fifty years and has been used on just about every supers T.V. show ever made. "I'm ready. First fall?"

"Sure, but you may not be getting up again."

"Any reason I should hold back on you?" I ask, ignoring his jibe.

"No, any reason I should hold back on YOU?"

"I'll let you be the judge of that." It's a tactical response to add a little doubt in his mind to whether or not he can totally unload on me without killing me, which could affect how much he puts into his first couple of punches.

He picks up his pace as he closes within twenty feet of where I'm casually standing. I'm squared up to him with nothing in my body language to show I'm about to be in combat with someone in the top one percent of the top one percent of the top one percent of the population of the earth.

As Anvil gets within ten feet of me, I crouch down before launching into a full sprint to rush him. As I close on him, he tries to sidestep and begins drawing back his fist for a punch, but it's like he's moving in slow motion to me and I make my adjustment to bring me directly in front of him. I punch both fists up into his chest and trigger them to discharge the sixty percent charge built up in my force blasters. I'm using my fists to discharge so the blast will be spread across his entire torso, rather than the tight beam they would deliver by pointing my hands and contacting with my fingertips. The impact and discharge of power is incredible.

Anvil's flying forty feet up, and a good two hundred feet away, where he digs a huge gash in the ground to the sounds of oohs, ahhs, and gasps from the onlookers. Several people begin to applaud from behind me while those within my view look back and forth between Anvil and me to make sure they won't miss anything.

He's not moving for a second, so I ask Carly, "Is he alive?"

She sounds amused, "Oh, yeah. Shocked, and in some pain, but he's alive."

"Good," is all I get out before I see Anvil start to pick himself up and out of the gash he dug, mostly with his head and shoulders. The green light on my HUD is indicating my shields, and through it, my force blasters have completed recharging. "What's he thinking?"

Carly takes a second and replies, "Not sure yet. He's still working out whether he's going to kill you or...not kill you. Want me to help him make the right decision?"

"No. That's a line we can't cross with people we want to be our teammates. Because, if anyone gets killed on this mission, I don't want us to be the ones responsible for them being there. I don't need that kind of guilt."

Remaining silent until Anvil gets way closer than I want him to be without knowing his intentions, Carly says, "I don't know what he's going to do."

Great. I drop into a combat stance as I swing my war hammer and shield out of their sling and double strap on my back into a ready position, then ask Carly, "Would you mind dropping this guy if I get in over my head?"

"No problem," is her reply. She's calm as a cucumber, so I'm slightly less concerned this goon is going to squish me than I was a few seconds ago.

Anvil stops just out of my weapon reach and looks me over, "Can't say that's not the hardest I've ever been hit. What class are you?" He's smiling, and there is grass in his teeth.

Staying in my ready stance, I reply, "Join our team, and I'll tell you."

Stepping forward and putting out his hand to shake, Anvil says, "Where do I sign up?"

I stand up and contemplate the likelihood of Anvil sucker punching me, then switch my war hammer to my shield hand, turn off my repeller field generator and take a chance on shaking his hand. "Come on, I'll give you an application."

When I look over to Carly, she's handing out applications as dozens of supers in costume, and a number in civilian dress, are reaching out to receive their own applications.

It takes another thirty minutes to get all the applications handed out, and we receive most of them back. We have ninety-seven applications so far. The people in the crowd are enjoying themselves and showing off their costumes and powers and telling stories to each other, which allows Carly and me enough time to quickly go through the applications and weed the number of people we want to interview down to twenty-two.

We go through the applications as quickly as we can and focus on previous experience and that they have the minimum power levels we want to consider. The sheer variety of skills, powers, and experience of the applicants is pretty amazing. Nova Academy has a very diverse and powerful population.

We complete sorting the applications and I'm ready to address the crowd; they're all still here. "Okay, listen up! I want to thank all of you for coming out today and want to let everyone know that if you are not on this list, it is not a judgement of your abilities. We have a limited number of places open and want a certain mix of powers. If you are not selected, it is likely your powers are not a fit, or we just don't have enough knowledge about what you can do to figure out how you can fit on the team. Or it may be your powers are already adequately represented on the team. Please don't have any hard feelings." This gets a snicker from a few people in the crowd, as that is exactly what they're going to think — that we think they're not good enough. Ignoring the snickers, I continue, "If you hear your name, please stick around, everyone else, if something changes, we'll be in contact." I announce the list, which includes Anvil.

Chapter 55

    I set our first team meeting to be at Waukegan Ranged Weapons & Personal Combat Facility that is, conveniently enough, listed as a student resource on the Nova Academy website. "Okay, gather around. For this first meeting, we are going to become familiar with each other's powers and get to know you a little bit. I will be frank, this is a tryout. You were each chosen for the information you provided on your application, now it is time for us to confirm the accuracy of those statements and to see what else you may bring to the table that will benefit the team. We will be taking a total of six heroes on this mission so some of you will be in a backup position, or part of the extraction team we are thinking of using for moving the hostages, or maybe as reinforcements. We're still working out the mission details. Dreamweaver and I will also display our abilities, just to be fair, and to give you an opportunity to see who you have signed on with." Walking over to a nearby table in the large sparring room, I pick up a clip board and turn back to the group, "First, however, everyone in this room will sign a non-disclosure agreement that prohibits you from discussing the identity or powers of anyone else in this room. This is not negotiable, we all have identities to protect and, I believe, aspirations to become professional superheroes after our college careers," or villains, which I don't say, "There is one last thing you should all know that is not in the NDA. If one of you betrays us, any of us, the legal consequences contained in the NDA will be the least of your worries. I will personally see to it."

A person in the back, obviously female in a skin tight, black supersuit, with yellow lightning bolts down the side, says, "That's not a very superhero thing to say. Threatening us." She's set her hip and crossed her arms with obvious disapproval.

I remember her application. Her name is Sparks; she's a Class 3 Lightning Elemental. She has long blonde hair and is obviously very attractive, even with the mask hiding half her face.

I ignore her comment because I really don't care whether she approves of the threat or not, and continue, "First thing will be hand-to-hand combat. Anvil has volunteered...."

Interrupting me, a voice pipes up, "What if we don't do hand-to-hand?"

"It doesn't matter, for now. I want to assess everyone so we know who can handle themselves in a slugging match, and who needs to be protected from close-quarters."

"Okay. Anvil, will you help us out by being our sparring partner?" Addressing the group, "This is physical combat only. No exotic powers. Yet."

Anvil, with a big grin on his face, nods, and says, "I'd love to," then, more seriously, "But, make sure you tell me what your body can handle before we start so I don't accidentally break you."

Everyone has a go at Anvil; he's not even sweating when we're done. Mostly he's standing there letting each of them punch on him while he laughs at them and tells them how puny and weak they are. Unfortunately, he is our only

Class 4 strongman, but we have several Class 3s, and none of the rest are lower than a Class 2; it's nice I won't have to worry about having a squishy on the team. All of them also have at least some hand-to-hand combat experience, with the exception of Sparks.

I face Anvil and announce I'm a Class 2 strength, but with the suit, I believe I qualify as a Class 4 in my abilities for dealing damage. As soon as I say it, Anvil decides that's a go ahead to hit me with everything he's worth. No warning, just BAM! Which, if I were any slower, would have driven me through a wall. Instead, I'm able to shift enough I only take a glancing blow off my repeller field, and spin as I let my war hammer slip down from where I'm holding it in the middle of the shaft down to the handle, and use it to sweep Anvil off his feet as I spin around. I follow up with an underhand blow into his chest as he's standing up and he bounces off the ceiling of the training room.

He manages to land on all fours, like a cat and stands up laughing.

"Okay, Dreamweaver, you're up," is all he says, brushing himself off. We have a clown on the team. A very powerful, very dangerous, clown.

Carly steps up to Anvil and announces, "I'm a Class 2 strength and will wait until the next event to display my close combat. I'm not sure why she is holding back, she's pretty good at mixed martial arts.

"Okay then. The next event Dreamweaver is referring to is we are going through close combat one more time, this time it's for anyone who has exotic, or other, powers they're able to use in close combat. Anvil, I'll take it from here."

Anvil starts to protest, then shrugs and steps to the side.

"Okay, same order. If you don't have a power other than the physical attacks you showed us in the last event, just sound off when your time comes; you can skip this round." I step to the middle of the room and proceed to get electrocuted, burned, plasma blasted, and hit with a sonic attack as each of the recruits shows how they are able to incorporate their powers into close combat.

Approaching me with a sweet smile showing under her half shield visor, Dreamweaver picks me up and throws me across the room with her telekinetic powers before walking back to stand with the rest of the group.

As I stand up to walk back to the middle of the room, I hear someone say, "You're telekinetic!"

Dreamweaver responds, "Yes, I am. I'm also a telepath."

"Holy crap!" This comes from Anvil. "Since when do you guys go superhero?"

"There are a few of us out there. Not all of us are pacifists," is Dreamweaver's response. Which is kind of funny to hear when you know the entire telepathic community is aggressive to the point any one of them will rip the thoughts right out of your head if you so much as think of doing anything harmful to them or theirs.

There are a lot of murmurs and looking at one another going on, "If anyone is uncomfortable working with a telepath, you should pack up and leave now. Just remember that everything you've seen today falls under the NDA." If anyone leaves, they'll never violate the NDA as Carly and I have already agreed anyone that does not go on the mission will have their memory wiped of everyone else's powers and identities. They'll think they were never selected. She let me know it was not open for discussion that she is going to wipe them of both of our memories, and I figured if we are going to benefit from them being wiped, everyone should.

"Well, I don't want my mind being read all the time." This comes from Rock Slide, one of our two Earth Elementals, both of whom I was hoping to take on the mission for their strong defensive abilities. They have amazing powers for crowd control and team defense second only to shield bubbles.

Walking over to where everyone placed their bags along the wall, "I'm out, too," says Derelict, a Class 3 strongman who I wasn't all that excited about having anyway.

"Wait a minute," Sparks steps up, "Wait. I don't understand. What's the big deal with having a telepath on the team? I'd like to know what's bothering everyone."

"That's fair," I say, "Anyone want to explain your concerns?" I look to Dreamweaver; she's standing, head up, and not showing the slightest bit of being affected by the fact people are saying they don't want to be around her just because she's a telepath. She gives me a small nod that she's okay, and I'm feeling sympathy for her. Even more so as I realize she probably already knew how everyone here felt about being around telepaths.

Derelict and Rockslide stop and look to see if anyone speaks up, but no one does. Rock Slide starts to come back over to the group, but I look at him and hold out my hand, palm up. "No, you can leave now. You too, Derelict. Thank you for coming out, but I don't think we'll be able to use you on this mission."

They look at each other, shrug, and make their exit. Carly takes care of any NDA violation risks on their way out the door.

"Does anyone else have any concerns about Dreamweaver?" No one answers, "Okay, good. Let's move on. Grab your stuff; I have a multi-discipline firing range reserved for us." Leading off, I head over and grab my gear and walk out of the sparring room without looking back. Thinking about what just happened, it's a little enlightening that being afraid of telepaths isn't one of the negative thoughts they erase from people's minds. It is odd when you consider they won't hesitate to wipe out feelings of hostility. It makes me feel like they are benevolent wolves managing their herd of sheep.

To get to the firing range I've reserved, at considerable cost, you have to take an elevator underground to what feels more like a cavern than a firing range. It's huge, a hundred feet wide and two thousand feet long, covered by an eighty foot high domed ceiling. The entrance side of the range has blast barriers with copper mesh imbedded, one foot thick, safety glass for observers and a control panel for dozens of paper and solid targets that can be set at any distance down range. The team is impressed, which is good considering it is costing me $800 per hour to be here. It's become easier to count the number of inventions I have to sell to maintain my superhero habit than to count the dollars I've been spending. This expenditure costs one invention, this expenditure costs two inventions….

"Let's start with the ground rules. We'll be taking turns on the range, and there will be only one shooter at a time. Only two people can be on the range at one time. Me, as the safety officer, and the shooter. Everyone else is to be behind the blast shield and paying attention to what is happening on the range. You need to know what your teammates can do." Everyone is chattering away, excited that they're going get to use the full powers without any concerns for someone being hurt. For some of them, it may be the first time they've been able to let go. "Let's keep the chatter to a minimum. If you have a question, wait until you hear, 'Cease Fire,' and the, 'All Clear,' have been called." Looking at all of them as I speak, I am happy to see all of them are paying full attention. Even Anvil.

"If you see something that is unsafe, I want you to yell as loud as you can, 'Stop!' Shout it out as it may be hard to hear you from out on the range. If you hear someone yell 'stop,' cease whatever it is you are doing immediately. There is also a panic button behind the barrier you can hit that will sound an alarm and red lights flashing." Walking beyond the barriers onto the firing platform, I turn back to them, "You know what you are going to bring up here, and what it can do, far better than me. Keep your powers directed down range, and be safe. Okay, that's it. Who wants to go first?"

The ranged tryouts go well, with several candidates showing they're legit ranged fighters who will work out well supporting our tanks. Sparks sends a fan of lightning nearly thirty feet and a single bolt twice that far. Flamella, a fire elemental, puts up a barrier of fire and shoots a stream of flame like a flame thrower, which is as terrifying as it is deadly. Hit Point, our weapon specialist, is amazing in her agility and ability to throw anything and is accurately hitting targets at the far end of the range. Barrier, who can project multiple force fields about as powerful as my old repeller field generators, with the smaller power supply, is strictly defensive in his skills. It is a waste he has not learned to use his powers offensively.

Anvil and Granite are both pretty limited in what they can do in ranged combat. But, their talents lie in another area. Those of the rest of us who have ranged abilities are capable, but not impressive, and it's beginning to look like the primary team is becoming set. Dreamweaver and I are accurate out to fifty yards with our blasters, although she one ups me with some telekinetically directed knife throwing and sending one inch steel balls around corners. She's such a showoff.

We're only able to take a self-imposed six supers on the team, including ourselves. First, because four is the number of working neural neutralizers I took from the warehouse during our last fight. (Besides the one I took apart to see how it worked and the two I gutted to use on Dreamweaver and my shielding upgrades.) I'm afraid to bring anyone not protected from being mind controlled if they don't have one. And second, because I doubt my ability to lead more than a few people at one time.

Any applicants who make the cut, but are not included on the team, I am thinking of inviting to join as backups in case someone falls out, and to train against. I'm also still trying to decide whether or not to bring them on the rescue as a backup.

"Okay, I think that's what we need." The tryouts are enlightening. Seeing supers on the news using all of their powers is one thing. But it's not "real." More like a superhero movie where you know the supers are real, but you're still only seeing it on a video screen. Seeing this much power up close, where you can feel the heat and the electricity standing your hair on end, and the concussion of the force of a blow from a bare fist, it's just all kinds of cool. I never was able to let myself feel it when I was in the fight myself, and I've never been around so much power before. Then again, I've never been so powerful before, either. Carly has maintained a running a dialogue with me of the candidates through our comms, and she has already chosen the team. I do not disagree with any of her choices, so there is no reason to point out her lack of collaboration with me in her selections.

"Thank you all for being here and for placing yourself out there to be someone who is willing to make a difference. All of you have an incredible amount of potential, and I would take you all if I could. Unfortunately, only four of you will be chosen. The rest I would ask if you can train with us for the mission and stand in as a backup if someone on the team can't go." I'm looking at each of them in turn and can see all of them want to be chosen. Carly's already confirmed they are all in and gives me the nod to go with our chosen crew.

"Anvil. You're our heavy hitter, along with me."

"Granite. I'd like you to be a controller and provide defense."

"How's an Earth Elemental supposed to control?" asks Sparks.

"He can isolate, channel, and build barriers. It's the same stuff any Earth Elemental would do." I reply, wondering why Sparks does not already know this. Earth Elementals as controllers have been on dozens of superhero teams in recent years.

"And, Sparks. I'd like you and Hit Point to be our ranged hitters."

Looking to the remaining applicants, "For operational security, I'm going to end it here. Any of you who want to work with us to train and be a backup, let me know now. Otherwise, I wish you all the best of luck in becoming superheroes. I think all of you have the talent to make it."

Chapter 56

The team has its first meeting the next day in the Student Labs. None of them have been here before; a few don't even know the labs exist. The elementals have their own "labs" that are more similar to a military firing range and construction site than a science lab. And, Hit Point has only ever used the speed and agility facilities for the Atlas Quad students.

"These student labs are normally not empty. Most of this year you had to sign up on a waiting list a week in advance to use one of the private labs like the one we are in now. And, that's the reason we're here. The science and engineering students are missing. Our mad scientists and resident geeks have been kidnapped and, we believe, are under mind control. That's more than two hundred students." I pause to see their reaction and give Carly some time to sort through what they are thinking in case one of them is a mole. I only see surprise on their faces.

"The university's admins don't even know they're missing and we believe they've had their memories altered. We tried to get the college admins and the police for that matter, to realize what is going on, but they all seem to have had their memories altered and won't believe anything we say."

Every one of our new teammates is wide-eyed. Carly is listening in to their thoughts to see if they are going to believe what I'm telling them and, I'm happy to see her nodding to me periodically that they're not rejecting what I'm telling them as I go through the entire story. I start from the time of our first stake out and fight at the Technology Park and Henderson Robotics, to tracking down the students near Van, West Virginia. It takes a while. Thankfully, all of them keep an open mind and believe what I am saying.

Dreamweaver takes over, "We're going to make two – three man squads, for the mission. One squad will be led by Nova, the other I will be leading. Granite and Hit Point. You'll be with Nova. Anvil, Sparks, you two will be with me. That may change as we work out how we work together, or it might change in the middle of a fight if that is what's needed. It just depends on how it goes."

Hit Point, not one to wait patiently, jumps ahead, "So, what's the plan? When do we go? And where the hell is 'Van, West Virginia?' We gonna have to fight hillbillies?" She's got a silly grin on her face and is looking around to the others to see if she gets a laugh out of them. Crickets. "That'll be fun," she follows up, but without the smirk as she sees her hillbilly comment didn't go over with the others. This group may be a little too uptight. I'll have to keep an eye on them, or rather Carly will. She's the resident psychologist.

"You can always tell the speeders." Replies Anvil, with a good laugh. It's somewhat true. Hit Point is a Class 3 speed, same as me. We do tend to talk fast and expect immediate results. I'm a little different as I've had to learn patience working to build my inventions.

"Alright, be like that," Hit Point says and crosses her arms. Nodding, she quickly gets she's being made fun of.

"Hit Point, we'll discuss the planning in a few days. First, we need to get some work in together to see how we fit.

The mission is tentatively set for ten days from now, weekend after next," I tell everyone.

"Wow, we're going to wait ten days? Not much of a hurry to free these guys is there," chimes in Granite, his voice just as gravelly as his name. Everything else about him though looks entirely out of place for how I picture earth elementals. He's tall and gangly with long blond hair that hangs down over his eyes all the time. He habitually pushes it to the side.

"They've been gone for a long time already. Ten days won't make much of a difference, and I'm not going to take a green team into a mission without any preparation."

"No, I get it. It's just not like you see on the vid, is it?" Granite concedes.

Anvil pops off, "And what if they're killed before we get to them because we're screwing around for the next ten days?"

"Then they're screwed. Which will be terrible, but if we go in there without any preparation, we're likely to get them killed anyway." I'm ready to move on, "Any other questions?" No one speaks up. "Okay, good. Then let's get to the other reason we're here in the labs."

I pull out a student crate that projects are normally stored in and start pulling out neural neutralizers, "These are called 'neural neutralizers.' They're the same neural neutralizers being worn by the students that have been kidnapped. The difference is going to be, the ones being worn by the students are meant to keep their messed up minds – messed up. You'll be wearing them to keep your not messed up minds from getting messed up by any telepaths we run into."

"There's no such thing," Hit Point claims as she grabs one of the devices and studies it.

"Up until a few months ago, I'd agree with you. As it happens, they do exist; they're being used by this criminal organization to hide their mind controlling from other telepaths. And yes, the telepaths, even the ones here on campus, know about it. But, they are not interested in doing anything about it because they're pacifists." As much as I would like to tell them all about what is really going on with the telepaths, I don't. It wouldn't do them any good if I did as the next telepath they ran into would just take it out of their memory. Hell, I can't be sure Carly wouldn't take it out.

Sparks asks, "What do you mean?"

"I mean the telepaths do not get involved in anything that does not affect them directly. It's their 'hands off' policy to not attract attention to themselves, or to interfere with others."

"But what about Dreamweaver? She's involved," asks Granite.

"Dreamweaver has a different outlook. She's not a pacifist, and she's wants to make a difference."

"And they let her do that?" Sparks follows.

I give them what I can that may not be wiped from their memories by the next telepath they run into, "The telepathic community manages itself on a local level and is generally passive in nature. The telepaths here at school don't feel like it's their place to interfere with Dreamweaver being involved. Don't expect any help from them, but at the same time, we shouldn't expect them to interfere with what we're doing, either."

Finishing handing out the neural neutralizers, I get the purpose of the meeting back on track, "Okay, here are your neural neutralizers. Go ahead and put them on and we'll show you how they work."

The four new team members put on the devices. Granite has his on backwards, but I don't correct it as I'm curious if it will still work. "Press this switch one time, and the device turns on." I point to the stud on the inside of the edge of the cap on Hit Point's head. "You'll have to press the button five times in a row to deactivate the device."

Everyone turns on their device and Dreamweaver steps up, "Right now I'm trying to read each of your minds, and I'm also transmitting a very uncomfortable compulsion that you all need to go to the bathroom. Anyone feeling anything?"

Everyone indicates "no" while giving Dreamweaver a concerned look that she can even do that to them. I am satisfied to know Granite's backwards neural neutralizer still works when it is on backwards. That could make a difference in the middle of a fight.

Smiling, Dreamweaver continues, "Good. Anyone want to take off your neutralizer so you can tell the others what it would have felt like to have me make you want to go pee?" There are no takers. "Okay, well then you can just trust me the devices are working."

I take over, "You will all be wearing these during the mission. If it comes off, you need to immediately get it back on your head; you risk being mind controlled, if you don't. Trust me, it only takes a couple seconds for a telepath to shut you down, so be mindful."

"Was that a pun?" Dreamweaver asks, smiling.

"Yes. Someone's paying attention," I grin back at her.

Anvil looks like he ate a sour grape, "What about you and Nova?"

"I'm a telepath, so for me to wear one would be like cutting off my arm. Nova has his own protections." Carly says, not telling them my protections are built into my mind.

Heading for the door, I move things along, "Looks like everyone's is working. So, let's get out to the practice area and get some work in."

Breaking up into two groups the team takes Carly's Volkswagen Rabbit and Hot Point's beautifully restored 1970 Chevy Chavelle SS. The black Chavelle with its white racing stripes growls as it leaves the parking lot and I'd swear I felt Carly's VW Rabbit try to shy away from the muscle car.

I looked over to Carly, eyebrows raised.

"I think my bunny's a little intimidated," is her only response.

The practice area I found is located just South of the Illinois Beach State Park. No one goes out into the marshy area south of the park, and we are able to find a deserted stretch where we work in the heavy brush near the beach. We meet up with some of the other candidates who didn't make the team and break up into our two squads: me, or rather "Nova," leading Granite and Hit Point. And, Dreamweaver, leading Anvil and Sparks. The other candidates break themselves up into squads and set themselves up to be the Opposing Force. Even though we are careful not to hurt our glass cannons, and none of us wants to be electrocuted by Sparks, we are able to get some good work in supporting each other during the practice engagements and learn how to move together. The OpFor team gives us some tough competition. It also confirms I picked the right people to be on the team. Carly and I are able to coordinate through our suit communicators, which, since we were the only two able to communicate at a distance, is another reason we cannot be on the same squad together. I really hate the idea of her not being beside me so we can watch out for each other, but it's needed as she's the only one I completely trust to lead the other squad.

By the end of the training, everyone is exhausted and the ground we have been using is torn all to hell, mostly by Granite. I have Granite put the ground back to level, so there are no big holes or walls of earth left in the marsh.

It was a good day. Another couple training sessions like this one and we will be ready to go on the mission. We'll never be 100% ready, not with the amount of time we have, but our squads are effective and work well together. I'll take that.

Our last training session is on Wednesday, so we decide to leave on the mission on Thursday after classes. Friday is a light day for all of us, and no one has anything major going on for then, so we take it off in case the operation takes more than a day. Monday's a heavy load of classes for all of us, so no one wants to miss it if we don't have to. Although, now that I think about it, it is pretty sad to be superheroes who have to schedule missions around school.

Chapter 57

I rent a large tour van from a limo company in Chicago. It is a black Mercedes Mauck2 luxury van. It's loaded with leather bucket seats and a ton of room for our gear. I'm willing to go cheap on lots of things, but not on the chariot, or tour van, I ride into battle. I have three large gym bags with all Carly's and my stuff already loaded when we go to pick up the team at the science lab where we decided to meet. Everyone but Anvil is carrying a large bag. Hit Point's bags are even bigger than mine. Anvil's the opposite. He just has a half mask bandana in one hand, and a half full paper grocery bag tucked under his arm. I guess everything else he needs is built into his Class 4 body. The sun is just setting when we leave campus.

Granite and Sparks are sitting together, and it looks like they are hitting it off. Whereas Hit Point is decidedly ignoring Anvil's attempt to talk her up. It looks like he's used to it because he just keeps chattering away without expecting a reply to any of the sometimes personal questions he's asking her. Carly's up front with me; it feels like it did on our first trip together to Evanston, except for all the people in the back.

It takes about an hour for everyone to settle in for the trip. Anvil takes a nap, to Hit Points immense relief, and she is looking out the window watching the woods along the road pass by. I doubt she has ever taken a nap in her life.

Granite and Sparks are watching a movie on one of their phones. Carly and I are quietly discussing the latest images we received from the Dragon Tracker.

Rather than do the nine hour trip and go straight into battle, we decide to stop in Charleston, WV and stay until the following night in a local hotel. Charleston is about an hour and a half north of our destination.

The southern part of Ohio and all of West Virginia are some of the most beautiful forest areas in the United States. Unfortunately, we are passing through it at night and not able to see it in all its glory. Instead, we get to see the darkness with the fringes of the forest in our headlights as we drive down the freeway. Which, if you've travelled at night across country, is eerily beautiful and mysterious. We have the windows down and can feel the moisture and smell of the forest with its soft decay of old growth mixed with the lively smell of the trees. For me, it's a smell that can make me question why anyone would want to live in a city.

It's 3:00 AM when we enter the outskirts of Charleston and Sparks decides to ask the $64,000 question about our stay here, "How are the rooms going to be assigned?"

I'm tired. I don't want to play house mom, and I think it is better to let them figure it out, "You tell me. I'll get whatever rooms we need." A conversation breaks out between them, and it is a surprise to hear Granite and Sparks deciding to share a room, which leaves me getting separate rooms for Hit Point and Anvil.

After checking in, I let the team know Dreamweaver and I are turning in and to not expect us for breakfast, "Everyone is to meet in the lobby at noon and we'll go to lunch. Until then, get some rest and enjoy your stay in beautiful Charleston, West Virginia."

Carly and I go up to our room and immediately go to bed. Whatever planning there is to do can be done in the morning. I'm up by 8:00 AM, which is two hours earlier than I want to be, but there's work to be done, "What do we have from the Dragon Tracker?" I ask Carly.

"They're doing the same thing they've been doing every day. Up by six, and in the big building by seven. They're also getting sloppy in their patrols and have fallen into a routine. Same guards each shift, and they're walking the same route each round."

"Let me see," I ask, stooping over Carly while drying my hair.

"Hey, I already took my shower," she says in mock complaint.

"Sorry." I look over the pictures and it is immediately confusing to me, "They're laughing in all these pictures!" I keep going through the images downloaded from the Dragon Tracker, "How can they be so happy? It's like they want to be there."

Carly doesn't bother to look again at the pictures, "They are happy," she says, matter of fact. "They've likely had their minds altered; they will think whatever they are doing is the most important and fun thing they've ever done."

"It's that easy? Just change who someone is, what's important to them?"

"Yeah, it is." Carly looks back at me without shying away from what a telepath's powers, her powers, are capable of doing to a person.

"I don't see how the telepaths would be willing to allow this guy to do this without trying to stop him. If people see this going on, there will be a backlash. A big one."

"I know. But, keeping a low profile is what has allowed us to avoid attention. It's become ingrained in our culture. It's our survival instinct."

"All right. We can't worry about that right now," I reply, "What's important to me is what the students are going to do when we try to rescue them. It they're so happy, are they going to fight their rescuers?"

"There is a chance they will fight us. We have to be prepared to take them down without hurting them."

"How fast can you undo what's been done to them?" I ask.

"I can't do it during the battle. Better to just knock them out and unscramble their eggs later." Carly says it like it's not a big deal to have to knock out a couple hundred people.

We finish looking over the images from the drone, and I make some notes to discuss with the rest of the team.

Chapter 58

Heading down to the lobby, we run into Sparks and Granite. They both look refreshed and are noticeably playing new couple, which I think is great. Except that now I have to worry about them both having their judgement compromised during the mission if one of them gets into trouble. Nothing to be done about it now, but hoping for the best isn't really something I want as part of my game plan.

Down in the lobby, Hit Point and Anvil seem to have worked out their relationship, which is based on Hit Point not being interested and Anvil dealing with it. Overall they both look refreshed and not hostile to each other so much as indifferent. Hit Point is flipping a throwing knife with one hand and browsing her phone with the other, while Anvil plays with a one pound bronze ball he carries around and uses like silly putty.

"Good morning," I offer to the two who are not one and get a grunt from Anvil and a good morning in return from Hit Point. "You guys hungry?"

Both of them get up without saying anything and head to the front entrance to the hotel. *Okay*, I think, glad I have the two on separate squads. I look to Carly and can tell she's doing a little telepathic investigation to see what's going on between the two.

We decide to go to the Black Sheep Burrito and Brews because I want Mexican, and it has very good reviews online. The menu turns out to have a good bit of variety; the food is excellent. While we're here, we discuss the plan in detail in a back corner of the restaurant where we won't be overheard. I make sure everyone knows their role and what is expected of them. In case everything goes to hell, we designate our rendezvous point (making sure the location of the van is nowhere near the rendezvous to keep it from becoming a casualty if we're engaged while regrouping).

At the end, I pick up the tab and we all walk outside where I give them some last instructions, "We're rolling out at midnight, so I suggest you all go over your gear and make sure everything is ready to go. Make sure you get some rest; it's going to be a long night."

We split up at the hotel; Carly and I head up to our room. I don't bother looking back, leaving the rest of them to do what they will. Up in the room, Carly and I go over all of our gear in detail; everything is in perfect condition. Just like it was when I went over it in detail before we left. Once we are done with that, we decide to spend the next few hours exploring each other in detail, rather than sit around worrying about tonight. After, we take a long nap, and then do it all over again, this time in the bath.

We hardly notice the time pass until it is time to gather our gear and head out to the bus. My mind is clear and fresh; I'm ready to go.

Chapter 59

Everyone is quiet on the drive down, not showing any real interest other than in their own thoughts until we reach Van. Van is a little hole in the wall community that takes all of a minute to pass through as we head further south on State Highway 85. As we near the turn off that leads to the compound where the students are being held, we pass through an even smaller community than Van, called Wharton. If I take the turn off there, we will be on a dirt road for about five miles until we reach an old coal mine. The students are located another two miles passed there. Instead, we're going a different way. We can come up behind the compound by taking another dirt road that takes us about eight miles out of our way and snakes back to within two miles of the compound. We'll make our approach through the heavy woods that covers almost all of this part of West Virginia. If we're lucky, no one will see us coming. I added GPS and pathfinding programs to our suits before we left, so I'm not particularly worried about getting lost in the woods.

I pull our tour van off the dirt road and into the woods at our destination and we unload. The van is hidden that way so it can't be seen in the unlikely chance another vehicle comes down the road. Everyone starts changing into their super suits. Carly transforms into Dreamweaver and I into my new identity, Nova. My super name is definitely a one-off to never be used again after this mission. I only used it to because it is also the name of the Academy.

I have Dreamweaver take point as she has light enhancement in her helmet as well as her telepathy to identify potential threats. I take up the rear to make sure no one gets separated as none of the others has enhanced night vision. That I know of anyway. We travel a little over a mile; Hit Point is pushing branches out of her way and stepping over things, making it clear she has some kind of low light, UV, or thermal vision enhancement. Whatever it is, she can see better than most of us. Granite seems to have this relationship with the ground that he knows how it is shaped, maybe even knowing where the trees are penetrating the earth as he is having no difficulty. Sparks and Anvil are definitely struggling and catching their feet on the ground and the occasional branch in the face. Hit Point is helping Sparks, so it's not too bad for her, but Anvil is moving through the forest like a bull through a briar patch; I'm afraid he's going to knock down a tree and wake the entire forest. I have Granite give Anvil a hand making his way before he wakes up the dead. After that, we're finally making good time without making too much noise. I should have planned for this ahead of time instead of relying on the team members to take care of their own needs. Next time I will definitely investigate team members' ability to operate in the dark, even though I told them we would be working at night. For now, we'll have to make do and hope for the best.

We're a quarter mile out from the compound when I have Dreamweaver hold up. The team gathers together with Hit Point doing what she should be doing and scanning the area with whatever enhanced vision she has. Granite is just standing there, but I have a feeling he's using his power over the earth to detect anyone coming.

"Hey, Carly," I call over our helmet comms and immediately get corrected to call her Dreamweaver. "Sorry.

Can you bring up the aerial of the compound? It should be in the mission folder of your HUD."

"Got it," she replies after only a moment.

I review the plan with her, "We're coming in from the South. The main building is off to the East and directly ahead of us. That should be the sleeping quarters. The busses are on the other side of the main building." I'm identifying the buildings shown in the image, which Dreamweaver is already very familiar with, but she lets me do it anyway without saying anything. She knows I'm getting it all organized in my own head as much as trying to communicate what we are doing. "How much time do you think you'll need to work your way around to the East side?" I ask Dreamweaver, "The main building is where two of the sentries are stationed; they're fairly static, so I want to take advantage of knowing where they are and take them out first.

"Give us twenty minutes and I'll comm you when we're in position," Dreamweaver replies.

"Okay. While you're doing that, we'll make our way around the perimeter and see if we can get in position to take out the roving patrol." I cut off the comm channel and go back to my external communications, "All right, let's split up into our teams," I tell them, "Right now we're about a quarter mile south of the compound. Dreamweaver's team will make their way around to the East side and neutralize the sentries there while my team moves up and locates the roving patrol. We're about twenty minutes from getting this thing started, so shake out the kinks and get loose."

Dreamweaver pulls a short length of leather rope from her pouch. I'm not sure what she's going to do with it until I watch her hand part of it along its length to each of her teammates and use it to link them together with her so she can guide them through the forest. *Huh, good idea*, I think, being reminded Carly used to spend her summers volunteering at a school for the blind.

Once we get into the compound, the images from the Dragon shows there will be lights, so I tell myself to not panic over the team's inability to see in the dark.

We work our way to a position where a tree has fallen, and there is a low spot we can crouch in. We can see the lights of the compound to watch for any patrollers who may be walking the perimeter as they will be backlit against the lights as they pass. Dreamweaver and Team 2 are not in position yet, so we wait here until they're ready. Another ten minutes pass and Dreamweaver comms me to let me know next time she gets the heroes who can see in the dark. And, her team is making slow progress.

A shadow passes in front of the lights ahead; it's showing as a strong heat source in my HUD. Brighter than I would have expected in IR. The person patrolling stops, then casually backtracks a few steps into the shadows next to a building. I can only see her with light enhancement. For now, we stay low and wait for Dreamweaver's team to get into position.

A few minutes later I hear something coming through the forest off to our left. It's moving fast and not trying to be quiet; I'm pretty sure we're blown. "Granite, put up a wall between us and whatever's coming from over there," I order. Then, as I move out toward where the first patroller disappeared, I tell Hit Point, "Be ready," and break into a run while pulling out my shield and war hammer. There is someone over there, and I'm worried about how hot their IR signature is. Opening my channel with Dreamweaver, I let her know, "We're engaged." I'm not sure what she says back to me.

Granite raises an earthen wall about five feet high; a pit opens behind it. I assume the hole is where he got the earth for the wall. It's impressive how much earth he can move in a matter of seconds; tons of dirt is displaced. It doesn't help in this case though, except in inconveniencing whatever, or whoever is coming over it.

There's a sharp sound of something impacting the bark up high on a tree trunk above the wall. Hit Point is ready but has to adjust before throwing the handful of one pound bearings she chose to start out with. They're the least lethal things in her arsenal as she would prefer not to kill anyone. Her reluctance is soon to change.

Hit Point's arm is a blur as she starts the throw, but she doesn't release the bearing as the target is already gone. She can hear them crashing through the brush, now behind the team and working their way around, counter clockwise. She follows the sound and periodically is able to see a blur moving between the trees. Later she tells me she was able to track the guy using her infrared vision as he left a heat trail, but was only able to effectively target him when she could see him directly with her low light vision.

It, he, it is definitely a person, is moving too fast and there are too many trees for her to make an attack, so she uses this time to upgrade from the bearings she's holding in her left hand to a double edged throwing knife. As fast as this guy, or girl, is moving, they could close into hand-to-hand range far too fast for her to not have a close-in weapon not already in hand. The throwing knife is the best dual-purpose weapon she has.

I can hear the speedster behind me and have to assume it's a super speed villain from their rate of movement. I wonder if it is the same speedster I fought back in the Henderson Robotics warehouse first semester. For now, he's not my problem. Hit Point and Granite are going to have to deal with him while I deal with whatever is hiding in the shadows in front of me. I don't like the idea of allowing them to spring a trap from hiding as that looks like it's the tactic they want to use. The speedster is there to distract, and whoever this is, to hit us while we're trying to pinpoint the speedster. Not a bad tactic, but not one I'm falling for, either.

I angle to the left, away from where the speedster is running, and clockwise around the hidden patroller behind the edge of the building up ahead. The villain finally makes her appearance and steps out. I can tell instantly it's a woman because of the bright red, skin tight, costume she's wearing. She's showing some serious curves. Bolting directly for her, I flip on my repeller field, ready my shield and war hammer, and at ten feet away, I draw back the war hammer in a sidearm swing to make a sweep of the red lady's legs.

As I sweep her legs my IR in my HUD flares a bright white and I feel heat pouring over me. It's coming from her. I veer off to the right to put her on my shield side to block the heat. This is why my shield is sized like a Spartan shield. A smaller round shield like some other heroes use wouldn't be able to block nearly enough of the heat. I'm running blind with an over saturated HUD from all the heat, so I shut off the infrared in my HUD. I've got spots in my eyes and can barely see when I clothesline myself on a tree branch as I'm running away from her. Dammit. The branch is demolished, but manages to do its job and take me off my feet with enough force I do a back flip and land face down on the ground a good ten feet past the tree. I don't care how much armor, or how much shielding you have, getting clotheslined will disorient the bajeebas out of you.

Not hurt, but definitely shook up, I lift myself to a kneeling position, and before I can stand, a searing wall of flame engulfs my body. The repeller field shielding is holding out the heat to a large extent, but I can feel the heat begin to rise almost immediately and it's getting uncomfortable fast. The field is not designed with a fire attack specifically in mind, but it still gives a lot of protection.

Turning to the source of the heat that is pushing me back, I put up my shield again to protect myself and drop my war hammer on the ground. Reaching toward the direction the heat is coming from; I put out my open hand toward the red suited fire elemental and discharge a fifty percent force blast to get her off of me.

It definitely hits her, because the pressure of the raging furnace blasting into me stops. I can't tell how hard I got her, though, or if she's out of it as my HUD is having some difficulty with the super-heated air between us, something I'm going to have to fix. Later. If I live through this. While in an air conditioned laboratory.

Granite yells, "Nova!" And I duck down and grab my war hammer back up. Spinning toward Granite's yell, I put my shield between me and where I last heard the speedster. I feel a sharp blow against the upper portion of my shield, and let it spin me as I swing the war hammer and try to make a hit on the speedster's exit from my vicinity. Nothing. Clean miss.

Just like the last time. Whoever the speedster is, he's faster than me.

Trying to look everywhere at once, I am unable to see anything until the black spots in my vision go away that I can see again. My HUD display is showing me a green light for the enhanced vision feature, but IR is showing a bright red icon. There is no doubt it is burnt out as I can also sense a slight burnt electronics smell in my helmet.

I decide to go without reenergizing my low light feature in my HUD to limit the chances of any additional failures, and just use my own low light vision my parents blessed me with. I see the speedster run to the red lady who is a good forty feet away and slowly picking herself up off the ground. The speedster only stops for a moment to see that she's all right before heading off to our left, back into the woods again. Presumably to flank us.

We're standing at the edge of the woods as I watch him scamper off, and as Hit Point and Granite close behind me in support. I tell them, "This is for keeps. Put these guys down and don't hold back. If you do, we won't win this. We might not survive it, either." By the time I finish speaking, three knives thrown by Hit Point fly past me on my right toward the red lady. She ducks and dives and at the same time she flares flames in all directions in what amounts to a small explosion. Her entire body is on fire and flames are going everywhere. I've never seen Maria putting out that much heat, but I've never seen her in a fight to the death, either.

Granite runs past me on my left and mounds of earth are pushing up on either side of him as he goes. He's built a protective barrier from any attack from the sides as he rushes forward to put himself between us and the fire elemental. Hit Point begins moving to my right to flank the red lady, which leaves me to turn back to the woods and deal with the speedster as we swap opponents.

The speedster isn't trying to be quiet. I can hear his crashing through the woods as he circles and predict he is trying to get around me and take Hit Point from behind. Rather than give it away I know where he's going by calling out to Hit Point, I rush to intercept. I'm not going to reach him in time, but that doesn't matter as I switch to my force blasters again. This time I push the charge up to eighty percent and wait to unleash it with a fist to where I think it will intercept the charging speedster. It's a tighter blast than the open hand I used on the red lady, but I want the extra power when it hits. Hopefully, it will be broad enough to catch him as he passes. I want to put this guy down as I know how dangerous a speedster can be. A guy this fast could kill all of us before we even know we're dead.

Start here I can just see the smile come onto the speedster's face as he closes on Hit Point's back, she must know he's coming with all the noise he's making, but she's not turning to face him. I know she's not slow. She's as fast as I am. And she knows how deadly that can be. But, I don't see she's defenseless; I have all of my attention on the speedster. He's about to impact her and I finally see Hit Point come into my vision as I follow the speedster's motion. Just before impacting Hit Point, my force blasters discharge into the speedster in the side and drives him like he's been shot out of a cannon into a tree. There's a sickening meaty sound and breaking of branches, or bones. Making no assumptions about the speedster's ability to continue the fight, I run over to where he's lying and slam the head of my war hammer into his knee with a satisfying crunching sound. I don't care what level of speedster you are, you're not going to move very fast with a shattered knee.

Hit Point, still focused on the red lady, draws back and hurls three, one pound, steel bearings in rapid succession. The red lady dives to the side and narrowly avoids the first bearing, then runs into an earthen wall that wasn't there a moment before, just as she receives the second and third bearings: one in the ribs, shattering them, and the other in the kidney with enough force to rupture the organ.

First round goes to the Visiting Team.

Chapter 60

I turn from our defeated opponents and immediately hear a call for assistance through my comms. I wasn't paying attention to anything while I was fighting and I know I screwed up by allowing myself to get tunnel vision during the fight. Carly is screaming for me through my helmet comms for me to get my ass over there. At the same time I realize I screwed up, the double doors to the main building blast off their hinges and fly out into the open area between the buildings where we are standing.

"Granite, see if you can put a barrier around the barracks!" I shout, pointing to the barracks building to the right of the main building, "I don't want to have to worry about the students getting hurt." What I don't say is I don't want the students joining in the fight, either. "Hit Point, back up Granite!" Having given my orders to my team, I open my comm channel and reply to Carly's call for help, "Carly, hold on! We're coming!" I do this as I run to the now blown open entrance to the main building. Dreamweaver and her team should be on the other side of the building and the shortest distance between two points goes through whoever blew those doors off.

My war hammer is put away. I'm going in with force blasters to start and unleash a focused 40% blast on the first thing I see come out of the door. Whatever it was, it was big, and dark, and I doubt I'll ever know who it was as they are blasted back through the door and I hear them crashing through a wall inside the building. I'm becoming agitated as the seriousness of our rescue mission is hitting home. There is serious power here and we're not going to be able to hold back if we want to win this and rescue the students. The reality is setting in unlike anything I could have conceived of planning the mission. It's just not the same until you've done it.

My blast gets multiple responses, not least of which is the frame of the double door opening blasted out the same way as the doors. Someone inside the building is using a very powerful unfocused blast to get that result, but I won't know what kind of power it is until I go through the door. Actually, I think I would prefer to go through the window next to the door.

I see movement through the window and send another blast that blows out the window, sending glass shrapnel and wood splinters into the room. Screams come from at least two different people, then the entire side wall of the building blows out and catches me full on as I'm about to enter the building. I'm thrown back and land on my back. Fortunately, my armor and shield blocks what little gets past my suit's repeller field. Shaking it off, I roll off my back and out of the line of fire and am back on my feet before heading for the building a second time. Carly's on the other side and nothing is going to stop me getting to her.

Now I can see the people in the building, since most of the wall along this side of the building is blown all over the yard. There are six villains. Four are severely pissed off and looking at me with hate in their eyes, and two are on the ground screaming from the glass and wood splinters. I assume they're the two I heard scream when I blew out the window.

The four still standing start to make their moves. The biggest is more than twice the size of any of the others and broad as a bear. He's wearing a full length, black leather, trench coat and heavy black boots. He jumps out of the open side of the building and gives me a big toothy grin. There's no doubt in my mind he's a strong man, but I'm not seeing much in the way of speed as he jumps down. Speed guys can't really hide their speed, it's too hard to move that slow, so I'm hoping he's all muscle and no zoom. One of the others, a woman with her hair up in a bun with chopsticks and purple locks framing her face, is wearing a bright yellow, three-quarters length, open coat, with purple camo pants, and corfram shiny combat boots. A sure sign of too much manga in her diet. She must be the one who blew out the doors and wall as she's pulling all the material into a ball in front of her.

I'm pretty sure she's a telekinetic, and she's about to launch the ball of debris at me. So I blast the ball of material with a fist blast from my force blaster and blow it up in her face. None of it touches her, but a bunch of it hits the two already screaming people on the ground, and leather trench coat guy gives her an annoyed look as he's blasted from behind by the exploding building materials.

"Hey! Watch it!" He yells back at her.

When he turns back to me he's greeted by my war hammer in a full overhand swing coming down on his skull, which he promptly blocks. Turns out he's not as slow as he looks, and he may also be stronger. My war hammer slams off his arm that is now protecting his head. Using the momentum of the deflected blow, I spin and swing my war hammer around to build up momentum and sweep his legs. This he doesn't block and he flips head over tail with a deep booming "Gah!" I have a bad feeling about this guy, so I reverse my swing again and bring down another overhand swing onto his skull that gives a satisfying "Crack!" of hammer hitting head.

It smashes him into the ground and he's sprawled out. For about a second. I quickly back away from the strong man as he immediately sits back up and glares at me.

Holy crapola! This guy's a Class 5 strong man. He has to be. We are so screwed.

He looks at me standing over him, and, if I wasn't wearing my helmet, he would know I already know how screwed we are. So he wouldn't have had to say, "You're gonna pay for that." Which is exactly what he says.

Aww, damn. "Granite! I need you!" I yell as loud as I can, then add for effect, "Now!" as I keep backing up as fast as I can. The telekinetic launches a newly reformed ball of debris at me and I just manage to get my shield up and it explodes in a cloud of wood, glass, and insulation.

Granite has two walls up on the barracks and is moving around to do the other side when he hears my call. He and Hit Point both come tearing across the open area and Hit Point is about to start throwing things at the telekinetic, "Stop!" I shout, "Anything you throw at her will only come back at us. Leave her for me," I tell Hit Point. "Granite," I point at the Class 5 and am backing away, "I need you to bury that guy as deep as you can get him!"

Granite hesitates and looks at me, questioning the odd order I've given him.

I lose it and scream at him, "He's a Class 5!" which comes out distorted and barely understandable through my helmet speakers.

Granite's eyes bulge and I'm glad I don't have to explain it any further, so I turn back to assess the situation and account for all of the villains. I don't want any more surprises.

Granite starts heaving earth on top of the Class 5 and covers him up. It is immediately thrown off by the strong man, only to have more piled on by Granite. "Keep him occupied," I tell Granite.

Wondering how long it will take Granite to bury that guy, or get buried by him, I make a dash for the telekinetic. As I run I feel myself getting pushed back, so I activate the neural neutralizer modulator into my repeller field, and the feeling goes away. The telekinetic's eyes widen as she realizes she's not affecting me, and she starts to look around rapidly.

I see a broken beam lift off the ground and start floating towards me. I'm pretty sure it is meant to be used on me by the telekinetic, but I don't give her the chance as I give a quick twenty percent blast at her as I close in. At the same time my repeller field flares with electricity from one of the others still in the building who is still standing. The last two had just been standing there, which was fine by me up until now.

My repeller field holds up, but I can feel my teeth start to vibrate in my head from the electricity interacting with my repeller field. I think all the bones in my body are starting to vibrate. "Woah!" slips out of me as the feeling is pretty intense.

The amount of lightning flowing between me and the lightning elemental ramps up into a solid mass of brilliant arcs and flashes. My visor goes dark to protect my vision, something I had not set it to do earlier against the fire elemental.

Warning lights in my HUD tell me my repeller field is quickly being overwhelmed and I swing my shield up to put it between us. My shield includes a strong insulator, and it buys me the time I need to dive at the subfloor of the building and break through to the underside of the building, putting the floor between me and the elemental.

Sitting up under the building is difficult. I'm sitting on bare earth and my head bangs against the floor above me where I'm sitting in the crawl space beneath the building. I'm not thinking about it, or anything else, though as I become fixated on stopping the now painful vibration in my teeth that doesn't seem to want to go away. Giving up on feeling my teeth ever again, I realize I can't stay there and have to get back into the fight. So, I start looking around for an exit. It's pitch black in there and my HUD, which has automatically added heavy filters during the lightning attack, is adjusting back to low light. It takes a few seconds I don't have to get my vision back, so instead of waiting, I low crawl across the ground as fast as I can in the direction of the opposite side of the building until I ram into the other side and tear through.

Chapter 61

Before me are the backs of five supers that are majorly engaged fighting Dreamweaver, Anvil, and Sparks.

I can tell my team is losing. Anvil is in front being pummeled on by two heavies, while an ice elemental closer to me is trying to freeze him into a block of ice. Dreamweaver is using her telekinetic power to block the wall of bullets coming from two assault rifles being fired at her team by the two remaining hostiles. And, Sparks is down on one knee, bowed down holding her chest. They need me and I spring to action.

I raise both hands without getting off the ground and discharge a pair of forty percent blasts from my fists into the two guys with the assault rifles. Both of them are thrown through the air, one into a nearby tree to the satisfying crunch of breaking bones, and the other is thrown into the darkness to I don't know where. I hear a squelched scream come from where he went, however. This takes the pressure off Dreamweaver who reaches into her pouch and draws out two throwing daggers and throws them at the ice elemental. She adds a significant boost with her telekinetic power to the knives and the two blades sink into their target's chest up to the hilts and he goes down.

As Anvil shakes off the cold, the two strong men look back at the likely dead ice elemental. They are already aware of the two with the assault rifles being taken out as they passed by them as they flew through the air from my blasts. Both look from the ice elemental up to me as I come at them. The one I am facing turns towards me, while the other goes back to fighting with Anvil. I know they are tough, but they can't be any tougher than Anvil, or it would have been over for him. So, I dial up my force blaster to eighty percent and do something I have not done before. I use my pointed hand at point blank, discharging a narrow beam into the chest of the one I'm facing. The force rips through his chest and blows out his back. The man is dead instantly. Anvil and the other strong man trade blows and both turn in mid swing as the blood, bones, and pulped meat of my victim is blown all over them. Anvil doesn't show any surprise. I suppose he is already playing for keeps with his teammate, Sparks, hurt. He doesn't hesitate and follows through with the swing he was beginning when my opponent was killed. Anvil's opponent drops to one knee in seeing his companion killed instantly. I'm sure he didn't think that kind of thing was possible considering the guy likely could have taken a shotgun blast to the chest and come away with no more than a rash. Anvil drops in behind the guy and puts him in a choke hold while I rush over to Sparks.

Sparks has fallen on her side. Her eyes are open and there are tears running down her cheeks. Her eyes are glassy and her mouth is hanging open as a deep breath leaves it. There are multiple bloody holes in her chest from the assault rifle bullets. There is nothing I can do, but I am still down on one knee and rolling her onto her back to check her wounds. "No, no, no, no," was all I can say as I turn her over.

Dreamweaver touches my back, "She's gone, Theo. We can't stop now. Come on." Her first three words have compassion and hurt in them. The last six are hard as steel.

I look up to Carly and can't see her through the face shield on her armor, and I can't feel her mind touching mine. I am lost. Alone in the moment. I just killed a man, and he isn't even a thought in my mind. Only my teammate. The one for which I have responsibility. Only she matters. "No," is all I can say as I look up at Carly.

Dreamweaver is mentally much stronger than I am and smacks me in the back of my helmet with her gauntlet and yells, "MOVE! NOW! "

I shake my head, not because her smack hurts, she could have smacked me with my hammer and it wouldn't have hurt. I shake my head to clear the emptiness, if that makes sense. I need to focus on my course. Focus on my path through this. I can't think about Sparks right now. Turning off my neural neutralizer circuitry, I immediately feel the strong telepathic emotions coming from Carly. It is something I have not felt before from her.

I jump back to my feet and run to the main building's back entrance. My people are still in danger and could end up like Sparks. The door to this side of the building is still intact, so I blast it with my force blasters and pile through the door on my way back to the other side. Dreamweaver follows while Anvil puts the finishing touch on taking out the second strong man. I don't know if he will kill him or just choke him out. I don't care.

Moving through the building and blasting open walls where there is no opening and where closed doors stand in my way, I move back to the other side where I left Hit Point and Granite. I don't see anyone else in the building until I come through the last door that is already open and leads into the rooms where the outer walls have been blown out. I can see Granite is still piling earth on top of the Class 5 strong man and has also built a wall up between the building and where he is standing. Lying on the ground in front of the building is the lightning elemental with a large throwing knife sticking out of his chest.

The strong man is screaming in frustration and cussing Granite and telling him what he is going to do to him once he gets his hands on him. We'll have to make sure, for Granite's sake, that doesn't happen.

Hit Point is in her own duel. Her with a pair of khukuri knives like the Nepalese Gurkhas use, and her opponent, the manga girl gone ninja, of all things, with two short swords that are twice as long and look like they came out of a ComicCon convention. The blades are jagged, with half guards, and stylized circle cutouts that are whistling as they pass through the air in blinding fast, coordinated swings. Hit Point is doing all she can to fend off the attacks and is being pushed back continuously. Her opponent may be a little faster, but they otherwise look evenly matched. I am more concerned with helping Granite, so I point at Hit Point and tell Dreamweaver to help her. Dreamweaver, reaches out a hand and the manga girl gone ninja's movements slow to a crawl as Dreamweaver switches to using her telekinesis to try to hold the ninja in place. The ninja is too powerful to stop completely with telekinetic powers and is fighting them with her own telekinetic powers, but at least now she is moving at closer to Class 2 speed. Hit Point sheathes one of her khukuri's and grabs a blob of something out of a pouch behind her lower back and throws it in the face of the ninja. The blob attaches itself to the ninja's face and encases her head.

When the blob hits her face, the ninja forgets everything else, drops her blades, and struggles to rip the blob off her face. Hit Point then reaches back into a side pouch on her combat backpack and pulls out another wadded up mass and throws it at the ninja. The wad expands into a steel net with a small box attached, wraps up the ninja, and proceeds to electrocute her. Hit Point moves in and secures her and somehow touches the blob on the ninja's face to make it release. The ninja is still jerking and twitching from being electrocuted, making her one less to deal with.

I see this only paying half attention as I am trying to see how I can help finish the fight between Granite and the Class 5. I don't see anything I can do, except get in the way, so instead I suggest a change of tactic, "Granite, open a hole underneath the son-of-a-bitch and drop him in it."

Granite gives me a quick look and I can see his concern of being killed get replaced by a smile he might live through this.

"Keep it opening as deep as you can go and I'll make sure he goes down it," I tell him.

With that, Granite opens a large hole underneath the Class 5 and the strongman goes from trying to throw off earth from on top of his head, to trying to stand on air. He falls into the hole, screaming he's going to kill us all the whole way down. Thrusting his hands and feet into the walls of the hole, the Class 5 stops himself from falling to the very bottom of the hole opened up beneath him.

I can't let him climb out and he has to go all the way down, so I move to the edge of the hole and begin blasting the walls wherever he tries to grab on, and the great ape falls into a hole so deep I can no longer see him. I turn on my IR imager and am able to see his body heat at the bottom of the hole, tearing into the walls and trying to climb his way out.

I yell down to him, "Stop trying to climb out or we'll fill in the hole and see how long you can hold your breath."

The Class 5 stops what he is doing and looks up at me with what has to be the ugliest damn face I have ever seen, "I'm going to kill all of you," he growls. His voice is chilling with its controlled rage and even conviction of this foregone conclusion. I'm guessing no one has ever heard similar words from him and lived.

I pick up a big dirt clod and drop it down on him, "No, you'll stop what you're doing and not make any more threats or I'll end you right now." This guy has never lost a fight, or even been challenged in a fight, in his life. I doubt he will get a skinned knee if he falls out of an airplane. How he manages the next couple minutes is going to determine if he lives long enough to learn some humility.

"Try it, punk! I'll squash you like a bug!"

He makes his choice, "Granite, keep opening that hole beneath him. Make it as deep as you can."

Granite grimaces, knowing what I am asking him to do, and hesitates.

Looking over to him, I repeat the order, "Granite, open the hole. He needs to go as deep as we can get him or he'll just dig his way out and kill us all."

Nodding in understanding, and without losing the new grimace on his face, Granite opens the hole even deeper. I have no idea how deep it becomes, "Now pile the dirt on top of him," I say, "But, don't pack it in." I'm surprised I am still hedging towards letting this guy live until I realize I was only saying not to pack it in for Granite's sake. Let him believe I'm not trying to kill the guy. He'll sleep better.

Granite fills the hole with dirt rather than closing the hole. That way it isn't solid bedrock collapsing on him. From under the mound of dirt we hear yells for a moment until they are muffled by the dirt. The yells have a little desperation in them that wasn't there a minute ago.

Granite is looking at me like I just killed his cat, so I ask him, "Can you move the dirt off the hole? We'll give him one more chance."

I can see the relief in Granite's eyes. He's tired, but holds up long enough to reopen the hole and I look down into the deep, dark hole. I can't see the Class 5 at the bottom, but I can hear him screaming and tearing at the walls. He's back to threatening us and telling us what he is going to do in tearing us limb from limb as he is scrabbling to climb his way out of the hole. Granite is dripping sweat from his face as he keeps the earth at the bottom of the hole churning to prevent the Class 5 from getting oriented so he can start climbing the walls.

I suspect jumping out of the hole is not an option for the strong man as he isn't moving very fast. He just doesn't have enough fast twitch snap in his legs to make it out by leaping. He is more like a press in a machine shop, able to press hundreds of thousands of pounds, but at a slow speed. This strong man is the human version of the press and isn't that much faster than a baseline human.

I turn on my IR in my suit's HUD again and can see him in the bottom of the hole, around a hundred thirty feet down now, "Hey!" I yell down. He stops and glares up at me, starting to say, "I'm gonna…," before stopping himself.

That's better, I thought. "If you stay down there until we are done without trying to escape, I won't fill in this hole and you can climb out when we leave. Deal?"

"I'm going to kill you! You're a dead man!" He yells back.

I shake my head and turn to Granite, "Fill it up," and walk away. Listening as I walk I can tell Granite is staring at my back just by the fact no earth is moving. I have to let him work it out on his own, though. He may very well be killing a man who looks helpless. But, he's not. Not by a long shot. That guy gets any opportunity at all he will kill all of us without even trying. We are just lucky we have Granite here to keep piling earth on him so he can't function.

When I reach the wall surrounding the barracks, I finally hear earth moving back into the hole. Granite has made up his mind. Sometimes being a superhero calls for you to be just as ruthless as a supervillain.

Chapter 62

I walk into the barracks and instantly see a couple hundred pairs of eyes staring back at me. No one speaks. All of them have a smock cover on their heads. Looking to Dreamweaver I say, "I'll send Anvil and Hit Point to help you. It's time to un-hijack these kids' minds."

Dreamweaver is checking them over visually, but can't read any of their minds right now with their hats still on, "They seem to be cooperative. Let's get them on the busses and I'll start on them there. I want to get out of here."

Dreamweaver's warning we need to get out of here is not lost on me. "You're right. I'll send Anvil and Hit Point to help load."

I go outside to send them in and see Granite, still with concern on his face. He's looking at the ground where the hole used to be. It is now a pile of loose dirt that I can see trembling from the human earthquake that is happening below. When I stop next to Granite, I can feel the ground trembling as the Class 5 is digging his way out.

"He getting out?" I ask Granite.

"Not as long as I'm here, he won't. But, eventually, yes. He's hollowed out a space down there and is digging his way out. I have to keep shifting the earth to keep him down there." Granite never takes his eyes off the ground, sometimes frowning in concentration.

"That guy's scary," I say.

"No crap." He gets a big grin on his face as the stress of the long fight with one of the strongest men on earth begins to fade.

Turning, I tell Anvil and Hit Point, "Can you go help Dreamweaver get the kids loaded onto the busses. I want to be out of here as soon as they're loaded."

They both give me a nod and start heading into the barracks, so I turn and start checking all the villains to make sure they stay out of the game. A couple are still conscious and looking at me and the two who were hit by the glass and door frame shrapnel have reduced their screaming to whimpers.

Everything seems to be under control for the moment. There is one more building on the property that looks like it might be the factory for whatever the kids were making. Going in, I find a full production line for the neural neutralizers, along with two other production lines for devices I have no idea what they do. Continuing through the facility, I find a storage area with boxes of the devices. After breaking the lock to the storage room, I pull a large canvas bag out of my belt I brought just for this purpose and help myself to as many "samples" of the devices as I can stuff in the bag. I also break into the manager's office and rifle through the files and find supplier information and shipping manifests. The devices are all going to a location in Maryland, by D.C. We're going to have to convince someone of what is going on. Along with the papers I rip out the hard drives of a half dozen computers in the lab and move out. I get a smile as I wonder what the new devices will do that disappears when I think of Sparks.

It takes twenty minutes to get all the kids loaded onto two of the two busses. None of the kids knows what is going on and we are fortunate they silently go along in the direction we point them. We start pulling off all their caps until Dreamweaver stops us. She tells us their minds are broadcasting incoherent confusion and visceral fear, and it will overwhelm her if we pull all of the caps at one time.

Granite is still standing where he was and has not moved the entire time as he monitors the Class 5 who is still trying to dig his way out. I can feel the vibrations of the earth beneath my feet, as they have grown in intensity. I leave him to be the last to get on the bus and he tells me we likely have about ten minutes before the Class 5 will be able to dig his way out.

It isn't until Anvil asks me about what to do with Sparks that I remember her and Granite were an item. He doesn't know yet. Damn. Damn. Damn. It will just have to wait a few minutes longer.

I go behind the building and get Sparks' body and place her in the back of one of the busses through the emergency exit. She's wrapped in blankets taken from the barracks. I don't know how I'm going to tell her parents, or even if I will be able to go see them without exposing my identity. They have to be told. The thought of it drags me down even more than the thought of having to tell Granite.

Once everyone is loaded up I head over to Granite. He is still watching the ground and I can feel the tremors of the Class 5 trying to dig his way out. "How's he doing?" I ask him.

"The guy is a tough son of a bitch. He hasn't slowed down," Granite replies. He then looks around and then at me, "Where's Sparks?" He has been paying attention to what is going on more than I realized.

I can hear the concern in his voice and it almost chokes me up, "I'm sorry, Granite," I tell him, without looking at him, "She didn't make it."

The muscles in Granite's jaw clench and I can hear his teeth grinding. The ground we are standing on begins to pack down by at least a couple feet. It concerns me for about a millisecond that the Class 5 may not make it out of that hole, until I decide I don't care if he does or not.

"How?" He asks, through his clenched teeth; tears are welling up in his eyes.

"She was shot in the chest before they knew they were spotted," I tell him, relaying what Carly told me.

Granite just nods his head and looks down. The ground stops compressing and I can once again feel the Class 5 trying to dig his way out.

We're out of time and need to get out of here, so I put my armored arm around Granite and lead him over to the busses. Once he is loaded the busses start to pull out of the compound.

I stay behind and watch them leave, then take a quick look around and see three more vehicles on the side of one of the buildings, not far away. It won't do to give them a way of pursuing us, so on the way out I flip over two SUVs and a sedan and take my war hammer to the transmission of each of them before heading back into the woods.

Chapter 63

While running back to our vehicle through the woods, I start thinking about Sparks. She was very good with her powers and I am more than a little shocked she is dead. I had expected her to dominate at range and no one would get close to her, but that was stupid of me to believe. All it took was a baseline with an assault rifle to take her out. It shouldn't have happened. I shouldn't have allowed it to happen. Supers you see on TV, real supers in the news, not the television show kind, rarely wear armor. I always thought it was stupid not to take every protection you can, but I guess they see it differently. Sparks wasn't wearing any protection. Where she was shot would have been right into the breast plate of a bullet proof vest. Although, I don't know that it would have stopped an assault rifle round.

I am second guessing my decisions and blame myself for her death for the entire run back to the van. It is not until I am back in the van and bouncing my way down the rut filled dirt road back to the main road that I think about how Dreamweaver must be feeling. She must be blaming herself, I know she is. In her eyes, she is just as much a part of leading this mission as I am, and Sparks was in her squad. She's going to put a lot of guilt on herself that one of our people, one of *her* people, was killed and she didn't stop it. *I can't be doing this right now*, I think to myself, *there is nothing I can do about anything right now and I need to stay focused.*

Going as fast as I can on the dirt road without running the van off the road, I make the drive back to the main road with the headlights off to keep from attracting attention. Not that anyone is out here. Using my low light vision in the HUD in my helmet, I can see clearly the road and forest around me. It's pretty tight in the driver's seat with armor on, but doable with the seat all the way back. The van is huge and a top of the line touring vehicle and I had this exact case in mind when I rented it.

When I get to the main road, I take the turn towards the truck stop we are going to meet up at that's about a hundred miles north of here. I knew when I laid out our routes I would be separated from the team and the kids during this part of the mission and playing catch up. There was no way around it unless I abandon the van. This is the most dangerous part of the mission as far as I'm concerned, and I would not have tried it if we had not wiped out the opposition at the compound.

Feeling even greater need to catch up to the others, I push the throttle all the way down until the needle is pushing over a 100 mph. Driving at normal speeds I would be a good twenty minutes behind the busses, but going a hundred miles per hour, it's more like twelve minutes. I catch up to them six minutes later. Sooner than I anticipated.

My HUD shows me large vehicles ahead. They must be my busses on the side of the road nearly a mile ahead. One of them is on its side, and there is a third vehicle pulled off the road a little further ahead that is perpendicular to the road, blocking it. There are a number of people — supers, they have to be, moving around, but I can't see what they're doing other than they're doing it fast.

I can see there are a handful of warm bodies lying on the ground as well. Damn. Damn. Damn.

The headlights on the van are still off and I barrel down the road until I'm about an eighth of a mile away before I stomp on the brakes. When the van gets to twenty miles per hour I jamb down the emergency break and throw it into park; jumping out of the van as I crank the wheel over and throw open the door. Sprinting over to join the fight, I ready my war hammer and shield and activate my repeller field.

Opening up a communications channel, all I get is Carly's heavy breathing. "I'm here," I tell her.

I bring up the monitoring system for Carly's suit and I can see in my HUD she has her fighting sticks activated. And, her neural neutralizer built in her repeller field is activated. Now that concerns me. The only reason she would activate the neural neutralizer is if she was in a telepathic battle, and losing. Which doesn't seem right because she's engaged in close combat right now, and I'm not sure if she can do both at the same time or not.

Wait, wait, wait. That's exactly when she would be in close combat; when she can't use her telepathic or telekinetic powers. Who is she fighting?

She had to have activated her neural neutralizer to stop an overpowering telepathic attack on herself. Ah, damn.

I finally quit using my obviously slow to catch on mind and start using my eyes. Carly's holding her own just up ahead. And, I can see she's overmatched and completely defensive. The other guy is faster than her and is blocking the powered attacks of her fighting sticks with his forearms while snapping punches back at her. Her reach is the only thing keeping it even. My HUD shows me her repeller field and sticks are fully powered. The power flow is fluctuating between eighty and ninety-five percent. Normal parameters for a fight with her strength. If she were stronger, she would be able to transfer more power from the repeller field into her hits. I have the same problem. The harder you can hit, the more power is transferred from the field into your hit.

The guy does not look armored in any way, so he's definitely a tough bastard and I now know who my first target is going to be.

Dreamweaver has her neural neutralizer activated, so I activate mine as well. I have no intention of leaving myself open to someone strong enough to make her activate hers. Taking a last look around, I see Granite has a barrier put up between the bus and a couple other supers and seems to be keeping his head down behind one of the barriers while spikes of stone randomly shove up through the earth in front of the barriers to keep them back. He can keep. Anvil is in a full double embrace with another super, and neither one looks to be getting crushed by the other — telling me they are on a par in strength. They've gone beast mode and are having a contest of strength, loser gets mushed in the arms of the winner. There's not a lot I can do except bust them apart, but since Anvil does not look like he's lost the contest just yet, I choose to let them go at it. For now. Hit Point is on top of the roof of one of the busses and is backing up Granite by throwing anything, and everything, at the supers they're dealing with.

My team is all accounted for, and I am wondering who the people are lying on the ground. I'm afraid they are students.

I finish my scan of the battle just in time as I reach Dreamweaver and her antagonist. I've already equipped my shield and war hammer and my first thought is to hit this guy with my war hammer, then I think about all the momentum I've built up and need to shed, so instead I go in shield first like you would busting through a wall, only I'm busting through Dreamweaver's opponent. I have to give the guy credit. He does not even try to get out of the way. He just drops his shoulder and takes the hit from me.

I'm close to full speed when I pile into the guy shield first and I dip at the last moment so I can rise up and thrust out with my shield to counter his set to absorb my impact. It's the same thing defensive linemen do to take the leverage advantage away from offensive linemen when they come off the ball. The lower center of gravity that can come at an up angle doesn't allow the other guy the ability to direct the force coming at them downward into their legs. It saves me a world of hurt.

When I impact the guy, I know I'm dealing with a Class 4 strongman, which is impressive as hell that Carly was able to go toe-to-toe with him at all. It's like hitting a truck. What evens up the exchange are my armor and shield, and especially my repeller field. Dreamweaver's opponent, now also my opponent, goes flying through the air a good sixty feet before landing in a pile and tumbling through the tall grass, head over heels, between the road and the woods. I'm feeling the impact through my suit. It rattles me, but the suit does its job and I don't take any real damage.

"He's the one!" Shouts Dreamweaver, "That's the telepath we fought in the warehouse!" She is pointing at him with one of her fighting sticks and I can see the blue glow coming off it as it dissipates heat from continuous use. I'll have to look into that when we get home. Heat buildup could be a problem. Wait. What did she say?

Chapter 64

Oh crap. No wonder she had her neural neutralizer active. "You okay?" I ask her through our comm system.

"Yeah," she responds. I can hear her breathing hard.

"What about the others?"

We both look over to their fights and it's still a standoff. "I think they're still in it. I was on the bus that flipped. The kids got banged up a lot, but I didn't see any serious injuries before the fight started." Her hands are on her hips and she's bowed over.

I don't ask about the people lying on the ground. They'll keep. They have to. "Good. You mind if I dance with this guy for a bit?"

Dreamweaver lets out a sharp laugh, "Hah! He's all yours, baby!" She starts to give me a kiss and we bang heads through our helmets. She lets out a guffaw, and bends over with her hands on her hips again; she's still breathing heavy as she turns and starts walking bent over, then straightens up and starts running over to help Granite and Hit Point.

She's tough as nails, I think to myself. Yeah, that's my girlfriend.

I look over to where the guy who is responsible for all of this is picking himself up out of the grass where I knocked him. I knew he wouldn't be out of it. He's standing there and looking at me, which I'm taking as, he's trying to use his telepathy, or telekinesis on me and not getting anywhere. So, instead of waiting for him to figure it out, and start heading over to me, I go ahead and start heading over him.

"You know, I still don't know your name." I say to him, amplifying my voice through my helmet speaker.

He takes a deep breath and shakes his head, then starts his own walk over to me. We're both taking our time for the moment, sizing each other up. "Ah, from the warehouse," he says, wagging his finger at me, "I thought I recognized the suit of armor your friend is wearing. She did not have the ability to block her mind last time, however. Nor did you. The neutralizer is a fantastic invention, but I had not thought to incorporate it into a field to defend against telekinetic powers. Ingenious. Is that your doing?" He pauses for a second before answering my question, "I did not give it. My name. Tell you what, you tell me your name, and I will tell you mine."

"That's fair. My name's 'Thor.' My teammate over there, whom you've already met, is 'CinderKilla.' " Hah! I'm not giving this guy any name that could lead back to me. Screw that. CinderKilla is a cool name, too. I hope Carly likes it.

"Not very original names, but thank you," he replies, then waving toward the others, he continues, "She has some talent. As, it seems, do you."

Jerk. Not very original my ass, "Appreciate it. You're not a pushover, either. Class 4 strength and toughness. Class 4 telepathy? Is that right? I'd guess Class 3 telekinesis?" I don't mention his speed, maybe he'll think he can surprise me with it and do something stupid. This could be hard for him to do, since he's nigh on invulnerable. What a freak of nature!

We're about sixty feet apart and start to circle. I go to my right, away from the other battles that are going on, so as to not put a potential threat behind me. I know it gives him an avenue to attack my friends, but I think I have his attention enough he won't go that route. If he does go for them, though, I will have to put one of my steel bearings into the back of his head.

"You are very observant. Reasonably fast. The armor is superior, if not underpowered. Excepting the shielding, of course. The combo of armor, hammer, and shield serve to make up for your inadequacies. Did you make them yourself?"

"No. They were a gift from Cyrella."

"Pity. I could use someone with some real technological talents," he replies, before realizing who I was speaking of, "Ah, Cyrella, yes. I read those comics as a child as well. So, a middle aged super who has found a way to extend his career. It will be a shame to see it end for you this way. Yes?"

This asshole is smart. Not smart enough, though, as he is drawing the wrong conclusions.

Cyrella was a comic book my dad collected when he was a boy. They've been out of print for decades, but I read all my dad's comics from when he was growing up. "Oh, I think I've got a few more years left before hanging up the cape," I say. Better to let him think of me as a middle aged super. Using the term, "hanging up the cape" is another way

I'm dating myself to be my dad's age. Capes went out twenty years ago and no one in my generation says that.

Offering me an out, he says, "Why don't you pull your team out while you still can. Before you get anyone else on your team killed like the girl back at the compound."

That's bull. He won't let us go. He's an arrogant SOB. And, he already knows about what happened at the compound. He is pissing me off talking about Sparks, though. That stings as I am feeling a lot of guilt about her right now.

This guy doesn't know me, though. I'm not the type to get pissed off and lose control. I'm more the type to take my rage and weave it into an ice cold noose that I am going put around his neck.

Leaving isn't an option, anyway. He won't let us take the kids, even if he did let us leave. "I don't think so. See, I'm going to have to answer to her in the next life and I won't be able to face her in the next life if I don't have your head on a pike in this one." This is another dated reference, this time to an old super metaphysical order, the Valtyr, roughly based on some vague Norse Mythos. They believed supers would see their teammates in the afterlife and have to answer to them if you failed them in this life. I really don't want this guy figuring out who I am outside of my armor. Truly, I don't. So, he can expect more bullcrap the more we talk.

"So, is it to be to the death?" He asks with raised eyebrows. The slight surprise he is showing is phony, and not accompanied by any concern on his part. He does not expect to lose this fight. Hell, I'm not sure he expects to break a sweat. Or if he has ever broken a sweat during a fight.

"Only to victory, and be what it may." I reply, with a traditional response of the Omega Corps. They're another old superhero team from way back that was copied by supers for a few decades after they were wiped out in an explosion when they assaulted the base of Dr. Nucleos.

I beat my shield with my war hammer three times to signal the beginning of the battle, gladiator style, and break into a trot toward him. The Gladiators were a super group from…, well, you get it. I might be overdoing the age old references a bit, but this guy scares me.

"You can call me Wagner." Is the last thing he says before changing direction towards me, pronouncing it in the German, "VAUG-nur." I guess he styles himself some kind of composer.

Chapter 65

Rather than barrel into each other we both break down into fighting stances as we come into range. He's doing a passing job of a loose fighting stance, which is a little concerning. He's also not running in wild where I can surprise him, which is also a little disconcerting. Most Class 4 strongmen don't bother learning to fight, because they don't have to. The ones that do are deadly — if they have the speed to take advantage of their strength. Without speed, they really only have grappling. Grab the opponent, break the opponent. Done.

I break down into a fighting stance I learned from taking lessons with a shield and war hammer from a German weapons master I used to spar with. You just can't beat the Germans when it comes to beating the hell out of each other with medieval weapons. I've been planning on a war hammer and shield to fight with in my suit for years. Ever since I read my first epic fantasy novel of a half-orc barbarian warrior named Ka-Dor. He was a badass who equally beat the dog snot out of heroes and evil doers alike, and a small part of me has wanted to be him ever since.

Anyway, my old master developed a modernized version of the teachings of an Italian fencing master, Filippo Valdi, from his treatise, De Arte Gladiatoria Dimicandi. I'm no master, but the training was exceptional, and I put a couple hours of practice in several times per week of what I learned from him.

We circle each other and adjust our stances a number of times. Him trying to get closer to rush inside my guard, and I am trying to keep him at a distance with the reach advantage of my war hammer. Wagner's eyes are constantly shifting from my footwork, to my war hammer, to my eyes, to my center mass. I know what he is looking for, that little opening. That momentary lapse. Just enough for him to step inside, so I gave it to him.

Wagner gives himself away as his eyes widen just before he breaks for the opening I've given him. As he comes in, it looks like he is going to get inside my guard, and inside my shield, but I step to my right (my weapon side) and pivot as I sweep my war hammer for his legs. Wagner sees my maneuver just the slightest bit too late, and catches the head of my war hammer on his hamstring. It doesn't flip him off his feet the way I want, but it does give a nice meaty feel to the impact. I hop-step back out of his reach as he grabs the back of his left leg and hops out of range. I could see the pain in his face, briefly.

He shakes his leg a few times and says, "Ow. That hurt," is all he says and begins to circle me again as if he'd never been hit.

Rather than let him circle me and put my back to the others fighting, I parallel his walk and keep him between us.

"You've some skills. Not a lot of power, but enough to leave a bruise, I suppose," is his backhanded way of complimenting me.

C'mon, you sorry bastard, I'll give you something to praise me for, I'm thinking, but not saying. No need to piss him off.

It raises my confidence a little, though, seeing him feel some pain. The swing wasn't the wallop I put into the hit on Welcoming Committee when I hit him in the head last year, but it was decent. It would have torn the leg off a Class 1, and pulped the muscle and bone of a Class 2. This guy can take a hit. But, him whining about it makes me think he doesn't do much real fighting. The kind you do off of a sparring mat. Dreamweaver says he's the most powerful telepath she's ever seen from our fight before, so he likely has never even needed to use his hands in a real fight.

I shift my eyes to look at the fight going on by the busses. Dreamweaver has joined the fight, standing on the top of the bus next to Hit Point. I don't like that they are so close together, but the two they are fighting don't seem to be able to take advantage of it. Dreamweaver is using her force blasters and I can see in my HUD that she still has her shields and neural neutralizer activated. The two they are fighting are still trying to break through Granite's defense and shrugging off Hit Point and Dreamweaver's attacks. They're not making much progress, though, as Granite is shifting and churning the earth they are standing on back as fast as they are moving forward. It's like they are in an earthquake while on a treadmill.

I spent too much time looking at the other fight and the distraction almost costs me. Wagner can't see my eyes through the visor in my helmet, but he might have detected my head move a little out of line from where it would be if I was watching him. In a fight with an experienced opponent, even a movement of a fraction of an inch in head or posture can give away information that can be used against you. Wagner rushes me, starting from flat footed, to bursting into a full on bull rush.

I'm as flat footed as he was. If it wasn't for the extra distance that separates us, I would never have been able to react at all. As it is, he is nearly on top of me when I get my shield up in between us. My war hammer is useless as I don't have it in position to take a swing and it is out of line enough I cannot thrust it into his chest to arrest his momentum.

Wagner hits my shield and I can feel his strength pushing me back, and down. He is high on me, being taller, and my being crouched as I take his impact. Normally this would be good, but now it puts me in a position of strength versus strength, and I do not have any momentum, and not nearly enough strength. Even with the leverage advantage, his Class 4 strength against my, albeit powerful, Class 2 strength, isn't even a close contest. It's more like a toddler trying to hold back an NFL lineman. I'm pushed back and my legs buckle.

Wagner reaches over the top of my shield to grab my head and I duck down further and raise my shield as best I can. Knowing the war hammer is doing me no good, I drop it. Wagner's middle and legs are exposed as my shield is up in his chest and covering his head and arms. Seeing the opportunity, I charge my force blaster with a quick thirty percent charge. I don't want to wait long enough for any more as I'm not sure it won't all be over by then.

I discharge my force blaster into his stomach with my hand pointed to make the narrowest beam possible. It won't knock him back as much as an open palm would, which is what I should have hit him with to get him off me, but it is enough as I hear the air rush out of his lungs and he is lifted off the ground a good six feet.

I snatch my war hammer back up and leap back from him as he comes down in a pile on the ground where we were.

Wagner is back up in a split second, but stops himself from coming at me right away. Rubbing his stomach, he once again says, "Ow." This time followed by an ominous, "I think I may have to kill you." There, I've done it. I've pissed him off.

I'm pretty sure my forehead is breaking out into a major sweat right after he says that. Not that I wasn't sweating in my armor already. My stomach clenches, and I don't even want to respond. What is there to say? Sorry? I'm thinking too much. This isn't like fighting Welcoming Committee. That fight did not have much on the line. And, that fight didn't come right after one of my team was killed.

This guy scares the crap out of me, which any Class 4 should do to anyone not also a Class 4, or higher. My confidence is shaken. Why, though? My suit is doing what it's supposed to and evening up the odds as long as I don't get into a grapple or strength contest. Like the one I just had. I'm just not sure I can put this guy down for the count. I glance again at my team and wonder if it is better if I just keep him engaged until they can come help me, or if that wouldn't actually make things more dangerous as they're a lot more squishy than I am right now. With his speed, they wouldn't be able to keep at range from him.

The realization hits me. Damn, I have to win this. And, I'm going to have to do this alone. They will just get themselves killed fighting this guy. Carly was lucky she lasted as long as she did.

It's pretty clear I'm defensive right now. He's just standing there, rubbing his stomach, and looking at me, while I'm down in a fighting stance, shield held out in front and war hammer half-cocked for a strike. I look like I'm waiting for him to come take my head off.

That has to change, but I decide to keep a defensive look about me just a little bit longer in hopes I can surprise him when I switch to the attack. He's too far away right now for me to make a move on before he can react. So, I need to wait until he closes the distance on me. I don't have long to wait.

Giving his head a twist to get the kinks out, then giving his arms a shake, Wagner's expression no longer looks amused. Now he looks pissed off. I know he's coming and he's going to come hard when he does. As soon as he finishes shaking out his legs, he squats and lunges toward me with a twenty foot leap before hitting the ground running for the last ten feet. It's fast, but it's also about what I expect. He's got no finesse, like most Class 4s and 5s. I raise my shield but don't stay directly behind it, shifting my body to the right. I drop my war hammer once again to free up my right hand.

Wagner opens up his arms in an attempt to grab me, shield and all. I slip under his left arm, leaving my shield for him to grab if he wants to and release it, then move behind him. I can see the shock in his eyes as his head twists to see my helmet come up behind his arm over his shoulder as I move in. I started charging up my force blaster in my right forearm before he even made his leap. I'm not going to have much of a shield for the next few seconds, so I better not screw this up.

Wagner starts to twist as I bring my hand up, pointed for the narrowest beam, and place it in the middle of his back. His twisting takes his spine out of the line of my fire, but I've run out of time to line up the shot. I am at 72% charge when the blast goes into his kidney. I think it might be just as good. I can feel his flesh rend and tear as the narrowly focused blast of energy discharges its massive force into the side of Wagner's body. He reacts like any prize fighter would when they catch a brutal punch in the kidney, lifting up his toes and trying to pull his body away from the impact, but like them, he does not have anything to push off from to move away and I have my free arm braced around his neck to hold him tight to me. The blast doesn't toss him as far as it would if I had used an open palm, but that was not my goal. It was a kill shot, pure and simple. The narrow focus is meant for cutting and penetrating rather than pushing. I've got my shield arm now wrapped around his neck and I'm holding onto him for all I am worth. Even so, he is nearly torn from my grasp as the discharge rips into him. It is like trying to hold onto a rocket launching.

I have a brief moment of thinking of the physics of the system as it appears I have managed to lift both him, and myself, off the ground. We fly a good ten feet in the air from the blast. How's that possible? I'm thinking it's like lifting yourself up with your own bootstraps. *Not really possible, but if you try really, really hard....*

Focusing back on the situation at hand, I recharge my force blaster as we come down. Wagner is in agony and his body has gone rigid. I know I penetrated his flesh, but I can't tell how deep, or if it is just the shock effect. I see my charge rapidly going up to forty, fifty, sixty percent, over the next few seconds. Wagner has not made another move on me, but is twisting in my grip, writhing in agony. I'm on top of him on the ground and my shield and arm are pinned under him. If he shakes off the attack for even a moment, he can grab onto my arm and rip it off. Then again, he could rip something off accidentally as well and not even know it. When my force blaster reads 97%, I discharge it again, this time into his solar plexus, pointed up into his chest. Pressing my pointed hand against his soft flesh in the v-shape of his ribs, I feel on my shield hand as it rips through his body and through his back with the discharge. His flesh rends, and I can feel his spine part as my hand pushes into his back and into the cavity where his heart used to be. The back blast completely covers me in blood and gore. The ground didn't allow any give, so he takes the full brunt of the discharge. My shield hand, still behind his back, is numb and I wonder if I blew it off, too.

    It's as close and personal of a way of killing someone as a knife fight could ever be. I feel his upper body tense, even as his legs go slack. A guttural gasp of breath leaves his body, followed by a shudder. His hand is on my shoulder and he squeezes my pauldron armor plate into a death sculpture of his agony as I hunch down my shoulder trying to get it out of the way of the crushing armor plating. He stays rigid, and for the first time in the fight I can feel a pressure against what's left of my recharging repeller field that I can't identify, but it's coming from Wagner. The repeller field power in my suit shows ten percent, then twenty percent, in the scrolling up it normally does as it recharges, but then stops and starts to go down, back to fifteen, then seven, then two percent. I leap back from Wagner, ripping my arm from under him and leaving my shield behind. 1%. I keep backpedaling and the power in my repeller field hits 0% momentarily and I'm lifted and thrown through the air. My shield is not just down; my neural neutralizer that works through my shield is down. Wagner just hit me with some kind of telepathic and telekinetic death scream explosion. I can't tell how far I'm thrown as I look at the stars while sailing through the air. My natural mental defenses feel like someone dropped a building on them and my mind is in a vice. Fortunately, as I'm flying, I am aware enough to see my repeller field strength begin to go back up in its usual rapid manner. I'm going to need it when I hit the ground. If I ever do.

When I hit, my repeller field is up to thirteen percent, but immediately goes back down to zero when the thing I impact is a very large tree. The impact jars me to my teeth and my head snaps back and impacts the trunk. Bouncing off the tree, I spin like a top and continue my travels along a new trajectory into the ground. Impacting for the second time, this time into the tall grass. My repeller field reads three percent for the second impact, but I don't know that. I'm not sure why I was keeping track of my repeller field power, it's not like I can do anything about it. Morbid curiosity, perhaps? It may be the engineer in me wanting to evaluate the suit's performance. I'll have to check the logs later as I'm not sure what it reads after I hit the ground as I promptly black out. *Maybe I should run two power supplies in my suit,* I think, but not until I wake up.

Chapter 66

I'm not sure how long I'm out, but when I wake, I turn my head and open my eyes to see my team surrounding the double clenched duo of Anvil and his Class 4 opponent. They are still trying to squeeze the life out of each other, neither seeming to have any luck. Hit Point rushes in from behind the other guy and pulls the cap off his head. A couple seconds later he begins shaking his head and screaming, "Noooo! Get out! Get out! Get out!" Putting on a burst of strength as he panics from the telepathic assault I'm sure Dreamweaver is putting on him, he lifts Anvil in the air and I can see Anvil start to lose his hold on the guy. Fortunately for Anvil, it only lasts a moment before the guy goes completely limp and collapses. Anvil, still gripping the guy and straddling his body, eases him to the ground.

I can't hear what he says to Dreamweaver, but he is not happy, whatever it was. Dreamweaver holds her arms out to her side and shrugs in response, then points at the guy as if to say, "I took the guy out, what are you complaining about?"

I drop my head back to the ground and look at the stars. The Milky Way is showcased in its full glory in rural West Virginia sky. There is almost no light pollution or smog and the air is crystal clear tonight. I don't wonder where the famous "smoky" part of the smoky mountains is. Wait, are these the Smoky Mountains? Are they in West Virginia? I honestly don't know right now. I'm not sure I ever knew. But, I think I am beginning to get my senses back.

Anyway, the Milky Way is a beautiful sight to behold. When I was a kid, we used to go all the way out to the desert in California to star gaze. Every summer we would go to Joshua Tree National Park and I used to stare up at the sky and wonder who was out there traveling between the stars, and when would they come to visit us. *Boy, will they be surprised when they get here,* I think. Smiling to myself in my helmet, I close my eyes and let my mind drift. No one is trying to kill me right now.

Hearing at least some of the team running over to me, one of them gives a, "Holy crap," as he passes what I assume to be Wagner's body. That could only be Anvil. I laugh to myself, as getting a "holy crap" out of him is pretty hard to do.

I feel someone bang into my armor as they run up and drop down next to me, and I give a grunt at the pain it causes me. Dreamweaver reaches down to pull my helmet off, but I stop her, "Wait," I say, "I'm in a lot of pain right now. I need a minute." I need to do an inventory before I try to move anything.

She gives me my minute, then tells me to turn off my neural neutralizer, so I do. "Hey," She says, softly, "you okay?"

"Not sure yet," I reply, "Wagner. That's what his name was, you know? 'Vaug-ner,' " I say, sounding it out slowly, "He put a hurt on me when I put him down. My shields were down, and it's like he just blew up."

"I felt it. It was intense." Carly says. She is doing a first aid sweep of my body, looking for broken parts and bleeding. I can feel her poking me through my armor and I think she is using her telekinesis to feel her way through my body. It feels weird.

"Heh-heh, stop it," I tell her. Not because it tickles. Because it is funny that she is trying to check me through my armor and it hurts to laugh. Wagner couldn't get through my armor, why would Carly's finger get through it. I might have a concussion.

Carly pulls back from me and I can feel her mental projection of concern briefly flip flop to annoyance I am stopping her, and back to concern. Hmm, that's new. I usually can't feel her emotions telepathically.

"Hold on for a sec, would you?" I ask her, and begin running diagnostics in my suit. As the diagnostics run, I start doing an inventory of my body. I'm hurting all over, but as I focus on each part of my body, starting at my toes and working my way slowly up my body, giving each location a little wiggle and flex of the muscles in that location. I flex and relax each muscle I can identify to see if it is working, or if the bone it's attached to complains at its use. Both of my legs hurt like hell, but it seems to be coming from my muscles. Mostly. I don't think any bones are broken, but I decide I better take it slow trying to get up. My butt and back hurts like someone just beat my ass with a two-by-four. Not surprising, I suppose, since that is what impacted the tree first. Fortunately, I don't know of any bones that could be broken in my ass. I guess I could have broken a hip, but I don't think so. Or, maybe my coccyx. I start laughing again, but quickly stop as it hurts too much. It's the next part of my search I'm more worried about. I have a lot of pain in my lower back. I can't tell if I have trauma to my spine, or if it's broken. I know my spinal cord is intact, or I wouldn't have been able to move my toes. But, if something is broke, I might sever it if I try to get up. Better to just work through the rest of my body check and see how things feel in a few minutes. I go through the rest of my body, and I'm amazed that I don't think anything is broken. A big smile comes over my face as I realize my armor is what saved me from being broken like kindling fighting Wagner. The smile makes the back of my head hurt like hell and I notice my helmet seems to be getting really tight. *I might have a concussion from hitting the tree,* I tell myself, again.

"I think I'm okay," I finally announce. By now the others are standing around me, "You guys all right?" I ask. I see a couple heads nod, but otherwise they just stand there and look at me lying on the ground.

Anvil speaks up first, "Get up, ya candy ass. We gotta get outa here before someone shows up."

"You just hold onto your Clydesdales, there Kemosabe. I need a minute." Anvil and I seem to be developing a tentative understanding. I think he thinks I'm invulnerable in my suit as I'm sure he was trying to kill me during training. But, I'm not sure he realizes how close to being killed I was. Unlike Wagner, Anvil never hit me when my repeller field was down.

"Well hurry it up, I'm going to need your help flipping this bus back upright," he tells me. The big liar.

"What for, you can lift that thing over your head if you want?" Hit Point asks him.

"Because, sweetheart, If I put that much force into a single point the metal's going to bend and we'll have a screwed up looking bus."

Hit Point gives him a dirty look over the "sweetheart" comment, but doesn't say anything more. I doubt she cares about the appearance of the bus, either.

Granite solves the issue; "I'll flip the bus back upright. It's not a problem. Just need to shift around a little earth." He sounds exhausted. He should be. I'll never underestimate the power of an earth elemental again.

I'm a little curious as to how it got on its side in the first place, so I ask, "How did it get flipped over in the first place?"

"That guy you fought, Wagner. He did it," replied Dreamweaver, "He was standing in the middle of the road when we saw him in our headlights. I could feel his telekinetic power when he picked the bus up completely in the air and just threw it to the side of the road." I could hear the awe, and fear, in her voice. "I knew it was him right then. I could taste the flavor of his mind from the time we fought him in the warehouse."

"What did you do then?" I ask, wanting to know what happened, and buying some more time before I have to get up.

"I turned on my repeller field and neural neutralizer right then," she pauses as she realizes she gave away one of my suit secrets, then continues, "Even before we hit the ground. I don't think that saved me in the crash. I mean, it wasn't that bad. I don't think any of the kids were hurt badly." She looks over to the busses to where the students are. I doubt any of us has checked on them yet. Some of them are sitting up and the other students are helping them, though.

"I didn't even turn on the repeller field to protect myself from the crash. The only thing I could think of was that I had to protect myself from his telepathic powers and had to get the neural neutralizer activated before he seized my mind." Dreamweaver pulls off her helmet while she is speaking and I see her face light up, "It worked, Theo! He couldn't get into my mind! He couldn't even use his telekinetic powers on me!"

"Awesome." I reply, enjoying seeing her excited, but not thrilled she is using my name out loud.

Hit Point takes over the story, "I hit the brakes and stopped behind them. We didn't realize we were being attacked, but we should have known. What else could have made the bus go airborne like that? Granite and I jumped out of the bus to check on them when those two thugs tried to jump us. I saw them just in time and was able to send a couple things their way and Granite was able to put up a barrier. I'm still not sure what their powers were, but they kept trying to get at us, so whatever it was, it wasn't ranged. Everything I threw at them they were able to dodge, though. Thankfully, Granite was able to hold them back, but they were a lot faster than that Class 5 strongman back at the compound and he wasn't able to cover them or open a hole underneath them. Whenever he tried, they just jumped out of the hole."

"Why couldn't they just jump over Granite's barrier," I ask, imagining the fight and trying to figure out how they could have attacked them, "Did they try that?"

"Yeah, they tried," Hit Point replied with a pretty satisfied tone, "But when they tried to make a big leap they weren't able to dodge my attacks. Unfortunately, I didn't start using lethal attacks until after they learned that the hard way. Otherwise, it would have been over for them the first time they tried to make the jump." I can see she regrets not resorting to lethal force from the beginning. If she becomes a superhero, she will have to continue doing it that way. I don't recommend it, though.

"Lesson learned?" I ask.

"In this situation?" she replies, "Yeah. I shouldn't have held back from the beginning."

"Right. But, I know you'll hold back most other times. And, you'll be right for doing it. Your trick will be knowing, and remembering, where things stand from the beginning." Hit Point is a good person, and I don't want her carrying the guilt of someday killing a punk that didn't need to die to be stopped. She'll make a great superhero.

"All right. I think I can do this," I finally declare, and slowly sit up with a groan. "Ahh, damn that hurts."

"How'd you do it?" Anvil finally asks me. "How'd you take that guy out?"

I know what he means. Even though I didn't know right then he had tried to fight Wagner at the beginning and Wagner had just lifted him off the ground telekinetically and started slamming him into the ground. It had taken Dreamweaver intervening to get him off Anvil. That's when Anvil was given a new dance partner with the guy he was doing the double embrace with. Dreamweaver, because she has the neural neutralizer built into her repeller field, was able to fight Wagner to an impasse, but she couldn't hurt him. From what I saw, Wagner may have been holding back. I think I got there just in time as the guy had a lot of options as a telekinetic if he wanted to start throwing objects at

Dreamweaver rather than try to use his powers on her directly. Maybe he just never had the problem of not being able to use his powers directly.

"It's all in the suit, my man. It's all in the suit," is the only explanation I give him.

Chapter 67

Dreamweaver walks with me back to the busses as we watch Granite manipulate the earth under the bus to tip it back upright. He places it as gently as a feather. Most of the kids are still on the bus, and you can see them scrambling a bit as the bus tips back upright. Granite takes it slow, though, and no one else gets hurt. We check out the kids, both on the bus and the ones who were lying in the dirt when I arrived, and no one is seriously hurt other than bruises, scrapes, and a couple broken bones, which Hit Point and Dreamweaver place in splints from a med kit found on the bus. Most of them have at least some physical enhancements and are either a Class 1 or Class 2 physically, along with some Class 3s. Neither Anvil nor Granite is much use with the first aid. Anvil has never had a use for it in his family as they are all Class 3 or higher physically, and Granite has never even skinned his knee. I've read that earth elementals just don't fall down. Me? I have first aid training, a good bit of it, in fact. Instead of helping, I nurse my own injuries. My head is at least starting to clear.

I forget to ask Dreamweaver how they finally took out the last two guys attacking Granite and Hit Point. Later I find out that, once I had taken down Wagner, Dreamweaver turned off her neural neutralizer and put the two down with her telekinetically directed throwing knives. It's a lot harder to dodge when the throwing knife follows you wherever you go and is flying a few hundred miles per hour.

We get everyone back in their seats and check out the busses. The bus that flipped grumbles and misfires a couple times, but then starts up and runs without a problem. I swap places with Anvil and have him drive the van ahead of the busses in case we have any more surprises, while I drive the bus that flipped, with Dreamweaver. It isn't until we get back on the road that Dreamweaver starts first aid on the more minor injuries. It takes a while to settle everyone down and get them patched up, but she does it efficiently and doesn't take any longer than it needs. The kids are like putty and just sit there until you tell them to do something. Once all the injuries are patched up, Dreamweaver starts, one at a time, taking the caps off the kids and going to work on fixing their minds.

It's exhausting work for Dreamweaver as she takes almost an hour with each kid. Wagner did a number on them, but had not bothered to erase any of their memories or personality. Instead he had just laid over a compulsion to be subservient and an extreme paranoia of failing to do whatever they were told. And, he made them believe he was their lord high master, whatever that was. Dreamweaver has to undo all of it, which takes her a while for the first few as she figures out exactly what he did, and how. Once she has the compulsion and paranoia removed, she goes in and edits the memories they have made while under them. Some of them are terrifying as they were made from the viewpoint of a person who was filled with terror and paranoia. The last thing she removes is their belief Wagner was their high lord master as she was using that as her authority in getting them to accept what she was doing. I have no idea how it works, she just said it makes a difference if they willingly accept what she is doing. Their reactions, once she has removed all the mental manipulations, are about what I expect from the arrogant jerks that make up the student body of the science department. Some of them understand what she's done for them and are grateful. Some of them try to help with the others. All of the students, however, are arrogant idiots who demand an explanation for how what happened to them was allowed to happen and are threatening retaliation and lawsuits against us as much as they are against Wagner. I have to stop the bus a couple times and put a couple them in their place.

Dreamweaver can put them in their place with a thought, but she's so exhausted from freeing the minds of the students in the first place, she just looks at them and shakes her head when they start acting like asses. I've had enough when one of them tries to assault her and she has to telekinetically throw him down the aisle. He slams into the front wall of the bus next to where I'm sitting in the driver's seat. Thankfully, she still has her suit and helmet on and his attempt at a sucker punch does not do any damage other than to knock her on her butt. After that she keeps her repeller field on low power in case one of the idiots is a Class 3. These arrogant ungrateful jerks are the reason why I don't live in the Oppenheimer Quad.

We drive the whole way back to Nova Academy, only stopping for gas. And at the half way point at a Grocer's Warehouse to buy five cases of water, ten pounds of lunch meat, and twenty loaves of bread and snacks for a couple hundred kids. Fortunately, they are nearly all still under mind control and don't complain about what is given to them. The few kids we have put back right are given the job of slopping some meat between two pieces of bread and handing them out to the others.

We finally make it back to campus early the next morning. All of us have been up for the last thirty hours straight, and chugging energy drinks for the last twelve to stay awake. We have a total of sixteen kids who have their minds restored, and that is as much as Carly can handle, and as much as I can tolerate. I am sick of hearing them try to blame us for everything that happened to them. Dreamweaver is mentally exhausted to the point she can't work on freeing any more of the kids' minds for fear she will screw up more than she fixes. Instead, she calls her roommate, Imelda, for telepathic reinforcements to meet us at the Erickson Quad Commons when we get there. We figure our best chance of getting the telepaths to help put these kids back right is to dump them in their laps in their own recreation area of their commons. If we try to get them to come to us, I doubt they will show.

I have the team stay in their super suits and keep their neural neutralizer caps on when we pull onto campus so we can have at least some chance of remaining anonymous. The telepaths don't need to know who we are any more than anyone else. I don't doubt all of them know who I am, and I can't see how they don't all know who Carly is, but we can at least try to protect the rest of the team.

It's still the middle of night out, but the common area is well lit and we can see Imelda and a dozen other telepath students standing outside of the Erickson Commons. Dreamweaver steps off the bus first, "Imelda, thank you for coming," then looking at the others, "Thank all of you."

"What have you done, Carly?" Imelda asks; arms crossed.

"The name is Dreamweaver. Please respect it," then adding with a little ice in her voice, "And you know why." Imelda still does not like that Carly is a superhero.

Nothing else is said and this is where things get awkward. When you're not telepathic and you're around a group of telepaths, it's awkward. They all just stand there looking at each other, having a conversation you can't hear. Occasionally they change who they're looking at, but otherwise they just stand there, sometimes with a vacant look on their face. They are having a conversation and I'm not invited. That's fine with me, though. So long as they take these kids off our hands and get them put back right in the head.

Eventually Imelda, and the rest of the telepaths who meet us, nod their reluctant agreement. Dreamweaver turns back to me, "They'll take them from here."

"Are they going to help them?" I ask, not really liking their reluctance now, and their outright refusal before, to be of any sort of help. I ignore the icy glare from Imelda. If she says anything I'm going to pop her one.

"Yeah. They know exactly what happened to them and what needs to be done to fix them. Don't worry, once they start helping the kids, the whole quad will step up. They'll have all the kids' heads back on straight by dinner."

"Okay," I reply, looking over the telepaths, who are all ignoring me now as they start taking the kids off the busses. I step over and pull the neural neutralizers off the kids' heads as they step off the bus then work my way up into the bus and grab them off all of the kids. Once I have them all I go out the back emergency door, and repeat the process on the other bus. The telepaths won't let the kids keep them anyway, so I may as well grab them. They might come in handy someday and it will be better if I don't have to build them myself when the time comes.

Imelda is staring at me and I can feel her telepathically trying to tunnel into my head, trying to break into my head like she has every other time I've been around her. I don't appreciate it any more than I have the other times she's done this, so I turn on my repeller field and neural neutralizer. See how she likes that. I swear I'm a half second from hitting her.

Her head snaps back and she blinks a bunch of times and I smile under my helmet. Keep out. That's what the sign on the door says, lady.

Dreamweaver sees her reaction and knows what happened, "I told you not to," she says with a shrug and shakes her head as she turns and walks over to me.

Carrying the bags of stuff I took from the compound, and gathering Hit Point and Granite at the other bus, I tell them it's time to go, and the team walks away from the kids and the busses over to the van. Our job is done.

Chapter 68

I want nothing more than to crawl into my bed for a week, but first we drop off the rest of the team and take Sparks' body into town to the city morgue. We leave her body on a gurney with a note and get out of there before we're seen. Sadly, she isn't the first super to die and be left at a morgue. Once the investigation begins when the students all show back up, we can let them know what she did to save all those kids.

Leaving Sparks is a reminder to us of what this mission cost and, reflecting on the ungrateful science students we saved, I'm not completely feeling like the rescue was worth the cost. It is going to be a while before I even think about saving someone who isn't important to me again.

Back at my dorm room, we change and I am able to see all the damage that's been done to my armor. The armor weave is damaged and torn in several places and shows burn marks all along one side from nearly being cooked by the fire elemental. It held up, though, as the damage is superficial. The repeller field, however, wasn't able to keep out all the heat, which I know because I was feeling myself begin to cook in my armor. I thought it would provide more protection from the heat than that, so I make a mental note to add a reengineering of the repeller field. Again. My to-do list for my suit is long and getting longer. My helmet has a pretty good scuff on it. That must be from the tree, or...I'm not sure where it was from now that I think about it. It, the helmet, definitely has some electronics issues that need to be hardened from impact damage. I think I burned out some of the sensors for low light and infrared as well.

Carly, now changed out of her suit and standing in one of the labs with me in her underwear, catches me frowning at my suit. She knows I am giving it the critical stare as she has seen that expression on my face many times over the last few months. "Hey," she calls to me.

"Yeah?" I respond, without looking.

"Your suit is awesome. You know that, right?"

"I was nearly barbecued last night." I reply, frowning. Grabbing the upper chest piece, I look at the damage to the material, "It wasn't strong enough."

"Are you kidding me? You went toe to toe with a Class 4 strongman who was at least as fast as you are, and who is telepathic and telekinetic. And, you won! You kicked his ass!" She steps up to me and pokes me in the chest, "You should be dead. You know that, right?"

I let what she's saying sink in for a minute before a grin starts to creep up on my face, "I did, didn't I?" Then back to critical, "Still, I can make it better."

"Okay, fine. Make it better. But, you better not go all mad scientist on me for at least a week! Don't make me kick your butt, because you won't have your suit to save you when I do."

Setting down my suit, I go over to the woman who is quickly becoming my better half and pull her into my arms, "Baby, I promise. You've got my full attention for at least a week." I know I'm lying. So does she.

"Don't you 'baby' me. I'm going to hold you to it," she declares, "You're officially on mad science vacation. And, no superheroeing, either." I can tell she's serious, even though she's stopped resisting me as she wraps her arms around me in return. I give her, or maybe she gives me, a slow kiss. It's good to be alive.

"Ow." I'm not sure which of us said it, or if we both did, but it hurts to kiss right now, and her arms around me are pressing on a huge bruise on my shoulder.

Pulling back, I say, "All right. Rain check."

I grab both of our suit bags and we take them with us. I can't leave them in the science labs anymore; the science students we just rescued will steal them.

Epilogue

I skip classes on Monday and sleep in until dinner time. Which is just as well; all of my classes are in chaos as the science students show up for classes and none of the professors know they're supposed to be there. Admittance doesn't help any as all their records for them are missing. Fortunately for the students, Carly's telepath friends step up and fix the memories of the professors and the admins.

The science students take care of the school's computer systems themselves by adding all of their own information back in. I have serious doubts as to the accuracy of what they put back in, though. There's no telling what changes they made to their records when they recreated them back into the school's database.

I am two months ahead in all of my classes from everyone else. Actually, it is more like a year ahead as I have been receiving one-on-one attention in all of the classes and I haven't wasted a moment; getting as much out of my professors as I possibly can. I do not get any extra credits for the year, however. What I do get is what I need to test out of the next two follow on courses in my engineering, metallurgy, and advanced math classes over the summer. I'll be able to start my theoretical robotics, nuclear engineering applications, and advanced manufacturing techniques in my sophomore year.

Unfortunately, being that far ahead doesn't sit well with my professors, so they make me substitute teach their classes for the rest of the semester. I'm up late grading papers every weekend until school lets out and I can't get Carly to hang out with me like she does when I am in the science lab working on projects. She says grading papers is too boring and there's nothing I can build for her with a stack of term papers. Nothing she wants, anyway. I have to agree with her, but I'm afraid I created a monster. One who has a gleam in its eyes whenever I build her something. She's the perfect woman for a mad scientist. I just know someday she's going to ask me to make her a doomsday device.

Two weeks after the rescue, the police show up. It took them long enough to figure out something is wrong as none of the telepaths ever did visit them to undo whatever Wagner had done to make them ignore a 200 person missing persons report. They are not ignoring it now, though. The administration doesn't know what they are talking about and, after they interview a bunch of the science students, they are back to being as confused as they were when I tried to report the missing students in January. But, they don't give up that easily. They bring in a telepath to scan all the science students who were abducted, except none of them have any memories of being abducted. No one was able to identify Wagner and his crew, or their rescuers. I'm sure the telepath can see their minds have been messed with, but he seems to go along with it. Interestingly, Carly's roommate is present when the telepath interviews take place, ostensibly to observe police interviewing techniques for her criminal law class.

I, of course, stand out like a sore thumb, as I am the one who reported the abductions in the first place. As well as being the only physical sciences student to not be abducted. They interview me for two hours but don't get anywhere. I have to come up with a story with Carly that makes the whole thing look like a sorority prank. Not that I'm in a sorority. In the end they call in the telepath again and we just stare at each other for a few minutes before he tells them I don't know anything about the abductions or the rescue. I not sure how he can say that considering he's not able to read my mind, but later Carly tells me the telepath was told everything by Imelda and her friends, and the guy agreed this wasn't something non-telepaths needed to spend a lot of time investigating.

When finals week comes around my professors let me in on the fact I have to take the finals with everyone else, even though I have been teaching the damn classes for the last month and they said I didn't have to. It pisses me off but I'm not worried about it. I have the material down pat and ace all my tests, which is a given since they make me grade the finals too. If I ever decide there is nothing left in this world I want to accomplish I think I'll start teaching at Nova Academy Science Department. The place is full of brilliant minds that have all gone soft.

Our last weekend before summer break I'm hanging out in the quad while Carly crams for some telepathy exam; this is not how I planned to spend our last weekend together. So, instead of getting all worked up about it, I do something about it and talk Carly into delaying her flight home until Monday (school let out on Friday, and her test was Saturday, so I get Sunday). I intend for our time to last me through most of the summer. We spend the weekend in the nicest hotel the rinky-dink little town has, and have a proper goodbye.

I call Mom that night to let her know of the change of plans and she complains about me not coming straight home, but I know she understands. Her little boy is all grown up and has discovered the joys of the opposite sex. Yeah, okay. I did that a while back, but it can take moms a while to come to terms with that particular realization.

Monday morning we're getting packed up and ready to head for the airport, so I turn on the television in the hotel. The president is addressing the nation about some trade agreement with the Chinese that no one cares about, so I pick the remote back up to put it on The Super News Channel. It is the only channel worth watching on the hotel's crappy channel lineup.

"Wait, wait! Turn it back!" shouts Carly from across the room.

Okay, geez. I didn't know she cared about international trade or politics. So, I futz with the remote because it doesn't have a "last channel" button. Finally, I have to down channel about twenty times until I find another news network showing the same press conference. The conference is just getting over and the president steps away from the podium and walks off to the right of the stage. The cameras follow him and that's when I see him.

"I killed that guy," is all I can say as I'm in total shock.

Carly doesn't say anything. She's just staring at the screen when I look over to her for confirmation of who I just saw.

"Carly? That was him, wasn't it?" I ask with trepidation. "Carly?"

"They're all wearing hats," she responds in a whisper.

"What?" I snap my head back to look at the T.V., but the talking head at the news network is back on the screen. "Who?" I ask Carly.

"The Secret Service agents. They were all wearing hats," she whispers again.

My mind is storming with conflicting thoughts: Since when does the Secret Service wear hats? How is this guy still alive? Regeneration? Twin? What do I do? After a dozen different questions flit through my mind, I come to a conclusion: I don't give a damn if they wear hats or not. I don't give a damn if this guy is still alive. He's not my problem. Finally I tell Carly, "This isn't our problem anymore. You may want to call Imelda and tell her the telepaths have a problem they need to fix before he takes over the world."

Carly stares at me for nearly a minute then, tight lipped, nods and reaches for her phone.

The End (of my freshman year)

Biography:

Scott is a California native where he lives with his wife, son, and their dog. A native of the West Coast, Scott grew up moving every few years in an Army family with his brother and two sisters. After high school, Scott spent five years working in mostly construction and maintenance until joining the U.S. Coast Guard where he worked as a Fire Control Technician working on CIWS. Scott married and completed his bachelor's degree in Business Administration then began a career in commercial real estate where he today national auction firm as one of the firm's brokers. Scott is a part time author, sometime gamer, and full time lover of science fiction and fantasy novels that he has been reading since grade school.
Nova Academy is Scott's first novel.

Manufactured by Amazon.ca
Bolton, ON